RSVP

RSVP

Tara Moore

W F HOWES LTD

This large print edition published in 2010 by
W F Howes Ltd
Unit 4, Rearsby Business Park, Gaddesby Lane,
Rearsby, Leicester LE7 4YH

1 3 5 7 9 10 8 6 4 2

First published in the United Kingdom in 2010
by Orion Books

ISBN 978 1 40745 544 0

Typeset by Palimpsest Book Production Limited,
Grangemouth, Stirlingshire
Printed and bound in Great Britain
by MPG Books Ltd, Bodmin, Cornwall

For Dr David Moore, my husband,
my love, my world!

PROLOGUE

APRIL 2008

New York

Coppelia Morrison lay sprawled on the satin sheets, her flawless skin almost copper against their whiteness, and her long hair, the colour of wet autumn leaves, fanned out across the pillow. Her almond eyes glowed in a shaft of sunlight as she stretched and purred.

Indolent, she turned to gaze at her sleeping companion, marvelling at the clean perfection of his jaw-line, the promise of strength in the face now so innocent and relaxed in sleep. Another ten years and Fintan Granville would be a man to reckon with, just like Carrick, his older brother, and others of the Granville clan. Now, at a mere nineteen, he was putty in her hands, a delightful toy to be picked up and played with when the mood took her. And the irony of it all was that Fin thought *he* was the one calling the shots, that she was just his version of Mrs Robinson, perfect for expanding his sexual repertoire. Little did he know that when someone had pointed him out to her in a nightclub one evening, it was the name – Granville – that had

1

interested her, far more than his gorgeous youthful body (although *that* was a definite bonus). Like everything else that caught her eye, it was just a matter of time before he was hers for the taking.

Snuggling closer, she flicked her tongue gently over the lobe of his ear. 'Mm, that was fun, baby.' The words were a whisper of breath, barely a sigh. 'But tell me, what's it like sleeping with the enemy?'

Young Fintan Granville dreamt sweetly on and heard not a word.

Her own lids beginning to droop, Coppelia slid an arm round his hard young body and surrendered herself to delicious dreams of revenge.

Carrickross House, County Kerry, Ireland

Honoria Granville sat in her spacious drawing room, gazing through the large bay window at the splendid view of lake and mountain before her.

'Rajesh!' she called, gripping the ivory boar's head that topped her favourite walking stick and tapping the gleaming floorboards twice to summon her servant.

Sensing rather than hearing his quiet approach, she smiled a little grimly to herself. There was a time when her hearing was so acute she could hear the maids laughing in the kitchen, a time when she could hear Henry turn the pages of a book in the library two rooms away, the tiny secretive clink of the crystal glass as he poured yet another whiskey and the soft hiss as he added the soda.

2

There had also come a time when, in the dark reaches of the night, she could hear the soft stealthy whisper of his feet padding across his bedroom floor and the oh-so-careful turning of the door-knob as lust led him out into the night and the soft welcoming arms of other women.

One woman in particular.

Her hand tightened on her stick, the skin over the knuckles stretched thin as rice-paper. All these years later, the memory still brought a bitter twist to her mouth, replaced almost immediately by an expression of satisfaction. Henry had paid the ultimate price for that piece of folly.

As Rajesh took up his habitual position, to the left of her chair but slightly behind it, she made no acknowledgement, knowing that when it became necessary he would move forward into her line of vision. Instead, she relaxed slightly against the back of the upright mahogany chair, where tigers prowled through an elaborately carved jungle.

Henry and the past faded and her gaze, penetrating as ever, fixed itself once more on the view outside her drawing-room window.

The daffodils had performed well this year, disporting themselves in a great and regal display – the baize-green lawn, as it swept between Scots pines and vivid rhododendron down to the water beyond, providing a splendid backdrop to the yellow gold. Across the lake, its shoulders forested, Nead an Iolair mountain – the Eagle's Nest – reared its brooding head over the scene.

At last Honoria spoke, her voice vibrating with its characteristically harsh timbre. 'They should be receiving their invitations soon.'

She could sense his smile, no doubt matching hers in grimness.

After a pause she spoke again, with a dry chuckle. 'What do you think they will make of them, Rajesh?'

The question demanded no reply. He laid a reassuring hand on the shoulder of her heavily embroidered silk kameez.

'Ah, yes, we've set the cat among the pigeons,' she said gloatingly, and, with a sudden surge of energy, rose to her feet and stepped forward between the heavily fringed curtains, into the great bay window. When she spoke it was as if she addressed the mountain looming across the lake.

'Come, Coppelia! Come and do your worst!'

As she swung about to face him, her silver hair piled thickly on her head and her face alive with gleeful malice, the years fell away and Rajesh saw in her once more the young memsahib with whom he had fallen in love long years ago and for whom he would still willingly lay down his life. Honoria. His queen. His rani.

A shadow crossed her face. 'Rajesh,' she asked abruptly, 'do you think this will be the last game we play together, you and I?'

'I doubt that very much, Rani,' he replied, a wry smile curving his lips. If propriety hadn't dictated otherwise, he might have taken her in his arms.

CHAPTER 1

MAY

Dublin

Ashling Morrison gave a quick check around the studio, slung her favourite Nikon camera around her neck, grabbed the handle of her Vuitton trolley-case and trundled to the door.

'Is that it? Are you off?' Moira, her assistant, shoved her head out of the darkroom where she'd been developing a batch of prints for *Irish Crème*, a new high-society mag.

'I am, God help me.' Slightly wild-eyed, Ashling fired off the usual last-minute volley of instructions. 'Now don't forget – email me those test shots on her ladyship asap.' 'Her ladyship' was an accurate nickname for Tempest O'Leary, an ageing supermodel whose unreasonable demands were legendary. 'And don't forget to lock up properly. You've got my contact numbers in case of emergency, and I've left both Rossa's number and the number for Carrickross pinned on the noticeboard. Oh, and tell anyone who asks that it'll be business as usual come Monday. I'm not

5

in a position yet where I can afford to turn down work.'

Moira flapped an impatient hand. 'Ah, would you get out of here, for God's sake! I'm not a complete eejit, you know. And, Ashling,' she called just before the door closed, 'remember, you're one lucky cow! I wouldn't turn down a ride on Rossa Granville's trike meself!'

Ashling grinned, letting the door slam behind her. Cheeky madam! But Moira was right. She was lucky, luckier than she'd ever dared to imagine. The great solitaire diamond shimmering on her left hand was proof of that – a Granville family heirloom. She checked her watch, her excitement rising as she thought of her financé who at that very moment would be battling the heavy Dublin traffic from the airport on his way to meet her. The thought made her spirits soar as she bumped her suitcase all the way downstairs from her studio, In Focus, set right at the top of an old four-storey Georgian building in Exchequer Street. Although she appreciated its classic design and history, this was one of those times when she would have sold her soul for the modern convenience of an elevator. Several flights of uneven creaky stairs were certainly not the ideal, but the central location was second to none and, with rents as exorbitant as they were in this part of Dublin, she felt blessed to have secured it.

Down she went past the firm of chartered accountants on the third floor, the kooky hypnotherapist's on the second and finally on down to the ground floor, which had been given over to a famous chocolatier. But there was no time today to stop and drool over the coffee pralines or strawberry liqueurs and she set off at a half-trot, dragging the suitcase behind her, swinging right at the junction of Exchequer Street and Grafton Street and heading up the glamorous pedestrianised thoroughfare towards St Stephen's Green. She had arranged to meet Rossa on the far side, where he had some hope of finding a parking space. Determinedly, she elbowed her way past the crowd of shoppers and tourists thronging the famous old street with its wealth of designer boutiques and eclectic book and art shops, past Bewley's, the world-famous coffee shop, from which issued the most beguiling of aromas. When time permitted, there was nothing she loved more than to linger, her photographer's eye constantly assessing the tide of humanity flowing past, marvelling at the change wrought in the demographics over the last few years. Today, foreign faces and voices were as much in evidence as Irish ones. Poles, Romanians, Somalians, Chinese, all in search of the Promised Land – an ironic turnaround from the days when it was the Irish who packed their bags and set sail for foreign climes.

Refusing to be distracted, Ashling pressed on, skilfully avoiding the crush, coming to a halt only when forced to at a pedestrian crossing opposite St Stephen's Green. She wasn't exactly late, but Rossa wasn't renowned for his patience and in her

7

mind's eye she pictured him drumming impatiently on the steering-wheel of his silver Aston Martin.

When the lights changed she scurried across, passing beneath Fusiliers' Arch at the entrance to the park, and on past the duck pond where a rather appealing tableau was being enacted: a mother and toddler feeding the ducks. Normally such a scene would have had her diving for her camera, but now she gathered pace, finally emerging, puffing and triumphant, on the far side of the Green.

Pausing to catch her breath, she gazed excitedly around and there, illegally parked in a busy traffic lane and intent on charming a hefty-looking female traffic warden, stood Rossa. Gorgeous, sexy Rossa Granville.

Abandoning her suitcase, she rushed to him and laughingly flung her arms around his neck.

'Whoa, steady on there!' He staggered playfully under her weight and winked at the traffic warden. 'That's the great thing about going away – guarantees an enthusiastic reception when you get back. Must go more often!'

'Don't even say that!' With a mock pout, Ashling went to pull away, but he held her tight around the waist, treating her to the full force of his megawatt smile. She grinned and relaxed against him. 'I was so relieved when you phoned from the airport this morning. I was worried that something might have come up to keep you in Thailand

and I'd end up rattling round Carrickross on my own. Oh, baby, I've missed you so much!'

'Missed you more,' came Rossa's muffled voice against the top of her head.

She pulled back again. 'Did you really?'

'Hey, what do you think?' He grinned like a naughty little boy. 'I can't tell you how boring it is being out there on my own!'

'Oh yes, Hua Hin is such a shit-hole.' Her tone was playful but a little dry. 'All that gorgeous sun, sea and sensuous dusky maidens! Cocktails on the beach, picture-postcard sunsets and midnight dips! Real penance, I should imagine!' She tried hard not to be jealous of Rossa's glittering career as a pilot with Thai-Orient, but, God, she wouldn't be human if she didn't sometimes resent the way it kept him from her for weeks at a time.

With a mischievous grin, Rossa picked up her case and stowed it in the boot of his car. 'Come on, love of my life! Let's get this show on the road. I'm hoping to make it onto the dual carriageway before the worst of the traffic hits. That way, we should be in Kerry well before Grandmother sends out the dogs.'

With total disregard for the motorists who glared at him as they changed lanes to get past the Aston Martin, he sauntered round and opened the passenger door for her.

'"Dinner will be at eight prompt!"' He did a perfetly impersonation of his grandmother's cut-glass diction, slightly nasal, über grand. '"Dress formal! No farting, burping or shagging in the hayloft!"'

'Rossa, don't!' Ashling giggled at such irreverence. Something of a throwback to the British Raj, Honoria Granville managed to really intimidate her, despite the fact that she had given the engagement her full approval.

As Rossa climbed in beside her, she laid a proprietary hand on his thigh, feeling the muscles contract as he slipped the car into gear and screeched away across two lanes of traffic, waving an airy two-fingered salute out the window to the fuming motorists. Ashling held on tight and prepared for a bumpy ride. But that was Rossa: a law unto himself. Like all of the Granvilles, Ashling reflected, still bemused by how her life had changed in just a few short months, and all thanks to a totally un-expected commission from Honoria Granville to do some formal family portraits at their magnifi-cent country estate in Kerry. In truth, the prospect had taken her aback. Although she had lately been touted as Ireland's answer to her all-time heroine, the American photographer Annie Leibovitz, and was becoming a 'name' in the cut-throat world of society photographers, she had thought her methods a little avant garde for such a grand old family. But, wow! What an experience it had turned out to be – what a family!

Never one to turn down a challenge, Ashling had excelled herself and the result had been a collec-tion of arresting and stylish portraits. Those of the twins, Indigo and Sapphire, were particularly remarkable. But then the subjects had been pretty remarkable in their own right: two beautiful beings, almost scarily perfect – blonde, blue-eyed, angelic – but with a hint of something disturbing behind their smiles.

Two significant members of the family were away on the day of the shoot. Carrick Granville, Rossa's elder brother, was in Japan on business and his Uncle Jaspar, by all accounts a colourful character, lived in Kenya. Ashling thought it strange that Honoria had arranged the photographic session in their absence. Disappointing, too. She had especially wanted to meet Carrick, who was much lauded by the press for his innovative architecture and 'green' credentials. But then it didn't take a genius to figure out that Honoria Granville marched to her own drum and perhaps Ashling shouldn't have been too surprised to find that whilst two key members of the family were absent, Rajesh, her Indian servant, was included in the family pictures.

As for Rossa, well, she had noticed him straight away. One look in those deep-set turquoise eyes and she had practically been down to her underwear. And he had been so kind and attentive, making sure she was well supplied with coffee and sandwiches, to keep her strength up, as he put it. When he invited her to dinner on the second evening at an amazing local fish restaurant – the first evening she had dined en famille – she didn't

11

even pretend reluctance. So beguiled was she that she could have eaten sawdust for all the attention she paid to the food. And, over coffee, when he had bashfully admitted to an interest in photography and asked her if she wouldn't mind having a look at his collection, she agreed without hesitation, although usually the prospect of looking at other people's holiday snaps sent her running for the hills. The snaps were good, not brilliant, but certainly better than average – land- and seascapes capturing the exotic beauty of Hua Hin where he had his base. There were pictures of the locals, too, and she couldn't help but notice that one bewitching young woman with waist-length hair and bold laughing eyes appeared several times. His girlfriend perhaps? She was surprised to feel a surge of jealousy.

But she needn't have worried. By the time she returned to Dublin, Rossa had made it plain that his interest lay not only in photography but in one particular photographer – her – and she found herself caught up in a whirlwind romance that would transform her life. Two months later they were engaged – and to Ashling's great surprise the severe Honoria unhesitatingly gave them her blessing.

Now here they were en route to where it all began to discuss arrangements for the Midsummer Ball, at which Honoria intended to formally announce the engagement.

'Penny for your thoughts?' Rossa took his hand

off the gearstick for a moment and lightly squeezed her fingers.

'I was just thinking ahead to the Midsummer Ball and your grandmother's plans.' Ashling allowed herself a small, goodhumoured grimace. 'We've spoken a few times on the phone recently and let's just say consulting with you and me appears to be something of a formality.'

The sun, already beginning its descent, slanted through the windscreen and Rossa pulled a pair of Ray-Bans from his top pocket and slipped them on. 'Oh dear, taking over the whole show, is she? I'm afraid old habits die hard.'

'You could say that! She seems to have covered all the bases, everything from a champagne fountain to a chocolate one – the last being Sapphire's suggestion, I believe. But I don't want to sound as if I'm moaning because, in fairness, she seems determined to make the event "appealing to the young folk".' She hooked her fingers around the expression.

Rossa laughed incredulously. 'Well, I'll be damned, a chocolate fountain. I've heard it all now! Trust Cousin Sapph to come up with a hare-brained idea like that. Still, what Sapph wants Sapph gets. Grandmother has forever been trying to make up to her for something or other. I've never been exactly sure what.' Rossa gestured to the glove compartment. 'I think I need a ciggie. Will you do the honours?'

While she didn't approve of smoking, Ashling

had to admit she did enjoy *watching* Rossa smoke. It was utterly sexy, conjuring up visions of Bogie and Bacall. She opened the compartment and pulled out a leather-covered cigarette case on which his initials had been embossed along with the insignia of his airline. There was a gold Dunhill lighter resting there too. Rossa had expensive tastes – but then he was a Granville. She lit the cigarette, drew tentatively on it, and when she was sure it was alight passed it to him, her eyes fastening on his strong brown wrist with its smattering of strawberry-blond hair. New watch too? Porsche, by the look of it. She'd photographed a display of them recently for one of the glossies and knew the genuine article would have set him back a cool four grand or so.

He took a hungry drag, exhaling a moment later in a tinge of blue-tinted smoke. 'Manna!' Pressing a button on the console between them, he lowered the driver's window to allow the smoke to clear.

A delicious quiver of anticipation ran down Ashling's spine. She could hardly wait for tonight and the feel of his rock-hard body against her own. Happily she thought of the gorgeous scanties from Agent Provocateur nestling in her suitcase.

'So have you told your mother the news yet?'

'What?' The question jerked her out of her complacency and the quiver that ran down her spine this time was more trepidation than fantasy. 'Um . . . not yet. She's still in the States. I'd – em – prefer to tell her in person. It's only fair.'

14

'You're not ashamed of me, I hope?' His tone was teasing.

'As if! It's just – it's just, well, Mother is not like other women. She needs careful handling.'

Rossa had heard of Coppelia Morrison. You'd have to have been living under a rock for the last umpteen years not to. Her photograph was forever splashed all over the newspapers detailing her exploits and the latest of her string of conquests, all stinking rich and many looking as though they were barely legal. He had been surprised that his grandmother hadn't balked at the connection. To Honoria's mind, Coppelia Morrison was the worst kind of woman – vulgar, social-climbing, walking fodder for the tabloids. One of her favourite sayings came to mind: *Lie down with dogs and you'll get up with fleas.* Yes, it was very odd that Honoria had remained uncharacteristically silent on the subject. She had to have known of Ashling's relationship to Coppelia even before she hired her for the photo-shoot.

'Anyway,' Ashling slipped into her Scarlett O'Hara impression, '*I don't want to think about that now. I'll think about it tomorrow.*'

'Fair enough. Let's have some music instead. Snow Patrol?'

'Perfect!' Ashling nestled back against the luxurious upholstery and a moment later found them both singing along to 'Chasing Cars'.

Ashling lurched awake as the car took a sharp bend to the right and started up a long side-road

15

snaking beneath an enormous vaulted cathedral of larch trees.

'Almost there.' Rossa touched her thigh lightly as she blinked herself back to full consciousness and gazed out into the purple dusk.

Ashling gave an involuntary shudder. They were nearly at Carrickross and this time she would enter it as an almost-member of the family.

Rossa noticed the movement. 'Cold?' he asked, and began fiddling with the temperature regulator on the dashboard.

'A bit,' Ashling lied, unwilling to tell him how scared she was; that as an only child she was nervous about becoming part of such a large family, worried about being accepted by all the others, about fitting in and finding her own niche. Something of her thoughts must have transmitted themselves to him anyway, because he reached across and squeezed her fingers reassuringly. Immediately she relaxed, covertly studying the strong lines of his face. She was with Rossa – Rossa Granville, the man of her dreams, soon to be her husband. Everything would be all right.

'I've phoned ahead to let them know we're nearly there,' said Rossa. 'Spoke to Noreen – you remember her – the cook?'

'Sure.' Ashling had grown fond of Noreen – and her cooking – on her last visit, short as it was.

As the car breasted and descended a final hill they found themselves skirting the old stone walls that surrounded the vast Carrickross estate. In the gathering gloom the iron gates rose up in monolithic splendour and Ashling's anxiety levels increased once more. They were not allayed by the sudden thundering of approaching hooves. In another moment, the headlights picked out the figure of Seán McCarthy, astride a magnificent Arabian stallion. Seán was the Carrickross groom, as well as gamekeeper-in-training, occasional chauffeur, odd-job man and jack-of-all-trades about the estate.

Jumping to the ground, he quickly tethered the horse to a nearby hitching post, then dragged the heavy gates open with a grating noise across the gravel. Greeting them both with a nod, he came and leaned on the window Rossa had slid open.

'Fuckin' great wheels, Rossa! Who did you have to shag for that?'

Rossa laughed, not at all put out by the familiarity. The pair had known each other since childhood. 'Wouldn't you like to know, me old son!' He gestured towards the horse, softly blowing streams of breath through its nostrils and crunching its hooves impatiently into the ground. 'How's The Sheikh? I must say, he looks in fine fettle!'

'Jesus, he's great,' Seán concurred. 'Not a bother on him. Carrick has a good eye for a horse.'

'Better than mine anyway,' Rossa agreed, ruefully referring to his well-known penchant for gambling.

Seán grinned, running a brazen eye over Ashling. 'Oh, I don't know, Miss Ashling is a grand little filly. Although why she doesn't show you a clean pair of heels is beyond me.'

Pretending pique, Rossa revved the engine. 'Ah, would you feck off, Seán, you cheeky beggar, and go and do a bit of work for a change!' Throwing the car into gear, he sped away up the long twisting tree-lined drive, leaving a chuckling Seán to lock the gates for the night.

Breaking clear of the last covering of trees, a thick huddle of Scots pines, Ashling caught her breath as Carrickross was revealed in all its splendour. In the dark, and with artfully arranged floodlights playing over its tall-chimneyed, multi-turreted facade, it truly was the stuff of fairy tales.

Rossa pulled up to allow her to drink in the view.

'Well, Ash, is it as good as you remember?' he asked with a note of pride in his voice.

'Amazing!' Ashling was overawed. She hadn't remembered it being quite so . . . overwhelming. But then, the first and only time she'd been here before had been on business and though she had admired it in the way one admires a beautiful hotel or civic building, her main focus had been on poses, angles and lighting meters – and, most of all, on people. Now she was regarding it in a completely different way. Now, it was personal. Slowly her eyes ranged over the pale limestone facade – quarried locally, added to and altered by

18

generations of Granvilles over hundreds of years. In daylight, she knew, an experienced eye could see the joins, the tell-tale colour variation where firstly the west wing was added and later, in another century altogether, the east, the pair reaching forward from the main building like arms, ready to embrace.

Rossa started the engine again and swept up the drive, swerving to a stop at the foot of the flight of steps that led to the main doorway. Ashling gazed around her, remembering it all. The drive circled round an oval of lawn which, with the clever placing of box hedging, had been fashioned to form a miniature maze. A sundial, the copper verdigris with age, sat directly in the centre on a base of granite inset with the Granville coat of arms. Satsuma-coloured light spilled in diamond facets from behind the many mullioned windows. The marble steps leading up to the door were bordered on each side by ornately carved balustrades, the newels of which were topped off by great ornamental urns out of which spilled a profusion of trailing ivy and lobelia in nursery pinks and blues.

Suddenly the great doors were thrown open and a figure trotted down the steps: Noreen McCarthy, the cook-cum-housekeeper and mother of Seán.

'Lord Almighty, you poor little thing, sure you must be exhausted! Leave the luggage – I'll have it brought in and taken upstairs for you.'

Grabbing Ashling by the arm Noreen helped her out and bustled her up the steps, leaving Rossa to fend for himself. She threw a disgusted look back over her shoulder at the Aston Martin.

'Them sports cars are all very well and good, pet, if you ask me, but if it's comfort you want, you're barking up the wrong tree. Come on in now and you can have a little freshen-up in the ladies' room off the hall before seeing the mistress. She's waiting for you in Little India.'

'Little India?' Ashling wasn't sure she'd heard right.

Noreen chuckled. 'Aye, Little India. It's what we call the main drawing room on account of it being stuffed with all sorts of heathen objects picked up by the mistress on her travels there. The small drawing room in the east wing is Little China – did you not see it last time you were here?' She rattled on without waiting for an answer as she led Ashling into the entrance hall. 'All Chinese lacquer furniture, silk carpets and great big ugly dragon ornaments that I, personally, wouldn't give you thanks for. But then, what do I know? Then, there's Little Africa – that's where Jaspar stays on his very occasional trips home from Kenya. The savage-looking things in there would give you nightmares. Big ugly masks and spears and the likes. Even a shrunken head or two.' Noreen shot her a mischievous look. 'And guess what we call the twins' suite? Little Bedlam!' She threw back her head and laughed heartily. 'Your own Rossa came up with that one. Didn't you, darlin'?'

Rossa smiled as he caught up with them and

dropped a kiss on her cheek. 'I hope you're not filling my beautiful fiancee's ears with tales of horror, Noreen?'

Noreen laughed. 'I'm just giving her the lie of the land, that's all.'

'Ready to beard the dragon, sweetheart?' Rossa steered Ashling towards the drawing room. 'Best get it over with!'

Noreen slapped his hand away sharply. 'For heaven's sake, would you give the poor girl a chance to freshen up, Rossa!' She rolled her eyes at Ashling. 'Men! They haven't a clue!'

Ashling laughed. 'You can say that again! Especially Rossa.' She flipped him an airy wave. 'You go on ahead. I won't be long.'

'Well, be it at your own risk. Grandmother may have reduced me to a heap of ashes by that time!' Rossa made a mock-grimace and set off, walking as though on his way to the gallows.

Unsympathetic, Ashling blew him a kiss. 'I doubt it. Anyway, aren't dragons supposed to be extinct?'

'Not this one. This one is very much alive and full of fire.'

Honoria had been standing discreetly by the window as Rossa's car pulled up in front of the house. Her lips had quirked slightly, then clamped together in satisfaction. How fortunate that Ashling had turned out to be so pleasing to the eye and Rossa so malleable! Her grandson, much as she loved him, had always been somewhat

21

shallow – a magpie attracted by bright shiny objects and tireless in his pursuit to make them his own.

'I, Rajesh, am a puppeteer,' Honoria announced grandly, turning from the window and levering herself somewhat stiffly into her favourite chair. 'The strings may not always be visible, but they are there nevertheless and now the curtain is set to rise on the greatest show of all.'

'Indeed, Rani.' Rajesh bowed from the waist and handed her a glass of ruby port, the facets of the crystal catching the light and shearing off along the walls like broken diamonds.

'She is beautiful, is she not – Ashling? Intelligent and principled too, the kind of girl any grandmother would wish for her grandson.' A tremor ran through her hand. The glass wobbled dangerously. 'All that *and* the daughter of my greatest enemy. Do not let me weaken, Rajesh. Remind me always. No mercy.'

'No mercy,' Rajesh repeated softly. 'Keep your enemies close and your enemy's daughter closer.'

Honoria smiled. 'Exactly so. You have always understood me so well.' She leaned back, sipped her drink and waited for the knock on the door that would announce the presence of her grandson and his fiancée.

She didn't have long to wait. Rossa erupted through the door and, sinking to his knees beside her chair, took her hand in both of his and kissed it. It was a typical over-the-top Rossa entrance, but Honoria lapped it up.

'Grandmother, how lovely to see you!'

'Silly boy!' She gestured for him to get up and looked over his shoulder. 'And where is the lovely Ashling?'

'Just gone to freshen up. She won't be long.'

'Such a wearying trip,' Honoria sympathised. 'One can see why Carrick keeps a helicopter.'

Any mention of Carrick's wealth, so much greater than his own, always brought out Rossa's petulant side. 'We've only come from Dublin, a mere four-hour drive. Anyway, it's not as though Ashling is some wishy-washy milksop. She might look fragile, but she's tough as old boots, really. Every bit as tough as you were when you sailed up the Ganges or climbed the Himalayas or led the Charge of the Light Brigade in your youth!'

'Led the Charge of the Light Brigade! What nonsense! Do you suppose I am two hundred years old? Besides, that was in the Crimea, you ignorant boy!' Honoria gave a loud sniff and her mouth pruned, but Rossa could see she was pleased with his sly flattery. 'Ah, and here is the delightful Ashling, just in time to save me from any more of your nonsense!' Honoria smiled and held her hand out graciously as Ashling approached. 'Welcome back to Carrickross, my dear. Please excuse me if I don't get up. Old bones, I'm afraid.'

'Oh, not too painful, I hope?' Ashling took the proffered hand and wondered if she should kiss Honoria. As she hesitated, Honoria solved the problem by drawing her down to sit in the armchair beside her.

'Some wine for the children, please, Rajesh! Despite your protestations, Rossa, I'm sure Ashling, at least, must be fatigued from the long drive.' She scanned her from head to foot with her penetrating gaze. 'Well, child, how lovely you look tonight! Rossa, I trust you know how lucky you are.'

Ashling smiled, pleased that she had chosen to wear her favourite Orla Kiely knee-length cashmere sweater dress. It never failed to make her feel confident and glamorous and the soft lavender colour really suited her complexion. She had added a bejewelled Christian Lacroix pendant with matching earrings. It was undoubtedly a statement piece of jewellery but what better evening to make a statement? Her shoes were Louboutin, not killer-heels, but high enough to show her slender legs to their best advantage. She had pulled her hair up in a soft wispy up-do and kept her make-up light. As her stepmother, Coppelia, was fond of saying, the only real adornment a girl needed was her youth. Pleased with her appearance, Ashling had nevertheless enlisted Noreen's opinion when she'd emerged from the cloakroom.

'Do you look all right?' Disbelievingly, Noreen had raked her head to toe. 'What do you mean do you look all right? Sure you look amazin', like one of them big filum stars from Hollywood.

24

I don't know whether to bow or to ask for your autograph.'

Now Ashling smiled as Rajesh presented her with a glass of wine, his peculiarly intent eyes fixed on her face. A sudden bout of nerves made the stem of the glass shake slightly in her hand. She took a sip, feeling slightly better as the liquid warmed her blood.

Rossa, of course, was experiencing no such qualms. Perching himself on the arm of Honoria's armchair, he continued both to charm and to annoy her in the way that came as natural to him as breathing.

'So, Grandmother, I hear you've been having a merry old time sorting out all this engagement stuff.'

Ashling's head came up, not too sure she liked their engagement being referred to in such casual terms, but Honoria seemed not in the least fazed.

'Engagements take a lot of organisation, young man,' she admonished him lightly. 'Things must be done properly and must be seen to be done properly. People look to the Granvilles for the lead in these matters and we must not let the side down.'

Ashling flinched inwardly, thinking of her step-mother, who considered nobody's side but her own. She imagined the scene when these two formidable women came face to face for the very first time. Clash of the Titans? The flinch became a full-grown shudder but, luckily, the older woman

25

was gesturing for Rajesh to bring her something from her writing bureau on the far side of the room and didn't notice.

'Thank you, Rajesh.' She took a cream vellum envelope from him and eased out a heavily embossed formal invitation which she waved under their noses. 'The invitation, my dears! I know you won't mind that I took the liberty of having these printed, knowing how busy you are, Rossa, flying round the world, and you, Ashling, pursuing your own, no doubt estimable career. Still, that can get quite in the way of important matters.' The last was said with something of a hard look at Ashling. Honoria tapped the invitation against her palm. 'In any case, you will be pleased to know that they are, as we speak, winging their way all round the world. So important to give sufficient notice, especially to those who have chosen to squirrel themselves away abroad.'

Rossa took the invitation from her, scanned it briefly, then handed it to Ashling. 'Oh, Grandmother, how lovely and how kind of you,' he said stiffly, 'but I think Ashling and I would have preferred—'

Honoria's hand scythed through the air. 'Tosh! These things are better left in experienced hands. In any case, I did, indeed, send a sample to you in Thailand, Rossa, and to Ashling also, but as neither one of you responded I'm afraid I took your silence as acquiescence. I apologise unreservedly if you feel I took too much upon myself.' There was a

26

sudden shine in her eyes and her hand trembled slightly in apparent distress.

Quickly, Ashling hurried to reassure her. 'Oh, no, it's fine. Honestly! It saves us the bother and I'm not surprised about the post. Mine goes astray all the time. Please don't be upset. We're both very grateful, aren't we, Rossa? Rossa?' She glanced at him as he made no reply, just sat looking suddenly pale and slightly sick.

He gave a slight jerk, suddenly recollecting himself. 'What? Oh, yes. Yes, of course we're grateful, Grandmother. I only wish . . .'

Honoria gazed at him stonily. 'What, Rossa? You wish what?'

His own gaze didn't meet hers and Ashling was aware of a strange undercurrent running between the pair.

'Oh, nothing. Nothing at all.' Rossa smiled unconvincingly.

'I'm pleased to hear it!' Honoria turned to Ashling. 'I did not, of course, forget your step-mother, Ashling, and I trust you will be pleased to hear that an invitation was sent to her suite at the New York Hilton.'

It was Ashling who looked pale and a little sick now, her eyes signalling Rossa's in a morse code of distress, as Honoria, having delivered this *coup de grâce*, rose stiffly to her feet.

'Now, if you two young people will excuse me, I shall leave you to dine alone. It has grown late and I find I am more weary than I expected to be. Age, sadly, must ever be one's master. Still, Noreen will take excellent care of you. There is trout, I believe, caught in our own river.'

Utterly dismayed, Ashling watched her exit the room, leaning heavily on her boar's-head walking stick, Rajesh, as ever, in attendance. Quickly, she put her glass down on a nearby table, but it fell to the floor and smashed in pieces.

'Jesus! Fucking hell, Rossa! My stepmother! She's told my stepmother. Christ, she's going to go ballistic! I wanted to tell her myself.' She fell to her knees and began to clear up the glass, uncaring even when a small shard pierced her thumb. 'Oh, I know you're pissed off she stole our thunder but at least no one's going to be out for your blood. But my stepmother will never understand. Not in a month of Sundays.' A hysterical note entered her voice. 'Take a good long look and remember me as I am now, Rossa, because, as of the moment Coppelia Morrison receives that invite, I am officially Dead Woman Walking.'

Honoria sat at her dressing table pondering the success of the evening. She chuckled as she recalled the expression on her grandson's face as he struggled to bring his panic under control. Her face hardened. Nothing and no one must be allowed to jeopardise her plan and if its success depended on a little manipulation here or a little bending of the truth there, so be it. As for Ashling, Honoria had never sent the invitation to her. She couldn't risk the girl telephoning Rossa for his opinion, unwittingly putting him on the alert and in a position to stay on in Thailand and intercept the invitation on arrival there. That was not what Honoria had in mind. Not at all.

Ashling stared at her image in the bathroom mirror in Rossa's suite, although she had been given her own opulent rooms across from his, Honoria doubtless being of a generation who liked to pretend nice girls didn't. Or, perhaps, she really was that naive. She raised nervous fingers to soothe the frown from her brow and the tension from her lips. Rossa was waiting for her in the bedroom, in the luxurious four-poster bed, but all the pleasurable anticipation she had been feeling had fled and she could think only of that lethal invitation winging its way to New York like a little ticking bomb. Obviously it hadn't arrived yet. She would have heard the explosion had it found its mark.

She had suffered a profound shock and now a potent mix of nervous tension, anger and sheer panic was coursing through her veins. Why in God's name had she neglected to tell her step-mother before now? There were reasons, yes – good solid rational ones like wanting to tell her face to face rather than over the phone – but all the reasons in the world were like feathers when weighed against this looming catastrophe. Besides, the real reason had been an instinctive one – she felt sure that her stepmother would pour scorn on this wonderful whirlwind romance, this fairy-tale engagement. But why should this frighten her so much? Did she feel that her newfound happiness was so fragile that one scathing look from Coppelia could shatter it?

Ashling resolutely shook her head to banish these thoughts. She picked up her hairbrush and vigorously began to brush her dark hair. Why did she always have to feel so insecure? She had come to think of her life as a jigsaw, of which many of the pieces had gone missing or didn't quite fit. Round pegs and square holes. She had been conscious of this even as a small child when her mother's remoteness had vaguely puzzled her. Eventually she had come to understand that the word 'stepmother' was the jigsaw piece that completed *that* part of the puzzle.

On the morning of her thirteenth birthday another jigsaw piece had awaited her, together with the solid gold charm bracelet from Tiffany's and an original black-and-white study by Annie Leibovitz. There had been an over-generous cheque, too, which, in her memory, seemed to hover unsupported over the silver serving dishes, her father's eyes the apprehensive backdrop. What had it been, that cheque? she had often wondered. Consolation prize, payoff, bribe? Whatever the intention, the knowledge that was served up with it had been a heavy burden to place on such young shoulders.

Ashling's father, Edward, had delivered the blow, stumblingly and with embarrassed tenderness. He had obviously rehearsed the words, coated them with honey, but still they cut like a knife. She was *special*. She was *chosen*. She was . . . adopted. Adopted! The word clanged, reverberating in the air between them. She recalled a sudden whooshing noise in her ears and her father's voice, echoey, seeming to come from a distance. Ashling had been adopted by him and his first wife, Margery, before her sudden decline and untimely death. Two years later, persuaded that the infant Ashling needed a mother, he had married Coppelia. He'd looked a little bewildered here and unhappy, as if he couldn't quite figure out how that had actually come to pass. They had agreed to keep the fact of her adoption a secret until she was old enough to understand.

Had Coppelia stage-managed the whole birthday revelation? Ashling couldn't help but wonder now with the benefit of hindsight. Coppelia always did wear the trousers in that relationship. They certainly made an unlikely pairing. Her adoptive father was a quiet bookish man, private, warm-hearted and old before his time – Coppelia, the antithesis, a social and exotic butterfly.

Ashling shrugged on the emerald-silk Agent Provocateur cami, enjoying the caress of the luxurious material against her skin. She stepped into the matching thong and stood back to view her reflection in the full-length mirror-tiled walls.

Sexy, definitely sexy! She spritzed on some Eau d'Hadrien and ruthlessly pushed away the old memories and the future fears. The past was past. Her father, darling man, was dead and more than likely, especially after Honoria's little bombshell, she and her stepmother would now drift apart, living their separate lives. She must learn to live in the here and now – and *now* it was high time she was in Rossa Granville's arms.

But when she emerged from the bathroom, Rossa was already asleep, his chest rising and falling steadily, small puffs of air escaping from between his lips. Feeling slightly ridiculous, she caught sight of herself in the dressing-table mirror, marble pale in the scraps of emerald-green underwear. All undressed and nowhere to go! Disappointed, she turned off the light, climbed into bed and slipped her arm around Rossa's waist.

As her eyes closed, she was unaware that his had opened and were fixed unseeingly on the wall opposite.

In the morning Rossa was up and dressed before she was even awake. Blinking the sleep from her eyes, she watched him run a comb quickly through his hair, straighten the collar of his shirt and pat on some Bulgari cologne.

'Rossa?' She struggled up on her elbow. 'Where are you going?'

He spun quickly round, then strode over and dropped a kiss on her lips.

'Oh, you're awake. I'm sorry I woke you, darling. And I'm even sorrier to tell you I'm going to have to leave you. I have to go back to Thailand sooner than I imagined. There was a phone call earlier. Seems someone cocked up the schedules and I'm actually due to captain a flight to Australia in the next forty-eight hours, if you can believe that. Incompetent bastards!'

'Oh no, Rossa! You can't be serious. Shit, we've only just got here. And what about me, Rossa? What about your grandmother? All the arrangements she wanted to discuss. She'll be gutted. *I'm* gutted.'

Rossa sat down on the side of the bed, picked up her hand and dropped a kiss on the palm, lingering. It sent chills up her spine.

'No more than me. What can I do, though? I'm between a rock and a hard place. There's no way I can let the airline down. It is my bread and butter, after all. You know that, darling. Comes with the territory, I'm afraid.'

'But it's okay to let me down?' Fearing she might cry, Ashling bit her lip.

'That's not fair! This isn't my choice, Ashling. You know there's nowhere I'd rather be than with you. Please don't make this any harder than it needs to be. I'll be back as soon as I can, promise. I'll just do this flight and get them to rearrange the schedules. Cheer up! You'll hardly have time to miss me.'

Ashling made a valiant attempt at smiling. 'Oh

well, I suppose I have no choice. Love you, love your job.'

Rossa's face cleared. 'Atta girl. Anyway, I'm going to have to get my skates on. So, do you want to stay here at Carrickross for a bit or would you prefer to decamp back to Dublin?'

'Drive back with you.' Ashling didn't miss a heart-beat, quailing at the thought of being at Carrickross without him. 'There's work I can be getting on with at the studio anyway.'

'Right! You get dressed while I go and break the bad news to Grandmother, although I'd sooner stick pins in my eyes!'

Rossa left a moment later, looking comically terrified.

And so, a little more than twelve hours after they arrived, a very disappointed Ashling found herself on her way back to Dublin and normal life. Really things hadn't turned out at all as she'd expected. She hoped it wasn't a bad omen.

Beside her, Rossa was altogether more stoical, humming some jolly little tune beneath his breath. She wasn't sure whether to admire this display of maturity or deplore the fact that he simply didn't appear to be quite as bothered as she was. As he dropped her off, causing a traffic snarl-up as usual, he took her face between her hands and kissed her soundly.

'Remember, I'll be back before you know it.'

'I hope so, Rossa!' She smiled a little sadly, then threw her arms around his neck. 'I do hope so.'

She stood watching as he drove away into the traffic.

In the car Rossa had hastily voice-activated his mobile phone.

'Hello, darling,' he cooed, as the handset was picked up at the far end. 'I've been to visit my grandmother like I told you. I'm leaving now – flying out this afternoon. I'll be with you before you know it.'

CHAPTER 2

New York

Propping herself up on one elbow, Coppelia Morrison smiled sleepily across at the open bathroom door.

'Hey, baby!' she called, as the mingled scents of hot soapy water and Missoni drifted out on a cloud of steam. 'Come back to bed!' Her voice had the texture of warm syrup poured over double cream.

'Can't!' The response, muffled from behind a face flannel, held a world of regret. 'You know I've got to be on that plane. I'm a whole week late as it is. Grandmere will have my guts for garters! I'm supposed to be studying for my exams!'

'So? Can't you catch a later flight?' Slowly raising one leg, she flexed her foot, *en point*, like a ballet dancer. Toned, tanned, lean and muscular, it could have belonged to a woman many years younger than the big five-O it said on her passport.

Butt-naked, fluffy white towel in hand, Fin Granville strolled back into the bedroom. Dark-blue eyes surveyed her as he ruffled his blue-black hair. 'Stop pouting, Pelia! You know there's nothing I'd like better but I have to go.' Firmly, he wrapped the towel around his slim young waist, as if to clinch the argument.

Emerald eyes brazenly raked him up and down, as idly she rotated her ankle first one way, then the other. 'Oh, well, please yourself . . . or please me . . .' This time the look she gave him was nothing short of lascivious and she was pleased to see a pulse begin to twitch in his cheek.

When Coppelia Morrison put her mind to it, there wasn't a man alive who could resist her and she put her mind to it now, running her hands tantalisingly over her breasts so that her nipples grew erect, then slowly down across her flat stomach to where the V of lush hair pointed, X-marks-the-spot, to the treasure below. And what little boy could resist a game of pirates?

'Coppelia,' he said thickly, 'please don't do this to me!' Aroused despite his best intentions, his eyes found themselves drawn magnetically to the long sensuously gliding fingers. Man, she was hot! Wait till he told the posse at school! Well, the few who could keep a secret. They'd go mad with envy.

'Do what?' she asked huskily, deliberately sliding her hand further down, her eyes, half hidden beneath a veil of heavy lashes, flashing a challenge.

'That!' Fin's voice grew thicker and he swallowed rapidly.

'You don't have to look if you don't want to.'

Her own voice dripping with desire, Coppelia raised a sardonic, perfectly arched, eyebrow. 'Anyway, wasn't there something about a plane?'

'Bugger the plane!' A moment later, control completely abandoned, Fin tossed aside the towel and practically hurled himself on top of her.

Content, now that she had got her own way, she traced the line of his spine with a sensuous finger. 'Heavens, how I shall miss you when you go back to school!'

'But you'll come and visit me, won't you? And pretend to be my "Aunty", like you did before?' His words came hot against her ear. 'You'll come and take me out for tea and cream buns and hot sex, won't you?'

'Why, of course I will! But only if you ask me in the nicest possible way.'

'Please, Aunty Pelia! Pretty please?' Coaxing, his tongue began to inch and slide its way along her skin, pausing at all the most sensitive points, exploring every shadow, every curve, every exquisite crease of her body.

He levered himself above her, sweat beading his brow, the muscles of his young athletic frame bunched beneath the skin as his forearms took the weight. Smiling, Coppelia wrapped her legs around his waist.

Later, much later, after Fin had finally left, a satiated Coppelia rolled out of bed, made straight for the bathroom cabinet and took out a small hand-mirror and a plastic bag with a few grams of white powder nestling in the corner. God, she really needed this. Like, *really, really needed this!* Tipping a small pile out onto the glass she carefully divided it in two and, with the aid of a razor blade kept specifically for the purpose, formed each half into a long narrow line. When she was absolutely satisfied that they were as neat and symmetrical as she could make them, she reached back into the cabinet and took out a specially designed straw in chased silver, a birthday present to herself. No one could ever accuse Coppelia Morrison of not having style. Closing off one nostril, she dipped the straw in the first line of powder and inhaled deeply, quickly following suit with the other. Then she dabbed up the residue with the tip of her finger and rubbed it across her teeth. As her eyes began to dilate to the point where they were nearly all black pupil with just the merest rim of green, she smiled at their fathoms-deep reflection in the bathroom mirror.

Now she was ready to take on the world. The *whole* world, including that wealthy little corner occupied by the great Honoria Granville and her too-big-for-their-boots, ride-roughshod-over-everyone-else family.

'Slowly, slowly,' she whispered, liberally sprinkling her specially blended Jo Malone ylang ylang and jasmine bath salts beneath the running faucet into the bathtub, 'catchee monkey!'

Still, she reflected, sliding sensuously into the

water, it was high time she got herself back to the Emerald Shit-Hole. It was a bore, but she had been away for almost four months. Risky! The media were so fickle and every johnny-come-lately and reality-show reject would be queuing up to take her place as the queen of Irish society. Not a crown she would relinquish easily.

By the time she emerged, her damp hair turbaned in a towel, room service had already been in with her breakfast tray. She surveyed it with satisfaction. One pot of freshly ground coffee, a croissant with a curl of yellow butter, and one perfect, ripe mango, peeled, sliced and sprinkled with lemon juice to stop it discolouring. All served on the finest of white bone china. Intriguingly there was a letter, propped up against the coffee pot.

For a moment, Coppelia's hand hovered apprehensively, although hers wasn't a nature normally given to fancies. Annoyed, she shrugged the feeling off, picked up the envelope and weighed it assessingly. The stationery was good quality – cream Basildon Bond in a linen weave – the handwriting a flowing copperplate in an unusual shade of violet ink. An Irish stamp depicting two fantastically elongated birds curved into a circle with interlocking tails and beaks sat squarely, almost grotesquely, on the right-hand corner like a harbinger of doom.

Chastising herself for a fool, she ripped the envelope open so that the gold-embossed invitation nestling inside fell out and landed elaborate-script-side up on the table.

40

As the words jumped out and seemed to pulsate in the air around her, Coppelia reeled back against the table.

'*No!*' The scream came knifing up from inside her, a physical demonstration of remembered pain and a rage so great she had to grab onto the back of a chair to stop herself from keeling over. '*No! No! No!*' And all the time the words of the unexpected invitation spun and swam, jumbled and rearranged themselves before her eyes – branding themselves indelibly into her brain.

Mrs Honoria Granville
cordially requests the pleasure of
Mrs Coppelia Morrison's presence
at the Midsummer Ball, 21 June 2008
on the occasion of the engagement
of her grandson Rossa Granville
to Miss Ashling Morrison . . .

Feeling as though the very bones in her legs had melted, Coppelia edged round the front of the chair and shakily let herself flop onto the seat.

Engagement? Dear God, when did that happen? When had Ashling even *met* Rossa Granville? And why had she kept it a secret from her mother? Her heart thudded deafeningly in her ears as her mind conjured up scenario after hideous scenario. She gritted her teeth so hard her jaw ached.

41

Whatever the reason for her daughter's silence, *that* was one wedding that would never happen! Not while she, Coppelia Morrison, still had breath in her body. In a fury, she picked up the invitation, ripped it to shreds and tossed the pieces in the ashtray, then set fire to them. Ashes to ashes.

Breathless with rage, she watched the last piece curl and burn. *R.S.V.P.* The letters faded to black and disintegrated, leaving only a small blue flame. It fanned for a moment, sputtered and died to a spark. Then that too went out.

Répondez s'il vous plait . . . By Christ, she'd respond all right! Just not quite in the way Honoria Granville expected! With trembling fingers she picked up the telephone, thought twice and replaced it again. An exchange of disembodied voices would not suffice. She needed to see her daughter face to face, to look deep in her eyes and make the foolish little idiot understand that hers was no boy-meets-girl-and-they-all-live-happily-ever-after fairy tale. Like hell it was! No, this was a challenge, an unmistakable gauntlet thrown down by Honoria Granville, who, Coppelia was in no doubt, had somehow engineered the whole sorry situation. It was too much of a coincidence that out of all the young, eligible men in Ireland, her daughter, Ashling, would end up engaged to her arch-enemy's grandson.

She drummed absentmindedly on the arm of her chair. Like a master chess player she needed to consider all the pieces, work out the different

42

permutations of this game. In using Ashling as a pawn, Honoria Granville had made the first move. Coppelia drummed harder. She would bide her time. She was familiar with the rules of the waiting game. She'd been playing it most of her life. A little more patience was all that was required.

CHAPTER 3

Carrickross House

Sapphire Granville trailed a graceful hand in the stream, enjoying the dual sensations of the water lapping over and through her fingers and the delicate kiss of the tiny tiddlers against her skin as they came to investigate the strange creature invading their world. Beside her, Indigo lay stretched at full length, a joint in one hand, eyes shaded against the glare of the sun.

'I wish I had a jamjar.'

'Eh?' He opened one eye.

'A jamjar.' She flicked her wet fingers at him, scattering prisms of crystal in the air. 'Like when we were kids, to catch tiddlers?'

He scowled, slightly irritated that she had broken his train of thought, which increasingly these days concerned his grandmother and his ever-growing dislike of her scheming. Take this whole Midsummer Ball thing. The way she was using it as a public platform to display her latest victory made him sick, though not nearly as sick as it was likely to make Carrick. Poor bloke, what a shock it must be to find the script you'd followed all your life suddenly ripped from your hands and the lead role given to a lesser actor who happened to be your younger brother.

Indigo inhaled deeply, held the smoke for a moment in his mouth then let it out in a long stream. Mind you, that Ashling was a bit of a hottie. He'd go there himself, given half the chance. But did she have child-bearing hips? That was the question!

His thoughts turned to Uncle Jaspar. In reality, he had more right to inherit than any of them, given that he was Honoria's only remaining son. But Jaspar's sexual proclivities had ruled him firmly out of inheriting Carrickross, from the start. Not that Honoria had ever come right out and said it in so many words, but everyone knew she didn't hold with such 'unnatural behaviour', especially not amongst the Granvilles. Besides, Jaspar seemed perfectly happy off in the wilds of Kenya and rumour had it his latest boyfriend was actually a Maasai tribesman. What fun if he brought him to the Midsummer Ball! Indigo only hoped the invitation hadn't gone astray. He knew for a fact it was the first one to be sent, as the post in Kenya was so unreliable. Trust Honoria. Any normal person would simply have used the phone or even email. Snail mail was so passe these days. Then again, so was his grandmother. Modern technology brought her out in a rash and had her wittering on about how much simpler life was in her day. Hence her refusal to go within fifty metres of a mobile telephone or, God forbid, install Sky TV. Something buzzed in his face and Indigo flicked it away. Thank Christ, her days of ruling the roost, ruling them all with a rod of iron, were almost numbered. The insect buzzed again and Indigo's eyes snapped open to find Sapphire trailing a blade of grass along his cheek.

'Earth to Indy! Earth to Indy! Come in, Indy!'

'Fuck's sake, stop that, Sapph!' Catching her by the wrist he pulled her down till her face was directly over his, her mouth so close he could feel the tangy sweetness of her breath. 'Those tiddlers you were banging on about just now – you always caught more than me . . .'

'Still do,' she grinned. 'Only the fish are bigger now!'

He chuckled. 'But, you know, fishing wasn't the only thing we did . . . even then. Remember?'

'Oh, indeed!' Locking eyes, she let her lips brush softly against his lower one and then nibbled it gently. 'Sometimes we caught butterflies!' Laughing, she leaped to her feet and began to dance, every delicate curve of her body visible as sunlight glanced through her flimsy ivory-hued dress. 'You liked that, didn't you, Ind? Remember the red admirals? Remember how, when we held them, all the colour came away on our fingers like paint?' Dipping and swaying, her hair arced out in a halo of silver. 'And the cabbage whites? They were your favourites. Remember how we chased

46

them with our nets and how you liked to pull their wings off and take bets on how long it would take the poor creatures to die?'

Indigo's blue eyes darkened instantly. He raised himself on an elbow and, turning his head, looked towards the house, which was just visible through the blaze of rhododendron and the stand of Scots pines that guarded its south-western corner. 'Talking of creatures and dying, what are the latest odds on how long it will take the Black Widow to turn up her toes?'

With a last shimmy, Sapphire came back to sink on her knees beside him, her jewel-bright eyes meeting his gaze. 'Granoria? Oh, *she'll* never die. She's immortal, a giant spider at the centre of her Carrickross web shooting out her sticky strands,' her arms formed waving tentacles, 'and drawing us one by one into the centre,' she gave a dramatic shiver and finished in a quavery voice, 'so she can suck the very life-blood out of our veins!'

Indigo groaned. 'Don't be so moronic, Sapph! How often must I tell you? She's not immortal. She's bloody ancient and it's nature's law that the old should die and make way for the young.'

An expression of discontent narrowed Sapphire's normally plump lips into a straight line.

'Oh, I do wish she'd get on with it, Ind. She scares me the way she constantly watches us. I'm so afraid she'll send us away again.'

'Hush!' He reached out and silenced her with a finger across her mouth. 'You're imagining things.

Did you forget to take your medication this morning?'

She pouted, shaking her head indignantly.

'Anyway, we're not going anywhere, do you hear me?' he said. 'Not me. Not you. Carrickross is our home and over my dead body will Honoria or anyone else, come to that, make us leave.'

Sapphire gave him a sharp look. 'You frighten me sometimes, Indy. You really do. You mustn't underestimate Granoria. And as for Rajesh . . .' Her voice trembled.

'Oh, don't fuss, Sapph. Those two old fogeys don't bother me.' He fanned a bored hand across his mouth. 'I'd take them both on with one hand tied behind my back. Now, tell you what, why don't we turn our minds to something much more interesting?'

With a lightning move, he reversed their positions so that she was underneath him, then tiptoed a finger all the way from her mouth, down her slender throat to where the shadowed hollow of her cleavage began. The pointed little nipples of her small breasts sprang immediately to attention, straining through her dress. He circled them each in turn and she gasped with pleasure. His breath came harder. 'You know I'll always look after you, Sapph, don't you?' Silent, she nodded, as he rose, yanked her to her feet and pulled her into the secret heart of a purple rhododendron bush. 'Starting right now!'

*   *   *

Up at the house, Honoria Granville glared down the length of the luncheon table, her piercing blue eyes bypassing the splendid Waterford glass centrepiece and lingering angrily on the two empty chairs placed side by side.

'You!' she barked at a maid hovering nervously nearby. 'Go and see what's keeping the twins. Those two will be the death of me!'

CHAPTER 4

Tokyo

The red-gold liquid swirled around the ice as Carrick Granville poured a shot of Black Bush into the heavy crystal whiskey glass. The taste of home.

Home. Carrickross, nestled among the woods and lakes of Kerry. A world away from this mesmerising spectacle that was night-time Tokyo.

He moved across the room, barefoot – a tautly muscular figure, dressed only in fine dark cords. Standing in the window – or rather in a prow-shaped extension of it which projected dizzyingly over the street far beneath – he felt like a bird of prey about to swoop on the defenceless little creatures scurrying along the street below. He raised his glass in a farewell to the teeming city, seemingly chaotic but in fact going about its business with Japanese precision.

His time in Tokyo was over. The job was done, his building finished. He had enjoyed the whole project immensely, but then he always did. The challenge had been to create a stimulating working environment for a small exclusive jewellery company on a narrow strip of land between two high-rise office blocks. Inspired by ancient Japanese *shinden-zukuri* architecture where separate domestic buildings were linked by corridors and bridges, he designed a structure that looked inwards on itself. So, while the oblong building had a clinical blank exterior, inside it was complex and intimate. It held the city at bay, creating a space poised in calm.

But now it was done and dusted, and tonight he would dream of the springy peat of an Irish woodland path beneath his feet, the earthy smell of leaves and fungus, the heavy aroma of pine. His two great wolfhounds, Zerakiel and Barakiel, would bound ahead of him and then they would emerge on the lakeshore and make for the boat that would take them to the island, *his* island.

Something tugged at the edges of his consciousness, something he had wilfully suppressed. Resigned, he placed his tumbler on a glass table and retrieved the envelope which he had thrust unopened into his briefcase earlier. An envelope with his grandmother's name on the back, its expensive vellum defaced by a cheeky rosebud of magenta lipstick – that would be Cousin Sapphire adding her mark, he thought, with a twist of the lips more rueful than affectionate.

With a sense of deep foreboding, he slit the flap and extracted a gold-embossed invitation from within. His eyes flitted briefly over the printed message, then, with growing shock, he read it a second time, more slowly. His grandmother, it appeared, was inviting him to the engagement of her grandson, *his* younger brother, Rossa.

Engaged? Love 'em and leave 'em Rossa? Inveterate playboy Rossa? In a pig's eye! Frozen to the spot, Carrick stared hard at the card, his dark face brooding, blue eyes glittering with their enigmatic gaze. When? When had Rossa become engaged? And why was this invitation the first he had heard of it, this coldly official invite? He didn't have to search far for the answers. It was his grandmother's own inimitable way of informing him that he was no longer the great white hope, that he had been disinherited. Such was her determination for a great-grandson to carry on the Granville name, it seemed she was prepared to go to any lengths. But, ironically, in so doing, she was likely to bring about the destruction of the very thing she loved most, Carrickross.

Tossing the card on the table, he picked up and drained his glass. He continued to brood, looking for the bigger picture. Honoria was never one to cut off her nose to spite her face. She knew Rossa's character better than anyone and how, even as a child, his pocket money had burned a hole in his pocket. The estate would be bankrupt in no time at all. So, what was she thinking? No doubt something so cunning, so elaborate, it would take the combined services of both Holmes and Poirot to unravel it. And what was the betting that he himself was a key player? But what exactly was his role?

The invitation had fallen face-up on the table. His glance went once more to the distinctive purple scrawl at the bottom:

Be there. Honoria.

By Christ, he'd be there all right, even if he had to swim all the way from Tokyo. But first . . . Picking up his mobile he pressed the memory key for Hua Hin and, when his brother answered, spoke without preamble. 'Carrick here. Firstly, allow me to offer my congratulations. And secondly, Rossa, what the hell are you playing at?'

Hua Hin, Thailand

Rossa Granville replaced the receiver and sank back against the pillows. Sweat beaded his brow, not all of which was entirely due to the dank humidity of Hua Hin. He'd expected the phone call, of course, and Carrick had been nowhere near as unpleasant as he had a right to be, but still he felt like an absolute shit. Well, damn it, he wasn't totally without a conscience. Dress it up how you would, the fact was that he'd stolen a march on his elder brother and colluded with his grandmother against him.

It had almost been accomplished by a sleight of hand. One moment she'd been reading him the riot act because he'd had the 'temerity' to ask for an advance on his personal allowance and castigating the arse off him for being irresponsible and a spendthrift. Then suddenly she'd changed tack and started whispering sweet nothings in his ear. Well, sweet somethings, actually. Very sweet.

There was a slight rustling sound and Rossa saw that an insect had come to grief in a spider's web his cleaner had missed high up in one corner of the ceiling. The sight depressed him. Was he being drawn into a web himself? And yet his grandmother had been in deadly earnest, her distress at Carrick's apparent determination to remain a bachelor very real. Some of Rossa's confidence returned. Carrick had had his chance and who else but he was the obvious successor? Jaspar had been ruled out years ago. No prospect of an heir there. Fin was only finishing school and far too young to think about settling down yet. As for the twins – that dissolute pair shouldn't be allowed to breed. Though it wouldn't surprise him if Indigo had fathered half a dozen bastards already – his matinée-idol looks made him a great favourite with women of all ages. But Honoria's old-fashioned morals would never countenance a child born on the wrong side of the blanket. Or only as a last resort, which wasn't quite the case just yet, especially since Ashling had turned up so fortuitously. Feisty, intelligent Ashling. Marrying her was really no hardship at all.

54

Indeed, any red-blooded man would agree that Ashling was beautiful. But she just wasn't Priti!

As if his thoughts had conjured her up, a beaded screen rattled on the far side of the room and his young Thai lover glided, proudly naked, towards him, drops of moisture from the swimming pool clinging to her delicious toffee-tinted skin. Her breasts were high, round, perfectly formed and had cost him a bloody fortune. Her face, with those amazing cheekbones, looked stunning – but just now her long almond eyes flashed fire and her mouth with its bee-stung pout turned down at the corners.

He extended a conciliatory hand. 'Come here, darling. Lie beside me.'

She tossed her head, waist-length hair switching about, a very lovely, but very angry Eve.

'No. Fuck you!' She stood glaring down at him. 'Fuck you big, Rossa!'

He sighed, aware that yet another quarrel was in the offing. It had been one scene after another ever since he'd arrived back and Priti had come dashing out of the house and hit him round the head with the invitation announcing his engagement to another woman.

'Oh, sweetheart, how much longer are you going to keep this up? I know you're angry. I'm angry too. I never expected my grandmother to send out that bloody invitation. I intended to tell you myself first, to explain everything.'

'Yeah, yeah, I know, you said. You doin' it all for

me. You gonna marry some bitch woman for me.' Priti scowled. 'Thank you, *darlin'*, that make me very happy. That very nice present.'

It was amazing how she could take a term of endearment and turn it into a weapon. Jesus Christ! Rossa felt a great wave of weariness wash over him. 'I told you, angel, it's not like that. This won't be a *real* marriage. It's a means to an end. Fuck's sake, Priti, look around you!' He nodded to indicate their surroundings, the luxuriously appointed villa that was her dream home, a Hollywood-style hotchpotch of marbled walls and floors, white bespoke Italian furniture, fanciful fluted columns and ornate ceilings plastered and gilded in the Roman style.

Outside, through the open door, he could see palm trees waving gently in the light tropical breeze, sparkling white sands and the mercurial sea that, depending on its mood, changed from jade, to azure, to marcasite, and in the evening when the sun went down to a mass of blazing pinks.

'This little pile doesn't come cheap. It all costs money. Lots of it! More than I could ever hope to earn on just my pilot's salary. The upshot is, if I don't marry Ashling and shoot out a great-grandson to ensure that Carrickross is safe for the foreseeable, she'll castrate me financially, cut off my annual allowance from the estate. Don't you get it, my love, my balls are in her hands! On her say-so, all this will be history – the land, the house, the boats, the cars. Game over! And I don't think you would like that at all, would you?'

Sitting up, he swung his legs over the side of the bed, made a grab and caught her round the waist, pulling her to stand between his knees. 'Answer me, Priti!' He bent her head gently downwards. 'Eh? Would you like that?' Her eyes slid away, giving him his answer. 'Good, so let's have no more tantrums. Just comfort yourself with the thought that soon Carrickross will be mine, to do with what I will, regardless of the old bat. And you and I will have more money than we'll know what to do with. You can even have that cosmetic surgery you're so desperate for, not that it's remotely necessary – you're perfect as you are. Still, if it makes you happy.' He placed his hands on her hips, admiring the pretty diamond stud in her navel. 'Now, how about you making *me* happy?'

Slightly mollified, Priti climbed onto the bed and within seconds her expert mouth was milking him to ecstasy.

Afterwards, sweat-soaked, Rossa's hair several shades darker than its normal strawberry blonde, he lay and watched her sleeping, this woman-child who had first entered his bed and, of late, entered his heart. A cloud of perfume rose like butterflies from her hair, an exotic blend of orchids and spice overlaid with something of the sea. It was as if the very essence of the island he had fallen in love with was captured in her lithe young body. Gently, so as not to wake her, he dropped a kiss on her forehead, the tip of her nose and finally her lips. Her eyes sprang open.

'Do you love me, Rossa? Really love me?'

'One hundred per cent.' His hand traced a heart-shaped doodle on her stomach.

'Good. Cos if you don't . . .'

Something in her tone alerted him, made him look searchingly in her face.

'Cos, if you don't,' she repeated softly, coal-black eyes probing the turquoise depths of his own, 'I promise, Rossa, I come kill you. Wherever you are, Priti find you.'

And though she was smiling as she made the threat, her full lips curved softly, invitingly up at the corners, Rossa Granville felt a shiver go through him as if, just for a moment, the sun had died in the sky.

CHAPTER 5

Dublin

Ashling sat nervously in the Westbury Hotel's chic Mandarin Bar, waiting for her step-mother who, true to form, was running late. Not that Coppelia meant to be rude. It was just that she considered little niceties, the pleasantries that oiled the wheels of life, to be for other people. Ashling fancied a drink, a strong one, something to quell the butterflies that had taken up residence in her stomach. Tempting; on the other hand, this was going to be no cosy tête-à-tête. She would need a crystal-clear head for the encounter that lay ahead.

Anxious, she bit her lip. Why oh why hadn't she told her stepmother that she'd found the love of her life? Why had she delayed and delayed, only to find herself pre-empted by Honoria? Christ! Now Coppelia was going to make her pay.

Far from sanguine now, Ashling pressed her closed fists against her increasingly queasy stomach. *Oh, dear God, she's going to kill me*, she thought, as Coppelia's figure darkened the door, pausing for a moment for full film-star effect, before regally sweeping into the bar.

Amused, Ashling watched heads turn. Coppelia was undoubtedly a fashionista's dream, the epitome of glamour and sophistication, a living echo of the truly great film icons of the 40s and 50s. Grace Kelly meets Sophia Loren. Fire and ice, an odd but successful pairing that combined to make men want her and women want to be her.

Today, she was attired in a superbly tailored black Yves St Laurent suit, the skirt cut to just above the knee, showing off her long shapely legs. Sheer barely there black tights and sky-high scarlet Louboutin heels punctuated the outfit. An ecru lace camisole peeked out from beneath her jacket, cleverly emphasising her tanned cleavage, and her slender throat was encircled by a ravishing silver torque. A present from her latest admirer? Her make-up was flawless, understated and classy, those much-lauded almond eyes of hers outlined in shades of smoky grey, her lips in a nude shade of lipstick that somehow managed to emphasise her full sensuous mouth far better than if she'd opted for a more obvious shade. The abundant tawny hair – her crowning glory – was glossed back in a French chignon with a pair of black-framed Versace sunglasses perched on top, like an expensive afterthought.

Ashling's photographer's eye took it all in, reflecting ruefully that her own 'formal' best – a beautifully cut, dark-grey Stella McCartney trouser suit over a silver top – was dull by comparison. Even the jaunty Pucci scarf draped around her neck failed to enliven it. Until Coppelia's entrance, she had felt quite stylish and modern, but now, as ever, she felt overshadowed. Not for the first time, she wished that even a fraction of Coppelia's natural glamour had rubbed off on her.

As she neared the table, Ashling was conscious of that strange brew of emotions Coppelia always stirred up in her: envy, admiration, resentment, pride, hurt . . . and love? But uppermost today was acute nervousness.

'Darling.' Wafting her signature scent, Estée Lauder's Private Collection, Coppelia slid onto the soft leather opposite.

'Hello, Mother.' Ashling leaned across the table and kissed her cheek.

A waiter approached, retreating a moment later with an order for a bottle of Château Lafite Rothschild 1982 – only the best for Coppelia! Settling herself comfortably, she propped her exquisite Mulberry bag on the seat next to her, nodding her thanks as the waiter reappeared with lightning speed, the linen-wrapped bottle cradled against the crook of his arm. He poured an inch or so into her glass and paused but, dispensing with the whole tasting pantomime, she motioned him to continue.

'I do hope I haven't kept you too long, Ashling.' She raised her glass. 'Cheers, my dear.'

'No longer than usual.' Airily, Ashling raised her

own glass, pleased she had managed to sound so composed. 'Anyway, it's good to see you. You've been away quite a while.'

'Indeed, almost four months. An eventful four months for you, it would appear.' Wasting no time, Coppelia arched an interrogative eyebrow. 'So, tell me, child, what's the real story here? What's with this *sudden* engagement? Are you pregnant? Is that what it's all about?'

'Mother!'

'Oh, come now!' she sniffed. 'Let's not have a fit of the vestal virgins. Yes or no? Only I can see no other reason for such underhand behaviour. And even if you have been stupid enough to get caught, long gone are the days when you had to sell yourself into penal servitude. There are alternatives these days, Ashling – abortion, adoption, single—'

'That's enough!' Scarlet with embarrassment and mounting anger, Ashling cut her off. 'I am *not* pregnant. And "underhand." hardly describes a formal announcement at the Carrickross Midsummer Ball! Hell, most people would give their right arm for such an opportunity!'

'Most people are fools,' Coppelia hissed, 'but, until now, I never took you for one.' She drew a Fabergé-style cigarette case from her handbag and offered it to Ashling, disregarding the national smoking-in-public-places ban. Let them challenge her if they had the balls. No one dared. 'Cigarette?'

Still reeling from the accusation, Ashling shook

62

her head. 'No thanks. Smoking is bad for your health.' Her voice, even to herself, sounded prim and mimsy.

'No kidding?' With a careless shrug, Coppelia slid her cigarette into an ivory holder. 'Well, if one thing doesn't get you, something else will. Or *someone*!'

'Oh please, Mother. I know you're pissed off, but spare me the riddles.' Ashling rolled her eyes.

'Fair enough. I'm referring to the fiancé from hell – *your* fiancé.'

'Fiancé from hell? Rossa? That's a bit strong, isn't it, considering you haven't even met him?'

'I never met Hitler either, but I still know he was evil.' Coppelia took a sip of wine, regarding her daughter steadily over the rim.

Ashling couldn't help herself. She laughed. 'Hitler! Jesus, now you really are talking in riddles!' She banged her glass down on the table. 'Tell me, are you quite well, Mother? Not been hearing any strange voices lately? Doctor hasn't given you any little pills?'

Coppelia shrugged off the insult, her eyes drawn to Ashling's engagement ring as, agitated, Ashling twisted it round and round her finger.

'Ashling, why didn't you tell me about this engagement of yours? I mean, in person? I know I may not have been the best mother in the world, but I do believe I deserved better.' Tears came into her eyes and she looked genuinely upset. 'You have no idea how I felt when that – that – invitation came like a bolt from the blue. What a shock it was. How humiliated I felt! How small!'

'Oh God, I truly am sorry.' Guiltily, Ashling reached across the table and squeezed Coppelia's hand briefly. It was a rare display of public affection, since her mother usually frowned on such gestures. 'I honestly had intended to tell you myself, but then Honoria – Rossa's grandmother – sent out the invitations off her own bat, silly old moo. I was well pissed off. But I didn't really feel I could say anything. It was too late anyway – the horse had bolted – so it wasn't worth upsetting her.'

'Big mistake, Ashling, to write Honoria Granville's actions off as those of a "silly old moo" and simply bow to her wishes.' Coppelia dabbed at her eyes with a lace handkerchief. 'The Granvilles of this world are not as others. They require total fealty and obedience. Give them an inch and they'll park their car in it. You've set a dangerous precedent, my girl, and from here on in they'll walk all over you. You won't be able to call your soul your own.'

'*Fealty?* What old-fashioned nonsense! You don't know them, Mother. You—' Suddenly her eyes widened. Her mouth dried. 'Mother . . . ?'

Coppelia did not respond immediately. She drew deeply on her cigarette and then, for lack of an ashtray, flicked an inch of ash onto the carpet.

'Yes, Ashling, I *do* know them.' Even in the muted lighting of the bar, Ashling could see her stepmother's eyes change into two hard pieces of green flint. 'And because I know them, I also know this marriage *must not* take place.' She nodded for emphasis. 'As of now, this wedding is off!'

'What? Are you mad? Have you gone completely off your rocker?' Shocked, Ashling gave a half laugh, half groan. 'Is this some kind of sick joke?'

'I am neither mad nor joking, I assure you.' Coppelia spoke very slowly, enunciating every word. 'Read my lips, Ashling. This wedding is a non-event. It is *not* going to happen. *Not! Not! Not!* And the sooner you accept that, the better for us both.'

Ashling's head spun. The blood rushed to her face and suddenly she was assailed by a wave of such fury, such red-hot contempt, that her arm actually jerked with a barely controllable impulse to strike her mother. An image of Coppelia's perfectly made-up cheek with the red finger-marks branded across it flashed temptingly through her mind's eye. Then the anger ebbed away again, leaving tears in its place.

'Dear God in heaven, tell me I'm not hearing this. Tell me it's just a nightmare and I'm going to wake up any second now and laugh at my fool-ishness!' Her voice skidded into the high octaves, causing a number of heads to swivel in their direc-tion. 'For fuck's sake, Mother, *why? Why are you doing this to me? Why* do you want to ruin my life and spoil my happiness? Surely it can't simply be that you weren't the first to know? No, I refuse to believe that. Way too petty, even for you!' Her hand

65

knifed suddenly through the air. 'Don't interrupt! I paid you the courtesy of listening, now it's your turn to zip it. Just remember, I'm over the age of twenty-one, Mother. I don't actually need your permission for anything, not to marry Rossa or to live my own life. I make my own decisions. Hell, I've been pretty much taking care of myself since I was just a kid because, let's face it, you were too busy filling column inches and jetting off round the world.' She took a deep breath, made her voice strong, painfully aware that every nerve, every sinew in her body was on edge. 'You always had to be *numero uno*, the centre of attention. Neither poor Dad nor I ever got a look-in, except on the occasions it suited you to trot us out, when you'd dirtied your bib in the press, perhaps, and wanted to claw back respectability by playing happy families. Well, no way, José! This time it's not about you. It's about *me*! It's about me and Rossa, *our* wedding and *our* future. Oh, you're still on the guest list, Mother, and I hope you'll be at the Midsummer Ball. Really, I do. But if you're not, I'll survive.' Her strength suddenly deserted her and, blinded by tears, she stumbled to her feet.

Coppelia's hand shot out and locked onto her wrist.

'Sit down, Ashling!' she hissed. 'We're not done yet.'

Green eyes blazed white fire as Coppelia forced her stepdaughter back down into her seat. Her grip left red marks on Ashling's skin. She lifted her wineglass with slightly trembling fingers and drank deeply.

'Okay, I was hoping I wasn't going to have to go down this route, but you've left me with no alternative. Hard as it may be for you to believe, the truth is I'm actually trying to protect you.'

'Funny way you've got of showing it.' Ashling rubbed pointedly at her wrist.

'Granted.' Coppelia sighed. 'You know, I really handled this very badly and I'm sorry for that. My only excuse is fear. Fear for you! My tongue ran away and made me tactless.' She sighed again. 'Nevertheless, I won't lie to you. I am utterly against this marriage. Not from spite. Not from temperament. Not because I am a control freak or for any of the hundred trivial reasons you might think, Ashling. Sadly, I have very solid reasons.'

'Solid reasons?' Ashling felt perspiration break out under her arms. Oh God, what was her stepmother hinting at? Her heart thudded uneasily against the wall of her chest.

'Solid as a rock. I give you my word. Unfortunately, what I can't give you at this moment in time are the details, only to say that the Granvilles, this laudable family to whom you are so willing to sell your soul, once came close to ruining my life. Oh, it was long ago but I carry the effects with me every single day.' Coppelia reached across the table, stroked the red marks on her daughter's wrist that were gradually fading. Her voice was urgent. To save her daughter's heart she had first to break it. 'Heed me, Ashling. The Granvilles are an evil bunch. A nest of vipers. To get involved with any one of them is to play with fire.' Her breath struggled up through her chest. 'God help me, it hurts to remember, let alone speak of that time. And worst of all, I must keep you in ignorance of the details and I beg you to take all this on trust. Oh, Ashling, at the very least, reconsider! Take your time. If Rossa Granville loves you, truly loves you, he will be content to wait for you.'

As Coppelia faltered to a close, Ashling broke into a slow handclap. 'Bravo, Mother! You missed your vocation. I never realised what a very fine actress you are. Such melodrama. Such histrionics. Such a load of old cobblers! Truth is, you've told me jack shit. You really don't know me at all, if you believe I would give up the man I love on such a flimsy basis!' She grabbed her glass and gulped at her drink. 'And, do you know, even if any of it were true, even a smidgin, it has got nothing to do with me and Rossa. *Your* past is not *our* future. We're not mafiosi, we don't carry on blood feuds.'

'It's true, Ashling. I swear it. Every word.'

'Crap!' Ashling yelled, totally oblivious now to the other patrons in the Mandarin. 'I love Rossa Granville and Rossa Granville loves me.' She flashed her engagement ring, this time deliberately, provocatively. '*We* are engaged and *we* are getting married. We love each other and nothing and no one is going to change that. Ever!'

68

Coppelia's lips twisted, her eyes hardened. 'Foolish girl. Pray your words don't turn around and bite you on the ass. Will you not *see* your blue-eyed fiancé for the scoundrel I know him to be? Oh, don't look so shocked. Of course, I've done some poking around and, guess what, it didn't take long before—'

'I don't want to hear it!' Once more, Ashling jumped to her feet. 'You know, you disgust me, Mother. You really are plumbing the depths and if you think I'm going to stick around while you slag off my future husband, then you really don't know me at all. But let this be your consolation. The scales have fallen off my eyes all right and now I can plainly see *you* for what you are: vain, bitter, shallow and twisted.' And with that she snatched up her bag and strode away.

Coppelia sat on at the table alone, looking older than when she'd first arrived, face drawn, brooding, as she continued to light cigarette after cigarette and work steadily through the bottle of wine.

CHAPTER 6

Dublin

The burger was shoe-leather, the cheese-slice plastic and the Coke both flat and tepid. But Maggie O'Keefe was ravenous so she forced them down as she drove.

Considering it was May, the weather was awful – dank, wet and miserable. The traffic was bloody awful too. In theory, the journey into the city centre from her flat in Fairview should have taken no time at all. The reality, thanks to the grid-locked Dublin traffic, was that she was facing a good forty-five minutes. What was it about the rain that brought all the traffic to a standstill? This was Ireland, for God's sake. It rained here. Buckets! Wouldn't you think the Powers that Be would have got a handle on it by now? Still, with a well-deserved holiday in the offing, nothing, not the wet weather, the traffic, nor the smell of the River Liffey, could dampen her spirits today. As she stopped and started her way over the Matt Talbot Bridge, she stole a glance at the screaming headlines on the front page of the *Independent* on the passenger seat. *Quelle surprise!* Bad news all the way. Iraq. Afghanistan. The state of Irish hospitals. Another crooked politician exposed. Resolutely, she turned her attention back to the windscreen, jumping as behind her a cacophony of horns blared. The traffic was moving again and her inattention had cost the commuters of Dublin a full three seconds. Pathetic!

Thank God, she would be away from it all soon, holed up in her cousin Deirdre Butler's lovely little cottage on the Kerry coast. She gave herself up to dreams of long walks on beaches pounded by Atlantic waves and evenings down the local pub listening to live ceilidh music and shooting the breeze with the locals. Then, at the end of each evening, happily exhausted, she would curl up in Deirdre's feather bed with a good thriller. Well, maybe not a feather bed. But who cared!

When her cousin had mentioned she was going away to California on holiday and needed someone to cat-sit, Maggie had nearly bitten her hand off with excitement. Maternal cousins, both she and Deirdre had been born and bred in 'The Kingdom', as the natives called County Kerry, but, while Maggie had eagerly made for the capital as soon as she could, Dublin had never held any appeal for Deirdre and she had sensibly remained where she was, happily teaching in the local primary school. But the joys of the 'Big Smoke' had lately begun to wane for Maggie and more and more she felt herself possessed of a real longing to go back to Kerry. Though she loved her work as an investigative journalist, and was damn good at it what's more, it could sometimes be stressful. It took her into areas of Dublin's underbelly that were well off the tourist map. Just this morning she'd tailed an errant teenage girl to the home of a small-time drug-dealer on an innercity sink estate. It hadn't been pleasant. More like Dante's seventh circle of hell. Her mind roamed over the appalling scenario she'd come upon – the poverty-stricken homes, the buggies laden with dirty underfed children, their wheels ploughing used condoms and needles into the mud. She shook her head of wine-red corkscrew curls. 'Dublin's Fair City'. Fair in the sense that it was certainly very beautiful, with its parks and churches and stunning Georgian architecture. Definitely fair, if you were numbered amongst the privileged and the massive new crop of nouveau riche. Hell, pure hell, if your only source of income was a giro from the local dole office.

Still, there was a definite up-side to her profession. By the end of the day, the drug-dealer would be safely behind bars and the teenage girl would have some hope of living a decent, normal life. That was the pay-off. That's what kept her from throwing in the towel and going off to be a secretary or a nurse or God knows what. That, plus the determination to justify her late, beloved father's faith in her. All her life, Andrew O'Keefe had been both hero and role model to her, a strong, principled man who when life handed him lemons, went straight out and made lemonade. Just like when he was made redundant from the teaching post that had been his life for well over thirty years. He could have retired, spent his remaining years surrounded by his books and the garden he loved. But that would never have suited his quick mind so, instead, he had picked himself up, dusted himself down and restyled himself as an investigative journalist. Fresh from college and fired up by his enthusiasm, Maggie had joined him and they had worked as a team for a strenuous satisfying five years. Until a massive heart attack had snatched him away from her. She missed him dreadfully. He'd been everything to her – father, friend, colleague all rolled into one. Working with him had been tough but fun. Now, it was often just tough. No time to eat, drink, sleep. Or have sex.

Roll on, Kerry! Roll on a nice tasty Kerryman who would, hopefully, be more adventurous and have more stamina than the metro-sexual version of Irish manhood that populated Dublin. She scrunched up her takeaway wrapping while moving her car forward another yard, imagining a dark-haired Kerryman grinning a laid-back grin and laying on the Blarney: 'An investigative journalist? A gorgeous-lookin' creature like yourself chasing great big criminals and vicious drug-dealin' fellas? I've heard it all now!' And then he'd buy her a pint or two and with a bit of luck, before you knew it, he'd be revealing far more of himself than she could print in any paper.

Back and forth went the windscreen wipers. More lights, another wait. Idly, Maggie flipped to the next page of the newspaper and found herself riveted by an unsmiling face that stared out at her. *What extraordinary eyes*, was her first thought. *What a hunk*, was her second. The third was X-rated. Framed with dark hair, the face was full of a brooding intensity. Dark brows, sensitive mouth.

Carrick Granville – Man of Stone and Steel, the caption under the photo read. Oh, yes, the architect – his family had a massive great estate in Kerry. She seemed to recall he owned a private island in a nearby lake and holed up there whenever he wasn't jetting all over the world lobbing up fantastical buildings. Nice for some! She stared intently at the inset picture of his latest feat in architecture, an oblong box of concrete and steel squeezed between two office-block buildings on a Tokyo street. Try as she might, Maggie could see no obvious connection between the clinical postmodern lines of the structure and the primitive man-the-hunter intensity of its designer's face. She ran the Kerryman scenario in her head again, this time using Carrick Granville as the benchmark. Oh yes, that worked – that worked brilliantly!

Suddenly the rain cleared and the elusive sun peeked out through a break in the clouds. Maggie decided to take it as a good omen.

CHAPTER 7

Carrickross House

Honoria closed her eyes and let her book and reading glasses fall to the spotless linen counterpane. Fifty winks, that's all, and then she would rise and dress for dinner, a mammoth task these days, where once it would have been a pleasure. Such was the penalty one paid for daring to exceed one's allotted three score and ten, but at least her mind was as sharp as ever, galvanised with a new energy as she watched her grand scheme blossom.

She could have dined in her suite, but indolence was not to be encouraged. Now, more than ever, she must stay in control. It was imperative that the family see her at the helm, her hand firmly on the tiller. And so, as long as she could dress, as long as she could walk, she would take her place at the head of the table, stepping aside only when she was satisfied Carrickross was in the safe hands of a young, worthy and vigorous successor.

She sighed and let her mind drift back . . . back . . . to a time when she, too, was young and vigorous – standing on the deck of the *Bombay Star*, watching the coast of India draw nearer. Multicoloured scarves of dawn still streaked the sky and yet the air was already uncomfortably hot and sticky, redolent of a curious mixture of un-familiar spices, raw sewage and paraffin oil. A light breeze flattened the white muslin of her summer dress against her body, outlining her breasts, her small waist and long legs, whilst a long strand of henna-red hair unpinned itself from her chignon and flicked playfully at her lips. Laughing, she tucked it behind one ear, not completely unaware of the admiring glances thrown her way by the other predominantly male passengers.

She experienced a clutch of excitement in the pit of her stomach as the ship nosed its way into dock. There, a mass of people swarmed like flies – the men with bare torsos, the muscles of their tawny-skinned bodies slickly delineated by a fine sheen of sweat; the women, their long black hair streaming, arrayed in a rainbow of saris, midriffs bare, gold jewellery glittering at ears, wrists and ankles. The noise was quite overwhelming, a barrage of banging, clattering and native sitar music, overlaid with the babble of a thousand foreign tongues.

A tall, deeply tanned European man on the quayside raised a khaki-covered arm and waved to someone on board the ship.

'Tim! Tim!' Beside her, her cousin Laura began to wave back furiously. 'That's Timothy. Timothy

Villiers, my husband's best friend. He said he would send him for us if work detained him and he could not get away himself.' She slid a sideways glance at Honoria. 'Such a perfect gentleman, Honoria, and quite unattached – not for the want of trying, however, on the part of many a young lady and her ambitious mother!'

Honoria laughed. 'Oh, no, you don't, Laura. Save your matchmaking skills. I am here for your benefit, remember? To help with the children. *Not* to find myself a husband.'

Her cousin pursed her lips, as they prepared to descend the gangplank. 'You could do worse, cousin dear. He is rather well-heeled, you know, and,' a mischievous twinkle came into her eye, 'not in the best of health.'

But marriage was the furthest thing from Honoria's mind at that moment, with the panoply of India spread out before her like a jewelled banquet just waiting to be enjoyed.

No one was much surprised, however, when Mr Timothy Villiers came assiduously a-courting, least of all Honoria. What did surprise her was her willingness to return his affections, even if, in truth, her heart wasn't really moved. But Timothy was personable and passably handsome and life in her cousin's household quickly showed itself to be boring and predictable. In fact, she found herself with very little to do, since the family's needs were taken care of by a whole retinue of ayahs and retainers and Laura, due to her family commitments and poor health, barely left the house, much less socialised. More and more, young Honoria found herself longing for a change of scene, to be part of the ex-pat community with the never-ending round of balls and tea-parties and excursions she often heard tell of. What surprised her even more was how quickly she fell in love with India, its people, its beautiful land-scapes, and how little inclined she felt to go back to Ireland, even to her beloved father and Carrickross.

Less than four months after her arrival in India, she married Timothy Villiers, renouncing with huge regret her maiden name of Granville. When her father died there would be no one else to carry the name on, with the exception of her cousin Henry, a somewhat feckless though charming character. And there had *always* been Granvilles at Carrickross. Always.

Honoria remembered her wedding night clearly even now – it had proved to be a huge disappoint-ment. Almost immediately after the wedding breakfast, Timothy was laid low with one of the ever-increasing bouts of hepatitis to which he was prone. Helpless, Honoria stood by and watched as his servants stepped in – one, in particular, Rajesh, a strikingly handsome Indian with a bearing worthy of a prince, taking charge and devotedly nursing him back to health. But, even when he was well again, Timothy made no attempts to consummate the marriage, just smiled apologetically whenever she made a tentative approach, setting her gently to one side with a kiss on her forehead, as one might kiss a child, or murmuring about not being quite fit yet, asking for her indulgence and begging her to give him time. Eventually, it all proved too much to bear and her spirit sank under the crushing weight of her disappointment.

And then one day as she wept at the foot of a banyan tree at the bottom of her garden, Rajesh came to comfort her. After that, she didn't cry any more.

'Rani!'

A hand shook her gently. Her eyes flew open.

The solid walls of Carrickross surrounded her. But India was there still, smouldering before her in Rajesh's gleaming eyes.

'Come, Rani, leave your dreams for now,' he said softly. 'Time to ready yourself for dinner.'

She smiled and stroked his face, then watched with pleasure as he moved about the room, graceful and precise, laying out the clothes she would wear.

Rajesh. Ah, Rajesh! His name meant king, lord, ruler, and to the heartbroken young woman bewailing the loss of her Indian dreams at the foot of that great banyan tree, he was, at the very least, a prince among men.

All those years ago he had crept into her presence silently, his shadow falling across her face in a shady veil. Brushing her tears away with the back of her hand, she had looked up into the most lustrous pair of eyes she had ever seen. Without waiting for an invitation, he had hunkered down before her, his handsome tawny-coloured face regarding her gravely.

'Dear Memsahib . . . dear lady, why do you weep?'

And somehow the habitually aloof Honoria found herself opening up and the whole sorry tale came tumbling out: her unhappiness and disillusion with her marriage and the fact that she felt herself more trapped now in the conventions of the ex-pat community than she had ever felt as a single woman in Ireland beneath her father's roof.

He had allowed her to talk on and on, passing neither comment nor judgement, simply listening, those solemn eyes probing deep into her soul. When finally, exhausted, she stuttered to an end, it seemed like the most reasonable thing in the world that he should reach for her. Rajesh – king, lord, ruler. That night he had made her his rani, his queen.

By the time she had walked back along the winding path to her home, her tears were a distant memory, the moon was a crescent of silver and every inch of her skin tingled and burned with remembered kisses and caresses.

She didn't shower that night, didn't want to wash his scent from her body. Instead, she lay naked upon her bed, cooled by the crisp white linen below and surrounded by swathes of bride-like mosquito netting, retracing with her own fingers the path his had taken earlier – hard, cool, seeking, eager, trailing like butterflies across her high full breasts, down along her flat stomach and thighs.

Passion had made them foolish. They vowed that next time they would take greater care.

When morning came, ushered in by a sun as bright as a newly minted penny, Honoria had found herself completely and irrevocably in love. *Rajesh!* She had tried his name on her lips. It fitted perfectly.

And it still did.

'Rani? Rani, my love?'

Rajesh was gently stroking her hair.

'You were dreaming again, I think,' he said softly.

'Waking dreams, Rajesh,' she smiled.

'Of India?'

'Of India.' She sighed. 'Perhaps a cup of tea, to wake me up?'

He smiled and pointed to the silver teapot keeping warm on its burner. As usual he had anticipated her.

'Will it ever leave me in peace? India?' she asked wryly, as she struggled into a sitting position while he adjusted the pillows behind her.

'So long as you draw breath, never! India is in your soul now and in your heart, just as it is in mine. Just as you, Rani, are in mine.' He poured tea into a china teacup, added a slice of lemon and handed her the cup.

She fell silent, staring at the vibrant segment of fruit floating in the amber liquid. Even that

81

reminded her of that vast continent that shaped her life.

'Rajesh, had I not been married to Timothy . . . you and I, would we . . . ?'

His reproachful gaze silenced her. 'Rani, it was not our destiny. This you know.'

She blew on the hot liquid. 'Perhaps, but sometimes I can't help but wonder what might have happened had we been brave enough to cast off the shackles of convention, kick sand in the face of the world and follow our hearts. Oh, Rajesh, how differently might our lives have turned out! What pain might have been avoided!'

He shook his head. 'No, Rani. Your family would have been shamed and, one day, our love would have soured and spoiled from your sorrow. Your heart would have hardened against me.' He removed her empty cup. 'Now, Rani, enough of the past. It is the present to which we must attend. Besides, I have news of Carrick. He is coming home,' he paused for effect, 'tomorrow.'

'Tomorrow!' With sudden renewed vigour, Honoria, eyes gleaming, threw off the bedclothes. 'Coming home *and* coming to his senses, I hope!'

Rajesh knelt and slid her slippers on her slender feet. 'For your sake, Rani, I wish it may be so,' he said.

His head was bent and so she did not see the look of scepticism that flashed across his face.

CHAPTER 8

Carrickross Estate, County Kerry

D awn was breaking over the rook-teeming turrets and chimneys of the Granville ancestral home as Carrick approached it. He was carrying only his laptop and travel-bag, having left his luggage at the station. A taxi had dropped him off at the East Lodge Gate.

He preferred it this way, to approach the house slowly, moving gradually into its presence.

Far to his right, the lake glimmered through the drifting mist. With criminal disregard for his soft leather brogues and the ends of his dove-grey suit trousers, he vaulted over a fence and took a shortcut through a dew-sodden stretch of pasture. Prize Black Kerry cattle raised their heads lazily and, dismissing him, got on with their grazing.

Soon he came upon a grassy track running at right angles to his course. With only the slightest hesitation he turned up the path and followed it towards the edge of the pasture where the woods sheltered the ivy-covered ruins of a small Franciscan abbey. He skirted the ruins, catching a glimpse of the ancient tombs within the crumbling walls, and slowed as the Granville family chapel came into view – a little building, laden with fanciful decoration. It was not much more than an oratory and used only on the rarest occasions: family christenings, memorial services, funerals.

There hadn't been a christening since the birth of Fin. But funerals . . . ah, yes, there had been funerals.

The two black marble stones were simple enough, the starkness of the tragedy echoed in that simplicity. Honoria's grief had been such that for once she forsook her taste for the ornate. No angels loomed, no sentimental verse embraced the headstones. No, the devastation of the Granvilles was there for all to see, point blank, no subterfuge.

Carrick stared, feeling the same frozen sense of bewilderment he had felt the day they buried his parents, William and Ella, together with his Uncle David and Aunt Agneta in this spongy ground. The same horror at the image of the four figures, roped together, hurtling through the mist from the cliff edge into the dark lake below. He always felt as though he were a mere boy of eleven again when confronted with this tragedy.

'There will be no blubbering, children,' an ashen-faced Honoria had decreed as the children stood before her in the library that dreadful morning. 'Remember you are Granvilles. Do not shame your parents by snivelling at their graveside. Cry by all means, but do so in private and not in front of the vulgar curious.'

Carrick remembered how at that point, despite her warning, Rossa had let out a loud wail and his grandmother had rounded on him sharply.

'Rossa! Control yourself!'

Oh, how he'd felt for his younger brother, his face blotched and drenched with tears beneath his carefully combed hairstyle, mouth quivering, eyes red-rimmed, nose running. Instinctively he'd moved a little closer to him, unwittingly drawing his grandmother's eye.

'Ah, Carrick, Carrick, my dear, what a responsibility you now bear on your young shoulders. I would not have wished it so, but . . .' she pulled him towards her, 'now you must accept the mixed blessings of becoming the heir to Carrickross. From now on the others must take their cue from you. You will set the example and always remember duty must take precedence over personal gratification. You may be called on to make great sacrifices.' There had been something in her voice and a far-seeing look in her eye. 'But, in the grand scheme of things, only Carrickross counts. We are the care-takers, you and I.'

He hadn't really understood the import of her words then. But that's when the promise had been made, all those years ago, the promise that he, Carrick Granville, would inherit Carrickross. Yet now it would go to Rossa.

Carrick stayed by the graves musing a little

longer, standing so still that a little robin flew down and landed on one of the gravestones, gazing at him with curious bright eyes, before spotting something more interesting in the grass nearby and fluttering off to investigate.

Strange how sound travels even from the past, how after all this time he could still hear those voices crystal clear in his head, including his own, young and puzzled.

'But, Grandmother, what about Uncle Jaspar? He's your only son now . . . shouldn't he be the heir?'

She'd rounded on him then. 'Carrick, please do not attempt to tell me my business. Jaspar, for reasons well beyond your ken, will never inherit Carrickross. He is selfish and irresponsible, reliable only in that he has consistently proved himself to be a disappointment to me. Where is he today when his brothers and their wives are about to be consigned to the earth? In Africa, that's where.'

Thankfully, Indigo interrupted, his small face pugnacious, determination blazing from those amazing blue eyes. Sapphire, as usual, was glued to his side.

'Grandmama, may I hold Sapphire's hand at the funeral? She's only small and she's a girl and she's frightened.'

Honoria had unbent slightly, smiling wanly at the two little blonde black-clad figures, replicas of their Swedish mother Agneta. 'Indeed you may, Indigo. How lovely to see you showing a sense of responsibility. From now on it will be your duty to take care of your sister. Look after her well.'

The day itself had been crisp, dry and autumnal. He remembered the glint of sunlight on the windows of the four hearses that carried the remains of his parents, uncle and aunt, the black plumes waving gently above the horses' heads and the clouds of breath frosting the air as they snorted gently and shuffled their hooves on the gravel outside the main door of Carrickross.

And, at the end of the short clip-clopping journey, he still recalled with horror the two freshly dug graves awaiting them, two coffins beside each one, draped with the family coat of arms. Because the chapel was too small to accommodate the large number of mourners, the ceremony was carried out at the side of the graves, kept short for the sake of the children. Family friends, dignitaries, staff and villagers had drawn back to allow the sad little cortege to take pride of place, more than one soft-hearted woman wiping a tear from her eye.

The priest's voice rose thin and dry, discordant against the background sounds of nature: water, air, birds, insects. There had been a deer. It emerged from the woods, stared a moment in wonder, then disappeared in a flash of red.

He tried not to look at the coffins, frightened lest he might imagine the broken bloated bodies inside. Instead he had focused all his attention on the edge of the woods where the deer had disappeared, imagining he saw his parents standing there hand in hand: his strong and smiling black-haired father, his fearless mother, her hair like a field of wheat . . . they waved at him and were gone into the trees.

When, despite his best efforts to control himself, Rossa had broken down, Carrick had thrown an arm about his slight shoulders, hoping to imbue him with some of his own strength, and willing him to read his mind. *Come on, Rossa. Come on! We'll still swim in the lake and throw sticks for the dogs – we'll still ride and fish and hunt rabbits and pheasants and shoot the rapids between the lakes . . . We'll do all of the things we used to do with Dad. We have each other still and baby Fin. We can teach him all of the things Dad taught us. You have me, Rossa, you still have me!*

Opposite, beside the open maw of their own parents' grave, the twins stood hand in hand, like two little blonde angels of death in their identical black coats. Motionless, emotionless, frozen – identical blue eyes staring horror in the face. Something about their stillness was unsettling – the complete lack of tears. Weren't little children who had just lost their mother and father supposed to cry – even if they were scared of making Grandmother cross?

Honoria too had remained composed, at least outwardly, her erect posture betraying no weakness.

Later, when night had fallen and long after all the mourners had gone, Carrick heard the eerie sound of someone crying, sending him rocketing from his bed, heart pounding. At first he thought he had dreamt the noise and a quick glance at Rossa in the other bed showed him sleeping soundly, exhausted from the rigors of the day, the skin round his eyes still patchy, red and swollen. Then the sound came again, this time more muted, and on bare feet so as not to disturb Rossa, he went to the nursery to check on baby Fin. He, too, was sleeping serenely, his infant dreams undisturbed by the tragedy of the days events. From the annexe next door came the reassuring soft snoring of his nanny. Carefully Carrick had pulled the little teddy-bear quilt up to the baby's chin and moved on to the twins' room. Like two peas in a pod, they were fast asleep, entwined in each other's arms, Sapphire's long blonde hair trailing across Indy's face, his breath fanning it ever so softly. He'd reached out a hand to push the shining tendrils back, then stopped – Indy wouldn't like him to interfere. He might even be angry – like he was when Noreen, the cook's daughter, had offered to come and sleep with the twins in case Sapphire needed comforting in the night. 'I can take care of my sister,' he'd snapped. 'She's mine. Grandmother gave her to me. I'm to look after her, always!' And though he was not yet five years old and Noreen twenty-five, she'd backed off without another word.

But then, just as he'd reassured himself that all was well, the cries came again, shockingly loud and terrifying. His heart thudding fit to burst, he'd followed the sound along the corridors and up an oak staircase to his grandmother's door, which was slightly ajar. Peering gingerly around it, he saw Honoria striding up and down the room, rending her hair like a madwoman, her eyes streaming with tears.

'It was she, Rajesh! Agneta! What other explanation can there possibly be? She jumped, I tell you. The she-devil jumped and took them all with her, shackled together as they were, to their deaths! Was God punishing me for my sins when he inflicted such a daughter-in-law on me?'

Scarcely able to breathe, Carrick lurked out of sight, hardly understanding her wild words, but horrified at the spectacle of his grandmother's grief and rage. His grandmother never cried. She hadn't cried while the men searched the mountain and trawled the corrie lake. She hadn't cried when they brought the bodies home or even when she viewed them in their coffins. No, throughout it all, she had remained strong, giving them their lead, allowing each and every one to draw strength from her. But now it seemed that she was their rock no longer.

Rajesh came into view, clutching at her elbow. 'No, no, Rani, calm yourself! You do not know this and those who do know can no longer speak. Why do you torture yourself with such wild imaginings?'

Weeping, Honoria shrugged him off. 'I tell you she jumped, Rajesh! She wanted to die and she took them with her! My God, it is more than flesh and blood can stand! My sons! My lovely sons! William and David *knew* that mountain, Rajesh!

Knew every rock, every cliff, every blade of grass that grew there. They could have found their way down blindfolded, mist or no mist! Oh, Rajesh!' Sobbing, she fell into his ready arms.

'Rani, Rani, it was an accident.' Rajesh's voice was soothing as he stroked her hair. He spoke slowly, deliberately, as if to a child. 'The mists came down . . . it was their karma!'

'It was no accident! Agneta was suicidal!' Honoria cried, beating weakly on his chest with her fists as he gently tried to restrain her. 'Unbalanced! Every year, when winter and the mists closed in on Carrickross, her mind disintegrated. They had roped themselves together for safety and she deliberately jumped! Oh why? Dear God, *why* did she have to take them with her? Had I not already suffered enough loss and grief in my life?'

'Hush, Rani, please! Calm yourself! You will be ill!'

She wrenched herself away from him and resumed her agitated pacing.

'David – foolish romantic boy!' she wailed. 'How easily she manipulated him with her blonde hair and blue eyes and sly ways! See where it has led him now! Off the mountain to plunge into the rocky depths of the corrie lake.'

Carrick, who had not heard the details before, gave a little cry.

Perhaps Rajesh had heard something, because his voice cracked suddenly, sharp as a whip. 'Rani, Rani, the children! Be careful or you will waken them!'

Carrick wondered that Rajesh should dare to speak to Grandmother like that. Surely she would be angry with him?

But his grandmother just dissolved into a bout of hoarse, gutwrenching sobbing in Rajesh's arms.

Carrick crept away then, his mind pulsing with horror, and that night and for many nights to come, the nightmare vision of four figures roped together, arms outstretched, moving blindly through the mist, haunted his dreams.

But more terrifying than that, every time he awoke that first night, it was to the distant sound of his grandmother's grief and rage.

With a deep shuddering sigh, he shook off the memories that haunted him and turned to his grandfather's more elaborate headstone nearby, complete with hovering marble angels.

The highly decorated inscription read:

In fond memory of
Henry Granville of Carrickross
Born 5 March 1923
Fell asleep 15 August 1981
Beloved Husband, Father and Grandfather
★   ★   ★
Till the day break and shadows flee away
And with the morn those angel faces smile
Which we have loved long since and lost awhile.

Is that so, Grandmother? thought Carrick with a grim smile, imagining – and not for the first time – that meeting. And what will Henry have to say to you, Honoria? What, indeed, will *you* have to say to Henry? And will Rajesh be there too? No, Rajesh would be reincarnated, of course, still stuck on the wheel of existence while Honoria went to meet her Maker alone.

Wryly pondering on what sort of animal Rajesh would be when reincarnated, Carrick strode towards the old carriage drive that linked the chapel to the house.

At last, feet planted firmly, he confronted it. He loved it, his childhood home, and yet there was always a sense of challenge when he faced it again. The battle he had fought to claim his own identity never seemed quite over, as if the house always hoped to lure him back. His eyes swept over the lawns to the lake below; scanned the lofty Scots pines and the giant sequoia, brought home and planted by an adventurous forebear; lingered on the glossy horses that reared their heads in curiosity in the field that bordered the main approach to the house to the south and the startled antlered heads of the red deer in the woodland to the north.

Rooks cawed, the masses of rhododendron and bougainvillaea released their perfumes and the scent of pine embraced him.

The human inhabitants of Carrickross had yet to stir.

So much the better.

He stepped forward, feet crunching on the gravel, and up the marble steps to the portico. Above him, the family crest loomed, a boar's head surmounting a shield. Then he pushed open the great timbered doors – rarely locked, in an attitude that typified the inhabitants of the house, somewhere between aristocratic arrogance and an ancient tradition of open hospitality.

Passing through the stone-flagged porch with its umbrella stands and boot-scrapers, he gently opened the inner doors with their frosted crystal panels and stepped into another age. Polished timber floorboards glowed, and stands for walking sticks, whips and outdoor shoes lined the walls, while the unfortunate victims of long-gone hunts glowered glassily at him from every direction: stags, foxes, eagles, trout.

In the main hall beyond, the magnificent Waterford glass chandeliers shed their gentle light on another battery of long-dead stags' heads, interspersed by more ancient trophies: crossed swords, daggers, muskets. He softly trod the thick crimson carpet towards the staircase.

Before he could put a foot on the first step, the door that led to the kitchens and sculleries in the basement opened, in the left-hand corner of the hall.

'Carrick!'

Looking for all the world like one of his childhood teddy bears in a golden-brown towelling dressing gown, her brown hair standing on end,

Noreen McCarthy was standing there, a large mug steaming in her hand. For an unwary moment, her hot mug hovered over the glossy mahogany of one of the ornate sideboards that lined the hall, then she scuttled along to place it on the antique stove which had kept guests' drinks warm in the long-gone days when they were welcomed with mulled wine and wassail.

Beaming with surprise and pleasure, she came bustling to meet Carrick, arms wide.

'Noreen! How are you?' Carrick embraced her with genuine warmth, lifting her clean off her feet.

'Ah, sure, no complaints! Welcome home, Carrick! Welcome home! Now, put me down, ye devil!' She hammered on his shoulders with her fists. 'You have the breath knocked out of me!'

Laughing softly, mindful of the sleeping household – and particularly of the sleeping or perhaps wakeful Honoria – Carrick dropped her to the ground and fondly tousled the teddy-bear hair.

Mock angry, she aimed a swipe at him. 'Ah, let me alone, will you? You have me all mussed up!'

Carrick could not imagine Carrickross without Noreen. Her mother had been live-in cook when he was a child and Noreen, from an early age, had been trained to replace her. Many's the winter afternoon he had spent in the warm, welcoming kitchen, sitting at a corner of the great wooden table with his schoolbooks, listening to the laughter of the women, while he acted as willing 'taster' for the cakes and buns emerging from the great ovens.

95

Buttery rock buns were his favourites with their spiciness and fat sultanas – but then there was golden sponge-cake springy to the touch, chewy fruitcake, melt-in-the-mouth pancakes. The kitchen had always been his haven of comfort, the women there his surrogate mothers even before his real mother had been killed.

'You must be dead tired, God love you, with all the travelling,' Noreen was saying, shooting him a searching look, 'and famished too, no doubt. And will you look at your shoes and the ends of your beautiful trousers! Soaked! Were you walking through the wet grass again? Will you never learn?' She shooed him in front of her. 'Come on and I'll settle you in the library – the fire should still have some life in it. Sure, wasn't your grandmother sitting up there till all hours last night. Well, when you get to her age, you don't need as much sleep, but,' she dropped her voice to a whisper, conspiratorial, 'it strikes me, with this engagement and everything, the poor woman has a lot on her mind. In you go now and I'll rustle you up some breakfast in two shakes of a lamb's tail. Seán will take your bag up later, when he bothers to get up, the lazy scut!'

In truth, Carrick would have preferred to breakfast alone in his room, feeling his way quietly back into his space so that his feet were firmly planted on home ground before the inevitable confrontation with his grandmother. Any meeting of his with Honoria could best be described as a confrontation,

96

but now, with Rossa's engagement in the offing, it would truly be battle-lines drawn.

'Here we are then!' Following him into the library, Noreen glared at the fire, which had died to mere ashes, as if it had done her a personal disservice. 'Ah, will you look at that! Cold as a six-week-old corpse. The rads are on but you'd need a fire – I'd better plug in the electric.'

'It's all right, I'm fine, Noreen . . .' Carrick began, then subsided, knowing Noreen's stubbornness of old.

And, sure enough, she paid him no attention whatsoever, just plugged in the fire and drew it close to him. 'That's it, sit yourself down there now on the sofa and take the weight off your feet.'

Carrick sat as ordered.

'Give me those wet shoes . . . there! They can be drying at the fire while I get the breakfast. The Full Irish. I'll tell you what, I'll bring you out a cup of tea and a bit of toast while you're waiting – sure, you look like death on wires. Good strong Irish tea. None of that green muck!' She grimaced and shuddered, her plump shoulders shaking as she headed for the door, halted, swung around and gazed at him intently. 'Or a scone? A hot scone, with maybe a nice bit of butter and raspberry jam. You were always a divil for the raspberry jam.'

'Excellent! But don't put yourself—'

She was already gone.

Sighing, Carrick sank back against the soft leather of the sofa and gazed around.

The library was small by Carrickross standards and a favourite of his for that very reason. On a winter's night, with the fire blazing and everything aglow – the rose-coloured Persian carpet brought back by the same intrepid relative who had planted the sequoia, the gleaming oak floor and book-cases – one could relax before the fire and achieve something approaching cosiness. Even now the room was glowing, as the morning sunlight slanted through the tall windows.

For all he refused to live in it under Honoria's thumb, Carrick truly loved the house. The archi-tect in him loved it for the splendour and grace of its design. The romantic in him loved it for its sense of history. The soul in him loved it because it had formed him and become part of him. He had always believed that it would some day be his. But now it would be Rossa's. That was Honoria's revenge for Carrick wanting to be his own man.

'Here we are!' Returning with a tray, Noreen intruded on his thoughts.

Two cups, he noticed. The 'Full Irish' would be a long time coming.

She plonked herself down beside him on the sofa. 'Thanks for the card from Japan, by the way, though I'm not sure what to make of those geisha girls!' A coy look. 'And the little monkey sitting in the hot springs – Christ, Carrick, wasn't he the image of my Tom?'

Carrick grinned. 'The spit!' Tom, the game-keeper, was Noreen's husband.

She laughed and began to pour the tea, then stopped and put the pot down. 'I nearly forgot!' Plunging her hand into the deep pocket of her dressing gown, she pulled out a pair of heavy woollen boot-socks. 'There! They're Sean's. Put them on or you'll get your death.'

She finished pouring as he gratefully stripped off his wet socks and pulled on the cosy pair, warm from drying on the kitchen range.

'I always think your Uncle Jaspar should bring us some monkeys from Africa,' she chattered on. 'They'd be happy as sandboys swinging out of the trees outside and we could allow visitors in and we could make a bit of money! Sure, don't they have lions in England in those stately homes?'

'Longleat? Yes. But that won't happen while Honoria is alive. Too vulgar by half.'

'No, but she might go for monkeys. They had them in India. Put a bit more of that raspberry jam on your scone. Anyone would think you were on a diet.' Not trusting him to do the job properly, she did it for him, piling the jam high and preparing a second scone in readiness. Just as though he were still a child and not a grown man of thirty. 'There you are! I suppose you'll be wanting to see the horses immediately? I'll tell Sean the minute he gets up, the lazy article! Eat that scone now.'

Carrick ate the warm scone – it was bursting with plump sultanas and dripping with butter. And the tart home-made raspberry jam was the crowning glory. Memories of sushi were fading fast.

'Carrick . . .'

Alerted by a new note in her voice, he stopped munching and looked at her enquiringly. Yes, her pose and expression promised a lecture of some sort. He felt like a very small boy again.

'Now, look, love – I've got to get something off my chest. I don't want to speak out of turn, but this business with Rossa isn't right.' She held up a hand to forestall any argument. 'Not that I have anything against Rossa. Don't I love him like my own son or young brother? But we're none of us so blind that we can't see that that young man pleases himself – always did. Not a responsible bone in his body. Sure, if your grandmother wanted a ne'er-do-well to inherit, didn't she have Jaspar? Although,' she elbowed Carrick in the ribs and winked hugely, 'she's no fool, and she knew hell would freeze over before Jaspar would bag himself a bride! Drink a sup of tea there.'

Carrick found himself drinking obediently and, irritated, put down the cup firmly, leaned back into his corner of the sofa and fixed Noreen with a sombre gaze.

'But Jaspar apart, aren't you yourself the eldest son of her eldest son – God rest your father's soul? Carrickross should pass to you.' She shook her head and her teddy-bear hair stood out more than ever. 'What is the woman thinking of at all? And you her favourite, too, for all you don't always see

100

eye to eye! But then one of you is as stubborn and bloody-minded as the other.'

Carrick kept his voice steady. 'Well, there's nothing to be done now, Noreen, but grin and bear it. I'll still have my private income, after all – as we all will.'

But Noreen wasn't quite as fatalistic. Her eyes flashing, she put a maternal hand on his knee. 'Now! Now! Now! What sort of lie-down-and-walk-all-over-me attitude is that? You have to fight it, Carrick! Your poor father must be turning in his grave. I said it to my Tom, just the other day. "Tom," I said, "Carrick should fight it. He should fight it tooth and nail. And if he can't see that for himself, then he needs his eyes tested!"' With that, she picked up her cup, staring into it like a fortune-teller trying to divine the future.

'Look, Noreen, I cooked my goose when I stood up to my grandmother, end of story. But in all conscience, how could she expect me to marry and produce an heir at the drop of a hat? That might have been a solution for her, but not for me, not for the poor woman roped in as an incubator and certainly not for the child of such a manufactured union.' Disconcerted to find a note of bitterness in his voice, he made an effort to sound upbeat. 'So that's the long and the short of it and I'm damned if I'm going to whine. That was my decision and now I'll live with the consequences.'

Noreen cocked her head, teddy-bear eyes

suddenly narrowing shrewdly. 'Ah, Carrick, isn't it natural that she wants to see you settled and Carrickross secure for the future? But it was too much to expect you to marry that one you were seeing a while back! Sure anyone could tell you had no real interest in her at all. No more than Rossa has in that Ashling, if you'll excuse me saying so!' She busied herself topping up his cup, then waded in where angels feared to tread. 'Though, mind you, Carrick, 'twould be no harm for you to be thinking of settling down now . . . life has a way of slipping by . . . and d'you really think your grandmother would be dangling a carrot in front of Rossa's nose if she had even a *promise* that you'd consider getting hitched in the next few years?' She flicked him a glance and his icy expression told her the subject was taboo. Wisely she chose to drop it and embark on a different tack. 'I suppose you'll be shakin' the dust of this house off your feet in no time and takin' off to that island of yours?'

Carrick smiled, his expression lightening immediately. 'You better believe it.'

'So, maybe you have us all fooled? Maybe it's true what Indigo says and you've got a woman stowed away out there?' She slid him a sly sideways look.

'Indigo's a liar,' said Carrick laconically.

'Ah, well, more's the pity if you haven't! Anyway, I suppose I'd better go and see to that Full Irish.' She heaved herself to her feet and gathered up the tea things. 'By the way, I suppose you don't know – your Uncle Jaspar has arrived.'

'Really?' Startled, Carrick raised an eyebrow. 'Jaspar? Here? Already?'

'Aye, indeed, surprising and all as it is, seeing as how he makes no secret of how much he hates the place. If you ask me, he came early to sniff out the lie of the land.' Noreen halted, tray in hand, at the door. 'Could be that while he was content to let you step into Honoria's shoes, the prospect of Rossa taking over is a horse of a different colour. Sure, he might want to shove in his own tuppence ha'penny's worth after all. And, as your grandmother's only living son, he'd have a good case for it, for all she wants to forget he exists! Jaspar and Rossa, eh? Talk about being between the devil and the deep blue sea! Sure, the pair of them would bankrupt the place in no time and we'd all be up the creek without a paddle. No jobs, no thanks, just an up-yours!'

With that parting shot she made a grand exit, leaving a thoughtful Carrick behind her.

CHAPTER 9

Carrickross House

T he old-style free-standing bath was filled to the brim, the gin and tonic mixed just so and Jaspar Granville, his nut-brown wiry frame chest-deep in the steaming water, was engaged in washing his mother right out of his hair. He lofted his glass.

'Bugger you, Mother!' he said with feeling, and not for the first time. 'So here we are, dear boy, back in the bosom. Yes, when the mad old bitch decides to hold court, we all must attend. All in fear, don't you know, lest she give us the chop. When she says jump, then, dear Ehu, one really has no choice but to levitate. I, myself, have spent nearly fifty years dancing to her tune, with that Indian viper, Rajesh, forever hovering in the background. I wouldn't be surprised if he weren't plotting to poison us all. Lucrezia Borgia in a turban!'

That his companion had never heard of Lucrezia Borgia bothered him not one whit – as always, Jaspar was talking for his own entertainment. He downed half his drink and smacked his lips.

'But what's the real agenda, I wonder? This engagement business just doesn't ring true. Seriously, what's with summoning people from the ends of the earth for an *engagement* party! Not a wedding, which might be understandable. No, Ehu, the old witch is up to something. Nothing will convince me that she is prepared to hand over Carrickross lock, stock and barrel to Rossa, which is what will happen if he goes through with this farce. And as for his fiancée – Ashling, isn't it? One really has to wonder what she sees in him, apart from his looks and the Granville charm, which he obviously inherited from me. Could she really have no inkling as to his true nature? Or is it that the prospect of inheriting Carrickross has blinded her? Is she, in effect, just another gold-digging bitch with an eye to the main chance?' His normally good-humoured face drew itself into a thunderous scowl. 'Oh, I can't be doing with all of these shenanigans! Would that I were financially independent! Would that I were able to stick two fingers up at the whole scheming lot and live out my days in Kenya in peace. But my fate is to be dependent on the matriarch for my every penny – work doesn't suit me, as you know.'

Thoughtfully, Jaspar swirled the drink round in his glass. 'But you know, maybe the time has come to shake her up a bit. If she's really thinking of handing Rossa the estate, maybe I should step up to the plate myself. After all, it should be mine, you know, Ehu, as the only surviving son. And

105

quit with the face like a mass bereavement! I have no intention of staying here enduring a living death, but what's to stop me from disposing of it to the highest bidder and high-tailing it back to Africa? We'd live like kings on the proceeds – or,' he tittered, '*queens*, if we preferred!' He held his glass out for a top-up. 'Stepping aside for Carrick was one thing – he'd always see a fellow right – but Rossa is all for himself. As different as chalk and cheese, that pair. Carrick is as sound and steadfast as a rock, which is what his name means in Gaelic, you know, and although I do wish he'd lighten up a bit occasionally, he's also generous and loyal. But Rossa? Dear oh dear oh dear! That young man makes Yours Truly here look like the Virgin Mary. Not sure I can stomach him taking over the joint.'

Ehu re-filled his glass, then raised an eyebrow as Jaspar ignored the proffered drink and fell into uncharacteristic silence.

'But, getting back to that Indian, Rajesh . . .' he said at last, something that sounded oddly like fear replacing his bluster. 'I was joking about him poisoning us – if he hasn't done it by now he never will. Still, a part of me always wondered if he didn't have some role to play in my father's "little accident". "Fell" in the lake, did Henry, whilst in his cups – the self-same lake he'd swum, fished and boated in, drunk and sober, since he was knee-high to a duck? Odd, very odd!' A prolonged pause. Turning a languid little-boy-lost look on his companion, he reached out and braceleted his slender mahogany wrist. 'I'm so glad you've come along for the ride, dear boy. It means so much. Might just prevent me from going completely doolally.'

Nodding his elaborately plaited head, Ehu smiled his blindingly beautiful smile, his fingers idly playing with the little beaded gourd suspended on a thin leather thong from his neck. Of course he had come – and brought his little supply of poison too. Jaspar Granville would not walk into any spider's web without Ehu at his side. If there was any poisoning to be done, then *he'd* be the one to do it.

CHAPTER 10

JUNE

Dublin

Ashling put down the phone after a marathon session with Rossa's grand-mother and flopped into the fabulous retro Henrik Thor-Larsen egg chair that had cost her almost two months' wages. Funny how she felt she had to stand to attention whilst speaking to Honoria, almost as if she was a lowly private parading in front of her commanding officer. Well, Honoria certainly was commanding but Ashling had to admit the old lady had come up with a fabulous idea for the wedding – a winter theme. The picture she'd painted had been irresistible: huge log fires, hot punch, shimmering Christmas trees, holly and mistletoe, candles glowing . . . a traditional jaunting car to the church with a high-stepping horse decked out in bells and the Granville crest on the side. Might as well go the whole hog! And, hopefully, it would turn out to be one of those bright sparkling wintry days. She would enlist a designer to work on some kind of fabulous cloak or coat – that wonderful Helen Cody, maybe, whose speciality was bespoke couture pieces. Ashling had recently photographed her collection for the Dublin Fashion Show and fallen head over heels in love with several of the garments. Who better to commission to do her very own Dr Zhivago fur-trimmed cloak? Not real fur, of course. Ashling would rather go naked, as the famous ad slogan ran.

Idly, she let her eyes roam around her open-plan loft apartment. Occupying the whole of the top floor of a converted old biscuit factory overlooking the Grand Canal, it featured bare brick walls and the original floor-to-ceiling factory windows with Georgian fan-effects at the top. For most of the day, it was flooded with light, and, at night, the lights of Dublin city bled across the floor in soft stained-glass colours. Ashling loved her apartment with a passion. Buying it had been a real milestone in her life, her first major accomplishment as an independent adult. And how she had enjoyed stamping her mark on it. Everything from the vintage bone-handled teaspoons in the cutlery drawer, the vibrant rugs and kilims picked up in Marrakesh to the utterly ludicrous hurdy-gurdy propped in one corner, she had chosen not for their functionality but purely because she loved them. And, of course, there were framed copies of her own photographs every-where, a disproportionate number of which featured Rossa. Yum! What a gorgeous subject he made, especially nude! And soon she would be living with him full-time and all this would have to go. Ashling's heart gave a little lurch, just as it did every time she remembered. But they had to be practical. Spacious though her apartment was, it simply wasn't big enough for both of them. However, Rossa was proving rather elusive whenever it came to the matter of where exactly they would live.

When she'd raised the notion of moving to Thailand to be with him, there had been no pros, but many cons, apparently. Firstly, Hua Hin was only a base for so long as he was working for Thai-Orient and his contract was due to be reviewed any day now. Two, his accommodation was very basic, plus he shared with three other pilots – not exactly ideal. Three, he was beginning to get sick of the place and besides he wanted to start married life somewhere new. Ashling had been disappointed. She'd never been to Thailand and it sounded so beautiful. Four, her business was really taking off and her portfolio of clients was growing by the day. Could she really see herself giving it up, after all her hard work? She had to admit she couldn't. Not really. Apart from Rossa, photography was her great love and not one she could imagine relinquishing easily.

And there was the final clincher – children! She, herself, was in no great hurry but Rossa seemed keen on the idea of becoming a daddy, like yesterday, which was really very sweet and quite unexpected. Rossa was such a free spirit and children, no matter how adorable, took over one's entire life. But, as Granvilles, he was adamant that any children they had should be raised in Ireland, maybe even at Carrickross. It had crossed Ashling's mind to wonder what Carrick would have to say about that, given that as the eldest son he would surely inherit. In truth, she hoped he would. The prospect of living at Carrickross was pretty daunting, especially if Honoria was still in residence.

She stood up and walked to the window. A plane was tracking across the darkening sky, red lights winking on the end of each wing, vapour trail cork-screwing off into the distance. On the canal below a swan drifted slowly past, its head tucked under one wing, sound asleep – amazing! But equally amazing was the fact that Ashling was marrying the man of her dreams and whilst she would be more than sad to leave her apartment, hell, she'd live on the moon with him if he asked. And what would Coppelia have to say to that? The thought of her stepmother depressed her and sent her mind rocketing back to that fraught meeting at the Westbury and the nightmare of bewilderment that followed. Since then no amount of nagging, cajoling or threatening could persuade Coppelia to elaborate on her history with the Granvilles. The mere mention had her swearing dramatically that she would almost sooner see her daughter dead than in the clutches of such an evil mob.

Bugger! Why didn't Coppelia just sod off and

leave her alone? But then their relationship had always been complicated. And antagonistic. She was naturally closer to her father in temperament and had found herself taking on his gentility, patience and kindness like a cloak. An ascetic, academic man, he had no great appetite for the material things of life that his wife craved – and Ashling had followed where he led, immersing herself in books, in art, and eventually in photographs. Generous both with his time and with his love for his little adopted daughter, she had blossomed in his presence and had been devastated by his sudden death.

Ashling walked over to her favourite picture of Rossa and traced the lines of his face with a fingertip.

'I really, really love you!' she whispered aloud.

With a soft smile she went off to pour herself a glass of wine and catch up on the latest episode of *The Brides of Franc* – with a bit of luck Franc might even be organising a winter wedding to fuel her fantasies.

N7 Motorway

At last Maggie O'Keefe was on her way, Dublin and traffic fumes at her back and before her Kerry, the wild Atlantic and her cousin Deirdre's cottage on the coast. Foot down, amber eyes fixed on the road before her, Maggie slid into a waking dream, seeing a small cottage in her mind's eye, the walls festooned with seashells, the Atlantic Ocean to the front, the bleating of grazing goats round the back and, as in every good dream sequence, a dark and brooding male figure waiting to tend to her every need. Maggie laughed and shook her head, curly tendrils of hair bouncing before her eyes. The twee dream cottage was as far removed from Deirdre's state-of-the-art all-mod-cons renovated-to-within-an-inch-of-its-life one as you could get. And as for dark and brooding males, she should be so lucky.

Her mind inevitably slid to Carrick Granville. Now if she could get close enough to him to scoop an interview – that would be a stroke of luck. One eyebrow raised in a musing expression, Maggie eagerly headed south-west to 'The Kingdom'.

Dublin

There were new lines around Coppelia's eyes and mouth. Nothing her plastic surgeon couldn't erase, but still they pointed to the fact that she was no longer in the first flush of youth and, to someone as vain as Coppelia, the thought was sheer anathema. Her looks were the tools of her trade, something she had always played on, a passport that paved her way through life, giving her access to money, privilege and power. But Coppelia wasn't shallow enough, or stupid enough, to depend on looks alone. Still, it had initially been her startling looks and then her vibrant, spirited personality that had captured the eye of her first lover, James, long years before. That first conquest had made everything else that followed possible. James. God, she still missed him and thought of him often, especially at night in that nebulous state between waking and sleeping when, freed from the day's demands, her mind was apt to slide back- wards to the rawness of those early days of her childhood – the pain, the degradation, the grinding poverty.

He had rescued her from all that; snatched her from the jaws of despair and presented her with the gift of a whole new life – education, culture, a place in society. A world she could look right in the eye and spit in the face of. But her life with James was long ago and Coppelia had become a very different creature since then. And, if she were being honest, not always one of whom he would have been proud. No, better he could not see her now. She had embarked on a certain path after his death and had come much too far now to retrace her steps. Despite the successful public face of her present-day lifestyle, there was still a part of Coppelia that was, and always would be, that poverty-stricken waif. Spurned. Cast aside like so much rubbish.

Ironing out the creases at the edges of her eyes with the tips of her fingers, Coppelia bent forward and gazed into the mirror. Just for a moment, her reflection seemed to waver and the face of Honoria Granville floated before her. The aristocratic, patrician-featured Honoria Granville, with those diamond-chip, penetrating icy-blue eyes. She gave a little shudder and the vision dissolved.

Slowly her eyes travelled down the length of the mirror. Rightly, she was proud of her figure, the taut firm breasts, the hand-span waist and shapely hips, the long slender toned legs, tapering to narrow size 5 feet. 'Lady's feet', one of her many lovers, a great romantic, had once remarked, commenting also on her delicate wrists and ankles, which he proclaimed as the mark of a thorough-bred. And he should know, he owned a string of them. Coppelia's chin came up. Yes, she was a lady. Yes, she was a thoroughbred. But this lady knew how to fight dirty. And if dear Honoria hadn't learned that by now, then she really was in for a rude awakening.

She turned to the bed where her customised Rigby & Peller underwear lay in a snowy mound of pure white silk. There really was nothing to beat the feel of silk against one's skin, she reflected as she stepped gracefully into the knickers, and nothing more titillating than virginal white silk when the wearer was anything but. The thought brought a smile, half-rueful, to her lips. Then a shadow darkened the brilliant eyes. Once upon a time there was a virgin Coppelia, but that was in another lifetime, a life-time that had been all too short.

Snatching up the matching bra from the bed, she

shrugged the straps over her shoulders, reached behind and despite the impressive length of her nails deftly clipped the hooks and eyes into place. Next she reached for a pair of sheer-silk lace-topped holdups and rolled them on smoothly. She picked out a Cavalli summer suit from her wardrobe – dear Roberto, one of the few men who never let her down! A tribute to the 1960s and Jackie O, it had a short boxy jacket braided in cream ribbon, and a beautifully cut sheath dress that moulded itself to her curves. The fabric was unusual, an uncrushable linen-silk mix in a soft lemon – perfect for travelling in. Make-up and hair already done, it only remained to slip on a pair of low-heeled cream Choos, collect her luggage and car keys and set out for the Non-Event of the Year. Her nose wrinkled. All this hoo-ha for something that wasn't even going to happen.

Moments later she left Merrion Square behind in a belch of blue exhaust smoke and a flash of fire-engine red. Four and a half hours and she would be in Kerry, that rainy and completely overrated county, lair of the Granvilles. And in another twenty-four hours or so she would be the wild card at her daughter's engagement party. The thought brought a burst of optimism. Everything would be okay. Everything would be just fine. Come hell or high water, she would make it so. Switching on the radio, she laughed out loud as Elton John burst over the airwaves with a song that exactly mirrored her thoughts: 'The Bitch Is Back'. You better believe it, honey! Stepping on the accelerator, Coppelia joined in with the chorus.

CHAPTER 11

Kerry

Fate! Maggie decided. That's what it was. Destiny, a sign that she and Carrick Granville were bound to meet. There she was, innocently waiting for her seafood chowder in Today's News, a pub on the Kerry coast, and there he was too, the man himself. Well, okay, not in person, but prominent among the dozens of framed photographs and local newspaper clippings decorating the walls. And damn, if he wasn't smiling! She squinted her eyes to read the small print of the caption beneath: *Carrick Granville, celebrity guest, at the opening of Today's News.* Funny, she wouldn't have tagged him as a cutting-the-ribbon type, but maybe the proprietor was a personal friend. Mentally, she compared the photo to the one she had seen in the newspaper that rainy day in Dublin as she tailgated her way through the city. God, it seemed an eternity ago – not a matter of what – a month?

But now the sun was shining and she was far away from tailgating. She stretched luxuriously, just for the joy of it, bare arms high above her head, fingers entwined, blue-jeaned legs stretched out under the glossy wooden table. Space, time and dry weather. What more could a body want? Content, she turned her head and watched the sea glitter beyond the quay wall.

The barman arrived with the Guinness she had ordered – a half pint only on account of driving. She took a long pull from her glass, wiped away her frothy moustache, and then rummaged in her shoulder-bag for the invitation she had rescued from a pile of junk mail in Deirdre's hallway. What had started out as just the glimmer of an idea was fast growing legs. Jesus, dare she? Did she actually have enough balls to turn up at the Granvilles' Midsummer Ball on the strength of her cousin's invite? It would be a right gamble but how well did they know Deirdre anyway? She certainly wasn't a friend of the family, that was for sure. They probably invited a certain number of local professionals and business people just as a courtesy. Anyway, with hundreds of people milling about at the ball, it was unlikely anyone would spot the deception. What's more, their shared genetics meant that on the face of it she and Deirdre bore more than a passing resemblance to each other, although her dark reddish curls were natural, whilst Deirdre's shade was 'Burgundy' from a bottle. Give or take an inch, they were roughly the same height and build, too. The more she considered it, the more she realised that it was definitely worth a punt. Anyway, what was the worst that could happen? She'd be rumbled and thrown out on her ear. Not the first time such an indignity had been forced upon her. In her line of work, it was pretty much routine.

Her seafood chowder arrived, accompanied by grainy brown soda bread and a small dish of Kerrygold butter – perfect. Tucking the invitation back in her bag, she blissfully inhaled the aroma, then took a sip of Guinness. Since she hadn't been planning on tripping the light fantastic, she had no clothes fit for a ball, but Deirdre had always been a bit of a clothes-horse and there was bound to be something she could borrow. Now that she had made up her mind, nothing could be allowed to stand in her way. Opportunities like this came along once in a lifetime. Imagine, carte blanche to go under cover at the Granville Midsummer Ball and winkle out the inside story on the rich and famous! Perhaps sell an article to one of the prestigious glossy mags and collect a tidy sum? Only a saint could resist and she was no saint.

Her eyes turned once more to a picture of Carrick Granville on the wall. She raised her spoon in a kind of salute. Hold on, baby! Maggie's coming.

Darkness had fallen and weariness had well and truly set in by the time Coppelia reached her destination. She pulled up in front of The Kerry Eden, a pretentious monstrosity of a building loosely based on the famous Burj Al Arab hotel in Dubai, famous not only for its seven stars, but also for the sail-like structure that dominated the cobalt skyline. Its meeker Irish cousin was far less impressive, looking to Coppelia's critical eye more like a ship sinking belly-up into the surrounding forest. That said, The Kerry Eden was unashamedly luxurious and a well-known haunt for celebrities like Tempest O'Leary, the Irish supermodel, and a coterie of young British actresses such as Sienna Miller and Kate Winslet, who wanted to get away from it all and indulge in the many therapies on offer. She'd pre-booked one herself, hot stones, and God she needed it after that drive.

Inside, the hotel lived up to its luxury billing. Crystal uplighters set into the ceiling rained down a light that was reflected back up from the highly polished marble floors which also contained particles of crystal. Combined, floor and ceiling served to give the impression of a galaxy of stars winking and blinking light years away. Huge modern paintings lined the walls and a Damian Hirst-style sculpture took up virtually one entire side of the lobby.

One look at her imperious face was enough to persuade the receptionist to halve the time of the normal check-in process. Thus, only minutes later, Coppelia stood gazing out the window of her sumptuous penthouse suite. Her eyes skirted round indeterminate shapes looming black-on-black against a blacker canvas, till they found what they were looking for. The lights of Carrickross. How safe and smug it looked, a crown of jewels in a black satin box.

Bang on time, the therapist tapped on the door and, having bidden her enter, Coppelia turned away from the window, disrobed and climbed onto the portable massage table. Sleek and satisfied as a cat she stretched out as the young woman laid heated basalt stones along her spine and shoulders, easing away the tensions of the day and the stiffness of her muscles. The heady scents of birch, ginger and peppermint oils, combined with soft music and the darkened room, almost sent her to sleep. But not quite. Coppelia's suspicious nature prevented her from ever letting go completely and although she allowed her eyelids to droop and her body to meld bonelessly onto the soft leather of the couch, her mind remained alert.

And lurking at the fringes of her consciousness, she could sense Honoria Granville nearby, felt almost as if her own aura and the old witch's had reached out through the night. Hers – hot, passionate, vengeful. Honoria's – ice-cold, manipulative and treacherous. And tomorrow, for the first time in so many years, they would be face to face. She would look deep into those arrogant eyes and hope Honoria would see reflected in her own the intense hatred she carried in her heart.

'Is that all right for you, Mrs Morrison?' The therapist replaced some of the hot stones with cold ones to help detoxify the body by encouraging blood flow along the meridian lines.

Coppelia sighed. 'Wonderful, just wonderful.'

Outside the darkened window, the lights of Carrickross went out, one by one.

CHAPTER 12

MIDSUMMER, 21 JUNE 2008

Carrickross House

On the longest day of the year, the sun was still high in the sky when a procession of sleek luxury cars made their way up the drive at Carrickross and deposited their glamorous occupants at the foot of the steps.

At the top, Rossa, a somewhat nervous Ashling, Sapphire, Indigo and Fintan stood ready to welcome them. Honoria, in deference to her age, awaited the guests inside and Carrick, to Honoria's chagrin, had yet to arrive from his island. Excited, as always, Sapphire could barely restrain herself, despite having attended every Midsummer Ball since she was just fourteen.

'Look!' she cried, her eyes flying to where one booted leg was emerging from a sleek red Ferrari, followed by a leather-clad body, topped off with a shock of jet-black hair and a pale, haughty face. 'That's Rocky Cashel. Isn't he just lush? I really didn't think he'd come. And that must be his girlfriend, Rosetta Stone, but I'll bet that's not her real name.'

'I dare say not,' Rossa remarked drily. 'You know, I'm quite sure the invitation clearly mentioned black tie.'

Sapphire gave a careless shrug. 'Oh, rules don't apply to Rocky. We're lucky he could make it. This is going to be the best Midsummer Ball ever! Don't you think so, Indigo?'

Her twin was eyeing up the rock star's scantily clad, big-breasted girlfriend. He nodded distractedly. 'Do you think those things are real?'

Sapphire giggled. 'Well, the silicone is.'

'Hush!' Rossa warned, as the rock star bounded up the steps towards them, leaving his girlfriend to totter after him as best she could in six-inch-heel Jimmy Choos.

'Hey,' Rocky greeted them en masse. 'Nice bricks 'n mortar. Let me know if you ever think of selling, right?' He glanced impatiently behind him. 'C'mon, Zetta, get your fat ass in gear!'

'Lush,' Sapphire said again as Rocky disappeared through the great doors. 'Super lush!'

'I gotta get my hands on those boobs,' Indigo said with a sigh, gazing longingly after Zetta.

'Shut up, you two!' Rossa glared at them, but a moment later found him graciously welcoming the American Ambassador and his wife, followed in swift succession by a well-known thriller writer and a Brazilian racing driver with his gorgeous Spanish wife. Ashling felt her head spin as celebrity followed dignitary and Rossa introduced her to them all as 'my beautiful intended, Ashling Morrison'.

Sapphire bobbed up and down in excitement, whilst both Fin and Indigo found themselves torn between checking out the female talent and the glorious array of cars, amongst which the undoubted star was a perfect replica of the Porsche 550 Spyder, in which the legendary James Dean was killed.

'Lucky bastard. I'd love one of those,' Fin muttered, watching in envy as Seán, acting as car jockey, drove it off round the side of the house to the guest car park.

'And I'd love one of those,' Indigo sniggered, as a Japanese businessman, one of Carrick's clients, escorted his exotic kimono-clad twin daughters up the steps. 'Tell you what, I'll have Saki and you can have Sushi!'

'Grow up, you two!' Rossa snapped, but Ashling noticed how his own eyes ran appreciatively over the almond-eyed pair. She suppressed a sudden twinge of jealousy. Rossa, after all, was a red-blooded man and the two young women were very attractive. But she reminded herself, glancing at her engagement ring, *she* was the one he loved. *She* was the one wearing his ring. And *she* was the one being introduced as his beautiful intended.

'We're so pleased you could come,' she said with a smile, as the man and his daughters performed a small charming bow in front of her, more a dip of the head, really. 'I do hope you'll enjoy yourselves.'

'Yes,' Indigo said, his eyes speaking volumes. 'You must let me know if there's anything,

anything at all, I can do to make your evening more enjoyable.'

'*Lech!*' Sapphire slapped him playfully as the girls, fully aware of the subtext, tittered behind their hands and followed their father into the house. 'You'd better not desert me tonight, brother dear.'

'As if!' Indigo snorted.

'Well, I think that's it,' Rossa declared some time later as the stream of guests thinned to a trickle. 'We should go through just in case Grandmother is feeling a bit overwhelmed. Fin, maybe you could stay out here for a while and take care of the latecomers?'

Fin nodded. 'Not a problem.' His eyes lit up. 'Hey, I wonder if I could get a ride in that Spyder? Seán!' he yelled, catching sight of the Carrickross groom coming round the side of the house, and waving furiously. 'Hey, Seán, wait up a minute!' And he was gone.

Rossa rolled his eyes. 'Come on.' He slipped his arm round Ashling's waist. 'Let's go get some champagne. I feel we deserve it.'

'Great idea!' Sapphire spun on her heel. 'I'll race you, Ind. Last one in has to kiss Rajesh's bottom!' And with an undignified whoop, evening dress and high heels notwithstanding, she was off and running like a gazelle towards the ballroom, Indigo in pursuit.

Sapphire reached the top of the marble stairs leading down to the ballroom floor before Indigo caught her and scandalised onlookers by kissing her full on the mouth. She had been halted in her flight by the crowd of guests standing on the upper steps of the stairs gaping at the dazzling display above and below them.

First-time guests invariably stood for a long while on the sweeping stairway, mesmerised by the glittering white and gold rococo ballroom with its collection of gilded Queen Anne furniture, its ceiling where cherubs played in and out of white clouds in a blue sky, its cleverly placed mirrors, chandeliers and candles reflecting light around the room.

From her seat on a dais at the top of the room, Honoria, in imperial purple, her hair dressed with amethysts, cast a satisfied and regal eye over the scene. Her gown was of heavy satin, the full skirt billowing about her as she sat, a fichu of mauve lace preserving modesty despite the low neckline. An antique collar of amethysts encircled her neck, the matching bracelet worn over her elbow-length white-satin evening gloves. In her hand, another affectation of hers, was a mauve silk fan decorated with silver peacocks. As ever, Rajesh stood by her side, his costume complementing hers. And *that* would also be commented on by the press with much innuendo. He was dressed in a charcoal Nehru tunic, enlivened by a braiding of purple and gold around the edges and collar, and silken charcoal Jodhpur trousers. An amethyst-handled dagger was tucked into the purple satin sash around his waist.

Honoria greeted the steady stream of guests with a dignified smile and a slight bow of the head, only offering her hand when obliged to. She exuded pleasure, even triumph.

She had good reason to feel so. This year truly she had excelled herself. An invitation to the Granville Midsummer Ball was always highly coveted amongst anyone who was anyone but this year, combined as it was with Rossa's engagement party, people had been virtually stepping over bodies to be here. Members of the glitterati, politicians, movers and shakers of the media, arts and business worlds happily rubbed designer-clad shoulders.

And Carrickross was set to put on the most spectacular show in its illustrious history. No expense had been spared. Honoria's eyes ranged around with pleasure, noting with particular approval the deft movements of the team of black-and-white-clad waiters as they bore their trays of champagne, aperitifs and cocktails among the guests. Honoria always insisted on professionals – 'One *cannot* put awkward country girls out on a ballroom floor bearing trays of delicate champagne flutes!' She thought with satisfaction of the steady stream of drinks and tasty titbits flowing out to the terraces, rockeries, gazebos and to the boathouse by the lake beyond. There was a jazz band playing down at the boathouse for those who preferred that kind of thing – a notion of Indigo's – and a string quartet in one of the gazebos out on the lawn.

A champagne fountain tinkled seductively in one corner of the room, creating its own distinct melody. Less sophisticated was the chocolate fountain for which Sapphire had begged, a clearly popular draw with the younger set who dipped skewers of strawberries, marshmallows and mini-éclairs into the sticky depths, shrieking with laughter as they tried to avoid getting the chocolate all over their faces and expensive clothes.

Yes, all was exactly as it should be, Honoria congratulated herself. Except for one thing. The trap had been baited. But the prey had yet to pick up the scent.

Though the formal meeting and greeting had taken place at the main door, all around the house French windows were thrown open onto the terraces. Anyone could approach the house and simply walk in.

And Maggie O'Keefe, in a dress liberated from her cousin's wardrobe and clutching her cousin's invitation, did just that. She had progressed no further than the sumptuous drawing room when she caught sight of herself in a beautiful full-length Venetian mirror. She stared in dismay. Holy God! The dress, which in the dim light of the cottage had looked sophisticated and slinky, looked cheap and ill-fitting under the Carrickross chandeliers. Clingy and plum-coloured, it plunged sharply at the back almost to bum level. It struck her now as she took a discreet glance over her shoulder at her rear that only the narrow straps that criss-crossed at her shoulder-blades were keeping the whole shebang anchored in place. Added to this, Deirdre's big diamanté butterfly hair-decoration had come loose and her hair, 'artfully' bundled into a loose up-do, was threatening to cover her eyes, making her look like an uncut poodle.

This was so embarrassing. The pay-off had better be good – nothing less than a feature placed on the society page. Otherwise, she would be one very pissed-off undercover journalist.

'What a bunch of idiots!'

Startled, Maggie turned to find a rather stunning girl standing next to her, her eyes riveted on something going on outside the window. Maggie followed her gaze. A rowing boat weighed down by a bunch of young piss-heads was rocking precariously out on the lake, threatening to capsize at any moment. Not, judging by the shouts of laughter, that the occupants were in the least bit bothered.

The girl touched Maggie's arm lightly. 'Anyway, never mind those twits – I dare say they can swim. So, how is the acting going?' As Maggie gaped, searching desperately for a response, the girl looked faintly embarrassed. 'I have got the right woman, haven't I? You were in that benefit play here recently, right? To be honest, I've met so many people lately, names and faces have all become a bit of a blur.'

'Oh, I know what you mean! It can be difficult – especially in a situation like this!' gabbled Maggie.

Acting? What was the girl talking about? She

131

tried desperately to remember if she had ever met this person before. She thought not – with that classic Irish combination of black hair and dark blue eyes, she wasn't the kind you would forget. Couture-clad in a soft chiffon dress – ivory with a faint blush of pink – her skin was luminous, lit up from within, like a Greek goddess. In fact, the comparison was apt, as she did rather resemble a figure from Grecian mythology: one creamy shoulder bare, the soft, graceful folds of her dress tied about by a loose girdle of dark damask rose, delicate silver sandals on her feet and her hair piled up in ringlets. Her jewellery was simple: diamond drops at her ears and a spectacular rock for an engagement ring. Engagement ring! The bell clanged. Maggie just about refrained from striking her forehead. Of course, who else could she be but Ashling Morrison, the lucky girl who had nabbed a Granville?

Luckily, distracted again by the rocking rowing boat, the girl didn't seem to notice anything amiss with Maggie's tongue-tied state. Instead, she touched her arm lightly again. 'Anyway, I'd love to stay and have a chat, but duty calls and I've got to circulate. I just wanted to let you know I thought you were really great. Next step Hollywood, eh? Enjoy the ball.' Then, with an airy wave of her hand, she was gone.

Acting? Hollywood? What was that about?

Maggie grabbed a glass from the tray of a passing waiter.

'That girl who just left,' she said to him, jerking her head towards the door. 'That's Ashling Morrison, right?'

The waiter gave a great Gallic shrug, his dark eyes mournful. 'Madame, I am hired for ze night – I do not know ze family.' And with a sniff, he ambled off, no doubt to dispense cheer and helpful advice elsewhere.

Maggie downed her champagne in one. Things were off to a bad start. First, she had made a complete ass of herself with Rossa Granville's intended, then some little oik of a foreign waiter makes her feel about two feet tall. But, on the plus side, Ashling Morrison thought she was some sort of actress.

Maggie suddenly choked on her champagne. Of course, how could she have forgotten? Deirdre was into amateur dramatics. Could it be . . . ? Oh hell, it was, wasn't it? Her cousin had acted in some play at Carrickross. Maggie's eyes slid downwards over her slinky and, now that she thought about it, patently homemade 1920s-style dress. And instinctively she knew, beyond a shadow of a doubt, that not only was she in character as Deirdre, her cousin, but she was wearing the costume Deirdre had made for her am-dram performance. She honestly didn't know whether to cry or laugh.

At least there was no fear of any other woman turning up in the same outfit! And no one here knew her anyway. With a shrug and a swish of her plum-coloured gown. Maggie O' Keefe set off in search of a story.

The sun was sinking fast over the lake. Now, like the pieces of a kaleidoscope, all the guests converged on the ballroom where a small orchestra swept through the selection of classical waltzes that traditionally opened the ball proper.

At this point Honoria customarily retired to the ancient musician's gallery above the dance floor. There, opera glasses in hand, with just Rajesh for company, she could relax and amuse herself by scrutinising her guests and their undisciplined, uncoordinated flailing. One didn't have to look too far to draw a parallel between the decline of the arts and the decline of society. The waltz of yester-year had been gracious, genteel and romantic – the foxtrot fast, skilful and controlled, each movement perfectly choreographed. Even the tango, whilst sensuous, was never vulgar. Nowadays, the old song 'Anything Goes' appeared to have taken on a more literal meaning and, even here at the Midsummer Ball, many of the partygoers thought nothing of disporting themselves in public in the most hedo-nistic manner possible. As if to prove her point, a government minister, jacket discarded, shirt half untucked, commenced upon a series of vaguely obscene pelvic thrusts opposite a woman most definitely not his wife. Honoria's nose wrinkled disdainfully. And to think the same individual was in charge of the country's coffers!

As the musicians laid down their instruments and broke for refreshments, there came the distinctive whirring of rotary blades outside. Suddenly invigorated, Honoria's spine straightened. On the dance floor, too, there was a marked frisson, an almost electrical charge. Virtually every head, including her own, turned expectantly to the doorway.

A few moments later, Carrick walked in. Better late than never. Honoria suppressed a snort. Really, these days it was becoming almost impossible to lure him away from that island of his. Her eyes fixed on him greedily, glinting with pleasure at the number of young ladies who came flocking round him like butterflies, laughing animatedly, fixing their hair and checking their dresses, bosoms jutting invitingly forward. All desperate to attract his attention. It was not surprising: her eldest grandson had been attracting female interest from the day he had left the schoolroom and indeed before. All to no avail! Perhaps now that she had thrown down the gauntlet, he might be more inclined to come to heel and finally choose a wife.

Her eyes then went in search of his brother and found him apparently listening intently to something his fiancée was saying. How smooth he looked tonight in his tuxedo, his silk bow tie expertly chosen to complement the pale pinkish ivory shade of Ashling's gown. She suppressed a dry chuckle. Rossa might fool others, but never his grandmother. But, give the boy his due – he was playing the role of adoring fiancé well. One could almost sympathise with Ashling for her lack of perception, were it not for the fact that it was the same lack of perception that had enabled Honoria to reel her in. But Ashling was just the bait. Coppelia was the real catch and Honoria just couldn't wait till she swam straight into her net. She watched a waitress approach the couple with a tray of champagne – an oriental – just Rossa's type. She wondered if Ashling noticed the sly brushing of his fingers against the girl's as he took a glass. Probably not.

The musicians assembled once more, Strauss rang out and Honoria leaned back, reflecting that under different circumstances she would have been happy to welcome Ashling into the Granville family. Intelligent, charming and uncomplicated, there was an honesty about the girl and a quiet core of dignity. Her good breeding was evident.

Speaking of breeding, she wondered who that woman was standing alone, glass in hand, appraising Rossa and Ashling so intently? An old flame? Good grief! That dress! What a noxious colour and such ghastly cheap material, like something out of a . . . She did a double take. No, surely not! Yet there couldn't possibly be two such vile dresses in the world at the same time. There was no denying the evidence. It was the *same* costume worn in the play performed at Carrickross recently as a charity benefit, Noel Coward's *Hay Fever*. Who could forget that unsightly pucker down the back seam? The woman turned her head slightly and Honoria saw the large diamanté butterfly glittering at the side of her head. The same ugly dress! The same vulgar ornament! But definitely not the same girl who had worn it on the night of the play. Honoria was good with names and faces. Deirdre . . . Deirdre Butler? A member of the local amateur dramatics society. She had lined up with the others after the play and Honoria had congratulated her on her performance. To be sure, there was an overall similarity, especially that reddish hair colour, but she was certain she had never set eyes on this other girl before. Curiosity piqued, she turned to Rajesh, to instruct him to make enquiries, but he was already turning to her, his face alight with anticipation.

'Look, Memsahib! The vixen has broken cover.'

Her gaze followed his to where Coppelia was standing on the stairs leading down to the dance floor, scanning the room. 'Indeed she has.' Honoria's shoulders tensed with a kind of savage joy. 'And how I shall enjoy running her to ground!'

As if by telepathy, Coppelia lifted her chin and stared directly at Honoria, their eyes locking with an almost audible snap.

She had dressed to dramatic effect in a jet-black velvet vintage Schiaparelli gown, cut close over the bodice and hips and flaring gently out from the knees to fall in a small train at the back. The neckline was scooped enticingly low to reveal the tops of her breasts, and the sleeves, tight as far as the wrists, stole out in jewel-encrusted points over the backs of her hands. The same jewels decorated her slippers and the delicately wrought Juliet-cap beneath which every last strand of burnished hair was hidden, accentuating the wonderful bone structure of her face. Charcoal eye-shadow and ebony eyeliner exaggerated her already almond-shaped green eyes, fringed by lashes, thick and black. With a last challenging stare, Coppelia turned her head away and walked slowly down the steps.

'She imagines she is my equal, Rajesh,' Honoria hissed, her fists turning white at the knuckle.

He laughed coldly. 'As the sparrow before the hawk, Memsahib.'

Coppelia halted a few steps from the bottom of the stairs, as Fin accosted her, presenting a glass of champagne with both hands. A camera flashed and the moment was captured for ever. Honoria hissed in annoyance. No doubt it would be in all the next day's papers. She watched as Coppelia seemed to milk the pose, the silly boy grinning beside her. Accepting the offering, Coppelia blew him a kiss over the rim, before tipping the flute to her lips and savouring the contents. Waving a dismissive hand, she said something that elicited a cheeky grin from the young fool. Then, mercifully, he left Madame Morrison to descend the last few steps and make her way onto the thronged ballroom floor alone.

Honoria struggled to keep her composure.

'Rajesh, remind me to speak to Fintan. That young puppy needs his tail docked. High time he learned what being a loyal member of this family means.'

A sudden screech from an Irish bagpipe signalled that the 'cultured' part of the evening had ended and the *céilí* was about to begin. It was the cue for the rowdiness to start in earnest as the already inebriated guests lined up to try their hands at Gaelic set dancing and make a pig's ear of all the beautiful old dances that went back hundreds of years: The Siege of Ennis, The Waves of Tory, The Walls of Limerick. Behind her steely facade, though, Honoria took malicious glee in watching some of Ireland's foremost citizens making complete asses of themselves. A wave of impatience washed over her. She was getting too old for all this, too tired and, yes, occasionally too disheartened. She sought out Carrick again, Rossa, Ashling and, finally, Coppelia Morrison, then slumped wearily back against her seat.

'Only a little while longer, Memsahib,' Rajesh whispered with his uncanny ability to read her mind. 'Many dogs kill a hare, no matter how many turns it takes.'

Honoria smiled thinly. 'A Hindu proverb for every occasion, Rajesh? You are right, of course. Many dogs, or just this old bitch alone, will hound Coppelia Morrison to her death.'

Indigo Granville was watching his twin as she flirted shamelessly with a young man who stood about as much chance of getting her into bed as he, himself, stood of becoming Archbishop of Galway. Her glorious white-blonde hair rippling over her slender shoulders, Sapphire's eyes were sparkling like the precious stones after which she was named. Every now and again she threw Indigo a conspiratorial half-wink, a gesture meant to reassure, an affirmation that no one, man, woman or child, could ever come between them. And nobody *ever* would. He'd sooner see her dead first. He helped himself to a Martini from a passing waiter and continued his study, his own blue eyes, darker than hers, half-narrowed. She was like a water sprite, he decided, an insubstantial, half-mythical creature, shimmering away in that eau-de-Nil evening dress that made her look as though she were floating under water. Millais' Ophelia, only in de Lisi. Catching Sapphire's eye, he gave a slight shake of the head and a moment later she shrugged off her companion and came to stand beside him.

'No good?' Her eyes flitted briefly back to the young man she had left who shifted uncomfortably under their combined gaze, seeming suddenly gauche and unsure of himself as though suspecting he was the subject of their derision.

'A peasant.' Brutal, Indigo narrowed his beautifully sculpted lips. 'Not fit to kiss the hem. If we want to slum it, we've got Seán. Besides, tonight is a night for something softer.' His lips peeled back in a vulpine grin. 'Something . . . virginal. Read me?'

'Loud and clear,' said Sapphire. And with a swift kiss on his cheek she launched herself once more into the melee thronging the dance floor, callously shaking off the young man Indigo had rejected.

She had already spotted a likely target, a dark-haired young woman on the far side of the room standing pretty much adrift by herself, and like a guided missile Sapphire honed right in. The 'mark' was wearing a pretty dress in old ivory with a wide scooped neckline, falling Empress style from a coral satin band beneath her breasts. Galliano. Sapphire recognised the style. Last season's. Her hair was loosely piled up, threaded through with a string of pearls, imitation – Sapphire knew the real thing – with glossy tendrils hanging about her neck. There was a pearl at each ear, too, and a single teardrop pearl suspended on a narrow gold chain round her neck. Her wrists and fingers were bare, except for a crystal ring on the middle finger of her left hand.

Breezing up with a confidence that is the sole preserve of the very wealthy, the very famous or the very spoiled, Sapphire extended a slender hand. 'Hi, I don't think we've met. I'm Sapphire Granville.'

Up close, the girl was even more stunning, creamy-skinned with dark-grey luminous eyes fringed with thick black lashes. She had full pink cushiony lips of the kind you wanted to bite down on. Or, at least you did if you were Sapphire Granville. The thought caused her to smirk inwardly.

'Kathleen.' Formally, and with a slight nervous shake in her fingers, the girl reached out and shook Sapphire's hand. 'But my friends call me Kate. Kate O'Leary.' Softly spoken, she dropped her eyes, a faint blush staining her neck and cheeks.

Sapphire kept hold of her hand. 'Well, I certainly hope I shall be one of your friends. Nice to meet you, Kate.' Deftly, she steered her off to one side to a gold-covered chaise longue and pulled her down on the seat next to her. 'So, are you having a good time?'

'Oh, God, yes. It's fabulous, thanks.' Breathless, the young woman let her eyes stray over the glittering ballroom and the 'beautiful people' whooping it up, the colourful frescoes adorning the ceiling and up along the *Gone With the Wind* sweeping stairway. 'I've never been anywhere so beautiful in my entire life.' She dipped her head, nervously fingering the soft material of her dress. 'To be honest, I feel like a bit of a fraud, really. I mean, I'm only here because I won the Kingdom Rose competition and a night at the Midsummer Ball was part of the prize. This Galliano dress was another.' She slanted an uncertain look across at Sapphire.

Galliano. Sapphire gave herself a mental high-five. 'No false modesty, Kate – you deserved to win!' With a smile, she reached out and drew the back of a long reassuring nail gently down the other girl's cheek. 'I saw the photos in *The Kerry Eagle*. Ugh! What a bunch of ugly ducklings!' She moved closer in an all-girls-together way and patted her on the knee, letting her hand remain there just a fraction too long. 'You outshone them all.'

Her face burning, Kate waved the flattery away, but Sapphire could tell she was pleased and immediately pressed home her advantage with another compliment. 'Indigo thought so too.' She waved an airy hand. 'My brother – that sex god holding up the pillar over there and drooling in your direction.'

Kate followed the direction of Sapphire's hand, her face flaming deeper as she caught sight of Indigo Granville, lounging halfway up the marble stairs, lofting a glass in her direction.

'You may recognise him. He's playing at being an actor at the moment and has become a bit of a media darling since his success in that new Irish black comedy *Switch Off*. Have you seen it? He played the part of an assassin. All old hat and been done to death a million times before, but the public loved him.' Merriment shone from her eyes. 'It cracked me up.'

'Oh, yes, I did see it,' Kate confessed.

'See?' Sapphire quirked an amused eyebrow as Indigo treated them to a broad wink. 'Smitten. Absolutely smitten. I must introduce you. She looked around. 'Unless . . . your boyfriend?'

'Oh, I haven't got a boyfriend!' Kate's answer was a bit too eager.

'No boyfriend?' Better and better. Sapphire widened her eyes. 'Good heavens, I don't believe it. Unless . . . unless . . .' She twinkled roguishly. 'Oh, I get it! You bat for the other side.'

Kate looked first confused, then horrified. 'Oh, no, nothing like that. Actually, I was seeing someone until last Christmas. *Seriously* seeing someone. Seems he wasn't quite so serious, though. He . . . he met someone else.' She attempted a little carefree laugh, but it was clear she was still smarting from the rejection, making her, in Sapphire's eyes, more likely than ever to be 'amenable'. 'I had asked a friend to come along with me tonight but she came down with some sort of bug at the last minute. So here I am, Johnny No Mates.' She looked a bit anxious. 'I hope it was okay to come on my own? I just knew this opportunity wouldn't come along again.'

Sapphire gave a mental crow of delight. 'Good grief, it's more than okay! I can't tell you how nice it is to see a new face – we're sick to death of the same boring old fogeys, year after year. Just look at Indigo – he looks like he's won the Lotto. So, come on, let's put him out of his misery! Let's really get this party started and see if we can't give Cupid a bit of a leg-up whilst we're about it.' Or, better still, a leg-over.

Smiling, she pulled the other girl to her feet, who, had she not been feeling quite so flustered, might have noticed that behind the smile her young hostess's blue eyes had lost some of their friendliness.

As Sapphire led the way across the floor, her grip

144

tightening almost imperceptibly on the girl's wrist, she flashed a triumphant look at her brother. There was a tautness about him now, a sense of expectation that hadn't been there earlier. Across the distance, their eyes met in silent and perfect communication. No one must be allowed to spoil their fun. She looked warily around for Carrick and found him, as ever, surrounded by women. Good! All clear.

'Come on, Kate.' Quickening her pace almost to the point of impatience, she urged the other girl forward. 'Indigo and I are going to give you a night you'll never forget. Would you like that? Think of all the girls who would give anything to be in your shoes!'

'Oh, yes. I'd like that very much.' Hardly able to believe her luck at being singled out for such an honour, the young woman lifted up the skirts of her evening gown and obligingly matched her pace to that of her hostess.

But their departure didn't go altogether unnoticed. From different points around the room, a number of heads turned discreetly as the Kingdom Rose allowed herself to be led away. Like a lamb to the slaughter.

Ashling politely took her leave of yet another well-wisher. Her jaws ached from smiling, her hand from having it crushed vigorously in congratulations. More than anything she longed to escape just for five minutes, to marshal her thoughts.

145

Vainly she looked around for Rossa. Over to one side she could see his brother, Carrick, fending off, not altogether successfully, the attentions of a whole coterie of women. Hardly surprising. In the flesh he was even more handsome than in photographs. And what a spectacular entrance he'd pulled off, arriving by helicopter! If she didn't already know his reputation as an all-round good guy, one might even have accused him of trying to steal her and Rossa's thunder. And that was part of the problem. She still only knew him by reputation, as neither Rossa nor anyone else had seen fit to introduce them to each other and she was much too shy to simply put herself forward. Craning her neck, she caught sight of the actress woman on the far side of the room determinedly making her way towards the French doors. Dear, oh dear, that dress did her no favours at all. Still, she had seemed pleasant enough, open and friendly. And down to earth, which was more than could be said for a lot of the guests present. Ashling wondered if she shouldn't go and have another word with her, but that would bring her within close range of Carrick and really she couldn't possibly just walk past him.

Absentmindedly she fiddled with the sweet mimosa display on a plinth next to her. A leaf came off and she crushed it in her hand, releasing its delicate bride's-bouquet scent. Appropriate, for soon she would be a bride and judging from what Rossa had chosen to divulge only the previous night, casually dropping it into the conversation, she would also be mistress of all she surveyed. She was still struggling with the news, trying hard to get her head around it, trying to gauge how she felt about it all. Any normal girl would be thrilled but actually the situation wasn't quite so clear cut. No matter how much Rossa insisted that Carrick had brought it on himself, she couldn't quite rid herself of the feeling that it was wrong to deprive him of his inheritance and that no good would come of it, for any of them.

Where in heaven's name was Rossa? His absence was beginning to irk her. Of course both he and she were circulating, spreading themselves around among the guests, the demand on him being much greater as she knew relatively few people here. But ever since the official photo-shoot at the start of the evening and the free-for-all press shoot that followed, they had managed to snatch only the odd moment here and there. This was not how she had ever imagined her engagement party. Tears sprang to her eyes. Furiously she blinked them away and when her vision cleared, she found herself looking into the open smiling face of her brother-in-law to be.

'You're going to do that poor plant a mischief.' Opening her hand gently, he removed the crushed leaf and placed it in a nearby ashtray. 'I'm Carrick, by the way, Rossa's older brother. And you are the beautiful Ashling Morrison, who has stolen his heart.'

147

And your inheritance, Ashling thought unhappily, as he bent and dropped a kiss on her cheek.

He linked his arm through hers. 'Come on, let's get acquainted before Rossa comes hurtling back demanding to know what I'm doing with his beautiful lady.'

Ashling laughed, immediately warming to him, as he led her away to replenish her drink. 'Oh, Rossa's not the jealous type.' *More's the pity.*

Coppelia tucked a stray copper tendril under the edge of her Juliet-cap and gazed at her perfect image in the mirror. What a mistake it had been to underestimate Honoria, to think for one moment that age would have withered that arrogant, regal bearing. Whatever new lines there might be on Honoria's face, the eyes themselves were as sharp as ever, obsidian in their hardness, and when they fixed on Coppelia, she had felt them pierce like daggers. Once before, Honoria had looked at her like that. Once, long ago, over a newly made grave.

Outside the cloakroom someone rattled the doorknob impatiently, but the noise didn't even register. It was important that she take this little interlude to marshal her thoughts and strength before engaging any further with the enemy. In the past, there had been no option but to retreat and lick her wounds. No longer! The battle lines were clearly drawn and finally she was ready to advance her army. When the smoke cleared, there could only be one victor.

Oblivious to the line of women outside and the barrage of dirty looks that came her way, she was heading back towards the ballroom when a sibilant hiss brought her head spinning round. Rajesh.

Coppelia's perfectly groomed eyebrows rose to form two half-moons. How dare he hiss at her! Her lip curled.

'Ah, Honoria's familiar! *Quelle surprise!* Sent by the old bag to harass me, no doubt? I wondered how long it would take.'

He bowed, the courtly gesture totally at variance with the hatred glittering in his eyes.

'Memsahib Morrison, you are invited to join my mistress for a drink in her private sitting room.'

The hairs on the back of Coppelia's neck prickled. *Come into my parlour, said the spider to the fly!*

'Wants to swap recipes, I suppose. Her Seville marmalade for my gin sling. No? How disappointing.' Dropping her flippant tone, she made a point of checking her watch. 'Given up on pressing the flesh and queening it already, has she? Why, it's scarcely past the witching hour. Dear, oh dear, the old girl must be losing her touch.'

But it was not wise to goad Rajesh. Instinctively she felt that, one day, he would try to kill her. His brand of death would be swift, merciless, her throat slit cleanly from ear to ear with that infernal dagger he carried. Or, like Honoria's late husband, Henry, perhaps she too would meet a watery end, her head submerged by those killer hands till every last breath had been forced from her body.

Her chin lifted. She wasn't dead yet! Dismissive, she shooed him away.

'Tell Honoria I might join her and, then again, I might not. The excitement of finding out which will do her good.'

'Very well. In that case you may ask one of the servants to direct you.'

She flapped her hand. 'Oh, run along, you verminous creature!'

Rajesh bowed, his expression inscrutable, and left without another word.

Rattled despite herself, Coppelia stared after him.

'Ah, there you are, Aunty Pelia!' Fin's voice roused her from her thoughts. 'I feared the party rabble might have scared you away already.'

'Nothing of the sort, my boy. *I* am the ultimate party animal. I thought you knew that.'

Fin laughed. 'A pussycat?'

She growled. 'No, a tiger . . .' Her green eyes glowed with sudden promise.

Gulping, Fin opened the door of an anteroom, checked to see if it was empty, then pulled her inside and into his arms.

'Well then, Aunty Pelia,' he murmured, his lips seeking hers hungrily, his hand rising to cup the fullness of her breast, 'I'm very happy to offer myself as your prey.'

The growl changed to a purr. As a first course, Fin would do very nicely. The main kill would come later.

★　★　★

150

Maggie was finishing her drink on the terrace outside, taking a break from the hurly-burly of the ballroom and sharing the available air with a number of smokers who had emerged when there was a pause in the dancing. She was glad when the music struck up again and they all scurried back inside.

Despite the dress debacle, she was feeling very mellow, so mellow it was difficult to make the required effort to talk to members of the Granville clan. She needed to add weight and sharpness to her proposed glossy-mag article. But her body had switched to holiday mode and was discovering a talent for indolence. She tipped up her glass and savoured the last drops, torn between going back inside and pursuing matters or exploring the rose garden she could see at a short distance from the house. She rose to her feet, plonked her glass on a little table, and teetered off down the steps in Deirdre's strappy too-high heels.

Drawing closer, her senses were assaulted by the heady scent of mixed roses and the melodic splashing of the garden's centrepiece, a wonderfully ornate fountain, itself encircled by a huge latticework laden with violet-blue wisteria that hung in heavy grape-bunch clusters. A string of delicate white lights was threaded through the latticework, lending the heart of the wisteria a gentle glow. To the relief of her aching feet, there were also a number of marble benches with candlelit tables before them tucked into the interior of the wisteria circle and by some strange fluke none of them were occupied. Gratefully, she sat down on the first one to the right of the entrance, kicking off her shoes in an extension of the same movement. Bliss!

After a moment, lulled by the enchanting sound of water falling on water, her eyes closed, then shot open almost immediately as a sudden crash sounded behind her. Then she heard two agitated voices, lowered but furious. Maggie strained to hear. Some poor sod was plainly getting it in the ear. Standing up, she tiptoed to the entrance of her latticework cocoon and peered out. Rossa Granville was at the bottom of the terrace steps, apparently giving out stink to one of the waiters who stood there, tray in hand, its contents smashed into smithereens at his feet. But was there really any need for Rossa to go through him for a shortcut?

The thought was hardly born before Rossa came striding towards her, leaving the poor waiter gesticulating and protesting in his wake. And, Maggie observed with satisfaction, finally giving Rossa the two-finger salute. Quickly, she scurried to her seat, shrinking back against the trellis and hoping that in the darkness the wisteria's heavy tendrils would conceal her. After all, no one likes to be caught spying.

Rossa Granville came to a halt at the entrance to the wisteria circle, almost within touching distance, his stance one of extreme tension. His face, illuminated dimly by the fairy-lights, bore what could only be described as a look of sheer despair.

The happy bridegroom-to-be, thought Maggie. Last seen schmoozing with his beautiful fiancée, now savaging waiters and looking like Godzilla on an off day. She scented mystery.

Then she tensed as she heard someone call his name.

Rossa jumped at the sound of his brother's voice, then took another deep drag from the cigarette he had just lit and turned away from the fountain. There was no putting off the moment any longer. He had been steeling himself for this encounter ever since Carrick's brief tight-lipped phone call from Tokyo. Conscience making a coward of him, he had not acquitted himself well then and had mumbled and stumbled through their conversation. No matter how many times he'd trotted out the old 'am I my brother's keeper?' line to himself, the tiny core of him that was still decent knew he was talking out of his ass. Regardless, there was no turning back. He was in over his head financially, deep in the brown stuff, and, goddammit, Carrickross was his only way out. Scruples were just one more luxury he couldn't afford. Besides, scruples wouldn't put bread on the table and scruples most definitely wouldn't put expensive designer clothes on Priti's gorgeous body or jewellery round her slender neck. It could be argued that his brother's pig-headedness had been his own undoing, so why shouldn't Carrick's loss be his gain? Carrick had hung up the phone on him that day, ominously ending the call with a curt 'Till Carrickross'. Rossa had been relieved upon arriving home over a week before to find that Carrick was going through one of his reclusive phases out on his precious island. But now the reckoning was at hand.

Dropping his cigarette onto the gravel walkway, he crushed it beneath his foot, and forced a jauntiness into his voice.

'Ah, Robinson Crusoe returns! I thought we might have seen you before this, that you might have come to lend a hand in the preparations for the ball.'

'I'm not sure I would have been entirely welcome.' Carrick gave a slightly grim smile. 'Besides, I suspect I was better off away from all the fuss.'

Rossa almost winced. 'Well, yeah, it was pretty manic – an asylum of women all shouting each other down in the quest for perfection. A million miles away from Tokyo, I expect?'

'True. Tokyo was fascinating but, mission accomplished, it's on to the next project now – a neo-Goth Cathedral in Wicklow. Needless to say, I'll be using all my powers of persuasion to alter that particular brief.' He stepped beyond Rossa, apparently to stare at the fountain. In reality, he was steeling himself to deal with the problem head on, to prevent this catastrophe if he could, for all their sakes – but, most of all, for the sake of Carrickross. Let them all play their little games. He, at least, would be straight.

He turned back, his face still giving no hint of his thoughts.

'And Thailand? Still enjoying it, are you? Still in thrall to all the exotic delights on offer?'

Rossa froze for a moment. Was this some veiled reference to Priti? Did Carrick know about her and, if so, who else did? He had always been paranoid about keeping his private life exactly that – private. But Carrick's countenance was so open, so devoid of any guile, that the panic subsided almost immediately.

'Yeah, Hua Hin's good. Blue skies, sandy beaches, sunshine. What's not to like? It suits me, anyway.'

'Better than home?' Lightly touching Rossa's elbow, Carrick steered him to a garden bench by the gravel walkway, facing the fountain.

Rossa sensed the real business was about to begin. Sitting down, he tried to relax, loosen his limbs, give the impression that he was calm and in control. Yet his heart was pounding, his pulse racing.

Carrick, on the other hand, sat slightly forward, staring straight ahead. He sighed deeply. 'Okay, cards on the table, Rossa. Why are you going along with this?' He gestured back towards the house, all lit up like a toy train, lights at every window, music issuing in a thin falsetto stream. 'This – this charade?'

Rossa lit up another cigarette. It was an effort to keep his voice steady. 'Charade, Carrick? Hardly! I know it's all happened rather quickly but there's no legislating for Cupid's little arrow. The long and the short is that I love Ashling, Ashling loves me and we're getting married.' He drew the smoke down deep into his lungs, wondering if his words sounded as false to Carrick as they did to his own ears. 'And I'm sorry if the by-product is that Honoria has kicked you in the nuts. But really, it's unreasonable of you to expect the rest of us to put our lives on hold till you've bucked up your own ideas about matrimony.'

Turning to him, Carrick's shrewd eyes seemed to bore into him.

'Quite so, Rossa. And, indeed, on the face of it, it all sounds like the perfect whirlwind romance and Ashling is an exceptionally lovely young woman. I spoke with her in the ballroom. Odd, though, how speed and greed rhyme, isn't it? Odd, too, how Grandmother *hand-picked* her for you.'

'Nothing odd about it at all,' Rossa snapped, guilt mixed with panic forcing him onto the back foot. 'I don't deny Grandmother introduced us, but isn't that generally how people meet, via a third party?' He changed tactics, went on the attack. 'Anyway, why the inquisition? Is it really my future that concerns you, Carrick, or this pile of old stones?'

A pulse beat at the side of Carrick's temple. 'This *pile* of old stones, Rossa, is our birthright and damn right I'm concerned about it. You don't want it. You never wanted it. Neither the responsibility nor the work entailed in keeping it in good repair. Its history means absolutely nothing to you. It never has.' Impassioned, Carrick jumped to his feet. 'But it's different for me, Rossa. When I look at Carrickross, I see in every stone, every slate, every ivy-covered piece of brick, the blood, sweat, tears and pride of all the Granvilles who have gone before us and who made us what we are. That old house, this land, is our birthright, don't you see that? Its real value is incalculable. It's not simply something that can be broken down in pounds, shillings and pence, prefaced by a "For Sale" sign.' Spinning round, he glared off into the distance, as if he could no longer bear to look directly at his brother. 'And that's all it comes down to with you, Rossa, isn't it? Money! Left to your own devices, you would milk the place dry.'

He sat down again, rubbed his eyes, suddenly weary and dispirited beyond belief.

'But there's the rub, Rossa. No matter what promises she's made or what carrot she's dangled in front of your eager nose, Honoria will never leave you to your own devices. She has Carrickross in a death grip. She'll sacrifice anything and anyone to keep the Granville name alive and the estate intact.' His voice dropped to barely more than a whisper. 'Be careful, Rossa, that the sacrifice doesn't turn out to be you.'

★   ★   ★

157

When at last the Granville brothers fell silent and Maggie heard footsteps angrily crunching gravel, retreating towards the house, she waited several minutes to make sure the coast was well clear before daring to leave the shelter of her wisteria-covered hidey-hole, the straps of her shoes looped over one wrist. Tentatively, she edged round the front of the trellis then shrieked in shock as another figure came round from the far side and almost knocked her off her feet.

'I beg your pardon!' A hand came up and steadied her. 'I hadn't realised anyone was there.'

Carrick Granville. Shit! She'd thought the pair of them had gone. 'I . . . er . . . I was . . .' she said lamely, feeling her cheeks flame and glad of the dim lighting.

'There all along?' His eyes glittered.

'Fraid so. But, listen, it wasn't intentional. I was here taking a breather and by the time it became apparent that you two were involved in a barney, it was kind of too late to come clean and reveal my presence.'

'Too late or too intriguing?' Carrick stepped closer.

She could feel his breath warm on her face. Involuntarily, she took a step back.

'Both, if I'm honest,' she said cheekily. 'Anyway, isn't discretion supposed to be the better part of valour? And what would *you* have done in the circumstances?'

To her relief, he smiled. 'Oh, probably the same.

But then I would have wiped it clean from my mind. And that's just what you're going to do too, isn't it?'

Maggie didn't reply, just smiled back winningly. Let him read what he liked into that. Then she glanced at her watch and gave an oh-my-God-is-that-the-time start.

'Well, I'd better be getting back to the house,' she said, stepping round him nimbly. 'It's been nice meeting you.'

Carrick's gaze flicked to the shoes looped round her wrist. 'You too, Cinderella. Although one could wish it were under different circumstances.'

Maggie grinned, twiddled her fingers at him and took off at the double regardless of the gravel digging into her bare feet.

The lavish suite of rooms occupied by Sapphire and Indigo was still known as the New Wing, despite the original having burned to the ground at least a hundred years before.

Perched self-consciously on the edge of a regency-striped chaise longue, clutching the second gin and tonic Indigo had forced on her, Kate felt like Alice in Wonderland. Everything in the Granville mansion was so big and so very rich. She, by contrast, felt very small indeed and although she was an unsophisticated country girl from a modest farming background, she knew enough to recognise real wealth when she saw it. The Granvilles' wealth wasn't the nouveau-riche kind she read about in celeb magazines like *Okay* and *Hello!* Far from it. This reeked of old money.

'Hey, loosen up! Let's party!' Sapphire playfully shook her arm as, her head turning like a child let loose in a fairground, Kate strove to drink in her surroundings and commit them to memory.

'Sorry!'

'What is she like, eh?' Sapphire said, directing the question jokingly at her brother.

'What *is* she like?' Raising his eyebrows a fraction, Indigo smiled, his eyes glimmering with an artificial brightness that owed not a little to mind-altering chemicals. 'Good question, sis. That's just what I intend to find out.'

Alive to a sudden intense charge in the atmosphere, Kate's gaze jumped uncertainly from one twin to the other, but any hint of uneasiness was banished immediately as they both smiled cheerily at her and Sapphire gave her fingers a fond squeeze.

'Drink up, my beauty!' said Indigo. 'You're not really making inroads into that gin. Would you prefer something else?' Without waiting for her response he began to rummage amongst the bottles in the well-stocked drinks cabinet, lifting this one and that and inspecting the labels. Then he snapped his fingers and smiled meaningfully across at Kate. 'Of course. Champagne! Well, it's got to be, hasn't it? In honour of our lovely Kingdom Rose.'

'Absolutely,' Sapphire agreed, seating herself

beside Kate. 'Only the best for the Kingdom Rose Beauty Queen!'

Slightly overcome by all the attention, Kate grasped the flute of Cristal that was pressed into her hand almost as though it were a lifeline. In truth, she didn't really like champagne – or any alcohol much. It made her tipsy in no time, and she'd already had far more than she was accustomed to, but Sapphire and Indigo were being such kind, thoughtful hosts and she was terrified of coming across as a party pooper.

'To the Rose!' Sapphire raised her glass, clinked it musically against Kate's.

'The Rose!' Indigo touched his own glass to each of theirs. 'And all who sip from her fair petals!'

And then he and his sister were suddenly convulsed with laughter.

Out of her depth, Kate sipped shyly at her drink.

'Yes, I know we're totally crazy!' Indigo gave a whoop. 'Poor Kate, what must you think of us?' Pulling her to her feet, he slipped an arm around her slender waist, holding her so close she could smell the fresh lemony tang of his aftershave and thanked her lucky stars once more for the chance to be part of their company. With a swift kiss on her forehead, Indigo released her. Too much too soon would only scare her off. She was still too keyed up for the real fun to begin. Heading over to the state-of-the-art Bang & Olufsen stereo system at the far side of the room, his latest little toy, he began riffling through a large stack of CDs

161

piled carelessly to one side. 'Hey, let's have our own private party, just the three of us, away from all the old geezers and Grandmother's all-seeing eye. Scissor Sisters, anyone?'

'Yeah, way to go!' With a little shimmy, Sapphire kicked off her high heels and strode out into the middle of the room as the first notes of 'Take Your Mama Out' blared from the stereo. She beckoned to Kate. 'Come on, Kate! Time to shake your cutie booty!'

Slightly woozy, Kate eased off her own high heels. 'Listen, I have to warn you I'm not much of a dancer. I was once chucked out of Irish dancing classes for having two left feet.'

'Really? How amusing!' Sapphire burst into her habitual effervescent laughter and Indigo joined in, guffawing disproportionately.

Their hilarity must have been catching because, a moment later, Kate found herself giggling away too, despite the fact that it was hardly the funniest anecdote ever. Still, the twins were hugely amused and she felt herself relax enough to join in their manic dancing, almost pathetically grateful to be their friend. So much so that, a little later, when Indigo produced a large spliff seemingly from out of nowhere, lit it up and offered it to her, she found herself unable to refuse in case it spoiled the mood or they should think her ungrateful.

Sapphire, who had continued to dance energetically, flopped back down on the chaise longue, stretching her long slender legs out in front of her.

Taking the joint from Indigo, she took a deep pull, coughing a little as it hit the back of her throat. 'Wow! That's powerful! Let me guess. Moroccan?'

'Right first time. Kashab Black to be exact, one of the newest mixes. Potent.'

'Laced?' Sapphire took another drag and narrowed her eyes suspiciously.

Indigo gave a careless shrugh. 'Whatever. But hey, what's a little Charlie between friends?'

'Charlie?' Kate asked, her grip on reality already beginning to slip under the combined effects of too much alcohol and laced weed.

Sapphire's lip curled in amusement. Lord, but the girl genuinely was an innocent.

'An old friend,' Indigo answered, his mind running along exactly the same track as his sister's. A thought struck him. Could it possibly be that the delicious Kate was still a virgin? His loins tightened pleasurably at the thought. He couldn't wait to find out.

'Another drink?' Without waiting for an answer, Sapphire refilled Kate's Waterford crystal glass right up to the brim. 'Come on, bottoms up! You've a long way to go before you catch up with Ind and me.'

As the champagne flowed freely and the cocaine-laced spliff did the rounds again and again, Kate found herself feeling nauseous. Then the room began to spin like a Wall of Death. Sweat broke out on her forehead, her stomach churned and suddenly she was falling . . .

When at last she opened her eyes again, it was to find a nightmarish scene unfolding before her. Sapphire and Indigo were still in the room, only now both were completely naked and standing so close together that Sapphire's perfect breasts were touching her brother's chest and his hand was cupping one of her buttocks. His other hand was supporting the back of his sister's neck, his mouth voraciously seeking hers. Horrified and sickened, it seemed to Kate that time had become suspended as she watched his tongue and his sister's dart out and writhe serpent-like around each other in a macabre incestuous dance. Incest! The word resounded in Kate's fogged-up brain like a funeral bell and the gorge rose and lodged somewhere in her throat.

'No!' Involuntarily her hands came up in front of her as if she could shield herself from the terrible spectacle.

The expletive caught the twins' attention and, disentangling themselves, they moved with one accord towards her.

'Ah, so the Rose has blossomed back to life!' Indigo's voice sounded hollow to her ears, his lips moving out of sync like an actor in a badly dubbed movie.

'Seems to me she wants to join in the fun.' Sapphire's speech too seemed badly bent out of shape, muffled, as though she was speaking under water, her face looming and receding like a reflection in a fairground mirror.

In vain, Kate struggled against the heavy fog that had her in its grip, lashing out wildly as Indigo advanced on her.

'Leave me alone! Oh, please, leave me alone!'

'Whaddya think, Sapph?' Indigo mocked, pinioning her hands and rendering her helpless. 'Will we leave her alone?'

'Oh no, I don't think so.' Sapphire adopted a little-girl sing-song voice. 'It would be bad manners to leave her out!'

'Bad manners? That would never do.' Indigo's grip tightened on Kate's wrists, causing her to cry out in pain.

Terrified, the girl struggled uselessly against him, but when Sapphire went to his aid and between them they hauled her to her feet, her legs gave way totally and a moment later she lapsed back into blessed unconsciousness.

Honoria was sitting by the fireside in her private sitting room, erect as a sentinel, hand clenched on the ivory boar's-head of her walking stick, when Coppelia swept in without even so much as a perfunctory knock. It was four minutes past two.

Tall and slender in her black Schiaparelli gown, Coppelia's face was an unreadable mask.

'You came.' Honoria's eyes fastened almost greedily upon her. 'You assumed I would wait up for you?'

'I *knew* you would,' Coppelia countered.

165

'Indeed.' The older woman chortled, a sound like the rasping of dry leaves.

Looking about, Coppelia spotted Rajesh, half-hidden in the shadows at the back of the room. 'What's he doing here? I thought this was supposed to be a tête-à-tête – just you and me, Honoria.' She pointed an imperious finger 'You! Piss off!'

'Rajesh stays,' Honoria said with finality. 'I keep no secrets from him.'

Leaning heavily on her walking stick, she rose to her feet so that the two women stood virtually face to face. Neither moved and yet the impression was of two predators slowly circling one another, each looking for the chink in the other's armour.

Coppelia tapped her watch. 'Ten minutes, Honoria. Ten minutes to say your piece and then I walk.'

'That will be more than adequate. And yet it seems such a paltry amount of time in which to ruin someone's life.'

Coppelia rolled her eyes. 'Cut to the chase. Some of us have better people – oops, I mean things, to be doing.'

Honoria's expression darkened. 'As you wish. You must have some inkling as to why I invited you here tonight?'

'Yes, of course. You're waiting for me to congratulate you on orchestrating this whole marriage fiasco. What else?' Coppelia's nostrils flared slightly.

'Honoria didn't deny it. Instead she smiled

humourlessly. 'So clever of me, don't you think? And what a lovely couple they make!'

'Bullshit!' A pulse began to throb at Coppelia's temple. 'There's more love between you and me than between Rossa and Ashling, on his side anyway. He spent most of this evening ogling the serving staff and not for their canapés.'

Malice shone from Honoria's eyes. 'Love? Hah, of course he doesn't love her. I doubt if he loves anyone other than himself. The boy's always been thoughtless and self-centred. But, his selfishness and permanent state of indebtedness worked to my advantage. After all, he who ends up as master of Carrickross pretty much ends up master of his own destiny.' Her hooded eyes blinked rapidly. 'Ashling is not without her charms. I like her, in fact. I didn't expect that. But then she's not cut from your cloth at all. Ashling is so obviously her father's daughter.'

Coppelia laughed dismissively. 'Dear, oh dear, you have been a busy old witch!'

'Well worth it,' Honoria snapped. 'And *so* easy. I laid the trap and Ashling sprang it all by herself. Poor girl, the lack of a proper mother made her desperate for affection, you see, and, bang on cue, enter the gallant and gorgeous Rossa. Truth to tell, he didn't have to work very hard, just blinked those turquoise eyes of his a few times, treated her to a bowlful of sugar-coated words, held out his arms and in she tumbled.' Taunting, she wagged a finger. 'You weren't a very good parent, Coppelia. You didn't protect her.'

Coppelia's hands clenched into fists, her long nails cutting crescents into the soft flesh of her palms. There was some truth in what the venomous old cow had said. She had chosen to keep Ashling at a distance. She had played the indifferent stepmother all too well. If Ashling grew up craving affection, it *was* her fault.

She realised that her enemy was eyeing her keenly, intent on reading her thoughts. She must not betray any signs of weakness.

'But why Rossa?' she said coolly, her face now a careful mask. 'Leaving aside the no doubt vexed question of Jaspar and his – er – proclivities, isn't Carrick the more obvious choice? More fitting I would have thought and less likely to bankrupt the estate.' She shot Honoria a speculative look. 'What's really going on here? I don't believe for one moment you are prepared to just step aside and throw Rossa the reins.' Coppelia paused for a beat. '*You* who once committed murder to preserve control!'

'I take it you are referring to Henry's unfortunate death?' Honoria smiled. 'My beloved late husband. Of course, that's when we last saw each other, wasn't it? The grieving widow and the tart, meeting across his freshly dug grave.'

'Where he was put by you and that *thing* sitting in the corner.' Coppelia felt tears prick her eyes, her grief at losing the only man she had ever really loved still raw even after all these years. 'You couldn't bear it that he was leaving you for me!'

'You were nothing!' Spittle flew from Honoria's mouth. 'Just another Jezebel in a long line. Henry's little *affaires de coeurs* meant nothing. I knew all about them. They didn't matter, only Carrickross. *You* didn't matter either. But that was my mistake, Coppelia; I didn't see you for the serpent you were. Unlike the other whores, the crumbs from my table weren't enough for you. You wanted it all. *Everything*! My husband! My home! My world!'

'Convenient for you then that Henry "accidentally" drowned before he could leave you. Although we both know there was nothing accidental about it. Were you there, watching from the bank, as Rajesh rowed him into the middle of the lake and pushed him in? Right in front of the summerhouse, wasn't it? Henry's Folly, I've heard you call it. Is that your idea of a joke, you sick old hag?'

Honoria lifted her stick from the floor and pointed it accusingly. 'Henry was a fool. He would have destroyed everything for the sake of a selfish red-haired whore hell-bent on ruining me.'

'The pity is I didn't succeed, you filthy, murdering bitch!'

'And never will.' Honoria threw her a look of triumph. 'Besides, since you seem to have worked it all out, why did you not go to the police with your suspicions?' She answered her own question. 'Because you had no proof. Because they would have taken one look at you and seen you for just another cheap, mischief-making, gold-digging trollop!' She banged the tip of her stick back down on the floor. 'And so you chose to slink away like a thief in the night instead and like a thief you stole something from Carrickross. Something precious . . .' Tantalisingly she let the accusation trail off, an air of barely suppressed excitement pulsating about her.

Jesus, surely not! A bead of sweat rolled down Coppelia's forehead. Her breath began to come in short gasps. There was no way Honoria could possibly know. She'd been so careful, paranoid almost. All that secrecy over all the years. The complexity of the subterfuge.

'I had eyes watching you.' The old woman's words fell over her like a shower of icy water. 'Always. Everywhere you went. I made it my business to know everything about you, no matter how trivial.' She sniggered at the growing look of horror on Coppelia's face. 'Even the midwife who delivered you was in my pay. Oh yes, Coppelia, I knew about Ashling's birth within fifteen minutes of her delivery.' Her expression iced over. 'My *husband's* daughter, the treasure you robbed from Carrickross, the secret you thought was safe.' Her hand sliced through the air. 'No! Don't try to deny it. Ashling is Henry's. And she should have been *mine*!' The last word was anguished and her lips peeled back in a snarl. '*You* didn't deserve her! You *gave her away*, like she was nothing! The daughter I wanted so desperately! *Why*? So you could continue your worthless life, unfettered by

170

a child! So fortunate that the childless Morrisons offered a solution. Rich, respectable, desperate for a child, they could be guaranteed to give Ashling a good life whilst salving your conscience at the same time.'

Shaking with the after-effects of shock, Coppelia made a superhuman effort to pull herself together. 'I didn't do it lightly, no matter what you think. My reasons were sound. It was better for Ashling. Safer.'

'Safer? Why? Surely you could have protected your own daughter?' Honoria looked sly. 'Unless you were worried about something – or someone in particular. Me, for instance?' She shook her head. 'Poor deluded creature. I could have taken Ashling any time it suited me. Instead, I sat back and enjoyed the whole pantomime. What a dilemma when the adoptive mother, Margery Morrison, so inconveniently died! How you must have fretted over the situation – Fate had made your little daughter motherless. And how ingenious of you to seduce your way into Margery's marriage bed, marry her grief-stricken husband and proclaim yourself stepmother to your own daughter! I take my hat off to you, Coppelia. Only a real psychopath could pull off a stunt like that.'

'Desperate times, desperate measures,' said Coppelia with as much control as she could muster. 'If Ashling knew I was her birth mother, at some point she would have demanded to know the identity of her birth father. I couldn't afford to tell her about Henry or her connection to the Granvilles. Most of all, I couldn't afford *you* finding out about her connection to me.' Her face darkened. 'Like I said, I was keeping her safe.'

'Not safe enough.' Goading, Honoria hummed a snatch of the Wedding March.

Coppelia shrugged. 'Which brings us full circle. The wedding can't take place. Since Ashling is Henry's daughter, that also makes her half-aunt to Rossa and as far as I'm aware incestuous marriages are still against the law. Knowing this, Honoria, why go to the trouble of orchestrating such an elaborate charade in the first place?'

'To watch you squirm like a worm on a hook. To see how you would try to extricate yourself from the mess. From the moment you found out about the engagement, all you had to do was open your mouth and tell Ashling the truth.' She smirked. 'You didn't, though, and shall I tell you why? You hate me and my family so much that it would have been anathema to you to tell her that she is one of us Granvilles. But there are other reasons. If you tell her, not only will Ashling see you for the stinking hypocrite you are, but *pouff* – her prospective marriage to the man she loves goes up in smoke. In fact, she discovers she is his aunt! And, worst of all, you will have to admit that you are her *real* mother and not the stepmother you led her to believe you were for all those years. Years of lie piled upon lie. She'll hate you. For ever.'

Feeling quite faint, Coppelia groped for the back of a nearby chair and leaned on it. Everything the old bitch said was right! Ashling would never forgive her.

'Unless . . .' said Honoria.

With a feeling of dread mingled with hope, Coppelia realised Honoria was about to offer her an alternative.

'Unless you leave Ireland immediately, take yourself away as far as possible without offering even one word of explanation, one excuse or goodbye to Ashling.' The scent of victory sweet in her nostrils, she administered the death blow. 'From this moment on, you must never ever contact her again. Because, if you do, I will make fully sure that she is told the whole sordid truth. Believe me, I will spare her nothing.' Her teeth locked around her prey. 'Coppelia Morrison, you will be dead to your daughter. Comply and I will make it my business to call off the wedding without giving a reason. And, believe me, my grandson will cooperate. Refuse and you will destroy your daughter as surely as if you were to put a gun to her head.'

Coppelia stared, fighting back tears, unable to believe what she was hearing. 'No, Honoria. Not even you could be so evil as to expect me to simply disappear from my daughter's life!'

'You did it before when you gave her up for adoption. Besides, think about this rationally. Ashling will be hurt whatever the outcome. She will be hurt that her marriage to Rossa never takes place. But she'll recover from that. She's young, beautiful and intelligent and one day she will meet a man who will actually love her as she deserves to be loved. How much more hurtful and longer lasting to discover your treachery, Coppelia, and the way you have deceived her all her life! For once, do the honourable thing. Walk away.'

Still leaning on the chair, Coppelia gazed unseeingly at the carpet at her feet, her mind in overdrive as she considered her options. Then, drawing herself erect with an effort, she faced her enemy.

'So, this then is your vengeance, Honoria. An eye for an eye, a daughter for a husband?'

Honoria savoured her triumph. 'The punishment must fit the crime and your punishment is to suffer every day of your life, just as you once planned for me and mine. And when I am dead, there are others who will continue to see that my orders are carried out. Your banishment is complete. It is for ever. It is irrevocable. But . . . tell her if you will. Destroy her. Destroy yourself. I shall enjoy that too. The choice is yours.'

The clock on the wall chimed a quarter past two. It had taken Honoria slightly longer than the allotted ten minutes to devastate her rival's life.

'Come, come, Coppelia,' she said abruptly. 'I need to retire to bed. It has been a long day. What is your decision?'

'Very well,' Coppelia said with a shuddering sigh. 'I will leave first thing in the morning.'

'And, in the meantime, I have your word that you will not seek Ashling out?'

Drained, Coppelia nodded. 'You have my word.'

'Very well. It is agreed. Leave me now.'

Without another glance or word, Coppelia turned and left.

Rajesh closed the door behind her.

'The circle is complete, Rani. Tonight your dreams will be sweet indeed.'

Suddenly cold, Honoria drew nearer to the fire. 'I wish it may be so, Rajesh. And yet, instinct tells me we have not seen the back of Coppelia Morrison.' She gazed into the flames. 'Like me, she is a fighter. It troubles me that she gave in so easily.' A cinder flew out and sizzled into nothingness on the hearth. Honoria shivered.

When Kate surfaced, it was to find herself lying on a circular bed, her head pounding. Beside her Sapphire lay sleeping, curled on one side, thumb in mouth, looking curiously vulnerable and child-like and bearing almost no resemblance whatsoever to the drugged-up, sexually perverted creature of earlier. Head spinning, she let her eyes wander down along her own body, realising with a start that she was totally naked and aching all over. There was blood staining her thighs and a rosary of bruises traversing her stomach and wrists. Kate was in no doubt. She had been raped. Disjointed memories raced through her brain like bizarre hallucinations. Sapphire dancing, shrieking, urging, goading.

175

Indigo plunging, pounding, penetrating. Pain. Hot red flashes of pain! *Her* pain. An image of herself protesting, pleading, imploring, yet no words emerging from her clumsy paralysed mouth. Gazing, as she floated above it all, at the spectacle of a naked helpless girl being ravished.

A sudden movement to the left brought her eyes swivelling fearfully round to where a naked Indigo sat hunched over a table, a line of cocaine in front of him which he was busy dispatching up his nose. The detritus of the evening's debauchery littered the floor: broken glasses, empty champagne bottles, shoes flung hither and yon, heaps of discarded clothing, somewhere amongst it hers . . . The room seemed to lurch. Vomit rose in her throat. She willed it back, hung onto the bed until things steadied a little. Given that Indigo was between her and the door – and she was naked – Kate knew there was no hope of escape. Quiet as a mouse, she tried not to attract attention to herself, but just at that moment, Indigo turned his head and slurred at her.

'Want some?'

'No, thank you.' Her voice came out sounding cracked. Her lips felt sore and there was the metallic taste of blood in her mouth.

'Suit yourself!' Indigo shrugged carelessly. 'How about a bit more fun then, Katie? A little light bondage, maybe? Now, shall *I* tie you up or *you* tie me?' He pretended to consider the matter. 'No, I think it had better be me doing the restraining.

Otherwise you might even try to escape. And that would be no fun at all.'

Kate's last conscious thought as he stood up and walked towards her, a length of cord stretched taut between his hands, was to wonder how anyone so beautiful, so angelic looking, could be so utterly depraved.

CHAPTER 13

Awakened by the sound of a pneumatic drill, Maggie O'Keefe opened her eyes and squinted painfully round. She was lying spread-eagled on a couch with a cushion under her head and a knitted rug partially covering her. It took a few moments to realise that actually the drilling was confined to her own head. Her stomach rebelled as she struggled to sit up.

After Ashling Morrison had introduced her to Jaspar Granville and Ehu, his Maasai sidekick, the evening before, it seemed as though her glass was magically never empty. She was introduced as Deirdre Butler, of course. But Maggie had really liked Jaspar and soon found herself confessing all to him about her masquerade. He thought it was hilarious.

Maggie lay back again as embarrassing cameos from the night before came back to haunt her. Ehu, elaborate beads and plaited hair bouncing, blood-red toga draped around him over his leather 'shorts', teaching her a tribal dance in which she had joined with uninhibited gusto. And, groan, did she really recall Carrick Granville standing on the sidelines with all the other spectators looking at her like . . . well, looking at her like something. Her brain wasn't up to deciphering quite what just yet, but she doubted if it was complimentary. Later, Ehu, plainly unused to alcohol, had gone completely mad and had run belligerently round the ballroom with a Zulu spear and shield he had snatched off a wall somewhere. Efficiently, Carrick had disarmed him, which gave rise to Jaspar muttering something about some people being far too high-handed and Ehu vowing darkly that if Carrick wasn't Jaspar's nephew, he might be tempted to teach him a lesson. At which point he had ominously patted a little beaded gourd suspended from a leather thong around his neck.

'Poison!' Jaspar told her with a huge wink. 'Never leaves home without it, the dear boy. Wouldn't hurt a fly, really.'

Maggie sat up again, groaning, her eyes tracking round the room and lingering on the number of sleeping bodies festooning the beautiful furniture who, like her, hadn't made it home.

Maggie had to admit, her behaviour last night hadn't exactly been inconspicuous – or professional. Whatever happened to her plans for a career-enhancing article – a rundown on the beautiful people at play? She shook herself in an effort to sober up, felt worse than ever and flopped back down again. Soon, she promised her conscience. Soon she would get up and do the *necessary*. In the meantime, another five minutes' kip could only do her the world of good.

Cradling her head between her hands, she drifted off again and, sure enough, when she woke a short time later, she felt marginally better. Well enough to sit up without throwing up. Tentatively she swung her legs over the side of the couch and eased herself to her feet. Shaky, but at least she was upright. Fresh air and a strong cup of coffee and she would be ready to join the human race again. Like a toddler learning to walk, she staggered uncertainly towards the back patio.

It was a beautiful morning. Making a visor of her hand, she looked around. The birds were about their business but, apart from their chatter, it was extraordinarily quiet. Then she remembered Jaspar mentioning that the morning after the Midsummer Ball was traditionally a half-day holiday for the servants – *staff* other people would have called them these days but the Granvilles were seemingly exempt from political correctness – in recognition of their working for most of the night. Also, it served as a courtesy to still-drunken guests who wouldn't appreciate being roused from their comas. Of course, Jaspar had added with a nose-tap, it also gave any media-shy politicians, celebrities, errant husbands and closet gays the opportunity to tidy away their 'midsummer madness' and do a runner before any unofficial paps arrived on the scene.

She drew a lungful of fresh air and cautiously

descended the steps, flinching as the gravel pavement bit into her bare feet. A flash of black caught her eye, way over to her left, alerting her to the fact that someone else was awake after all. Squinting, she caught a glimpse of Coppelia Morrison, mother of the bride-to-be and current muse of the paparazzi – that copper mantle of hair was a dead giveaway. Not alone either, but wrapped around some man she couldn't see quite well enough to recognise. Dark-haired, tall. Who was he? Her reporter's antennae twitched. The next scandalous liaison in La Morrison's vast repertoire of scandalous liaisons? She flinched suddenly at a twinge beneath the joint of her big toe where a sharp piece of gravel had become embedded. She tried to dislodge it by rubbing it against the shin of her other leg, but when that didn't work, squatted down and flicked it away. By the time she had straightened up again, the couple had vanished. Ah well, none of her business anyway and whilst she wasn't averse to a satirical article in one of the glossies, she drew the line at the catty gossip columns. Though the money would certainly come in handy.

Maggie circled her shoulders in an effort to loosen the stiffness brought about by sleeping on the couch. A sudden flutter at the ornamental fountain attracted her attention and she smiled to see that a robin had alighted on the edge and was attempting to dip his tiny beak into the water without falling in. The pleasant roar of the fountain was silenced, the water still. Maggie wandered over into the circle of wisteria and sat on the edge of the fountain. There were some plastic bags and other detritus floating in the water, another clean-up job for the no-doubt overworked and underpaid skivvies of Carrickross.

Talking of clean-up jobs – her hand went up to her brillo-pad hair – she herself was not a pretty sight, she guessed. Leaning over the water she checked for confirmation, then slid off the edge of the fountain in pure shock.

Her heart juddering in her chest, she checked again to make sure she hadn't been hallucinating. No, there was a woman's body in there all right, long dark hair floating in Medusa-like tendrils round her head, like a parody of that stupid shampoo advert on the telly.

On closer inspection the plastic bags turned out to be the wispy material of a ball gown breaking the surface. Maggie peered closer, trying to see past the slightly murky water and the rogue strands of hair partially obscuring the poor woman's face, but it was difficult to get a clear look.

'Good morning!' A deep male voice brought her spinning round.

Carrick Granville, handsome as ever in hacking jacket and wellington boots, was standing behind her. He took a step forward. 'Hey, are you all right? You look awful.'

She shook her head and gestured urgently to the fountain. 'There! In the water!'

He gazed at her as if he thought she might be still drunk. But then he moved over to the fountain's edge and peered in, recoiling just as she had done.

'Jesus! What the hell happened?'

'I don't know,' Maggie quavered. 'I only just found her. Too much to drink, maybe?'

'My God, she may have only just fallen in! She could even be alive!' Carrick tore off the thick Donegal-tweed hacking jacket which, bizarrely, he was wearing over his tuxedo trousers and dress shirt, and flung it to the ground.

'No point.' Maggie caught his arm. 'She's dead. I've seen enough bodies in my life to know when someone's past saving.'

'No, we've got to try.' Ignoring her, Carrick plunged his arms into the fountain and reluctantly Maggie moved forward to help. For a moment he struggled to lift the body, then suddenly he stopped and straightened, letting the woman slide back beneath the surface. Maggie looked at him questioningly, but his face was suddenly wiped clean of any expression.

He stepped back a little, cleared his throat. She noticed that his hands were shaking.

'Listen – you'd better run to the house and get help.' He scooped his jacket up from the ground, fumbled in a pocket and pulled out his mobile phone. 'I'll stay here and phone the guards. And an ambulance, too, I suppose, although you were right. The poor girl is long past saving.'

He flipped the top open on his mobile, then glanced up at Maggie. 'You never did tell me your name?'

'Maggie. Maggie O'Keefe.'

'Right, Maggie – can you run back to the house and tell Noreen, the cook, to send Tom and Seán? They're probably in their beds but if I know Noreen she'll be up and about in the kitchen – it's over there.' He pointed to a basement entrance. 'Okay?'

Maggie nodded.

'Play it down and don't go into any detail. Just say there's been an accident,' he continued crisply. 'Tell her not to wake the guests – the last thing we need is an audience. In the meantime, I'll phone Rossa and alert the rest of the family.'

Maggie couldn't help but be impressed at the efficient way he took charge. 'Right. Tom and Seán, you said?'

'Yes – Noreen's husband and son.' As she turned to go, he grasped her elbow. 'Better tell Tom to rouse the other servants too – just the men. Ask him to assemble them on the patio there as quickly as possible. I'll get them to form a cordon and make certain no one wanders over here either accidentally or out of curiosity. Got all that?'

'Got it!' Maggie confirmed and sped away, this time scarcely noticing the sting of the gravel beneath her bare feet.

The cook, as Carrick had guessed, was already up and making tea in the kitchen. Quickly, Maggie delivered her message and Noreen in her capable way hurried off to rouse her husband and son. Maggie didn't hang around either, but having delivered her message hurried back to the fountain, finding herself outstripped en route by a young man she recognised as Fintan Granville, Carrick's youngest brother. Without hesitation, he dashed straight over to the fountain, leaned on the edge and peered in.

'All done,' Maggie told Carrick, slightly out of breath.

'Thanks.' He touched her arm, a faint smile on his lips. 'You've been a big help.'

His fingers felt warm against the coolness of her skin, causing an involuntary little shiver to ripple through her.

Immediately he was concerned. 'How inconsiderate of me! You're cold. Probably the shock.' Picking up his hacking jacket, he draped it over her shoulders.

She waited silently by his side till Tom appeared at the patio doors and Carrick hurried to meet him. 'Fin,' he called over his shoulder, 'make sure no one goes near the fountain!'

Fin nodded, his young face serious for probably the first time in his life.

A little while later a straggle of pale and bewildered male servants appeared at the top of the steps. Maggie noticed Carrick's natural authority as he positioned some of them at the patio doors and others at the entrance to the fountain.

Next, like the animals boarding Noah's ark, the Granville family began to arrive two by two, most of them still in their dressing gowns and wearing expressions of complete disbelief to go with their hangovers. Rossa Granville and his fiancée, Ashling, were first on the scene, followed by Ehu, a hung-over Jaspar in tow. The Maasai was wearing a long white robe that made him seem taller than ever, while Jaspar was royally arrayed in a peacock-blue silk dressing gown that gave him an air of Bertie Wooster.

Behind the pair came Honoria Granville, leaning heavily on her boar's-head walking stick and flanked, as usual, by her Indian servant. Bringing up the rear were those startling twins, drifting casually along, hand in hand. They stopped and stood a little off to one side, a unit complete in themselves. Dressed in matching white towelling bathrobes, they looked almost ethereal in the morning light, like babes in the wood, were it not for their too-knowing, jewel-bright eyes and the expressions on their faces that hinted almost at an avaricious excitement. Maggie sensed that there was something very wrong there. Without doubt, there was more to Sapphire and Indigo Granville than met the eye.

Just as she was about to turn back to the fountain, there was a further distraction in the shape of Coppelia Morrison emerging from the house. For a moment she paused at the top of the steps, almost calculatedly, like an actress on a stage waiting for

186

that first moment of audience recognition, the first round of thunderous applause. Her hair, that enviable mantle of copper, streamed loose about her shoulders. She was still wearing her black ball gown, over which she had thrown a matching black-velvet wrap.

As Coppelia approached the little group huddled silently, a respectful distance from the fountain, Maggie wondered where she had disposed of her recent paramour. Then, with a jolt, a thought came to her – was Carrick the man she had seen earlier with Coppelia? He clearly hadn't been to bed, given that he'd still been wearing his dress shirt and tux trousers beneath that hacking jacket. It was certainly a possibility.

As Coppelia reached the group, Carrick began to speak.

'I'm sorry to be the bearer of such grim news—' he began but found himself hushed immediately as his grandmother, apparently enraged by the audacity of someone choosing to drown themselves in her ornamental fountain, erupted into a full-blown tantrum.

'Carrick, get that woman out of there. Immediately! Remove her at once!' She banged on the ground with her stick. 'This is insupportable. Insupportable, I tell you!'

Carrick waved a calming hand. 'No, Grandmother. We must wait for the police to get here. There are procedures that need to be observed in cases such as this.'

'Procedures!' Honoria gave a dismissive snort. 'What do I care for procedures? Tom!' She looked about her, found him cowering at the back. 'As my grandson insists on disobeying me, it falls to you to have her removed. If the guards see fit to make a fuss, then *I* shall take responsibility!'

'No can do, Grandmere.' Fin waved Tom away, much to his relief. 'Carrick is right. You can't just go shunting dead bodies about the place. They'll need to call a coroner and all sorts.' He knew that. *Waking the Dead* was his favourite TV programme, with *Cold Case* a close-run second.

'I take it resuscitation is out of the question?' Coppelia forced her way to the front and, pushing Fin unceremoniously out of the way, peered into the fountain for herself.

'Please, Mrs Morrison!' Carrick attempted to steer her away. 'You really shouldn't—'

She shrugged him off and bent to stare in the fountain, then turned back to the group. 'No. I can see there was no point. Dead. And for quite a while, too, by the looks of things.'

'Who is the girl?' thundered Honoria. 'Does anyone recognise her?'

'Well?' Coppelia raised her eyebrows at the others. 'Come and have a look.'

Reluctantly, almost dragging their feet, the rest of the group, bar Maggie and Fin, shuffled forward and peered over the edge of the fountain, looking as though they might bolt at any second. A chorus of gasps arose as their eyes adjusted to the murky depths and fixed upon the young woman's body in its watery grave, thick sodden strands of her heavy dark hair waving about her face, one blood-shot eye staring back up at them. The women drew back immediately, except for Sapphire who seemed to be frozen in fascinated horror.

'Well?' Honoria barked again. 'Who is she? Somebody must know.'

'Oh, God!' Sapphire's voice rose on a shriek. 'It – it's Kate! Kathleen O'Leary!'

'A local girl, then, I take it?' The relief in Honoria's voice was palpable. 'One of the serving staff?' It was clear to see how her mind was working. It was easier by far to play down the death of an unknown young woman than that of one of the VIP guests.

'No! She was the Kingdom Rose. Oh, Indigo! Indigo!' With a sudden hight-pitched cry, Sapphire launched herself at her twin, burying her head in his chest. His arms snaked round her, crushing her to him protectively. 'She's dead! Kate's dead!'

Maggie wondered if she was the only one to whom the words sounded almost like an accus-ation, but a sound, somewhere between a hiss and a gasp, emanating from Honoria Granville made her think not. For a fleeting moment, Honoria's face became a mask of rage and horror as she glared at the twins. Was it possible that Honoria actually suspected her grandchildren had something to do with the death?

'Oh, God,' Ashling quavered, breaking in on her thoughts, 'the poor girl! I spoke to her last night, you know.' Looking as though she might crumple to the ground at any second, she clung to Rossa's arm for support. 'She seemed so nice, not at all vain or in the usual vacant beauty-queen mould.' She was prattling with shock. 'She told me she had won—'

Brutally, Honoria cut her off. 'Nice or not, she can't stay here!' She jabbed at Carrick with her walking stick. 'No more nonsense, Carrick. I insist you have her removed immediately. Not into the house, though! The summerhouse or the carriage-house, perhaps. It can't much matter to her where she is laid, now. Only make sure she is out of sight of the servants and guests.' Her gaze sprang from him to Coppelia, harpooning her with those lancet eyes. 'I will *not* have a breath of scandal attaching to Carrickross. Is that clear to you all?'

Coppelia drew herself up. 'Nonsense, Honoria! You cannot move that body. Even you must know that a murder scene needs to be protected as much as possible. As it is, we may all have done untold damage by contaminating it.'

Murder. The word clanged and echoed through the group like the discordant jangling of a prison bell.

'Murder?' Furious, Honoria rounded on her. 'This is no murder. It must be clear to a blind man that the poor girl met with an unfortunate accident.'

Coppelia flicked her hand towards the water. 'By *accidentally* tying that cord around her neck too tightly, do you mean?'

'Mrs Morrison,' Carrick dragged a weary hand through his hair, 'did you have to? I'd hoped to spare everyone that particular bit of information.'

There was a moment's frozen silence, then they all surged forward again, peering more intently into the water this time.

Coppelia's sharp eyes had spotted something the rest had not: a ligature was wound so tightly around the drowned girl's throat as to be almost invisible in the folds of her skin, camouflaged further by the long strands of wet hair that had plastered themselves across her face and neck.

Honoria staggered and Rajesh leaped to her aid.

'Indigo . . .' Sapphire's mouth struggled to form his name. Spinning suddenly on her heel, she turned and fled back to the house, her usually graceful body flailing awkwardly. Instantly, her brother turned and sped after her.

'The gardai should be here any minute,' said Carrick. 'I suggest we withdraw to the house to await their arrival. This whole area is a crime scene and, as Mrs Morrison pointed out, we may already have contaminated it.' He looked around ruefully. 'Grandmother?'

Honoria nodded, leaning more heavily on her walking stick than was her wont. 'Perhaps that would be best.'

'Very well,' said Carrick. 'Tom, I'm leaving you in charge here till the gardai arrive.'

Gravely, Tom nodded assent and the family began

to troop back to the house, the shaken Honoria being supported between Carrick and Rajesh.

Unsure whether to follow them, Maggie hesitated, but Carrick turned and beckoned to her to join them.

Trailing behind the group, she couldn't help but reflect on the irony that it had taken a murder to make her an official guest of the Granvilles.

CHAPTER 14

Sapphire lay sprawled across her four-poster bed. Her porcelain skin was flushed and wet from the tears that just seemed to keep on coming, despite Indigo doing his best to comfort her.

'I-I just can't believe it,' she sobbed. 'W-what happened to her, Ind? What happened after she left us?' Red-eyed, she spluttered into her hands, her shoulders shaking with the force of her weeping. 'Oh, God, who could have done such a thing? It's so awful. P-poor Kate!'

'I don't know, Sapph. I really don't know.' Indigo could see his own face, a death mask, staring back at him from the mirror on her dressing table.

'I don't remember much of what happened last night,' Sapphire confessed, desperately trying to recall the events of the previous evening. 'All that drink we had, all that Charlie.' Gradually, in a series of vignettes, it all started to come back to her. Indigo pouring champagne, a thin stream of golden rain into crystal glasses, his head thrown back to reveal his even white teeth, laughing uproariously at something somebody had said;

Kate, her bare, lightly tanned feet stretched out in front of her, drawing inexpertly on a joint and trying not to disgrace herself by coughing; Indigo, pumping up and down on Kate's naked body, the muscles of his back and buttocks bunched, Kate's drugged eyes staring as if detached from what was happening; she, Sapphire, goading him on in a frenzy of sexual excitement. In the cold light of day, the memory almost made her throw up.

Struggling into a sitting position, she gazed at him, wide-eyed with horror. 'How many people saw her leave the ballroom with us? Supposing someone puts two and two together and tells the gardaí? They'll blame us, Indigo – they will!' Panic-stricken, she clawed at the front of his robe, breaking off one of her long red nails. It lay like a crescent of blood against the white linen. 'What time did she actually leave, Ind? I-I don't remember. I-I must have been asleep.' A thought struck her, so shocking that she reeled back. 'Oh no! Oh, please no! Don't let it be true . . . did you . . . ? Oh God, was it you, Indigo? Was it you? Did *you* kill Kate?'

Indigo pushed her away so hard she toppled off the bed onto the floor. 'Don't be so fucking stupid, Sapphire! Of course I didn't kill her! Yes, I got a little bit rough with her! Yes, I had a little more fun with her after you passed out, but she was alive when I finished – she was still *alive.*'

Sapphire implored him. 'Indy . . . Indy . . . you and I don't tell lies – not to each other! Never! Please, tell me the truth!'

'I *am* telling the truth!' he shouted, the veins in his neck standing out like ropes. 'Kate was alive when I last saw her. Living, breathing, alive!'

But Sapphire was terrified. Never in her life did she have to ask Indigo what he was thinking – his thoughts were transparent to her as hers were to him. But now, in this terrible moment, his thoughts were obscure. He was hiding something from her, she was sure of it! For the first time in their lives, she sensed a barrier between them.

A shudder ran through her. She couldn't bear being closed off from him. Her mind plunged into a jumble of despairing thoughts.

'We hurt her,' she groaned. 'We enjoyed hurting her, didn't we? But she's not like one of our butterflies that we could tear the wings off. She has a family. People who care about her. They're going to find out, you know that, Ind, don't you? They're going to find out about everything we did. They'll say we're evil and sick. They'll want to lock us up. Because nobody else understands what it's like to be us.'

'Yes, yes, yes, we hurt her. But we didn't *kill* her! *I* didn't kill her!' Indigo insisted. Yet despite the brave face and the blustering bravado, inside Indigo Granville was terrified. This time, a little voice told him, he had gone too far. But he hadn't . . . no, he definitely hadn't. He would have remembered . . . wouldn't he?

'I'm not going to jail!' Distraught, Sapphire ripped at her long hair. 'I wouldn't survive it, Ind.

All those filthy, verminous people. All those common criminals! I'll kill myself first, I swear I will.'

With a monumental effort, her twin made his voice as strong as possible, as much to reassure himself as her. 'Get a grip, Sapph! Neither of us is going to prison. The whole filthy mess is nothing to do with us. We just need to have our story straight, that's all. Do you understand that, Sapph?'

Sapphire gulped. 'Okay, but w-what time did she leave, Ind?'

Despairing, Indigo threw up his hands. 'I don't know,' he confessed. 'I-I must have passed out at some stage or other. When I woke up, she was already gone. Oh, take that look off your face. Shit! It's the truth. I swear it!' Angrily, he strode into the bathroom, banging the door behind him as, with a fresh bout of tears, Sapphire buried her face in the covers again.

When she surfaced a little later, Indigo was moving purposefully around the room. 'What are you doing?' she asked hoarsely.

'Destroying the evidence.'

The scene at Carrickross could not have been more different from the previous day. Instead of Italian sports cars and designer-clad partygoers, an assortment of police vehicles lined the driveway and uniformed gardaí and white-coated forensic experts stood dotted about all over the place, even on the lawn, despite a 'keep off the grass' sign.

196

The State Pathologist had arrived earlier, but she was now gone and poor Kate O'Leary's body had been removed from its watery resting place and was on its way to a mortuary somewhere.

The Granvilles, having been questioned, had all gone to ground in their various rooms and Maggie, still dressed in Deirdre's stage costume, was sitting in the kitchen sharing a cup of tea with Noreen. The cook had been good enough to lend her a long green woolly cardigan and a pair of her own bedroom slippers. Pure bliss.

Maggie's interview with the police had been a walk in the park. In their view, bizarre behaviour and journalists went hand in hand. Anything less would have been a disappointment. A simple phone call to a startled Deirdre in California confirmed her story and she was free to walk, with the standard caution that she should stay in the area for the present.

Dredging up the strength from somewhere, she had managed to phone in a piece on the Carrickross murder to one national newspaper and a bunch of provincial ones, but now she was wilting, drained and suffering the residual effects of her hangover.

'Another cup of tea? Well sweetened. Sugar is good for shock and sure, God help you, that was a terrible thing finding that poor wee girl in the fountain and the neck wrung off her.' Talking nineteen-to-the-dozen, Noreen poured for Maggie and herself. 'Such a terrible waste and so sad. And her only just beginning to get her life back on track after the boyfriend giving her the elbow last Christmas!'

Maggie's ears pricked up. An ex-boyfriend? Could there be a motive there?

'Threw her over for a one from Dingle he'd been seeing on the side, the dirty article!' Noreen snorted. 'And now I hear the pair of them are engaged and due to be married soon.' She took a sip of her tea. 'But that's Dingle girls for you. Short skirts, low morals and high speed!'

So the boyfriend was out of the picture, Maggie noted. Content to let Noreen rattle on and hopefully reveal other vital nuggets of information, she sank her teeth into a delicious fresh scone.

'We all said how it was one in the eye for him when she won the Kingdom Rose competition. There are a lot of perks to that, you know, as well as the thirty-grand in prize money – for all the good it is to the poor craythur now.' She added another spoon of sugar to her tea. 'Mind you, if they had still been together, she probably wouldn't have entered the competition in the first place and would still be alive today.' Noreen shook her head in morbid satisfaction and fell silent as both women dwelled on the fickleness of Fate.

'Do you think it was just a random killing, Noreen?' Maggie ventured. 'A drunken guest?'

Noreen adopted a musing expression. 'Jesus, but who could have done a terrible thing like that? I mean, for all that the guests got a bit rowdy – and they do every year – I can't imagine anyone having that kind of badness in them, can you?'

Maggie thought about that. She had seen plenty of badness in her time as an investigative journalist, things that would make Noreen's hair curl, but never anything quite so awful or so evil as had befallen poor Kate O'Leary. But before she had a chance to reply the cook had shot off on a tangent.

'I knew from the start no good would come of it all. And amn't I proved right now?' Pursing her lips, she looked to Maggie for confirmation.

'Would come of what, Noreen?' she asked, after a pause.

'This engagement.'

'Really? And why is that?'

'Because you can lead a horse to the water but you can't make him drink,' said Noreen with an exaggerated wink.

Maggie took a guess. 'You mean Rossa? Doesn't he want to marry her then?' What was it that Carrick had said to him last night, something about his grandmother hand-picking Ashling for him?

Noreen made a noncommittal noise in her throat.

'He's being pressured into it, right?' Maggie prodded. 'By his grandmother?'

Noreen threw her a shrewd glance. 'Oh, so you've rumbled that, have you?'

'I might have overheard something,' Maggie admitted.

'Well, you overheard right.' Noreen leaned in

confidentially. 'The mistress has the ring through that young man's nose for sure!' She wrinkled her nose. 'But Rossa isn't the horse that the mistress is leading to the water. It's Carrick.'

Maggie's brow creased into a hundred furrows. 'Carrick? How do you mean?'

Noreen put her plump arms on the table, leaned forward until her fluffy brown head almost touched Maggie's, and opened her mouth. But just then they heard a sound from the doorway and their heads swivelled in unison.

Seán was standing there, looking from one to the other of them, a strange expression on his face.

'Seán! What's the matter with you?' said Noreen. 'Why are you gaping like that?'

'They've got the twins.' Seán's voice sounded thick, as if his tongue was swollen in his mouth. 'They're taking them away.'

'Who's got them?' Noreen asked in confusion. 'Away where?'

'Please, Carrick,' Sapphire sobbed, as a garda folded her head down into a police car, whilst his colleague shepherded a handcuffed Indigo into a separate vehicle, 'don't let them take us away. We're innocent, really we are. Kate was our friend. She was our *friend*!'

Carrick gave her his best reassuring smile. 'Don't worry, Sapph, I'll get our lawyer on to it straight away. You'll be back at Carrickross in no time at all.'

As the police drove the forlorn pair away for further questioning, gravel spraying in the wake of the car like little bullets, Carrick sighed. Brave words, but from what he had gleaned by piecing together the gardai's inquiries, evidence, at least circumstantial, was beginning to mount up against the twins. Several guests had witnessed Kathleen O'Leary leave the ballroom in their company. One so-called witness, with a particularly colourful imagination, had claimed to have seen Kate O'Leary being dragged screaming through the corridors of Carrickross. As if! Another claimed to have seen a figure 'very like Indigo Granville' carrying 'what looked like a body in the early hours, but 'didn't think it peculiar at the time'. Forensics had had a field day in the twins' suite, despite indications that someone had made a thorough job of cleaning up. Not thorough enough for modern science, though, with its all-revealing chemicals. Considering the sexual reputation of the Granville twins, it was something of a giveaway that not a trace of porno-graphic material was found, not a single sex toy or piece of equipment. A few common-or-garden copies of *Playboy* were artfully and no doubt delib-erately displayed. Indigo had been a busy, busy boy. Perhaps too busy and too smart for his own good.

Examination of the bed itself showed that there were curious scuff-marks on the bedposts that might have indicated the use of restraints, which in itself didn't mean all that much. Lots of people were into mild bondage but, taking recent events into account, it couldn't be entirely discounted as evidence, given that there were a number of bruises on the victim's wrists, which had been consistent with the use of restraints. The bed linen was rumpled but, on examination, turned out to be almost pristine. Impossibly so, considering that the twins had admitted to all sorts of bedroom shenanigans. A search had discovered some blood-stained sheets under acres of other dirty laundry in the basement where they were kept prior to washing. That might have been quite a clever move on Indigo's part, assuming it was he who had hidden the sheets, because even if the blood proved to be that of the Kingdom Rose, the possibility of cross-contamination would undoubtedly be seized on by any barrister worth his salt.

Ostensibly the apartments were clean as a whistle, till the sniffer dogs were called in and traces of cocaine turned up here, there and everywhere – in the carpets, in the beds and on virtually every surface. But the use of drugs was not evidence of murder. Nor could it be proved who had used them.

In any case the twins, Carrick thought wryly, had done a pretty good job of putting a noose around their own necks, confessing not to murder, but to an orgy in which Kate had played the starring role. Not that they had put it like that, of course.

'We were just playing,' said Sapphire.

'She was well up for it!' said Indigo.

Returning the twins to their habitual playground was going to be anything but easy, thought Carrick.

Part of him wondered if it was even desirable.

CHAPTER 15

After Sapphire and Indigo had been taken away, a deep depression descended on the family who, marshalled by Honoria, had assembled in one of the smaller reception rooms at Carrickross. Set off in one wing of the house, it was reached by a long narrow passageway and was more private than any of the other rooms. With the exception of Rajesh, as always glued to her side, Honoria didn't trust anybody, not even faithful servants of long standing. Apart from the twins, the only other family member not present was Jaspar, who had retired to his room with a migraine and Ehu in attendance.

Honoria sat erect at the head of the table. She grimaced as she realised that Fate had allowed Coppelia to escape her trap – if only temporarily. She, like everyone else, had been ordered by the police not to leave the area. Her 'banishment' had been put on hold. But after the morning's unfortunate events, Honoria had more on her mind than her arch-rival, namely the fear that Carrickross and its inhabitants might become tabloid fodder.

'Poor Sapphire.' Listlessly, Ashling gazed into

the cup of tea somebody had pressed into her hand. Plates of ham and cucumber sandwiches lay untouched in the middle of the table. Nobody could bring themselves to eat – but the brandy bottle was doing the rounds. 'The poor kid looked frightened half to death.' Even as she said it she wondered why she always thought of Sapphire as a child, despite the fact that she was only a couple of years younger than herself. Yet that's the impression she gave. An immature, sometimes naughty little girl.

Standing behind her, Rossa stroked her soft, silky hair. It reminded him of Priti. God, under this terrible stress he was more desperate for her than ever, desperate for the feel of her toffee-coloured limbs wrapped about him, her rosebud pouting red lips working their magic up and down his hungry body until he almost died from the sheer pleasure of it all. Jesus, but he'd got himself into a right mess! Panic rose in his throat as he wondered if he would ever be free again. Free from the tentacles of Honoria, Ashling and Carrickross. Free to be with Priti. He made a huge effort to bring his thoughts under control. A cigarette would have helped, but Honoria had banned smoking anywhere within the hallowed precincts of Carrickross. Too many priceless paintings and antique wall coverings had been damaged by nicotine in the past. He arrested the brandy bottle as it did the rounds again and filled his glass.

'How could anyone think for a moment that

Sapph or Indigo could be guilty of anything so horrible?' Ashling continued. 'Okay, so maybe they're,' she chose her words carefully, 'a little unusual, but there's no real harm in them.'

'They're not as innocent as you might think.' Rossa's voice dropped like a stone into the middle of the room. 'They have a dark side to them – Indigo, in particular. Don't look at me like that, Grandmother. You know it's true.'

'But that doesn't make him a killer,' Carrick snapped from where he leaned against the marble fireplace, his brow corrugated into deep lines of worry that made him look older than his thirty years.

'Indeed it does not!' Honoria glared at Rossa, and rapped her walking stick sharply against the floor. 'Rossa, your attitude is most unhelpful. More than ever, this family needs to stand shoulder to shoulder, especially as we shall no doubt soon have the gutter press descending upon us in droves.'

'When we shall wear our united public face,' Rossa agreed evenly. 'But here, in the privacy of our own home and amongst each other, isn't it time for some honesty? Isn't it time to stop pretending that Indigo is some sort of innocent sacrificial lamb? Remember how he tortured that cat once, when he was only five?'

Ashling turned a horrified face towards him. 'Rossa!'

Ignoring her, he gazed fiercely at his grandmother.

'And Sapphire simply stood by and watched. Or maybe she helped, as Indigo always maintained. Odd that, don't you think? Most little girls love puppies and kittens and go all squeamish at the sight of blood. The poor animal had to be put down by the vet and even then the rotten pair showed no remorse. As I recall, you had a hell of a job hushing it all up, Grandmother.'

'Rossa, please!' Ashling protested, bewildered and disturbed at the gruesome picture he'd painted. 'That can't be true!' But no one appeared to hear her.

'The children had just lost their parents,' Honoria snapped, furious that he had resurrected a memory that, like the unfortunate cat, was best left dead and buried. 'People cope with stress in different ways, sometimes in ways they would never dream of ordinarily. One has to make allowances.'

Horrified, Ashling realised Honoria's words were an admission. She bit back a torrent of questions. She would ask Rossa about it later, in private.

Unusually for him, Rossa didn't back down. 'Ah, but perhaps they were quite themselves, *truly* themselves. Have you ever thought of that?'

Fin nodded pensively. 'And, face it, Grandmere, it's not going to look good for Indigo and Sapph that lots of people saw that young woman being hauled off out of the ballroom by them. I don't remember seeing any of them after that, and I bet other people have told the gardai the same.'

In a flash, Carrick turned on him, almost dislodging an antique ormolu clock from the mantelpiece. 'And what about you, Fintan? You also disappeared. Where exactly did you go? Because you know the police will want an in-depth catalogue of your movements too. You do realise those brief interviews this morning were only preliminary investigations? They'll be back – and who knows, perhaps they'll release the twins after questioning, satisfied they aren't guilty – and then they'll descend on the rest of us like vultures pouncing on carrion. So, before you go lining Indigo up against the wall, you might like to think about drumming up your own alibi!'

Wrong-footed, Fin flushed angrily. He did have an alibi, but not one he was willing to share with his family.

Seeing tempers beginning to blaze, Ashling thrust aside her shock and attempted to bring some perspective to the proceedings. 'Look, flying off the handle is not going to help matters, is it?' Her hand reached up and clasped Rossa's, her fingers stroking the heavy gold signet ring she had bought him as an engagement present. She made an attempt to move things on. 'Have you contacted your solicitor yet, Carrick?'

Carrick nodded shortly and glanced at his watch. 'Yes, of course. I'm meeting him at the garda station in thirty minutes. In the meantime, I've warned the twins to say and admit to nothing whatsoever until he counsels them. It's unfortunate that they gave a preliminary statement, but then we all did and if there's anything untoward in it, we can always argue it was given under duress.' His brow wrinkled. 'In fact, I would like to be present at the interviews, but I doubt if I'll be granted permission.'

'You are a Granville!' Honoria barked, in the tones of one who has never been denied anything. 'That gives you the right.'

Ashling was glad to see the old girl rallying a little. She seemed to have shrunk over the past few hours, her face a withered walnut shell of anxiety. 'You really mustn't worry too much, Honoria,' she said gently. 'We all know the twins are innocent. And soon the real murderer will be found and everyone else will know too. It'll all blow over, you'll see.' But in her heart a tiny voice was recounting the story of the dead cat again, and she was now much less sure. Would the death of their parents really have affected them temporarily in such a way? Or were they, as Rossa and Fin seemed to suggest, still very disturbed?

With something akin to desperation, Honoria fixed her gaze on her. 'Sensible girl! And the voice of reason. You are right of course, my dear. The twins are innocent. We must never lose sight of that.'

Why then didn't she sound more convinced? thought Ashling.

'But if they are innocent,' it fell to Fin to give voice to the next disquieting thought, 'that means someone else must be guilty. But who?'

As everyone fell silent, speculating, Rossa wound a strand of Ashling's hair round his finger. 'That's the sixty-four-thousand-dollar question,' he said.

Honoria's eyes sought those of Rajesh. Coppelia? Could their actions of last night have resulted in her doing something so monstrously evil? How far would she go to shame Honoria personally and drag the Granville family name through the dirt? She shook the thought away. No, whatever base conduct Coppelia Morrison was capable of, even she was likely to draw the line at murdering a complete stranger to score a point.

'What do we know about the girl's family?' asked Ashling. 'Is there likely to have been a domestic motive? Don't the police routinely examine those closest to the victim first?'

'They have done so – and, no, they were a close family and she was an only child, apparently. In fact, everyone who knew her seems to attest to the fact that she was something of an angel whom no one would have wished to kill, more's the pity,' said Honoria, entirely unconscious of voicing anything insensitive. Then a random image of Maggie O'Keefe flashed across her mind. 'Has anyone checked on that reporter woman? Wasn't she using a false identity? Perhaps she had a grudge against the beauty queen?'

'She was deceitful, certainly.' Carrick tried not to bristle. The fact was that he felt disproportionately annoyed by the fact that Maggie had turned out to be an undercover journalist.

Journalists were never his favourite people and yet there had been something about her which had appealed to him. 'But she's not in the frame and the gardaí let her go immediately. Besides, garrotting takes a lot of strength. No, if you ask me, our suspect is definitely male.'

'But they did caution her to stay in the area,' Fin pointed out.

'They cautioned all of us,' Carrick snapped. 'Even Grandmother, the most unlikely suspect of all.'

Fin rolled his eyes. 'All right, all right, keep your hair on, Carrick! God, since when did it become your job to defend the honour of journos and gatecrashing gossip-columnists?'

'At the same time it became your job to defame people you don't even know!'

'Whew! She's certainly managed to light your fuse, hasn't she, bro?' Fin leered and was about to add something else when Honoria intervened angrily.

'In heaven's name, be quiet, the pair of you! That woman is, and should be, of no consequence to this family and it is the *family* that matters! Remember that, all of you.'

'As if we could forget,' Carrick said drily, aiming a sly punch at Fin, who, risking his grandmother's wrath, made kissy-kissy lips at his brother.

Back at the Kerry Eden Hotel, Coppelia stepped out of her black velvet gown and kicked it carelessly to one side. Its work was done and she wouldn't be needing it again. Some little country chambermaid was going to think all her Christmases had come at once.

Weary now, she stepped into the luxurious shower, big enough to accommodate an entire rugby team, turned the gold-plated lever and gasped with pleasure as the first healing spray of warm water washed over her. Eschewing the complimentary hotel toiletries in favour of her own Jo Malone ylang ylang and jasmine shower-gel, she revelled in thoughts of how Honoria Granville must be suffering. How exultant the old witch had been last night, how triumphant! Pride comes before a fall and hopefully this fall would be in direct proportion to Honoria's pride and arrogance.

Coppelia experienced a charge that was almost sexual. She could hardly wait to see how the whole event would be portrayed in the evening news. Sensationalised, salivated and chewed over the length and breadth of the land by those who thrived on seeing their betters brought low. Wonderful. The murder itself was disgrace enough but the twins being dragged off in handcuffs was truly the icing on the cake. Just when Honoria thought she had her over a barrel. Really, she couldn't have planned the whole thing better herself and, hopefully, Ashling would now come to her senses, see the Granvilles for what they were and of her own accord give up the idea of this marriage.

Vigorously she rubbed foam into her arms. Oh, how the sands had shifted since last night! Not that she'd had any notion of bowing to Honoria's insane demands anyway.

Slathering a palmful of shampoo onto her hair, she worked it well into the roots. Her thoughts strayed to Ashling and her positive feelings began to ebb. Ashling, her darling daughter, for whom she had sacrificed everything. Suddenly tears gathered in her eyes. She had made the ultimate sacrifice to protect Ashling, to ensure she had a happy secure life – a life that she, Coppelia, had never had as a child and had so hungrily craved. And now it seemed it had all been for nothing. Honoria Granville had known all along. And nothing Coppelia could do now would spare her daughter searing emotional pain.

Coppelia moaned aloud and shook her head violently as if to push the dark thoughts away. Resolutely she banished Ashling from her mind, a skill she had learned through necessity long years before when she had given her up for adoption and had used again in her role as cold-hearted stepmother.

That look on Honoria's face this morning! God, it had been priceless. She had almost been able to divine her thought processes, when first the news had been brought to her. *A body! A body in my fountain. How tacky! Dispose of it, Carrick, at once!*

Carrick. Now there was a man to reckon with.

A man in the true sense of the word. She felt a little shiver of pleasure. Beneath those expensive but understated clothes of his, he exuded that raw animal power that made women, whatever their age, go weak at the knees. Those artistic hands one simply knew could navigate the female body like an Ordnance Survey map. With a little imagination, she could almost taste those lips on hers, sensitive yet demanding, provoking responses from her body. What would it feel like, those powerful arms enveloping her, the warm, solid mass of him, driving into her welcoming body . . . ? Taking the showerhead in her hand, she directed the flow, trailing it over her warm wet skin like a lover trailing kisses.

Yes, Carrick Granville was definitely worth a fantasy or two, she thought, rinsing off the last of the sudsy water. Given the opportunity, he might even be worth a dally with. It would certainly be no hardship and the fact that he was a Granville and the only one of them who appeared to be genuinely incorruptible, as well as Honoria's favourite, would add a certain piquancy to the experience. As with young Fin, every act of love would double as an act of revenge, a rape of the Granvilles. Coppelia felt no guilt in using Fin to slake her lust. On the contrary she savoured it, savoured her power over him and, by proxy, her power over the haughty Honoria. But Carrick, now he would really be a feather in her cap.

In the meantime, she would have to settle for

his younger brother – again, no hardship. His youthful hunger was exciting for its own sake, even discounting the whole Honoria angle. And there was a playful boyishness about him that she truly enjoyed and appreciated. Completely uninhibited and anxious to learn whatever she could teach, he was certainly a great improvement on the men of her own age, all of whom tended to be sexually jaded connoisseurs of the missionary position, perverts or habitual users of Viagra. Fin was fresh, exciting, willing and had boundless stamina. That little 'Aunty Pelia' game of theirs never failed to arouse her. Would the intense Carrick be amenable to such naughty little role plays? She hardly thought so. Both she and Fin were risk-takers, courting rather than shying away from adventure and scandal. He made her laugh too, something few men had ever learned to do.

As if that thought had conjured him up, the glass door suddenly slid back and Fin, naked and already primed for action, stepped in.

'Money talks,' he told her, flashing the key to her room, then chucking it over his shoulder behind him. 'Fifty quid and worth every penny.' A moment later he was on his knees in front of her doing what he did best.

Arching her back, so that her hips thrust forward, Coppelia thanked God she was such a good teacher.

Later, still damp from the shower, they made love all over again, till exhaustion and their rumbling stomachs reminded them that neither had eaten for hours. Coppelia ordered from room service – lobster salad, champagne, strawberries and cream, which Fin fed to her by hand, occasionally smearing the cream on her nipples and licking it off.

A little while after, sated in every way, he propped himself on one elbow and leaned over her. 'Pelia?' His voice was hesitant, suddenly unsure of itself.

She smiled lazily up at him, her wonderful tangle of hair and soft naked curves reminding him of the pictures of Botticelli's *Birth of Venus* in the history of art book he'd had at school. He loved the fact she was secure in her absolute desirability as only an older woman with no hang-ups about her sexuality can be.

'*Aunty* Pelia,' she corrected him.

For once he didn't play ball. 'I need you to provide me with an alibi for last night. I've thought about it and, believe me, if there was any other way . . .' The words came out in a rush. He shrugged helplessly, a lock of hair falling forward onto his forehead. Impatient, he brushed it away. 'Grandmère won't like it, of course, but with the gardaí sniffing about . . . what can I do?'

Coppelia's answer was swift and sure. 'Absolutely not!' Her mood of relaxed pleasure shattered in a moment, she climbed out of bed and strode across to the dressing table, glaring at her reflection in the mirror. 'I will not be drawn into this mess, Fin, do you hear me? What's between you and me must stay that way. I've always been crystal clear on that, so don't go moving the goalposts, there's a good boy.'

'But we *were* together,' Fin said, remembering with pleasure how they had sneaked back to her hotel the night before for a few hours of mind-blowing sex and how she had driven him back to Carrickross first thing that morning, both still in their dress clothing, in case anyone asked awkward questions.

Twisting the lid off her Crème de la Mer moisturiser, Coppelia scooped out a large dollop and smeared it liberally over her face and throat. 'Yes, I know that and you know that, but nobody else does, Fin, and that's the way it's going to stay.' Until she was good and ready.

Fin began to protest, then broke off, startled, as a knock sounded on the door.

'Room service, back to take away the dirty dishes, most likely,' Coppelia said in answer to his raised eyebrow.

Fin covered his modesty with a sheet draped around him toga-style and made for the door.

'I just hope it isn't Grandmère, lured from her den,' he joked, 'come to lecture us on our debauchery! Or even worse, Carrick!'

But, possibly worst of all, it was Ashling.

She stepped inside.

Horrified, her eyes darted from one to the other. It didn't take Einstein to figure out exactly what had been going on in the bedroom. Apart from the fact that her mother was naked as the day she was born, as indeed was Fin under his sheet, the unmistakable smell of sex hung on the air. Every bit as shaken, Fin beat a retreat to the bathroom, grabbing his clothes en route, while Coppelia barely moved a muscle, let alone made any attempt to reach for her robe.

'Oh, hello, dear! And to what do we owe the pleasure?' Wiping off the expensive face cream, she tossed the used cotton-wool pad in the bin and twisted round to face her daughter.

'Mother! I can hardly believe my eyes!' Furious at this display of brazenness, Ashling marched into the centre of the room, her fists balled at her sides, as if she might be tempted to strike something or someone. 'Fin is Rossa's kid brother! And young enough to be your son! What *can* you be thinking of?'

Coppelia stood up, reached for her white silk dressing gown on the back of the chair and drew it on. 'I should have thought that was obvious. Didn't they teach you anything at school, Ashling? Did you skip the lesson on the birds and the bees? Were you truanting?' Listening to her own contemptuous voice, she marvelled that she had slipped so effortlessly into her self-appointed role of Wicked Stepmother after her earlier emotional episode. Well, she had been playing at it so long it was second nature by now.

'Maybe,' Ashling gritted her teeth, 'but I

218

was definitely present for the one entitled "dirty old woman corrupts child". You, Mother, are a *disgrace*!'

'Fin is hardly a child.' Coppelia arched a meaningful eyebrow as she knotted the sash round her narrow waist. 'And we are both of us over the age of consent.'

'It's depraved!' Ashling stamped her foot. 'Honestly, what kind of a woman are you? What's the matter with men your own age? Must you go preying on young boys? Does it make you feel young, Mother? Is that what it is? Does it help you forget the passage of time and the fact that you need the occasional shot of Botox these days to rev up your confidence?'

'Shut up!' Her vanity coming under attack, Coppelia immediately lost her composure, not quite as secure in her own desirability as the innocent Fin might imagine. Sparks of fury crackled between the two women. '*You* know nothing of what I feel. *You*, who have always led a privileged life, pampered and waited on from the day you were born, riding high on the crest of a wave with nothing to disturb the equilibrium. Yes, *you*, Ashling, with your life all planned out for you. You've never had to do any more than lift your little finger and everyone comes running.' Far from calm now, Coppelia picked up a pillow and flung it violently across the far side of the room. 'So, tell me what right have *you* to take the moral high ground?'

'He's Rossa's brother!' Ashling shouted back. 'He is going to be *my* brother-in-law. Good God, it's virtually incest!'

Fully dressed, Fin emerged tentatively from the bathroom. Shuffling from foot to foot and more the schoolboy than ever, he looked to Coppelia for his cue.

'Oh, just go!' Ashling hissed at him. 'I'm surprised at you, Fin, really I am. Rite of passage thing, was it, screwing an older woman? An older, *desperate* woman!' She drew out the last words in a slow vicious underscoring, designed to inflict maximum injury on her stepmother. Right at that moment she hated her.

'Yes, go, Fin.' Coppelia dipped her head, winded by the attack. 'Ashling and I clearly have some talking to do. Best if you're not around to witness it.'

As Fin almost left a vapor trail behind in his hurry to leave the room, Coppelia subsided onto a chair and pointed Ashling into one opposite. 'Now then, young lady, let's see if we can't get on to a slightly more civil footing.'

Ashling sat but she wasn't in the mood for civility. 'You make me sick. Thinking only of your own gratification – and today of all days, with that poor girl murdered and the whole family in shock!' Angrily, she glared at her stepmother. 'I mean, I can't get my head around this. You *hate* the Granvilles! And now I find you shagging my young brother-in-law to be!' Frustrated, her voice rose

220

again. 'It doesn't make sense, Mother. None of it makes sense!'

'Believe me, it makes perfect sense, Ashling,' said Coppelia in a low voice and, if Ashling hadn't been so caught up in her own pain, she might have noticed that her mother's hands were trembling.

'Bullshit, Mother!' Ashling leaned forward in her chair and, lips parted, gazed searchingly right into Coppelia's eyes. 'I'm beginning to wonder why I even call you Mother,' she whispered. 'You have never once behaved like a mother to me.' Tears sprang to her eyes, spilt over and began to roll down her cheeks.

'Ashling,' said Coppelia through suddenly ashen lips, 'that is utterly untrue. I swear I am thinking of your welfare. But you'll never be happy married to a Granville. Surely you can see that, now that those vile twins have been arrested for that depraved crime?'

'They didn't do it, Mother! I know they didn't! And anyway, suppose they *did*, what has any of that to do with Rossa?'

'But don't you see, Ashling? That murder is the visible seeping pustule of the secret Granville rot!'

'The secret Granville rot!' cried Ashling, flaring up again. 'What exactly is that supposed to mean? Are you *crazy*? Have you completely lost it?' Then she clenched her fists and calmed herself with a visible effort. 'Come on then, explain yourself.' She took a deep shuddering breath. 'I'm ready and willing to hear whatever it is you have to say.'

Coppelia leaned forward and spoke with passionate sincerity. 'Ashling, that whole family is like a virulent disease. They are utterly amoral. Look at young Fin – are his actions those of a decent, balanced young man? *Are* they, Ashling? Seeking his own gratification and today of all days when his family is in desperate need of him? And he's just the baby of the bunch! I am telling you, Ashling, for your own good, that the Granvilles are corrupt and they destroy everything that crosses their path!' Deflated suddenly, the passion went out of her voice, leaving behind a deadness, a flatness, as if she had fought too hard for too long. 'And I should know . . . because they destroyed me.'

Standing up, Ashling came to kneel in front of her stepmother, placing her hands on her knees and looking searchingly up into her face, willing her to tell the truth. 'How, Mother? How did they destroy you? Please tell me. I want to understand. I want to understand *you*. I feel there is so much you have always hidden from me – about yourself, about your past. I feel . . . I feel this mystery about the Granvilles is only the last in a long line of secrets. Please, trust me, tell me.'

Coppelia stared into Ashling's pleading eyes. Could she tell her the truth? Could she at last share the pain of losing her and the pain of retrieving her only to live a life of pretence? How wonderful it

222

would be to take her daughter in her arms and explain how *much* she loved her, how every action she had taken had been for her protection. How she still thought only of her safety.

But to truly protect Ashling, she must keep the truth from her at all costs.

Coppelia stood up abruptly, shaking off her daughter. 'Oh, Ashling, I cannot tell you. I simply cannot. Why can't you just believe that what I say is true? And that all I want to do is to keep you safe?'

The hope in Ashling's eyes drained away, her hands slid from Coppelia's lap, her head drooped. When she looked up her expression had hardened.

'Fair enough. I won't ask again.'

Then she stood and walked from the room without a backward glance.

Coppelia sat at her dressing table again and, dropping her head in her hands, willed her tears away. Then, with shaking hands, she continued to apply her make-up.

CHAPTER 16

Having spent a sleepless night, Ashling rose with the early bird and went down to the Carrickross library, leaving Rossa tossing and turning in bed. Outside, the sky still carried the faint watermark of the moon. Pink and blue-edged clouds stealing in from the east gave promise of another glorious summer day. Paradise, indeed, were it not for the dark undercurrents she now sensed lay beneath the surface of Carrickross.

Yes, she had to admit that her confidence in the Granvilles had been undermined. Her stepmother's bitterness and hatred had to spring from *something*. If only she could find out what.

Turning away from the window, she plopped down on to the old brown-leather sofa and tucked her feet up underneath her. On the wall opposite hung an assortment of small landscapes by Jack Butler Yeats, here and there an empty space where a painting was on loan to the National Art Gallery. Rossa had divulged this bit of information almost carelessly, as if it was the most normal thing in the world. As if every well-to-do family had masterpieces hanging on their walls. But then the

Granvilles weren't normal. They were like the Kennedys in the States or the Guinness dynasty, both of which had also been beset with tragedy and scandal. Could it be that the Granvilles were equally cursed?

Ruefully she reflected that the murder of Kate O'Leary had well and truly wiped the gloss from her fairy-tale romance. Holding out her hand, she watched the rays of early sunlight catch the diamond in her engagement ring and flash a whole rainbow of colours. And Rossa was the pot of gold at the end of it. Or was he? What did she really know of her fiancé, apart from the obvious stuff? Trivia, really. His favourite colour? Purple. His favourite band? U2. Food? Thai, somewhat predictably. He loved old comedies, hated what he called weepies. Religion left him cold. He never ventured an opinion on politics. What else? What else? Almost in a panic, Ashling racked her brain. Fast cars! And photography. Shit, was that the best she could come up with?

And, when you came right down to it, what did he know about her? Considering she was the woman he proposed spending the rest of his life with, his lack of curiosity about her was remarkable.

Ashling took a deep calming breath. She looked at her ring once more, the tangible proof of Rossa's love. And that's all that counted, the fact that he loved her and wanted to marry her. That he didn't engage in meaningful dialogue was neither here nor there. Most men didn't – the old Mars versus Venus argument.

She must buck up, stay positive.

If only they could get away from Carrickross and the pall of gloom hanging over it. Perhaps she should go back upstairs and persuade him to go for a ride by the lakes or up the mountain tracks after breakfast? It would do both of them good. The idea brought with it a feeling of calm.

Yes, they needed to spend some quality time together. A ride would be lovely and Noreen would be more than happy to pack them a picnic brunch.

Energised by the idea, Ashling uncurled from the chair and made for the kitchen. She would grab a bite of breakfast and then go upstairs and see if Rossa was awake.

Rossa was in a state of tension as he sat on the side of the bed, one ear cocked for the sound of Ashling coming back to their room. She had dressed and left an hour earlier, sneaking out so as not to wake him. A lucky break for him, as some time later Priti had shocked him awake by ringing his mobile – something she was expressly forbidden to do.

'Honey, I no happy!'

This was the latest in a series of head-wrecking phone calls between him and Priti. No sooner had she seen Carrickross and its murder on Sky News than she was on to him: 'Oh, I so worried, my darling, 'bout you!' When in actual fact she was agog about the murder and wanted all the gory details. But soon she'd tired of the subject and reverted to her obsession: 'Pity it not that bitch woman you wanna marry got killed!'

'Look, Priti,' he tried again, 'I'm just waking up here. My brain is hardly in gear. Let me call you back in an hour and we can have a good long talk about everything.' He *must* get her off the phone before Ashling arrived back.

'But I wanna talk now! You just tryin' to get rid of me!'

It was hopeless. There was no reasoning with her. Yet he had to try. As Rossa drew a deep breath he heard the doorknob turn. Then a rapid triple knock sounded on the door.

'Rossa!' called Ashling.

'Who that?' Priti was immediately on the alert. 'That bitch woman, eh?'

'No,' Rossa muttered, grimacing down the telephone. 'Look, it's just the maid. She wants to clean the room – I must go now—'

'You lyin', Rossa!'

'I'm not,' Rossa panicked, as Ashling upped the ante.

'Rossa! Open the door! It's me!' The doorknob rattled impatiently.

'Sorry! Won't be a moment!' He cupped the receiver. 'Priti!' he said urgently. 'I must go but we have to talk again very soon. Okay?'

Then, to his infinite relief, Priti capitulated.

'Okay, fuckin-bastard, but remember what Priti say. You Irish bitch-woman, she gonna be sorry.'

Rossa hung up and wiped the sweat off his hands. After a moment or two to collect his thoughts, he made for the door.

'Sorry, sweetheart!' he said as a visibly irritated Ashling entered. He dropped a kiss on her head as she passed. 'I got a call from a friend – wishing me well on my engagement – I had to explain about the murder and all that. I didn't think you'd be back so soon and I didn't want to be disturbed by anyone else.' It was a weak excuse and he knew it.

Ashling threw him a rather sour look. 'A pilot, I take it? Only one of your colleagues would ring at this time of the morning. It's really ironic but you people seem to be less aware of international timelines than anyone else on the face of the earth!'

'Guilty as charged!' said Rossa with a shame-faced grin, making for the bathroom.

Mollified, Ashling called after him: 'Rossa! Do you know what I'd really love to do this morning?'

'What?'

'Go for a long ride around the estate with you.' She awaited his response with bated breath, wondering why she felt so nervous about making such an everyday suggestion.

'Great idea!' Rossa called as he turned on the shower. 'Let's do that.'

An hour later they were in the stables, stowing away Noreen's packed lunch in saddlebags.

Seán McCarthy was in attendance and obviously still in a state of shock about the murder but even more so about the fate of the twins.

'Tis a terrible thing,' he said as he led out a beautiful bay mare for Ashling, while Rossa saddled up Carrick's magnificent Arabian stallion, The Sheikh. 'I know they're a bit wild and Master Indigo is a bit of a head case, but murder?' He shook his head. 'Not at all! The police are barking up the wrong tree there.'

'I'm sure you're right,' said Ashling, relieved to find at least one voice at Carrickross whole-heartedly supporting the twins. 'Don't worry, Seán. The truth will out, as they say.'

What Ashling didn't know, what nobody knew except maybe his mother, was that Seán adored the twins to the point of idolatry. They had been part of his life for as long as he could remember. What people didn't understand, in his opinion, was that the twins were different. Special. They played by their own rules. He'd do anything for them, so he would. All they had to do was ask.

'Whoa!' Alarmed, Ashling stepped back as the mare pranced suddenly. 'God, I don't know if I can manage this lady! Skittish isn't the word for it!'

'Ah, she's a bit fresh today all right – aren't you, Morrígan?' said Seán, checking that the saddle was fastened securely. 'All the shenanigans around the place have unsettled her. Animals are sensitive to things like that.' He patted the horse reassuringly on the flank. 'Keep her on a tight rein, Miss Ashling, then after she's worn out a bit you can give her her head.'

'Morrígan?' Ashling asked, as he gave her a leg up. 'Isn't that the ancient Irish goddess of sex and battle?'

Seán grinned. 'Miss Sapphire's idea.'

'It would be.' Ashling smiled, gave him a small wave and followed Rossa and The Sheikh as they trotted briskly out of the stable yard.

Sex and battle, eh? Not a bad plan of action for the day ahead, she thought. A bit of passion would do them both good. In truth, there wasn't nearly enough sex in their relationship, mainly because of the demands of Rossa's job, which, right from the start – when lovers are supposed to be at their most ardent – kept them on slender rations. Which is why when they had an opportunity, like today, she intended to take full advantage of it. She sighed with frustration. Lord, but it had been ages since they'd made love – the lead-up to the Midsummer Ball had been so frantically busy that it had left them both wiped out at the end of every day, scarcely able to manage more than a good-night kiss and the briefest of cuddles.

She drew level with Rossa who was looking away from her, out across the lake.

'So, was this a good idea or what?' she remarked. 'It's such a beautiful day. It's wonderful to get away from it all for a while.'

'Yes, it's nice,' Rossa agreed.

Nice! Just nice! Ashling had hoped for a bit more enthusiasm than that. But, despite his healthy tan, Rossa was looking tired and drawn, the trauma of the past couple of days etched on his face just as, she supposed, it was etched on her own. Never mind, the day was still young. She broke into a trot.

'Come on, slow coach! Let's put some distance between us and Carrickross!'

'Who're you calling slow coach?' Suddenly galvanised, Rossa cantered past. 'What are you waiting for? Get your ass in gear, woman!'

Whatever about getting her ass in gear, Ashling wasn't so sure about getting Morrígan in gear, not if it ended up with her breaking her neck. With a nervous giggle, she set out after him, past the boathouse, through the woods and onto a glorious little crescent of white sand bordered with Scots pines that embraced a small cove. Idly they paddled the horses in the clear water, gazing out at the glossy expanses of the lake and the thickly forested Mullach Mountain that reared up on its far side.

Sheer unadulterated heaven. Carrickross, murder and her bloody mother with her ugly accusations, all receded into a parallel universe.

Elated, Ashling glanced at Rossa, hoping this clear and sparkling setting was working its magic on him, too.

'How about we circle the lake and go up Mullach?' he suggested.

'I'd sooner take the forest trail and go up past the waterfall on Ceanngairiff – you know, to that perfect picnic spot we went to once before. Do you remember, Rossa?' Ashling threw him a radiant smile, wistful now for a time that was so happy, so uncomplicated.

He smiled back, leaned across his horse and kissed her on the cheek. 'Course I remember. Come on then.'

After a glorious gallop across the sunlit parkland they set out on the slow clamber up the peaty path, shaded by moss-laden trees. When they reached the side of the roaring waterfall and the rushing torrent that fed into it, they took it easy, letting their reins drop and allowing the horses to dip their heads as they pleased and pick their delicate way along the path, which was crisscrossed with tree-roots sunk deep into the soil.

And then suddenly they emerged into a small bright grassy clearing that seemed almost suspended from the side of the mountain, so sheer was the drop in front of it. It was surrounded by a semi-circle of spruce trees and rhododendron, tangled with holly and ivy, but where the circle broke they had a view right over Carrickross Lake to the farthest side where Nead an Iolair, the Eagle's Nest, reared its head.

Tethering the horses to a tree trunk, they walked hand-in-hand to look at the view. Below them a doll's-house-size Carrickross sat sunning itself. Black Kerry cattle grazed on the parkland. The lake was dotted with white limestone islands, all thickly wooded, and small boats moved between them. Indeed, Ashling reflected, the whole estate was a child's playground – and her Rossa one of the lucky children who had run wild there in glorious freedom. Cabbage whites and red admirals flitted past, borne like confetti on a slight breeze, and the air was pungent with the sleepy, summery scents of pine and wild honeysuckle. Hidden from view in the long grass, crickets rubbed the dry kindling of their wings together producing that distinctive 'chirr-chirr' that sends every little boy out hunting with his matchbox.

Rossa turned his head to stare at the bleak rough bulk of the mighty mountain rising out of the forest slopes behind them. With the sunlight playing on it, it looked powerful but innocent. He shuddered, tried not to remember the terrible past – the loss of his beloved parents.

Ashling busily spread a plaid rug on the grass. 'Babe, can you stop dreaming and unpack the goodies, please? Rossa?'

Rossa started and turned to look at her. 'Sorry, did you say something?'

Ashling leaned across and straightened a corner of the rug. 'Yes, I asked if you could unpack the food. Hey, are you feeling okay? You look a bit—'

'No, no! I'm fine, just dopey!' He smiled reassuringly and went to empty the saddlebags, which had been filled to bursting by Noreen, who invariably thought she was catering for an army. 'It'll do you good,' she'd fussed. 'It's a grand idea to take that lovely fiancée of yours and go have a bit of fun for yourselves. Wasn't it a terrible thing to have happened on your engagement? I hope it wasn't some kind of omen.'

Understatement of the year, thought Rossa.

Ashling scanned the picnic fare with delight. 'Noreen's certainly surpassed herself. She really spoils you Granville boys, doesn't she?'

'Always did,' Rossa agreed, peering into a plastic container holding a selection of freshly made sandwiches with the crusts cut off. They had always insisted on having the crusts cut off when they were kids – and Noreen still hadn't dropped the habit.

Included in the bounty was a wedge of Carrickross Blue, some sweet green grapes, mini vine-leaves stuffed with rice and herbs, slices of chicken breast and ham, and a fresh fruit cocktail. The pièce de résistance was a bottle of crisp white Riesling, sandwiched between two icepacks to keep it cool. White china, silver cutlery and linen napkins were packed separately. No such thing as plastic knives and forks or paper plates for the Granvilles! Noreen's only grudging concession to the fact the items were to be bundled into saddlebags were the plastic beakers.

Ashling and Rossa chatted as they ate, touching on a range of non-contentious issues – her photography, his flight schedule – trivia for the most part and nothing that would upset the timbre of the day or force their thoughts down paths where neither wished to go. By unspoken agreement, neither one mentioned the subject of the murder. And for his part, Rossa took care not to look up at Ceanngairiff again.

After they had finished eating, Ashling packed up the leftovers and dishes, while Rossa lay down to relax in the sun, his hands cradling his head, his amazing turquoise eyes concealed by black aviator sunglasses. Though he tried to resist, his thoughts turned to Priti. The bane of his life; the love of his life. Was it too late to turn back the clock, to forget Ashling, his grandmother and Carrickross and high-tail it back to Thailand before any further damage was done? Before anyone else got hurt?

'Amazing mountain.' Ashling's voice intruded on his thoughts. 'Compelling, isn't it?'

'Yes.'

'What does it mean? Ceanngairiff? *Ceann* means head in Irish, doesn't it?'

'Yes. And "Ceanngairiff" means "rough head".'

'We must climb it some time.'

'Maybe.'

He had never told her that this was the mountain that haunted his dreams, that this was the mountain that had snatched his loving father and gentle mother away from him. His uncle, his aunt. That had ripped all their lives apart. This mountain she so admired was in disguise today. On the days when it was swept with bitter winds and shrouded in an evil mist, its true character was there for anyone astute enough to read it.

With a start he heard the rustle of Ashling lying down beside him and just about managed to suppress a groan. Not now. He couldn't. He just couldn't. But neither could he keep fending her off and making excuses. Ashling was a normal red-blooded woman with a normal red-blooded woman's needs. He'd known that when he'd signed up for all this.

'Darling . . .' Propping herself up onto one elbow, Ashling planted little kisses all down along the side of his face. His skin was warm from the heat of the day, slightly stubbly where he had forgone his daily shave. 'Darling, that fruit salad was very nice, but you know what I'd really like for dessert?' Her voice grew husky. Her fingers tiptoed their way down his trouser front to his crotch.

Pushing Priti firmly to the back of his mind, Rossa willed himself to respond. He opened his mouth to hers, kissed her deeply. He undid the belt of her jeans, thrust his hands inside and grasped her buttocks – he knew from experience that sometimes this worked if meanwhile he fantasised about Priti.

Nothing! Nada! His mind said yes, but his body had the casting vote.

Then, inevitably, she was looking at him with that hurt, bewildered face that made him feel so guilty, the offending member soft and unresponsive in her hand. Furious with himself for his failure to give her what she wanted – and irrationally with her for wanting it – he pushed her roughly away. Then, jumping to his feet, he strode over to a large tree and leaned his head against the trunk as he re-adjusted his clothing.

At a complete loss, Ashling stared after him, then rose shakily to her own feet. 'Rossa, what's wrong? Don't just walk away like that. Talk to me.'

Rossa's fist slammed into the tree. 'Fuck! I don't know, Ashling. I don't know. Maybe it's – it's all this pressure. I just don't know if I can take it any more. It's doing my head in.'

'I don't understand.' Her fingers made clumsy with nerves, Ashling straightened her own clothes. 'What pressure? Do you mean me? Our wedding? The murder? What?'

'No. Yes. I don't know, I told you.' He made a sweeping gesture. 'It's . . . it's everything! Oh bugger, I'm not a performing monkey, Ashling! I can't just get it up on demand.'

'*On demand?*' Furious all of a sudden, Ashling rushed over and spun him round with a strength she didn't know she possessed. 'What the hell are you talking about, Rossa? You call *that* "on demand"? Are you crazy?' She drew herself up to her full height. 'Listen, I don't know what demons are driving you, but why don't you just be a man and tell it like it is? I'll tell you what. Why don't I make it easy for you? You're no longer in love with me. There, I've said it. The genie is out of the bottle. Feel better?'

'No. No, that's not what it is,' Rossa protested, but when he tried to meet her eyes, his own fell away tellingly. 'You've got it all wrong.'

'Oh, indeed I have, but not the way you think, Rossa.' Trembling with hurt and anger, Ashling clenched her fists as she spoke. 'I got it wrong when I fell for your sweet talk and lies. I got it wrong when I believed you when you said you loved me. I got it wrong when I said yes to your proposal of marriage. I got it wrong by thinking that, despite the mounting evidence, things would work out for us and we'd eventually get to live happily ever after! Hah! You know what? I can't remember the last time we made love properly! And I mean *properly* – not just a quick tumble and fumble. You've always got an excuse. You're too knackered or too stressed, you're too hurried or too God knows what.' Her voice shook. 'You even went AWOL on the night of our engagement. And when finally you did show up, you were too off your face to do anything but sleep!'

Somewhere, way off in the distance, she could hear the thrum of a motor-boat moving across the lake, a bird singing its heart out, the pleasant thunder of the waterfall below them. All normal, soothing noises. The harmonious soundtrack to harmonious country life.

What she didn't hear was the sound of Rossa reassuring her. What she didn't hear was the sound of Rossa apologising to her for the fact that she should feel so miserable and unloved. Tears sprang to her eyes. She blinked them away and gazed off towards the mountain. When she spoke again, it was in a resigned tone.

'You know, Rossa, I'm really angry right now – more with myself than with you. Right from the start I've been completely open and honest with you. I'm an intelligent, educated, professional, independent woman. I scrub up nice and, actually, I am nice. I deserve better.'

A shadow fell across them both as a cloud passed overhead.

Even now, she hoped he might relent. Contradict her. Fight for her. For their relationship. For their future.

Nothing.

In the silence that fell between them, time seemed to stretch and expand. Afterwards Ashling had no idea how long she'd stood there, staring at Rossa's miserable face, her mind curiously numb, her body trembling, tears flowing freely down her face.

At last she turned and flung herself on Morrígan's back. A moment later she was moving back down the treacherous mountain trail at breakneck speed.

CHAPTER 17

Carrick Granville hung up the telephone receiver with a satisfied click. The gardaí had been surprisingly understanding about his pre-planned trip to attend a conference in Morocco and the difficulty of cancelling so late in the day as he was one of the guest speakers. He had provided both his contact details and his reassurance that he would be back as soon as possible and, simple as that, he had permission to leave the jurisdiction. Of course, reading between the lines, the fact that they raised no objection meant that they were pretty sure that they already had their man – and woman – in custody. Carrick sighed at the thought of the twins. What a God-awful mess. In some ways it would be a real relief to get away, even if it was only for a short while and work related. It would also be something of a relief to be away from the whole Rossa/Ashling/Grandmother debacle. Putting some distance between them might lend him a new perspective, even the will to tackle matters anew upon his return. The thought of positive action made him feel slightly better, as did the prospect of staying at the beautiful

Hivernage Hotel in Marrakesh. But first he needed to return to the tranquillity of his island to put the finishing touches to the lecture he was engaged to deliver. He would spend the night there and most of the following day, taking the helicopter directly from the island to Cork Airport without returning to Carrickross. He would be in Morocco a full two days ahead of the conference but, frankly, he would need that time to shake off the effects of the recent stress and bring his mind to focus on the job in hand.

Time to inform his grandmother of his plans. With a sigh and a rueful grimace he set off for Honoria's private sitting room downstairs. As he reached the hall, he halted as a flash of red hair outside a window caught his eye. Grim-faced, he made for one of the French doors to cut off the intruder, unable to believe the evidence of his senses and amazed at the pure cheek of that journalist woman, Maggie O'Keefe. As if the family hadn't been through enough in the past few days.

'Hey!' He stepped out in front of Maggie on the terrace and she came to an abrupt halt. 'What do you think you're doing sneaking round here? Trying to dig up more dirt, is that it?'

Feeling like a schoolkid who's been caught truanting by the headmaster, Maggie blushed. 'God, no! I'm . . . I'm . . .'

His face dark with fury, Carrick glared at her. 'Don't you people have any morals? No wonder they call you the gutter press. A young girl has lost her life, the family is in turmoil and still you go on snooping round – for what? A few bob more in your pay packet? A postage-stamp photograph over your by-line?'

'No – no, you don't understand—'

In her denim jeans, skimpy turquoise T-shirt and flat ballet pumps, she was a far cry from the Maggie who had graced the ball in that ill-fitting gown – younger-looking without all the make-up, even slightly vulnerable. But if Carrick was moved by that, he didn't show it.

'Oh, I understand perfectly well!' The last was said with as much sarcasm as he could muster. 'Your *profession*,' his lip curled, 'gives you the right to forego the common decency found in most of the population. Which is why you felt perfectly entitled to gatecrash a private party and eaves-drop on private conversations. Which reminds me, have you written your piece on my brother and me yet, complete with whatever embellishments you care to add?'

'Of course I have!' Maggie snapped, suddenly losing her own temper. 'In fact, I was hoping you might spell-check it for me and donate a photo of the pair of you at each other's throats.' Then she threw up her hands. 'Oh, look, I'm sorry. You've every right to be angry. You're right, I did sneak into the Midsummer Ball but, honestly, there was no malice intended. It just seemed like a God-given opportunity. And okay, fair enough, I was hoping to get some copy I could use, just a bit of social commentary really. I never meant to eavesdrop on anyone.' Her chin came up, her eyes sparkled angrily. 'And whether you believe it or not I have no intention of publishing that conversation now or ever.'

A pulse throbbed visibly in Carrick's forehead. 'And I suppose you expect me to thank you for that, just like I thanked you for helping out when Kate O'Leary was found drowned in the fountain,' the look of disgust he gave her made her curl up all the way to her toes, 'never for one minute suspecting that you were anything other than an innocent guest. Oh no, you were savvy enough to keep that to yourself until the police questioned you!' Savagely, he kicked a loose pebble from the gravelled path. It flew up and rebounded off a terracotta plant pot with a dull ping. 'That must have made great copy for your story! A body in the Granvilles' fountain and you conveniently on hand to discover it!'

'I hardly planned that!' Under the verbal onslaught Maggie felt tears spring to her eyes but she blinked them away, not wanting to show any weakness.

'I'm not implying that you did. But can't you just let things lie now? Surely even you must realise that the family are under considerable strain. What we need is time: time away from prying eyes, time to try to get to grips with this whole terrible tragedy. What we certainly don't need is any more meddling by people like you. Now, kindly leave the way you arrived, or do I have to arrange to have you escorted from the premises?'

Anger now replacing hurt, Maggie stood her ground pugnaciously.

And then Jaspar, with Ehu in his wake, came striding around the corner of the house.

'Ah, Maggie, Maggie, there you are!' His face wreathed in smiles, Jaspar wrapped her in one of his trademark effusive hugs. 'Ehu and I were beginning to think you'd stood us up. But now I see that that naughty nephew of mine wanted to keep you all to himself. Not that I can blame him—'

'Jaspar!' His face like a thundercloud, Carrick cut him off. 'Miss O'Keefe was just leaving.'

Puzzled, Jaspar looked from one to the other. 'Leaving, Maggie? And what's all this Miss O'Keefe business?' A frown gathered between his brows. 'Carrick, have you been upsetting Maggie?'

'On the contrary. *Maggie's* been upsetting me. Upsetting all of us, in fact, sneaking around the grounds with her bloodhound's nose on the sniff for another nice big bone of juicy scandal.'

'Nonsense! Maggie is here at my invitation. Not only is she exceptionally good company, but if you were to think outside of the box, dear nephew, you might realise that she is in a position to exercise a bit of damage limitation on our behalf.'

Carrick raised a sardonic eyebrow. 'Oh, yes, and how might that be?'

Jaspar sighed. 'I should have thought that was

obvious. Since the murder, the Granvilles have come under the spotlight even more than usual and for the most part, not in a good way. The fact that Maggie, a journalist, has carte blanche to come and go as she pleases and complete access to the Granvilles *en famille* can only do us good.' Jaspar looked pleased at his own cleverness. 'After all, we *have* nothing to hide. Let the Granvilles be as transparent as a pane of glass, that's what I say!'

'I see.' Carrick looked more cynical than ever. 'You want to keep her as a pet journalist.' He slanted an unamused grin at Maggie. 'I would ask if that goes against your principles, Miss O'Keefe, but as I've already noted, you people don't have any. Besides, Grandmother will never agree to it.'

'She already has,' Jaspar said triumphantly. 'Unlike you, she can see the benefits in a little positive press coverage. Don't forget, people already have the twins tried, convicted and hung by the necks. We need to use whatever means we can get our hands on to make sure they get a fair trial and whoever really murdered that poor girl is brought to book!'

'Ah, but do *you* believe the twins are innocent, Miss O'Keefe?' Carrick asked.

'I don't know,' Maggie answered honestly. 'But, as Jaspar said, they're entitled to a fair trial and I'm willing to keep an open mind.'

'Even if they are Granvilles! How very reassuring for us all. It will be a great comfort to me to know the family are in such safe hands while I am away in Morocco.'

'And it'll be a relief to the rest of us to have you there,' Jaspar snapped. 'Honestly, Carrick, you need to get over yourself. Maggie's a journalist, not a leper. And we like her, don't we, Ehu?' He linked his arm through Maggie's as Ehu, showing solidarity, linked her on the other side. 'So come along, m'dear. The jacuzzi is on and bubbling merrily away and the drinkies all lined up and waiting. I hope you remembered to bring your itsy-bitsy-teeny-weeny yellow polka-dot bikini?'

Maggie had a strong impulse to flick Carrick the finger as Jaspar and Ehu marched her off – but she restrained herself and gave him a level look instead.

Carrick watched them go. He really must have a serious word with his grandmother about the advisability of Maggie O'Keefe's presence.

'Master Carrick.' Rajesh had approached in his soundless way. 'Your grandmother wishes to see you. Will you come?'

'Actually, Rajesh, I was just on my way there now,' Carrick said.

'Excellent, I will go and inform her.' With a half-bow from the waist, Rajesh turned and hurried away, noiseless in his slippered feet. Inscrutable, as always.

Upon reaching the door to Honoria's sitting room, Carrick raised his hand to knock, but Rajesh was already waiting and it swung open as if by magic. Honoria stepped indoors from her small balcony which overlooked the sunken, paved flower garden on the western side of the house.

'Ah, Carrick. Will you join me in a glass of something?'

'Just a small port, thanks.' Carrick took a chair. 'Actually, I can't stay long. I'm off to Morocco tomorrow evening – I'm speaking at a conference in a few days' time. I'll sleep on the island tonight and go directly from there.'

'Really?' Handing him his drink, Honoria looked most disapproving. 'But the police . . .'

'Already notified. They're fine with it.'

Honoria sniffed. 'Well, personally I consider it most remiss of you to go gallivanting abroad, just when the family needs you most.'

'It's my *work*, Grandmother,' Carrick reiterated with emphasis. 'And this trip is something I committed to a long time ago. If it should happen that the twins are formally charged, I dare say Rossa and Fin, or even yourself, can attend the court. And my solicitor has been instructed to notify me immediately in the event of any untoward developments.'

Honoria looked sternly at him and took the chair opposite. 'You know, Carrick, you have been a great disappointment to me.' She held up a hand as if to forestall any argument, although he hadn't moved. 'No, hear me out. I shall have my say.' Behind her, the door closed quietly as Rajesh slipped discreetly away. 'You were my hope. When your father and uncle died, you became the repository of my dreams for Carrickross. I see by your face that you think it unfair to have an old woman's burdens placed upon your shoulders and, yes, you may even be right.' Her eyes took on a distant look. 'But who else? Jaspar? Never! I have sometimes wondered if my third and only surviving son was the result of bad karma being visited upon me.'

Carrick smiled at that. 'You were too long in India, Grandmother.'

Honoria glared at him. 'Do not patronise me, Carrick. There are things of which you have no knowledge – and do not ask what, for I shall never tell you.'

'We all make mistakes,' Carrick said mildly. 'And, Grandmother, I know you are of a different generation, but really Jaspar is not some sort of monster. I can't imagine he'd be too pleased to be referred to as bad karma.'

'Pah!' Honoria almost spat. 'Jaspar is not my concern. You are.'

'I can't imagine why.' Carrick set down his glass, sat back against his chair and stretched his legs out in front of him to their fullest extent, deliberately casual. 'The way I see it, Grandmother, I am no longer the *repository* of your hopes, now that you have deposited them in Rossa instead.'

'A ruse!' Honoria brought her heavily ringed hand down on the arm of her chair with a thwack. 'Designed to bring you to heel. Carrickross was meant for you. Always!' Her voice grew thready, whether as a deliberate attempt to elicit sympathy or not, he couldn't tell. 'My years are numbered. You are no fool – this you know. But whatever chance I may have of lying easy, I will have none at all if Carrickross is in the wrong hands.'

'Put there by you,' Carrick reminded her, unwilling to give in to emotional blackmail. 'Rossa and Ashling: you engineered it.'

'In the hope that it might spur you into settling down.'

'And into providing you with an official heir?'

'Yes. Yes. I will not lie. Are my wishes so very wrong?'

Carrick shook his head. 'No. But coldly manipulating others to achieve them is wrong, Grandmother. What about Rossa? You lured him into marriage with a woman he doesn't really love, dangling Carrickross like a carrot in front of his nose. And what if I was to jump suddenly to your tune? Would you so easily break your word to him? And what about Ashling? Is she simply to be discarded as collateral damage, because we both know that without Carrickross Rossa will never marry her?'

Honoria shrugged. 'Rossa will do well to learn a lesson. The boy is greedy and shallow. His appetites need curbing.'

'And Ashling?' Carrick persisted.

A closed look stole over his grandmother's face. 'Do not trouble yourself on that score. In any case, the girl is better off without him.'

Carrick's lips twisted. '*Double double toil and trouble!* Have you no conscience, Grandmother?'

Almost amused, she shook her head. 'Desperate times, desperate measures.'

Disgusted, Carrick slapped his glass down on the table. 'Listen carefully, Grandmother, because we'll not be having this conversation again. I will *not* marry simply to provide you with an heir. *If* and when I do marry, it will be to a woman I respect and love. Toss your head if you like, but I *will* marry for love and to a woman of my own choosing, *in* my own time.' He picked up his glass again, dispatched the remaining contents in one gulp. 'I love this old estate, every bit as much as you do, but if my soul is the price to be paid for it, then I must decline the transaction.' Pushing his chair away, so that it rocked precariously on its back legs, he got to his feet. 'Poor, stupid Rossa. He sold himself to you, body and soul, for what? Fool's gold! Let him have it!' With a last glance that mingled both contempt and pity, he walked out.

'Carrick!' Her bony hand lifted for a moment, reached out as if she would pull him back, then faltered and fell to her lap.

As Carrick hurried away to his helicopter, shouts of laughter from the jacuzzi reminded him that he had not had a chance to raise the thorny subject of Maggie O'Keefe with his grandmother. He gave a little shrug. It would wait.

★ ★ ★

Maggie couldn't help but brood as she relaxed, or tried to, in the jacuzzi. Carrick Granville brought out such mixed feelings in her. On the one hand, he was typical of his class – a touch arrogant, sure of his place in society and his right to occupy it. Silver spoon firmly in mouth, he was exactly the type of person Maggie most loathed. And yet, instead of resting on his laurels like many of his kind, he had done something worthwhile with his life and was now considered amongst the world's foremost architects. In a moment of insight, she realised that Carrick Granville, whatever the circumstances of his birth, would be a man to be reckoned with. On the flip side, there was also a sense of loss about him, an aloneness, which probably had its roots in losing his parents so young. Did anyone ever really get over such a tragedy? Was his answer to prevent others from getting too close to him in case he lost them too? Perhaps that was why he hadn't married yet or shown any signs of wanting to do so. After all, if he fancied a bit of female company, there were always the Coppelia Morrisons of this world to provide it, sophisticated older women who unlike their younger counterparts were only interested for the most part in a bit of uncomplicated fun. Thinking about it, she was pretty sure Carrick was the man she had seen with Coppelia the morning after the Midsummer Ball. He certainly fitted the bill.

Absentmindedly, Maggie took a sip of chilled

champagne, despite vowing in the throes of her most recent hangover never to touch a drop of alcohol again. She felt sick when she thought of the way Carrick had looked at her earlier, like she was nothing, the lowest of the low, a slug beneath his feet. But people had looked at her like that before, subjected her to far worse abuse and she had simply shaken it off like water off a duck's back. As a journalist, it went with the territory. But somehow this felt different. Somehow Carrick Granville's good opinion mattered and she wasn't quite sure why.

On the other side of the jacuzzi, Jaspar sighed luxuriously and relaxed back in the bubbles. 'You know,' he remarked conversationally, 'if I keep my eyes tight shut I can imagine I'm back at home. I can see the plains, the heat haze, the hazy horizon, leopards, elephant roaming free – hear the clink of ice in my G&T, the chattering of the monkeys swinging in the trees. If I open my eyes I expect to see one of them perched cheekily on the jacuzzi edge, hand out, waiting to be fed with nuts and raisins . . . and you, Ehu, the water making your skin gleam, your smile flashing in the sun, your almond eyes glistening—'

'Jaspar, Jaspar, please stop!' Startled from her musings, Maggie laughed out loud. 'You'll have poor Ehu in tears. I'm almost in tears myself. Put the weeping violins away, will you?'

Unabashed, Jaspar laughed too. 'Laying it on with a trowel, was I? Seriously though, Maggie, if you could just see Nyambeni.' He kissed his fingers. 'So beautiful, so tranquil, so not Carrickross! Ehu and I can't *wait* to shed the muck of this wretched corner of the earth and get back to the blessed red earth of civilisation!'

'Wretched corner of the earth? I should be so lucky!' said Maggie, gazing in awe at the magnificence of their surroundings and wishing she could take up residence in the jacuzzi for good. The lake danced with little white-crested waves. Nead an Iolair raised its craggy head out of its wreath of black-green forest while sun and cloud dappled the smooth head of the mountain to its right. 'I think it's wonderful. Don't you agree, Ehu?'

He shook his head. 'No. At home I swimmin' always in the lake.' He obviously thought she'd been referring to the jacuzzi. 'Sometimes in the lake here too. But it is more cold.'

'The lake! *Brrrr!*' Jaspar shivered dramatically. 'I don't do lakes. The boy is quite mad!'

Laughing, Ehu lunged playfully at him and Maggie noticed that, stripped down to his plaid boxer shorts, which left little – or should she say much? – to the imagination, Ehu was quite an eyeful.

'So where's your poison today, Ehu?' she asked, remembering their conversation at the ball. 'Don't tell me you've used it on someone already?'

With a great flash of white teeth, Ehu pointed to where his usual great rake of beads and charms hung from a nearby bush, and amongst them the little decorative gourd of poison. 'No, I don't use it yet,' he said. 'See, there it is. All safe.'

'And is it really deadly?' Maggie asked. 'Or just for show?'

'Oh, deadly!' Jaspar waved an airy hand. 'The Maasai take their poisons seriously. They don't mess about.'

'But, isn't it a bit risky, carrying it round the place?'

Ehu set his lips. 'A Maasai must always be prepared.'

'For what?' Maggie persisted. 'It's not like you're really going to use it, surely?'

'No. I told you before he wouldn't hurt a fly.' Jaspar chuckled. 'But it does lend a certain frisson.' And he burst into a camped-up version of 'Mad About the Boy'.

Noel Coward, of course, thought Maggie, and not without a blush at the memory of that wretched theatrical 1920s dress.

An idea flashed into her head. 'Hey, what would you two say to doing an in-depth interview with me? About your experience as a gay couple in Ireland versus Africa?'

So, three animated heads protruding from the bubbling jacuzzi, they began to discuss the gay interracial experience on two continents . . .

Back in her own rooms, white as a ghost and desperately upset, Ashling was throwing her clothes into her suitcases with the same wildness with which her thoughts were chasing themselves round and round in her head. The same thought came back to plague her over and over: Rossa didn't love her any more. And there was nothing really surprising about that. What was surprising was that he had ever loved her in the first place. What had it all been about? It wasn't as if he couldn't have had any woman he wanted. It wasn't as if there was anything particularly special about her, any way she could have enriched his life or career, other than by her love – which he didn't appear to want. False modesty aside, she was attractive, but so were millions of other women, some far more so than she. She wasn't especially wealthy – comfortably off, yes, but she didn't have a fraction of the kind of wealth the Granvilles were used to. Had he fallen in love with her but now had woken up to the fact that he could do better? She crumpled up the emerald silk camisole bought with such high expectations and shoved it into a corner of the case. How could her heart have got it so wrong?

Sitting down on the side of the bed, she dropped her head into her hands. A new thought came to her. Was his change of heart something to do with her stepmother's history with the Granvilles? Had his sudden coldness sprung from that? Bitterly, she reflected that Coppelia would shed no tears if that were so. On the contrary, she would be delighted.

And suddenly he was standing there, framed in

the doorway as large as life, looking as if he expected a shoe to come hurtling his way, or something worse.

'Ash? Can I come in?' He was wearing the naughty-little-boy face that generally ensured he got his way with her. Without waiting for an answer, he stepped in and sat down on the bed beside her. His weight on the mattress threw her slightly against him and she jerked away. 'I'm sorry,' he said, twisting his hands in front of him. 'I've been a complete dick! Can you forgive me?'

Ashling's head came up at that. She glared at him with naked hostility. 'And what exactly would you like me to forgive you for? For treating me like shit? For making me feel ugly and worthless and undesirable? For taking my love and making a mockery of it?'

'Ashling, I'm truly sorry. I—'

But she cut him off. 'Sorry is the cure-all for everything, isn't it? Put yourself in my shoes, Rossa. Try to imagine how it feels to find out that the person you love with all your heart, the person you have pledged to spend the rest of your life with, doesn't find you attractive enough to make love to.' A fat tear splodged onto the light fabric of her riding breeches. 'Over and over, I keep asking myself what I did wrong up on the mountain and over and over I keep coming back with the same answer. Nothing! I did absolutely nothing wrong, unless you count a gentle invitation to you to make love. Oops, I forgot – you saw that as a *demand*. What was it you said? "I'm not a performing monkey".'

Rossa sat, silent and ashamed. And in a trap of his own making: Ashling on one side, Priti on the other. To say nothing of Honoria if she thought her plans for the marriage were coming apart at the seams. What the fuck was he to do? In theory the plan had seemed beautifully simple. But he hadn't reckoned on Priti being such a loose cannon. And he hadn't reckoned on finding that he truly cared for Ashling. These new feelings were a most unwelcome complication.

Rossa closed his eyes with a sigh. He longed to be back in Hua Hin. He was beginning to think living in a beach shack for the rest of his life was infinitely preferable to continuing with this miserable charade. How had he ever persuaded himself it would all be plain sailing? He must have been completely delusional. Now every instinct in his body was urging him to throw in the towel, before he could do any further damage to poor, innocent Ashling. Before it got to the point where he lost every single ounce of self-respect.

Better to bite the bullet and make the break with Ashling right here, right now, when she couldn't deny that the cracks in their relationship were more like craters . . .

'Ashling,' he said, when she paused and made no further attempt to talk, 'are you telling me you want to call the wedding off? Is that what you want?'

He willed her to say yes, to save herself. And save him too.

'No, no, I don't,' she said in a very small voice, after he had endured several seconds of tormenting silence. 'God help me for being a fool, but I still *love* you!'

'And I love you,' he replied. And, as he said it, he realised it was true. He really did love Ashling. Somewhere along the line she had changed from being just a convenient means to financial freedom to someone he had grown to love. If only he didn't love Priti he could really make a go of it with this lovely girl. 'Ashling . . . I behaved like a prick today. My only excuse is the age-old one. I got cold feet. I'm – I'm not myself . . . the murder has rattled me terribly and suddenly . . . suddenly the idea of being the first Granville to marry and most probably provide Carrickross with its heir seemed much too heavy. So, you see, it's nothing to do with you, Ashling – it's the responsibility, living up to my grandmother's expectations . . . all that . . .' This had the beauty of being the truth . . . if not the whole truth.

Feeling a rush of tenderness, he looked at Ashling, *really* looked at her for what seemed like the very first time: her beautiful pale face framed with that cloud of dark hair like the most perfect picture, those stunning eyes swimming with tears, that perfectly sculpted mouth with those soft lips just begging to be kissed. He experienced a rush of desire he hadn't felt since . . . well, since Priti.

'So what do you say, Ash? Will you give me another chance? Please. Let's start all over again.' Even as he spoke he despised himself, aware he was trying to have his cake and eat it too.

No, no, no, thought Ashling. This was too much of a rollercoaster ride. She couldn't live like this: one moment cruising the stars, the next teetering on the edge of a precipice. But then, a little voice teased her, hadn't she wanted him to fight to save their relationship? In which case shouldn't she fight too? Wasn't it worth one last chance? And what he said was true. Bridegrooms often got cold feet, even at the very altar. And, as he said, the responsibilities Rossa was taking on must indeed be frightening to a man who had been so unfettered.

'Come here,' Rossa whispered, lust thickening his voice. 'I want to show you exactly how much you mean to me.'

'No. No. Not now,' she said with an effort, though she longed to lose herself in the pleasure of being in his arms. 'I need a little space. But . . . yes . . . maybe we should try again.'

'Thank you, Ashling,' said Rossa tenderly, stroking her hair gently. 'You won't be sorry.' But he sadly feared she would be.

In the revealing light of the late-afternoon sun, Honoria looked every one of her eighty-five years. Her face was drawn, a network of deep wrinkles fanned out beside her eyes and her hands, one linked through Rajesh's arm, the other clutched about the tip of her walking stick, were age-spotted. Hard to believe those hands still wielded so much power.

Slowly she allowed him to lead her down the long sloping lawn through the herb garden where insects flitted amongst the lavender and rosemary, past the fish pond where Indigo once killed all Henry's prize Koi carp by pouring bleach in the water, over a small stream spanned by a white wooden bridge to the summerhouse shaped like an Indian temple. Henry's Folly, the family called it. Another gift founded on guilt. As grandiose gestures went, it was no Taj Mahal, but Honoria loved it for its tranquillity and, after her sons died, it became something of a habit for her to sit there for hours on end, alone with her thoughts. Set in a slight dip, it looked out across the middle lake, mirror-still today but for the odd concentric patch of ripples where a curious fish broke the surface.

Great purple trusses of late-flowering wisteria cloaked the arched doorway, but for once the sight failed to lift her heart. Almost wearily she allowed Rajesh to settle her into a well-padded wicker sun-lounger.

'What would I do without you?' she asked, smiling her thanks.

Settling himself in the seat beside her, Rajesh, with a glance round to make sure they were not being observed, took one of her hands in his and stroked circles on the back of it with his thumb.

'Rani, my queen, you will never be without me. We are but one heart.'

'And one mind,' she said with a smile, finishing the sentence that had become their mantra down through the years.

They lapsed into silence then, and when Honoria spoke again there was a catch in her voice, a plaintiveness.

'Carrick is not for turning, Rajesh. He is as stubborn as a mule.'

Rajesh nodded but made no reply. He knew she was simply using him as a sounding board, trying to make sense of a situation that, thus far, had defeated her.

Honoria sighed, her eyes absently following the route of a vapour trail piped like icing across the otherwise clear blue sky. 'Why is life never simple? And why is it one's hopes and dreams seldom turn out as imagined?' She gave a dry chuckle, almost a cough. 'What madness possessed me to embark on such an absurd plan? What convinced me it would work? I *know* Carrick. He is an idealist, a man of strong principles, exactly the qualities that make him fit to be my heir. How could I have expected him to bend to my will?'

'Carrick is the commander of his own ocean,' Rajesh observed. 'Send forth your ship filled with treasure and he will quiet the winds.'

'Carrickross is my ship filled with treasure,' Honoria said bitterly. 'And who, if not Carrick, will keep it safe?' They sat silent for a moment

261

and when Honoria spoke again it was with a certain amount of resignation in her voice. 'I must cancel the wedding and prepare for the brickbats that will come my way, deservedly, as Carrick would be quick to point out. And yet, I fancy my plan has not been entirely unsuccessful, Rajesh, for at least one little birdie flew into my cage.'

Rajesh smiled too. 'Coppelia Morrison.'

'Indeed. Coppelia Morrison, soon to experience the bitter and excruciating pain of being torn from the thing she holds most dear in the world, her very own flesh and blood. My conscience is clear on that score, at least, for the rage still burns in me, Rajesh, as hot as ever and with every day that passes the flames grow higher and higher. I have condemned Coppelia Morrison to hell.'

Outside the summerhouse the air hung heavy and still, throbbing with the drone of a thousand busy bees. A transparent filament from a dandelion wafted by, reminding Rajesh of that first summer in England, when Honoria had shown him the dandelion clocks with their silky white globes. He recalled the redness of her lips, the whiteness of her skin, the adorable way her nose wrinkled slightly as she taught him how to tell time by the number of puffs it took to blow the filaments away. Most of all, he recalled the love in her eyes. 'Make a wish, Rajesh,' she'd told him when he got to the last one. And he had silently wished that he and she could be together always. And they had.

'Coppelia Morrison must pay for her sins,' he told her now. 'She did you a grave wrong. It is right that you should have your revenge. For all that she is still young and vibrant and you and I are ageing as the trunk on our beloved banyan tree, never forget, Rani, she is but one, and we, though one soul, are two heads.'

Honoria laughed softly. 'And two heads are better than one, eh, Rajesh?'

'Exactly so, Rani.'

CHAPTER 18

Honoria surveyed the breakfast table with tight-lipped disapproval. Only Rossa, Ashling and Fin were present. Carrick had taken off for his island after their little contretemps and would soon be on his way to Marrakesh. As for Jaspar – well, she didn't care where he and his *companion* were. Noreen had served up the Full Irish, but only the men were exhibiting signs of any appetite. Ashling nibbled desultorily on a piece of toast, while the egg, bacon, tomatoes and mushrooms congealed on her plate. Honoria never deviated from the same breakfast: half a grapefruit, a piece of fresh brown soda bread, sparingly spread with butter and thickcut Seville marmalade, and several cups of strong tea. Noreen circulated with a large silver teapot, making sure everyone was topped up.

'That will be all, Noreen,' Honoria dismissed her. 'Please ask Tom to have the car ready in thirty minutes, I'm going into town.'

Noreen dipped her head, placed the teapot on its matching silver trivet and hurried out.

Honoria cast her eyes around the table. 'In case

you are interested, I am going to visit my grand-children and demand that they be released immediately.' Disapproval folded her already thin lips into an almost non-existent line. 'It is unfortunate that I am forced to take the initiative in this matter, but it would seem your brother is engaged upon business he deems more important. *Business* that takes him to Morocco, whilst his innocent young cousins are rotting in jail.'

Rossa put down his teacup with something of a clatter. 'Bollocks, Grandmother, excuse my French! Carrick has done everything he can for the twins since their arrest and has been to visit them several times, which is more than can be said for the rest of us.'

'Rossa's right,' said Fin. 'But, you know, Grandmère, it's not entirely a bad thing that the twins are locked up – for the time being. At least, that way, they can't get into any more mischief.'

'Fin!' Honoria quelled him with a scowl. 'If you can't say something helpful, better you tie a knot in your tongue.'

Giving up all pretence at eating, Ashling pushed her plate away. 'Realistically, Honoria, what do you think are the chances of securing their release?'

'I do not know.' The elderly woman dabbed at her lips with a white linen napkin, carefully folded it and placed it to one side. 'However, I shall certainly pull out all the stops. Disgraceful! Who do these people think they are – to lock up a

Granville? *Two* Granvilles! It wouldn't have happened in the past. People had respect for the family then. Were it not for Carrickross, half this county would have been out of work.'

Rossa laid his cutlery across his empty plate. 'That was then and this is now, Grandmother, and even you must admit that on the face of it there is a certain amount of evidence against the twins. And for all we know Forensics may have come up with all sorts of other things which they're not yet ready to make public.'

'Such as?' Honoria's expression left him in no doubt that she was distinctly unimpressed with this line of reasoning.

Rossa faltered a little. 'W-well, by the twins' own admission, things got . . .' he cleared his throat, at a loss as to how to word this for his puritan grandmother, 'er . . . pretty steamy . . . and—'

Fin butted in where angels feared to tread. 'Yes, and what with those scuffmarks on the bedposts and the bloodstained sheets in the basement – you can't blame people for putting two and two together and—'

Furious, Honoria cut him off. 'Circumstantial! We know by now that the police have no witnesses. Anyone could have killed her. The house was swarming with guests that evening.'

'But only with one murderer!' came Jaspar's voice. 'Or two if the fair Sapph did have a hand in it!'

He had arrived just in time to catch the tail end

of the conversation, accompanied by Ehu in full Maasai attire who, like a bodyguard, took up position behind Jaspar's chair.

Honoria sent him a pointed look. 'Jaspar, we are having a meeting here – a *family* meeting.'

Jaspar shook out his napkin, tucked it into his collar. 'Oh, for goodness' sakes, Mother, Ehu is family – as good as, anyway, certainly as much family as that Indian flunky of yours!' He patted the empty chair beside him. 'Sit down, Ehu, do. You're making the place look untidy.'

'Insolence!' Pushed to the brink, Honoria exploded, her voice trembling with outrage. 'Rajesh has served this family well for more years than you've been alive! There is no comparison to this fancy of yours, this *circus* act you choose to inflict on us. Rajesh has dedicated himself to this family, watching over each and every one of you since the day of your birth. How dare you insult him so!' She wafted her hand at Ehu. 'You! Kindly leave the room. You may await Jaspar in the kitchen. Noreen will provide you with breakfast.'

Ehu moved not a muscle, looking right through her as if she was made of glass.

Jaspar bristled and rolled his eyes. 'Mother, I really don't understand why you persist in acting like some remnant from the days of the Raj. Even *you* are not that ancient.'

'Jaspar!' Her voice warned that she had reached the end of her tether.

Exasperated, he flapped his hand. 'Oh, for pity's sake! Go on then, scoot, Ehu! Anything to keep the peace. And kindly tell Noreen I am simply ravenous for my breakfast.'

'Please remember we are not on African time here, Jaspar.' Honoria glared after the departing Ehu. 'Carrickross runs to a strict schedule and Noreen cannot be expected to fetch and carry at your convenience.'

Diplomatically, Rossa steered the conversation back on track once more. 'Shall I accompany you to the garda station, Grandmother?' He hoped she would decline. He had no wish to put himself through that – he was under enough stress already. His face a study in innocence, he picked up a pair of silver sugar tongs and helped himself to two lumps.

Ashling shot him a look. She had hoped they might spend some time together, talk things over now that they both had calmed down and had time to think.

Honoria intercepted the glance but misinterpreted it. Poor girl, she thought. Let her enjoy the remnants of her fairy tale. Reality would bite soon enough. 'That won't be necessary, Rossa, thank you. But, perhaps you might think of taking Ashling on another excursion. She's seen little enough of the estate. You could ride up to the gamekeeper's lodge on the upper lake and boat back down to Carrickross – there is a narrow stretch of rushing water, Ashling, where the upper lake flows into the lower which is very exciting to traverse. The fresh air will do you good. You're looking decidedly peaky.'

Rossa seized on this suggestion. An excursion like that would give him an opportunity of redeeming himself in Ashling's eyes. An active, fun trip, which would allow him to avoid any soul-searching. He needed time to think things through, to explore his new feelings of tenderness and attraction towards her. 'Excellent idea, Grandmother.' He glanced at Ashling. 'If you agree?'

'Yes, sounds good.'

Registering the coolness of Ashling's reply, Honoria realised something was amiss in that relationship. Little wonder. She was well aware Rossa wasn't equipped to cope with a girl of Ashling's sensitivity.

Looking round the table, Honoria felt herself gripped by a huge sense of disappointment. Fate had robbed her of her finest sons, William and David, and left her with Jaspar, the runt of the litter. It was twenty years ago, but seemed like only yesterday when she had last watched them all congregate in the hallway planning that ill-fated expedition up the mountain. Dear God, some days she imagined she could still hear the echo of their well-loved voices as William, looking very much as Carrick did now, took charge, good-humouredly chivvying them along.

'Come on,' she remembered him saying. 'We

need to make an early start before the weather closes in.'

And David heckling him: 'Oh, don't be such an old woman, Will! There's not a cloud in the sky. The forecast is for fine weather.'

'You should know never to depend on the forecast, David. The weather on the mountain can change in a trice. Better to be safe than sorry.'

Oh, fateful words.

Honoria recalled how David had turned to The Swede, as she always thought of his wife Agneta. 'Netty? Are you really sure you're up to this. Shouldn't you still be resting?'

Foolish woman. She had just come out of hospital after yet another one of her famous nervous breakdowns. Honoria gave a mental snort. That was the problem with marrying out of one's own stable: tainted blood and weak minds. Despite her undeniable white-blonde beauty, poor besotted David had married a pig in a poke.

'Oh, I'm fine now, darling. I was just a little tired, that's all.' Agneta had slapped him playfully on the back of his hand, pouting in that ridiculous manner more suited to Sapphire, her young daughter, and Honoria had watched her son melt, as always, unable to deny her anything.

William's wife, the gentle, well-bred Ella, had begged to go too, even though Fin was but an infant still. The air would do her good, she insisted, looking earnestly up at him with the turquoise eyes only Rossa had been fortunate enough to inherit.

'Noreen will look after Fin and keep on eye on Carrick and Rossa. And it's simply ages since I've been up the mountain.'

Honoria had turned away then, her attention claimed by something else, something so trivial she couldn't even recall what it was, never for one moment imagining she had just seen her two precious sons alive for the very last time. Of her three sons, only Jaspar was left now. Jaspar with his predilection for pretty boys and unnatural practices. Jaspar, her bad karma.

A ray of sunlight slanted through the mullioned window, falling across Ashling's dark head. It was true, Honoria reflected, she really did like the girl. It was so ironic that she was the daughter of Coppelia Morrison.

A daughter. A daughter would have been such a joy, would have been a comfort and an ally. It sometimes seemed to Honoria as if she had been at war with the Granville males for as long as she could remember . . . father, sons, grandsons . . . why were they all so recalcitrant? It had hardened her, that unremitting war of attrition. Yes, she thought wistfully – a daughter.

Rising from the table, she left to prepare for her trip to see her grandchildren.

Ashling got up and crossed to the sideboard to help herself to more coffee. Rossa watched the curve of her willowy body, the fall of her black hair as she poured. He went over and stood behind her, tentatively wrapping his arms about her. It was the kind of foolish, romantic gesture she normally thrived on and he was relieved to feel her respond, relaxing back against him.

'Hi, beautiful,' he whispered into her hair and she turned her head and gave him a little smile.

Jesus, he thought, *I really do love her. But is it possible to love two women at the same time?*

Fifteen minutes later, Honoria, dressed in an old-fashioned driving coat and straw bonnet secured by a chiffon scarf under her chin, emerged from the house leaning heavily on Rajesh's arm. As always she carried her boar's-head walking stick in her free hand.

'The car's all ready for you, ma'am,' Tom touched the peak of his cap, 'and purring away sweet as a nut she is too.' Admiringly his glance roamed over the 1930s white Beauford convertible. Noreen, his wife, had often said that if he looked at her in half so loving a way, she would have been a happy woman indeed. 'Will you be needing Seán to drive?'

'I intend to drive myself,' said Honoria.

Greedily her own eyes swept over the car. She loved it with a passion that had never waned in all the years she had owned it. And even now, at the ripe old age of eighty-five, she was damned if she was going to be deprived of the pleasure of driving it while she still could. Henry had bought it for her shortly after they had married. She worked out later that it had coincided with his first little dally into the world of infidelity – a kitchen maid with bosoms more suited to a milch cow – generosity prompted by guilt. Poor old Henry. Other kitchen maids had followed over the years, and the guilt-fuelled presents had stockpiled: jewellery, pedigree dogs, horses and paintings, even the summerhouse, but nothing had ever stirred her quite like the Beauford. Long, white and sleek with a fold-down burgundy leather hood and elegant wire-spoked wheels, it stood foursquare on the gravel, majestic, a relic of a bygone more graceful era, just like its owner.

'Thank you, Rajesh.'

She allowed herself to be helped into the car. Her hand reached out and touched his, fleetingly. Their eyes met and held, sparked as old memories kindled and resurfaced. The car had been their sanctuary in the early years at Carrickross after she had pumped out in rapid succession an heir and two spares, William, Jaspar and David, thereby securing the future of the estate. Time was not on her side. She had, after all, been well into her thirties then.

She might have chosen to remain a widow after her return from India on the death of her father, were it not for the fact that Carrickross had needed an heir. Henry, the only male Granville of his generation, was self-indulgent and slow to accept his responsibilities to the family and the Granville name. She therefore had to take him in hand. She proposed marriage to him and he had accepted. He wouldn't have dared refuse.

Rajesh had waited for her, quiet and dignified, standing in the shadows of Carrickross, barely tolerated by Henry who mistrusted him, but for reasons he couldn't put a finger on. Never would it have occurred to him that Honoria might consort with a lowly Indian, much less fall in love with him. The irony that he, himself, consorted with the servant girls would never even have crossed his mind.

Lonely and exiled from his own precious land, made willing prisoner by his love for Honoria, tormented by the servants who were unable to pigeon-hole him, Rajesh waited till his beloved was free to come and lie with him once more. Duty done, she had not been slow to reclaim her life and her love.

The Beauford had made their assignations so much easier. On the pretext of taking Rajesh along for protection, Honoria would pack a picnic in the great leather trunk attached to the back of the car, and they would take off for long drives in the country, she dressed in full-skirted pretty summer dresses, her hair streaming out behind her, and Rajesh holding on to his turban for dear life as she took the corners on two wheels. Luckily other motor vehicles were still few and far between in rural Ireland. They became a familiar sight to the locals, the striking Mrs Granville and her Indian servant. Men touched their forelocks, heads swivelling to look admiringly after her, and the women stared in envy and awe, more than one half-hoping the Indian's green eyes would alight on her for more than just a moment. He really was a handsome devil and the devil himself some suspected.

Pulling up the car, Honoria would stop every so often to consult a map, then drive on for miles till they came to a pretty wood or stream, or a field of poppies or corn ripening in the sun. After eating, she would stretch out on the grass while Rajesh undressed her bit by bit, his lips expertly tracing a fiery path of kisses along every new piece of flesh revealed by his questing hands, before embarking on the process of making long, slow delicious love to her. When it came to the art of lovemaking he truly had no equal. Well versed in the ancient Eastern secrets of the Kama Sutra, he would take her to fever pitch time and time again, alternating between using his fingers, mouth, tongue and cock, before expertly timing his own pleasure to coincide with her last orgasm. Shuddering blissfully, Honoria would lie in his arms, content in a way she had never been with any other man and more truly herself.

'Rani? Dear one?'

Honoria started, returning to the present. 'Yes, Rajesh?'

'You will be all right?' Rajesh asked her now. 'I will come with you if you wish.'

'No need,' Honoria assured him, eyes still soft with recollection. 'Besides, I need you here. While there is mischief afoot in Carrickross, one of us must be here at all times. Be my eyes and ears, Rajesh, as you have always been.'

'Very well.' Rajesh inclined his head as she drove sedately away, a far cry from the days when she had careered blindly around corners and people and animals dived headfirst into ditches for safety.

An hour later a female garda was leading Honoria into a small, heavily barred holding-cell with nothing in it except for a table and a couple of chairs.

'Granoria! Oh, Granoria!' Sapphire rushed forward and threw her arms round Honoria's neck. 'Have you come to take me home? Oh, please, Granoria, take me home! I can't bear it in here!'

'No touching,' the garda barked sharply, only to be quelled by a glance from Honoria, who was shocked at the state of her granddaughter.

In the past few days the weight had dropped off, leaving her normally slender frame looking almost skeletal. The bones at her collarbone and wrists protruded in great ridges and her beautiful face looked gaunt and haunted, the features suddenly seeming too big and ill-fitting. Her eyes, those beautiful coloured jewels for which she was named, were sunk so far back in her head that they appeared to be nothing more than two dark holes, without even so much as a gleam to show that there was any life behind them at all.

'Leave us,' Honoria commanded the garda, who shrugged insolently and went to stand on the other side of the door.

Strictly speaking, she wasn't supposed to leave

the prisoners and visitors alone, but what harm could an old woman do?

'Oh, Sapphire, what have they done to you?' Gently, Honoria unwound the girl's stick-like arms from around her neck and held her gently away. 'Has anyone hurt you? Have they been unkind to you?'

'No,' Sapphire said honestly. 'I just hate it here. I want to go home.' A slightly hysterical note entered her voice. 'It's so noisy, people shouting all day and all night, I can't sleep. The food's awful and my bed is dirty. The sheets are all stained and the mattress is rock hard. I'm scared of the other prisoners too. You should see the way they look at me, almost as if they want to kill me. Please take me home. Take me home now!'

'I wish I could, but I can't.' Carefully, Honoria helped her into a chair at the table and took the one opposite, reaching across to cradle Sapphire's small white hands between her own age-speckled ones. 'But it won't be for too much longer, I promise. Carrick tells me they are likely to formally charge you and Indigo very shortly, after which it's likely the pair of you will be bailed into our care. I'll have you out of here and back home at Carrickross, just as soon as ever I can.'

Disappointed, Sapphire bent her head and wept, the tears pouring down her face and dripping off her chin onto her dress.

'Sapph . . .' Honoria usually despised the diminutive but somehow it seemed right for the occasion.

Comforting, normalising an abnormal situation. 'You must tell me. Did you and Indigo kill that girl? The truth, please.'

Sapphire's mouth made an 'O' of astonishment, stretching the skin on her face to a translucent parchment. 'No, of course not! Indigo and I are not murderers. We . . . played with her, that's all. Yes, we played games.'

Honoria didn't ask her to elaborate. She wasn't a fool. She knew exactly what the girl meant and her conscience smote her. Over the years she had taken the twins to see a succession of psychiatrists both in Ireland and abroad – to the best clinics in Switzerland and the USA. The consensus was always the same: the twins were terribly damaged. Psychotic! One of the psychiatrists had come straight out with the word. The best she could hope for was containment by medication. Although the verdict cut like a knife, it had come as no real shock. She had known that all along. Normal children did not torture helpless animals. Together with their striking eyes, white-blonde hair and astonishingly good looks, Sapphire and Indigo had received a further inheritance from their Swedish mother, Agneta – insanity.

Seeing that her grandmother's thoughts had wandered, Sapphire reached out and grabbed her wrist. 'But, Granoria . . . I fell asleep then . . . and . . . and . . .'

'Tell me, Sapphire,' Honoria prompted gently, knowing what was coming.

'W-when I woke up, Indigo was asleep at the table, but Kate was gone. I don't know what Indigo did with her.'

This was what Sapphire had told Carrick and the family lawyer, Honoria knew, though in her initial police statement she had claimed Indigo had fallen asleep before she did . . . while Indigo claimed the opposite. Now it appeared Sapphire had lied to the police to protect Indigo.

'I love you, Granoria,' said Sapphire and her eyes filled with tears.

'My dear!' Honoria was shaken and moved at this declaration. She patted her granddaughter's hand clumsily.

'I've always felt safe with you. I want to be back home with you *now.*'

'You soon will be, I promise you, my dear.'

'I've often been so mean to you, Granoria. I've been hateful. I'm so sorry!' Sapphire's face twisted with distress. 'It's so long since we've been nice to each other.'

Honoria stroked her granddaughter's blonde hair, which now seemed lifeless and lank. It was true, she thought. Dimly she remembered that once upon a time, despite her hatred of Agneta, she might have loved this strange girl. She had always wanted a daughter, after all. But Indigo had staked his claim early on, had placed himself between Sapphire and her grandmother, between Sapphire and the world.

'Yes, Sapphire, we were fond of each other once.'

An image of a little blonde figure in a white dress, flowers in her hair, danced, into her memory.

As if she could divine Honoria's thoughts, Sapphire gave a sudden thrill of laughter, leaped to her feet and began to dance, holding up the skirt of her dress and dipping and swaying towards her grandmother. Her tears drying as suddenly as they had begun, she tossed back her hair and began to sing, her voice pure and true, echoing round the ugly room, reverberating off the graffiti-covered walls.

'After the ball was over . . .'

Poor child! All her feelings of protectiveness towards Sapphire came welling up from where they had lain suppressed for years and years. And she vowed she would move heaven and earth to bring her granddaughter home.

Leaving Sapphire reluctantly to her jailors, Honoria set immediately to work. She made some heavy-duty phone calls – pulling in favours, offering bribes. Cajoling. Threatening. Demanding.

When the twins appeared before a judge and were formally charged, bail was granted to the tune of two million euros.

On their return to Carrickross, Sapphire was escorted straight to bed by her grandmother who had sent for her private physician. The sooner her granddaughter started back on her medication the better.

It was evident that Indigo had also suffered. He too had lost weight and there was no colour in him, except for his eyes, which glittered like bits of broken glass. But of course Indigo was all bravado, strutting back into Carrickross like he'd just stepped out of the OK Corral.

'Piece of piss,' he airily informed his cousins. 'No big deal. It felt like I was on holiday, really.'

Rossa and Fin exchanged glances, but said nothing.

'Welcome back anyway!' said Rossa, striding over. He made to do the manly thing and slap Indigo on his back, changed his mind and instinctively enveloped him in a bear hug. Indigo shook in his arms.

'We missed you,' said Fin.

'Well, I didn't miss any of you lot.' Extricating himself, Indigo mustered a weak grin. 'But I did miss a drink. I couldn't half murder a brandy.'

Not the best choice of words in the circumstances.

'Not till you've had a decent meal inside you!' Noreen came bustling over to him, dabbing her eyes. 'Sure there's not a pick on you!' She caught Indigo by the arm, steered him towards the doorway. 'Now, what about a nice shepherd's pie? Or there's some roast chicken in the fridge. Salmon, maybe? And rhubarb tart for afters . . .'

'Poor little bastard!' Rossa shook his head as Noreen's voice faded away. He glanced meaningfully at his brother. 'So what do you think now? Did he do it?'

'Wouldn't surprise me,' said Fin. 'We all know he's a sandwich short of a picnic, no matter how Grandmère tries to dress it up as high jinks. And Sapphire's loop the loop too.'

'I'm not so sure.' Gravely, Rossa regarded his brother. 'There's a big jump between being slightly off-the-wall and being a complete psychopath.'

'But he's not just slightly off-the-wall though, is he?' Jaspar chimed in, leaving the settee where he'd been making a vain stab at doing the cryptic crossword and loftily ignoring the proceedings. 'Indigo is barking. If you ask me, he's capable of anything. I'm surprised he hasn't murdered us all in our beds before now.'

An uneasy silence followed his words.

CHAPTER 19

Coppelia burrowed deeper into the plush bucket seat and crossed her elegantly shod feet on the matching footstool. On a silver tray at her elbow stood a bottle of Krug, Clos du Mesnil 1995, a gold-leaf-rimmed Venetian crystal flute and an ornate box of Belgian chocolates, hand-made especially for her. She would treat herself to one, no more, and possibly leave half of that. One didn't keep *soignée* by wolfing fat-laden carbohydrates.

Four million pounds' worth of Gulf Stream IV jet-propelled opulence – hers in return for a phone call. All thanks to the generosity of one of her old flames, a Texan oil magnate. For the price of the odd for-old-time's-sake shag whenever their paths crossed, she still had access to his seventy-two-foot Tayana yacht in Puerto Banus, his thousand-acre ranch in Kentucky, gothic-style, twenty-roomed mansion in the Hamptons, ski lodge in Val d'Isere, chateau in *la belle* Provence and any amount of holiday apartments and villas scattered all over the world. And, of course, the jet!

'Will that be all, Mrs Morrison?'

Coppelia ran an assessing eye over the young air steward: mid-twenties, good body, toned but not muscle-bound, dirty-blond hair, slightly long, big grey Bambi eyes, definitely worth fucking if the journey proved too tedious. She smiled to herself. That was one of the things men found so fascinating about her, her total elegance and femininity, coupled with a mouth like a navvy when she felt so inclined.

'Mrs Morrison?' the steward repeated. 'Will that be all?'

'For the present.' Coppelia licked her lips, made happily aware by the way the material of his trousers strained tightly over his crotch that there was more on offer than just champagne and chocolates. 'Thank you, em . . . ?'

'Steve.' The boy swallowed rapidly.

'Steve,' Coppelia repeated, making his name sound like a caress. 'You run along now and I'll buzz if I need anything.'

As a long-standing member of the mile-high club, it wouldn't be the first time she had experienced the delights of the jet's circular waterbed and jacuzzi with a hunky young flunky. Steve could well be on the menu before they reached Morocco.

But now her mind had already moved on to other things – Carrick Granville, principally, he of the wonderful achievements. Only thirty years of age and already an acclaimed architect. So bloody what! By the age of thirty, Coppelia had experienced far more and survived far more than Carrick, in his cosseted, protected world, ever would. Coppelia shifted slightly against the kid-soft leather of the seat, already savouring the battle to come. Battle? This would be a pleasure.

The Hivernage Hotel lived up to its five-star rating with high, elaborately plastered ceilings, marble columns and sumptuous fabrics, inspired by the indigenous colours of Morocco: golden cumins and turmerics, the colour of the shifting sands of the Sahara; pale and dark greens echoes of the coriander plant and mountain-fresh mint; azure, cerulean and cobalt blues fished from the seas, and mauves, rose-pinks and crimsons from the magnificent sunsets on the endless expanse of desert sky. Coppelia had been here many times before and now the manager rushed forward to welcome her like royalty. Taking her hand, he brushed it with his lips and gave an obsequious bow.

'Ah, Mrs Morrison, welcome to Marrakesh! How very nice of you to grace us with your presence. Our humble hotel is, as usual, greatly honoured.'

Coppelia gave a bare twitch of her lips. 'Thank you, Abdullah. My suite?'

'Ready as always, Madame.' He gave a snap of his fingers, barked a rapid series of orders in French, and a moment later a porter, who must have been seventy if he was a day, materialised seemingly from the ether, loaded Coppelia's bags onto a trolley and headed off towards the service lift moving in a surprisingly sprightly fashion.

Coppelia followed at a more leisurely pace, drawing glances of admiration from the richly attired male guests milling round in the foyer and daggers-drawn looks from their female companions.

She stopped for a moment before a large poster advertising a function that was taking place that evening in the conference room of the hotel: *Building the Future – Architecture for the 21st Century*. A series of thumbnail photographs of the guest speakers marched down one side. Carrick Granville's was second from the top. He was giving his lecture that very evening. Her timing was perfect and the fates were blessing her enterprise. Coppelia's lips curved into a satisfied smile. Bless Fin and his big informant's mouth. Little did he know how her ears had pricked up when he'd divulged the little snippet that Carrick was lecturing at this conference – too busy concentrating on his own prick, of course, to notice how his words had affected her or to realise that the sudden flame that ignited in her eyes had nothing whatsoever to do with his sexual prowess. Even as she crested the wave of a magnificent orgasm, her head was already off in Morocco scheming and dreaming. And now her body had followed it all the way to the penthouse suite.

Coppelia gave a cursory glance around her suite

to make sure that Abdullah was correct and that everything was as she liked it. The bed, king-size, oval, was dressed in the finest, whitest Egyptian linen. The fresh floral display by her bedside contained only her preferred flowers, a selection of delicate whites and gentle mauves, no vulgar oranges or acid yellows. The mini-bar was well stocked with her favourite champagne and mineral water.

Leaving a maid to get on with the unpacking, Coppelia went outside to her private terrace. She leaned on the wrought-iron balustrade and gazed out to where the inky outline of the High Atlas mountains and the nine-hundred-year-old Bad Jdid ramparts were etched in charcoal against a backdrop of black canvas sky. A sickle-shaped moon hung low in the sky surrounded by a million winking and blinking stars of Bethlehem. It was still hot, at least 26 degrees, and Coppelia was grateful for the slight breeze that blew down from the mountains and fanned her sticky skin. If she craned her neck she could just about make out Djemaa el Fnaa Square, where snake-charmers, fire-eaters and jugglers vied to part the tourists from their money and where a vast array of food stalls cooked up every kind of salmonella and botulism in the book.

She went back inside. The maid had gone and everything was neatly packed away, either hung in the huge walk-in wardrobe or folded away in the rose-petal-scented drawers of the cedarwood antique cabinets.

In the vast marble bathroom, the sunken jacuzzi, redolent of her favourite bath oils, was already filling. A glass of chilled rosé champagne stood on the side in readiness and a row of white night-lights in Moorish-style silver holders had been placed all around the edge. Shrugging off her clothes, Coppelia relaxed down into it, feeling the waters rise to meet her. Bliss! Closing her eyes she gave herself up to the sheer hedonistic pleasure of it, relishing the sensation of the bubbles breaking over her tired skin. So sensuous was the feeling that her nipples hardened, coppertipped, barely breaking the surface of the water. She opened her legs and felt the bubbles lap and caress her most private place. She reached for her champagne and took a sip. Her eyes gleamed, two green peridots in the soft filtered light of the sconces on the wall. She wondered how Carrick would react when she appeared in his suite. She planned to be there to welcome him when he returned after delivering his lecture. A little judicious bartering with the lift attendant had secured her not only his room number, but also a duplicate key-card. She raised her glass in a toast. Her reflection in the full-length mirror opposite toasted her back.

'To Honoria,' she said. 'May you not count your chickens!'

The telephone shrilled in Honoria's room. Rajesh picked it up, his face darkening as he listened to the voice at the other end.

'Who was that?' Honoria asked, emerging from her bathroom, a towel in her hand.

'The Hivernage Hotel in Morocco.'

'Carrick?'

'No, Coppelia Morrison. She wants you to phone her.'

The towel slipped from Honoria's hand. 'I don't understand. Coppelia Morrison is in Morocco? Surely it cannot be co-incidence?'

'Indeed not,' Rajesh said drily. 'She was calling from your grandson's room.'

Honoria let out an anguished cry. 'She is baiting me, Rajesh. Why? Why, when she knows the damage I can inflict upon both her and Ashling? Why, when I hold all the cards?' She stumbled slightly, steadied herself against the bed. 'Or, could it be that there's an ace missing?'

CHAPTER 20

C arrick hurried along the corridor to his suite, suddenly aching to get inside. He was looking forward to a nightcap, to top off the brandies his fellow-architects had pressed on him already to celebrate a very successful lecture. He was truly appreciating these few snatched days away from the pall that currently had Carrickross in its grip.

He wondered how that reporter woman would portray it. With sympathy for its inhabitants and the terrible shock they had endured upon the murder of the Kingdom Rose? Or would she approach it from the opposite angle, pillorying them for their wealth and privilege? An image of her rose to mind, taunting him, her merry brown eyes mocking him, her full mouth curling into a smile that said she didn't give a toss what he or his kind thought of her. He had no doubt but that she traded shamelessly on those gamine looks of hers to get under people's skin and elicit information from them. Well, her wiles might work on Jaspar, but they wouldn't work with him. He was no pushover. Not for Maggie O'Keefe. Not for any woman.

The key-card clicked in the lock, the light above it blinked from red to green, he threw open the door and stepped inside. The maid had been in since he left. A few lamps glowed softly around the spacious living room and there was the not unpleasant waft of joss sticks or incense of some kind. He dropped his laptop and briefcase without ceremony on the glossy marble floor. *Open Sesame,* he thought, looking round the Aladdin's Cave of a room – so mysterious, so opulent – surprised to hear the haunting notes of 'Scheherazade' playing in the background. Odd. Had he left the radio turned on?

Loosening his tie, he moved forward, then came to an abrupt halt as his eyes lit disbelievingly on a sinuous silken female draped across a golden couch.

His breath caught as she raised herself on an elbow, the copper of her hair signalling danger as filaments of lamplight caught it and turned it to flame.

'Mrs Morrison!' he breathed. 'Co . . . Coppelia? What on earth are you doing here?'

She raised a finger to her lips and pinned him with those incredible green eyes, glistening in the muted light. Her duskypink silken robe fell away to reveal her naked breasts underneath, full, ripe, luscious, setting up an immediate ache in his groin.

'Hush. Don't ask questions, just come!' Her voice was husky, laced with invitation.

Obedient, as one in a trance, he moved towards her. She took his hand and placed it on her breast, moving it gently over her erect nipple. 'Carrick . . .' she whispered, her lips parted invitingly.

A wave of savage longing possessed him. He bent towards her. Then jerked back as his brain kicked suddenly into gear.

Jesus, what was he doing? What was *she* doing?

'Oh, come on,' she coaxed, seeing him hesitate. 'You know you want to.'

Carrick did want to. Of course he wanted to. He was only human, damn it! But this was Coppelia Morrison, a woman with a most dangerous reputation. More to the point, she was Ashling's stepmother. Forbidden territory.

And with that thought the remnants of the spell disappeared into the ether. He turned his back for a moment and took a deep breath. When he turned round again, his face was completely impassive. 'Okay, Coppelia, so what's all this about?'

'Does it have to be about anything?' Suggestive, she licked her lips. 'Can't we simply take advantage of the amazing coincidence that has put you in exactly the same magical place at exactly the same time as me?'

'I don't believe in coincidence.' Carrick's voice was dry. 'Neither do I know what kind of little game you're playing and quite frankly I don't care. But, knowing something of your reputation, I doubt if I want to be on your team.'

To his dismay, Coppelia's eyes suddenly filled with tears. It was a most unexpected sight, making her seem a great deal younger and more vulnerable.

'God in heaven, Carrick! Do you have any idea what it's like always to be judged and more often than not by people you haven't even met?' Coppelia got clumsily to her feet. Her robe fell fully open revealing her long bronzed limbs and neat Brazilian. With trembling fingers she wrapped the robe round herself. 'Often, I don't even recognise the woman they're talking about, because whoever she is, the siren, the Machiavellian monster, whatever label is the order of the day, *she's* not me.'

'I'm sorry.' Carrick gulped rapidly, his eyes, despite himself, travelling down to a gap in her robe, pulled by a magnetic force far stronger than his will power. 'You're right, of course. I know enough about the press to know how vile they can be. But look . . . what are you really doing here?'

Coppelia heaved a sigh and one perfect tear rolled down her face almost as if it had been choreographed. 'You know what, I don't really know myself. I just couldn't stop thinking about what happened to that poor girl at Carrickross and when I learned that you were going to Morocco, and to my favourite hotel what's more, it suddenly seemed like the most marvellous idea for me to tag along too.' She gave a brave little shrug. 'And what can I tell you except that a kind of madness came over me.' She looked round the room. 'This place, well it's all so romantic, so seductive.' Her eyes appealed to his. 'And making love is so life-affirming, isn't it?' She looked down at the floor. 'I'm sorry. I didn't think things through. It was a really stupid idea.'

'Coppelia,' Carrick's voice was soft, 'we don't even know one another. We've scarcely exchanged more than a dozen words.' His hand ruffled his hair. 'I'm not denying you're attractive, very much so, but . . .'

Tentative, she reached out and touched his arm. His flesh burned with the imprint of her fingers.

'Loneliness makes one do foolish things, Carrick. Oh, to the outside world, I'm a social butterfly, flitting from glittering event to glittering event, surrounded by crowds of fashionable people. But, it's true what they say, one can be lonely even in the midst of a crowd.' She gave a little twist of her mouth. 'Don't worry, I wasn't expecting you to wave a magic wand and transform everything. I just wanted to be held by somebody decent and strong, someone who wasn't out simply to exploit me.'

And then, somehow, his body broke suddenly free of his mind and he took her in his arms. Oh, God, she felt good, so good, he was drowning in her, drowning in the warm scent of her body, the perfume of her tangled hair. Her skin was soft beneath his questing hands, pliable, welcoming. Urgent, he pushed her down on a thick sheepskin rug on the floor and raised himself above her, his blue eyes dark with passion.

Then the phone shrilled.

Coppelia wriggled out from underneath him. 'Hadn't you better get that?'

'It can wait.' He made to pull her back, but she resisted.

'What if it's something important? Something to do with the twins?'

'Blast!' He shot her a rueful smile. 'You're right. Terrible timing, though!'

Perfect timing, thought Coppelia.

'Hello? Yes, this is Carrick. Oh, hello, Grand-mother.'

Coppelia sat up and wrapped her arms around her knees, a small smile playing round her mouth. She could hear Honoria's disembodied voice squawking on the other end of the line.

Half-turning to look at her, Carrick's brow knit in puzzlement. 'Coppelia Morrison? Yes, she's here, but how did—' A click at the far end signalled that the caller had hung up. Thoughtfully, Carrick replaced his own handset. Then, with a groan of disbelief and growing anger, he moved back to stand over Coppelia. 'Okay, let's drop the pretence. You have some explaining to do, so be my guest.'

'Later.' Archly, Coppelia patted the rug bedside her, thrusting out her breasts invitingly.

'No, not later. Now!'

Coppelia shrugged and got to her feet. 'Oh, very well. What do you want to know?'

'Let's start with whatever it is that's going on between you and Honoria. I'm guessing your real agenda for showing up here has something to do with her.'

'Too right,' Coppelia announced matter-of-factly. 'I hate the bitch!'

Carrick frowned. 'A bit unfortunate that, don't you think, considering how your daughter is engaged to be married to her grandson?'

'Understatement of the year. She planned it all, you know, to get back at me.' Coppelia picked up a brass ornament from a nearby table, examined it unseeingly, put it down, picked it up again. 'The woman is twisted.'

'To get back at you for what?' Carrick asked. 'I wasn't even aware you knew each other prior to the engagement.'

'Oh, Honoria and I go back a long way. We have, as they say, history.'

Carrick let out a low whistle, almost of appreciation. 'The cunning old bird. She was playing us both along. You thought the whole set-up was to get back at you and she gave me to believe that it was to get back at me – or, at any rate, to manipulate me into doing her bidding. How she must have enjoyed pitting her wits against us.' He shot her a searching look. 'So what is this *history* between you?'

'Nothing you need concern yourself with.' Coppelia had a shuttered look upon her face. 'But this I know, she won't have the last laugh. I will!'

'And me and you . . .' Carrick waved a vague hand. 'This whole thing . . . the phone call informing her of your whereabouts . . . I'm guessing it's not unconnected.'

Coppelia tied the knot more firmly on her peignoir, tossed the mane of fiery hair back from her forehead and smiled brilliantly.

'Let's just say, that was a warning shot across Honoria's bows. She thought she had me on the run, but my race is far from over.' She ran a languorous hand down her body. 'Now, are you absolutely sure . . . ? I guess not. Shame. I've got a feeling we could have been really good together. Or really *bad*. Either way, it would have been a lot of fun finding out.'

When she had gone, Carrick poured himself a glass of champagne and sank down into a chair. Women! So complicated. Honoria. Coppelia. Maggie O'Keefe. Wearily, he closed his eyes, trying to blot them out, but one face kept coming back to tease him again and again.

In a hayloft high over the stables at Carrickross something was stirring, though Jaspar was lying fairly immobile on a horse blanket, an empty brandy bottle by his side. As the heavy warm scent of hay mingled with the powerful whiff of horses, Jaspar's lover was applying himself to his task.

But Seán had hardly climaxed and hit the hay when he was wondering already what the fuck he had got himself into. He should never have drunk that brandy. It was supposed to be 'only the one' to celebrate the twins' release. He was raging with himself for being so weak and with Jaspar for tempting him, the great fucking pansy!

Jaspar was worried too. Since Ehu, there had been nobody else. How utterly stupid of him to start drinking with Seán! One thing had inexorably led to another. If Ehu were ever to find out, God only knew how he would react.

Seán, meanwhile, could think of little else but Indigo. Ironically, he almost wished he was still in jail. He was terrified that he would find out about Jaspar. He would be furious, and no mistake.

After another hard day's soaking in the jacuzzi at Carrickross and schmoozing with the inhabitants, Maggie was back at Deirdre's cottage.

She uncorked a bottle of her cousin's Burgundy, grabbed a glass, located a large packet of roasted peanuts at the back of the kitchen cupboard and sat down in front of the telly. No satellite or multi-channel TV for Deirdre. The choice was between a programme on Irish farming techniques, a political debate, *South Park* in Irish or an endless repeat, *Sleeping with the Enemy*, which was already half over. No contest, really. Ripping off the corner of the packet with her teeth, Maggie poured a handful of peanuts into her palm and settled down to watch Julia Roberts setting up a bright new life having escaped from her husband, the menacing Patrick Bergin, a control freak with a passion for order. A whiff of Carrick Granville in a bad mood about this fellow-Irishman.

Inevitably, Maggie's mind strayed back to the Granvilles.

She was anxious to speak with Carrick, not only to complete her background research into the Granville family but also to do something to reverse his low opinion of her, although why she gave a stuff she really couldn't say. But it now appeared he was off on a dirty junket in Morocco with none other than La Morrison! Jaspar had overheard Honoria ranting about the whole situation. Talk about 'sleeping with the enemy'! Coppelia was clearly enemy number one at Carrickross, even if she was Mother of the Bride.

For some reason Maggie felt oddly upset that Carrick had fallen for the wiles of Coppelia. It wasn't as if what he got up to was any business of hers. It wasn't even a surprise, given that she had witnessed Coppelia wrapped around some tall dark male on the morning after the ball. Her instincts had been right all along. It must have been Carrick.

Maggie downed her glass of wine, poured another and tried to focus on the film. Julia Roberts was on screen playing a dressing-up game for her new love interest, looking cute in a variety of costumes and unbearably cute in a variety of hats. She was grinning so widely it looked like her face might split. By now she had created a new identity, by virtue of a change in address, a new hairstyle and even more importantly, a change in wardrobe. It just went to show. *Clothes maketh the man – or the woman.* Look how Ashling Morrison had seen her in Deirdre's plum-coloured dress with her butterfly decoration and thought she was actually Deirdre. But then Ashling had *expected* Deirdre to be there – she was on the guest list – so that had helped. Right location, right costume, right hair colour, right size and shape. Easy really to confuse one woman for another. An image of Ashling in her ivory Grecian robe, her ringletted hair piled high, her face slightly puzzled as she greeted the woman she thought was Deirdre, floated into Maggie's mind . . . then another images was super-imposed upon it.

Suddenly Maggie shot erect in her seat.

In a searing flash of intuition she understood.

Heart drumming, mind racing, hardly breathing, she sat there while a jumble of thoughts tumbled through her mind.

'My God,' she breathed, 'I know why the Kingdom Rose was killed.'

With that, another, more ominous realisation followed. And her heart sank like lead.

CHAPTER 21

'Ashling!' Maggie called.

Ashling was sitting on a ledge which formed a natural settee in the whitish limestone rock, a few yards down a little rocky cliff overlooking a small cove. With her fall of hair, her pale gold blouse against her golden skin, and her green trousers, she looked to Maggie like a mermaid. All she needed was a crown of seashells.

Ashling looked up, startled. 'Oh, hi, Maggie! Come and join me.' She patted the white and yellow lichen-covered stone. 'I thought you were the murderer come to get me.'

Maggie could tell by her face that she was only half-joking. She clambered down to join her. 'You definitely don't think it's the twins, then?' she asked. Below them the water lapped green, glossy and inviting.

'Definitely not.' Ashling shook her head. 'Call it gut instinct, but I don't think they did it.'

'So that would mean the murderer is still at large. Aren't you scared, coming down here through the woods on your own? And so early in the morning with so few people out and about?'

Ashling looked at her quizzically. 'Aren't you?'

'Touché.' Maggie sidestepped the question and continued doggedly. 'It's very isolated.'

'To be honest, I'm glad you came,' said Ashling. 'Although I refuse to believe we've got a serial killer in our midst, I did find myself beginning to get slightly jittery. Rationally, of course, I imagine that poor girl was killed by accident – somebody went too far. Sadly, these things do happen.'

'Possibly.' Maggie picked up a blade of grass growing between the rocks and nervously chewed on the end. 'I don't believe the twins did it either. It doesn't make sense. Why, in a house crammed with guests, would Indigo take the risk of carrying the body down from his room in order to dump her in that fountain? Quite frankly, they could have just stuffed her in a cupboard.'

Ashling winced at Maggie's callousness.

'Sorry, but it's true,' said Maggie. 'They could have hidden her anywhere – they must know every nook and cranny of that house. Her family would have thought she was still off partying and the gardaí might not even have arrived with a search warrant to Carrickross for several days – if at all. There would have been a world of time for the twins to dispose of the body far from Carrickross.'

'But . . . that's if they were acting rationally . . . You're forgetting the role of drugs in all this,' said Ashling, playing devil's advocate.

'No, I still don't believe it.' Maggie nodded shrewdly. 'It would take bucket-loads of crack for Indigo Granville to forsake his native cunning to that extent.'

'True. They've probably built up something of a tolerance.'

'So we're both in agreement on that much.' Maggie cleared her throat and Ashling looked at her enquiringly, sensing she was gearing up to something.

Maggie flipped the blade of grass away. 'Right, Ashling, I have a confession to make. I actually came to Carrickross today specifically to look for you.' She took a deep breath. 'You're not going to like this but I need to tell you regardless. Something struck me last night.'

'Go on.'

She had Ashling's full attention.

'It's going to come as something of a shock,' Maggie warned.

Ashling lifted her chin, as if to ready herself. 'Oh, come on, spit it out, Maggie. Whatever it is, it can't be that bad surely?'

'Oh, but it is. It's very bad . . . because . . . I believe that *you*, and not the Kingdom Rose, were the killer's real target.'

'Rubbish!' Ashling's shock was evident on her face. 'Why would you say such a crazy thing?'

'Please!' Maggie said. 'Just listen to me. You and Kate O'Leary looked pretty similar that night. Slim figure, same height and hairstyles – "Black Irish"

303

looks – dark hair, blue eyes, pale skin – Grecian-style dresses in a similar shade, simple jewellery. Kate was even wearing a crystal ring that could have been mistaken for an engagement ring.'

'Coincidence!' There was an edge of hostility in Ashling's voice. 'There were others there who weren't dissimilar either. No one who knew me could make such a mistake.'

'All cats are grey in the dark,' Maggie pressed on. 'And it must have been lightning quick, to prevent her crying aloud – there were guests sleeping all over the place – and he would have attacked from *behind* – putting all his effort into the act itself, not into IDing his victim.'

Ashling looked bewildered. 'But why me? Who would want to murder me? No, it's all nonsense. It makes no sense whatsoever!'

'Ah, but it does,' Maggie said softly. 'Think about it, Ashling. If your marriage to Rossa goes ahead, *someone* is going to lose out on a great deal of money. Money! One of the main motivators for murder.'

'Balls! So you're implying that one of my in-laws-to-be tried to bump me off? Carrick, maybe, or Jaspar, or perhaps all of them – were they all in on it, Maggie?'

'Oh, look, Ashling, I don't blame you for being cynical.' Maggie's heart was sinking by the second. 'But as you said, nothing else makes sense. This does! Any one of the Granvilles who stand to inherit the estate has a motive – or it could even be someone else acting out of misplaced loyalty.'

'Misplaced loyalty?'

'Yeah, like, well – Ehu, for instance, might think Jaspar should have the estate. Or Seán – according to Jaspar, Seán would lay down his life for the twins. Do you see what I mean?'

'What a load of old nonsense!' Now Ashling was openly angry. 'Whatever you might think of the Granvilles and their servants – they're not killers!' Ashling's eyes flashed and she pulled away from Maggie. 'You know, you disgust me, Maggie. The Granvilles have given you carte blanche to get to know them and, in return, you want to besmirch their reputations in the vilest way possible. But then your entry into the family was a little, shall we say, irregular. You began with deceit. Why shouldn't it end in the same way?'

Maggie shrugged. 'Look, I don't blame you for being in denial – anyone would be in your position. And I'm sorry you don't trust me, but I understand that too. Ideally, I would have much preferred to keep my suspicions to myself until I had some proof – but I had to warn you. I'm trying to *protect* you.'

'My ass, you are! You're a *reporter*, aren't you? What a great "scoop" you've cooked up!'

'Would that it were that simple.' Maggie shook her head. 'No, Ashling, I'm here to put you on your guard. It's my belief that somebody tried to kill you once. They may try again.'

Ashling's lip curled in scorn and she tossed her head, sending her black hair flying. 'Thought of a good headline yet, Maggie? Front-page spread, is that what you're after?'

Maggie willed herself to keep cool and sound rational. Besides, she could see fear in Ashling's eyes. For all her righteous anger, Ashling was scared. Maggie was getting through to her and that was the important thing.

'Be reasonable, Ashling. If the twins are not guilty, then somebody else is, which means we need to look for a motive. I've given you that motive.'

'And now I'll give you some. Sex. Drunkenness. Drugs. Jealousy. Need I go on?'

But no, she was wrong, thought Maggie. The Rose was garrotted, not strangled by some drunk's bare hands. Garrotting requires premeditation, an efficient, ruthless killer's method. Whoever did it had a steady and precise purpose.

'Ashling,' she said quietly, 'it doesn't matter what you think of me or my motives . . . please believe me, my *only* concern here is to warn you so that you can watch your back. Stay safe. Don't go out alone. Don't trust *anyone*. Even me, if it makes you feel better. And, for heaven's sake, don't *tell* anyone about this conversation. We don't want to alert them. It could be worth your life – or mine.' She got to her feet. 'Come on. Let's go back to the house together.'

With a little hesitation Ashling rose. They

climbed back onto the path and walked through the woods towards the house in an uneasy, if not hostile, silence.

As they reached the lawns Ashling halted and said with a certain acidity, 'I think I can manage to get from here to the house without a body-guard, don't you?' And she set off across the grass.

Stung, Maggie stood staring after her. Well, she'd tried. She could do no more. And, despite Ashling's hostility, she thought she had got through to her.

Back at the house she decided to circle past the stables and enter the house through the kitchen basement door.

'Miss O'Keefe!'

Maggie's head jerked up at the sound of her name and the ringing of hooves on cobblestones. Carrick Granville was riding towards her on The Sheikh, his jeans shoved into riding-boots and a dark-red plaid shirt rolled up to the elbows. No riding-hat. Not exactly Lawrence of Arabia, but he'd do.

Warily, she gazed up at him as he loomed over her. 'Had a good trip?' She couldn't help but inject a little irony into her voice.

'Yes, I did. Very successful. Got back last night.' Expertly, Carrick swung himself down from the saddle. 'I need to have a word with you.'

'Actually, I was hoping to have a word with you,' Maggie said, attack being the best form of defence.

'I'm supposed to be here getting the "in" on the Granvilles *en famille* – *all* the Granvilles – but everything has been delayed because you took off to Morocco with La Morrison!' Shit! Why did she say that? Damn the man! He seemed to wrong-foot her every time they met. Defiant, she glared at him.

He glared back, one eyebrow raised sardonically.

'I'm sorry if my absence inconvenienced you, Miss O'Keefe. I was under the misapprehension that my life was my own and that, of course, includes my private life.' He rapped his riding-boot sharply with his crop. She had the feeling he would like to rap her with it instead.

'I wasn't . . . I didn't mean . . .' Maggie felt a blush stain her face. 'Oh, I couldn't care less who you're getting jiggy with,' she blustered. 'I just want to do my job, that's all.'

'Which brings us back full circle. Look, you already know I don't think your presence here is a good idea. The family has had a huge shock. The last thing we need is an outsider poking and prying when people are at their most vulnerable.'

Hah, so that was his little game! He was trying to put her off the scent, worried that she might unearth something. She felt the blush die away and a real determination replace it.

She widened her eyes. 'Anyone who hasn't got anything to hide need have no worries. And everyone has been more than helpful. Well, *almost*

308

everyone.' There, the implication was clear. Put that in your pipe, Mr Carrick Granville, and smoke it.

'Well, that is exactly what I wanted to talk to you about,' he said in a tone that was mild coming from him.

'What do you mean?' Maggie was taken aback, both by his words and his change of manner.

'I've been thinking things over while I was away. I've decided I will agree to an interview with you. As lengthy as you please, with full permission to use all the material, *if* you agree to then leave Carrickross and its inhabitants in peace.'

'Yeah?' Maggie's eyes grew round. A no-holds-barred interview with Carrick Granville was the stuff of every journo's dreams. 'You're not just yanking my chain?'

'No yanking of chains, I promise. So, if you are agreeable, I would like the interview to take place on the island.'

Agreeable? Heck, Maggie would have sold her soul for the chance. Nobody, but nobody, particularly not one of the media types he seemed to detest so much, ever got the chance to visit Carrick Granville's island.

'Oh, fine, right, sweet!' The words tumbled out one after the other. She was unable to believe just how quickly her luck had changed. 'No seriously, thanks, that would be . . . great . . . yeah, really great.'

'Good.' Then he added with a grin that dazzled

her in its unexpectedness, 'It will make a change for you to see me in my natural habitat.'

'This isn't it, then?' she asked, indicating their surroundings.

'No,' he said as he mounted The Sheikh in one fluid movement. 'Maybe once, but not now . . .'

'Okay, whatever.' Maggie nodded, half-smiling.

'I'll be in touch then.' He smiled.

As Carrick rode off he hoped he had made the right move. The trip to Morocco and successful delivery of his lecture had cleared his head of much of the stress he had felt since the murder – and, indeed, since hearing about Rossa's engagement. And the encounter with Coppelia Morrison had forced him to rethink a number of issues. One of those issues was Maggie O'Keefe. Somehow he now felt his animosity towards her was out of proportion. In real terms, what had she actually done that was so terrible? Gatecrashed the Midsummer Ball – like no one ever had before? If anything she was gutsy, a trait that was to be admired.

That night, his thoughts filled with Maggie once more, Carrick found it hard to drift off to sleep. What on earth, he asked himself for the umpteenth time, had possessed him to invite her to his island, his haven of tranquillity? He had a feeling there would be nothing tranquil about Maggie. She was the kind of woman to keep a man on his toes. The kind of woman a man wouldn't grow bored with. Musing, Carrick finally fell asleep, with the vision of Maggie once more before him, her mouth pruned disapprovingly. La Morrison, that's what she had called Coppelia. Anyone would think she was jealous.

'So, come on, tell Aunty Maggie. What's the matter?' Maggie was in Jaspar's room, trying to cheer him up.

There was a prolonged silence, while he stared at the carpet with great intensity, then his words came out in a rush. He bit his lip. 'Maggie . . . I've done something terrible.'

'What?' Her heart skipped a beat. Not the murder! 'What have you done?'

'You mustn't tell anyone. Swear? I can't tell you otherwise.'

'I swear,' she said and felt like crossing her fingers behind her back like a child.

Tears sprang to Jaspar's eyes. 'I feel so ashamed,' he said, his voice breaking. 'I – I had sex with Seán!'

'*What?*' Whatever she had been expecting, it certainly wasn't that. Maggie pulled back and gaped at him. '*Seán?* Handyman Seán? Noreen's son, Seán?'

'See – you're shocked.'

'Well, yes, I am really. I mean, I thought you were truly in love with Ehu!'

'I am! I am! That's what's so appalling! What if he finds out?'

'Is that likely? Does Seán kiss and tell?'

'No. Absolutely not. He's terrified of losing his job and having to leave Carrickross. But, even more than that, he's terrified of Indigo finding out. He's even taken to threatening me about what he'll do to me if I spill the beans. I don't blame him. *I'm* terrified of Indigo finding out! Indigo can be very cruel. Ruthless. Truly, Maggie, he's capable of anything.'

Maggie frowned. 'So Indigo has a . . . a proprietary interest in Seán?'

'You better believe it! He owns him, body and soul. As does Sapphire. They don't like sharing their toys with anyone else – except each other, of course. Seán is absolutely obsessed with them and it would kill him if they decided to shun him. I told you before – he'd do anything for them.'

Even commit murder? wondered Maggie.

'Well, look,' she said, pouring oil on troubled water, 'what Ehu doesn't know won't harm him. My advice is to keep your mouth shut. Why tell him and break his heart? You can make it up to him in some other way. If Seán keeps shtum, as you believe he will, then you're home and dry.'

'Home and dry? With Seán making strangling gestures with his hands every time he catches sight of me? With a murderous look on his face! Like – like it was all my fault and he was the innocent victim. You know what, Maggie, I'm beginning to think it was *he* who throttled the Kingdom Rose!'

Jesus, was it possible? He certainly sounded twisted enough and his morals were undoubtedly questionable! Just suppose he'd had sex with Kate O'Leary and then, terrified that Indigo would find out, he'd throttled her? No, too farfetched! Besides, that idea flew in the face of her theory that Ashling was the intended victim. Still . . .

Intent on his own problems, Jaspar claimed her attention once more. 'But never mind all that. I do believe you're right. What's the point in telling Ehu? And I'll think of a stupendous way to make it up to him. Thank you, my dear.' And with that he embraced her, giving her a great smacking kiss on each cheek.

The door opened and Ehu entered.

'I was just leaving,' Maggie said diplomatically as Jaspar, beaming like a lighthouse, rose to greet his beloved.

'Priti, this has got to stop,' Rossa raged. It was the end of yet another phone call from his Thai lover. 'You must stop phoning me every five minutes! You're going to fuck everything up.'

'*You* fucking everything,' Priti spat sourly. 'I want see you, Rossa. I fed up being you dirty secret!'

Rossa groaned. 'Oh, be reasonable. I can't be in two places at once. Your jealousy is going to ruin everything. Can't you just sit tight and plan what you're going to do with all that lovely money?'

'No!' Priti roared and he could just imagine her stamping her small foot. 'I don't want money. I want *you*!'

'And I want you,' Rossa hissed. 'But to *afford* you I *need* money. Get it?'

'*I* get money,' Priti said, expertly winding him up as only she knew how. 'I go back to work in the bars, like when I met you, Rossa. Plenty of men with plenty of money.'

'Never!' Rossa was incensed by the idea, as well she knew he would be. 'I'm not having anyone else putting his stinking hands on you!'

'Pah! But it's okay for you to put your stinking hands on that bitch-woman in Ireland, eh?'

'For us, goddammit! For you and me.' He desperately hoped she hadn't rumbled his recent change of heart towards Ashling.

'But I just tell you I don't want that money,' Priti said, not unreasonably. 'So, no need for you to marry, eh?' She paused to let her words sink in. 'But if you still want marry her, then must be because you love her.' She paused again.

The silence was like icy water trickling down his neck.

Then Priti sing-songed down the line. 'So, honey, who you gonna choose?'

Ashling. He could just choose Ashling. That would put an end to all this. He'd have the girl, the estate, the Carrickross fortune. But somehow he couldn't bring himself to make that decision, to say the words that would cut him off from Priti for ever. It wouldn't be fair. At the very least he should tell her in person. Even as the thought formed in his mind, Rossa knew he needed to see

314

Priti for a very different reason. The very thought of her brought a bulge to his pants.

'Listen,' he said now, 'I don't know when I can come back to Hua Hin, but here's an idea. Why don't you take a flight and come and meet me somewhere closer – somewhere in Europe, anywhere you want!'

'Really?' Like a child being offered a special treat, Priti immediately sounded happier. 'Oh, honey, Priti would like that so much. Priti would be *so* grateful.' Her voice held a wealth of tantalising sexual promise.

'Great! So name your city!'

'Lonnon!' she said without hesitation. 'I always want see Lonnon. They got good shopping there. Nice shoes.'

Rossa groaned. He had been hoping she would say Istanbul, Athens, Venice, even Vienna! The further away from Ireland and Carrickross the better! London was far too close for comfort. 'London, Priti? Why London? It's a cold grey place. Why not Athens? Istanbul?'

'I got blue skies every day, Rossa,' she reminded him. 'Sun, sun, I sick of sun.'

She had a point.

'All right, all right! London it is!'

Having got her way, as usual, he could hear her smiling down the phone. 'Okay, sexy, I see you soon! Make sure you bring you wallet!'

'Sure will!'

But Priti had already hung up.

Just then Ashling opened the door to the room and came in.

'Fine, fine,' Rossa said hastily into the phone, assuming his professional tone of voice. 'I'll wait to hear from you with – the arrangements.'

'Problem?' Ashling asked as he put down the phone with a sigh.

'Kind of.' Rossa rolled his eyes. 'Bloody work! I'm sorry, angel, but I may have to go away for a couple of days. Half of the chaps have gone down with some lurgy or other and it's all hands on deck. They promised they won't call on me unless it's absolutely necessary.'

Ashling's face dropped. 'Oh, what a shame! Still, I expect you can't let them down and you've got to protect your career prospects.'

'Exactly. By the sweat of one's brow, and all that.' Excited by the prospect of seeing Priti, Rossa held out his arms. 'Now come here and I'll show you exactly how this man intends to work up a sweat on his brow and everywhere else.'

Later he lay and watched her sleeping, her beautiful face peaceful and serene, slightly flushed from their lovemaking, the contrast so marked in comparison to Priti, who, even whilst asleep, gave the impression of being a seething cauldron of unchecked emotion. In an ideal world, he would have both, one to balance out the other, one to soothe, one to excite. But, despite managing to fool himself for five minutes or so, he realised it wasn't an ideal world and such a choice did not exist. Peace of mind or a constant challenge? The known versus the unknown? Ashling, the safe harbour in which to weigh anchor; Priti, deep unexplored uncharted waters. Rossa was an adventurer. The choice was already made.

'I do love you, you know,' Rossa whispered, leaning over to gently lift a stray strand of hair away from where it lay on the sleeping Ashling's cheek. But Priti is my oxygen, he thought. Ashling deserves a man who will love her and only her. I can't give her that.

CHAPTER 22

Honoria waited in her sitting room, gazing from the balcony towards the stand of Scots pines where Indigo was walking, his arm lightly draped around Sapphire's shoulders. Since his sister's little breakdown, as they tactfully alluded to it, at the garda station, he had been more protective than ever.

'Rani.'

Honoria turned.

'Coppelia Morrison has arrived. She is in the library.'

Honoria frowned. 'I had hoped never to set eyes on her again.' She searched his face, looking for answers she knew he didn't have. 'What did I miss, Rajesh? There is something we have overlooked. When she phoned me earlier she sounded confident, her usual brazen self, in fact.' She made an impatient movement. 'Well, no point in speculating. We shall soon know. Bring the vixen here. She shall have a final hearing.'

When Rajesh returned a short time later with Coppelia in tow, Honoria was, apparently, totally absorbed in a game of Patience. Rajesh bowed and withdrew to the other end of the room.

Both women had power-dressed for the occasion. Coppelia in a tailored grey Versace trouser suit; Honoria in severe black Dior. Diamonds winked at Coppelia's throat and ears while a collar of pearls encircled Honoria's withered neck. Coppelia's luxuriant mane was tamed into a chignon held at the back by a fine net, equestrienne style; Honoria's pulled back into a bun, highlighting the clever, sharp angles of her face.

'So,' Honoria came straight to the point, 'you dare to renege on our deal? You should be far far away in some remote corner of the world by now licking your wounds. Yet you are not. What kind of madness tempts you to risk your daughter's happiness and peace of mind? What lunacy possessed you to fornicate with my grandson – *knowing* I can destroy you?' The sentence ended on a savage note.

'So many questions, Honoria,' Coppelia smirked, enjoying the barely concealed rage and frustration in the old woman's eyes, 'so little time. But I'll answer your last question first. Carrick is very . . . let me put this delicately . . . fuckable.' She flicked an imaginary piece of lint off her bosom. 'But I want you to know it meant nothing, nothing at all. I was merely toying with him and, by extension, toying with you.' Suddenly her eyes flashed fire. 'But the time for playing games is over. Today, Honoria, *I* am the one calling the shots. Be in no doubt of that.' Imperious, she clicked her fingers. 'You,' she said to Rajesh, 'you had better come here too. I think you'll be most interested in what I have to say.'

As Rajesh came forward, her eyes flicked from one to the other. Theatrically, she drew herself up.

'But first, I want you to take a long hard look at me and I want you to remember the last time you saw me. You thought I was beaten, that you had laid me low. And, admittedly, you did take the wind out of my sails, Honoria. I had no idea you knew about Ashling. Full marks, that was very clever – but not as clever as I have been!' Elated, she watched a look of barely concealed alarm pass between them. 'Now, why don't you both sit down while I tell you a story? You'll like this, Rajesh. It is a love story set, of all places, in your own country, India – and, as with all good love stories, our lovers are star-crossed. She is beautiful, an Irish woman, lonely, unhappily married and many miles from home. He, I'm guessing, is another ex-pat, the lady being an arch-snob and unlikely to dally with one of the natives – except, of course, when dishing out the orders.' She threw Rajesh a sneering look. 'You know the type, Rajesh. In any case, Cupid's arrow finds its mark and soon they are head over heels in love. They make assignations. Secretly, they bathe together in azure creeks and make love under azure skies. But then, disaster!' Coppelia grinned, hugely enjoying the drama of her own narrative and the obvious

320

impact on her listeners. 'Can you guess what comes next? That's right, the woman falls pregnant. She cannot keep the child. Her husband will know it's not his. He has, after all, been seriously ill, with neither the energy nor the inclination to engage in a spot of rumpy-pumpy.' The smile faded from Coppelia's face. 'But, of course, I may be embellishing the tale, romanticising what may simply have been a seedy drunken encounter with a one-night-stand. Who knows? Not I. But this I do know, there was a child.' She paused for dramatic effect, gazing at them like judge and jury. 'Oh Honoria, even you must appreciate the delicious irony of it. You uncovered the secret of my child – and I uncovered the secret of *yours*. Checkmate!'

She stood there for a few moments, savouring the utter shock displayed on their faces. But, by nature a consummate actress, Coppelia Morrison knew a good exit line and she had just delivered it. Turning on her heel, she walked out the door.

Had she waited just a moment longer, she would have been gratified to see Honoria slump in her seat, as though the bones in her body had melted clean away.

Agonised, she let out a cry. 'How, Rajesh? *How* did she find out? Nobody knew. I was certain of it. And now she will use my own deepest, darkest, most painful secret to ruin me!'

His eyes glittering with rage, Rajesh stalked over to the window, pressed his hands against the coolness of the glass and glared unseeingly into the distance.

'I will not let her harm you,' he said. 'Coppelia Morrison is dead. Do not trouble yourself.'

CHAPTER 23

Coppelia sat by her window, staring out into the night. The encounter with Honoria had left her feeling keyed up and unable to sleep. The moon, one quarter full, sat high in the sky, murky and unpolished, its brilliance dulled like a silver coin left too long in a child's piggy bank. Jigsaw-shaped clouds raced across its surface, sometimes obliterating it completely. Only one star, the North Star, shone brightly.

Her eyes cut a swathe through the woods towards Carrickross, although it was too dark to see anything more than the odd stripe of orange light through the branches of the intervening trees. A poem from her childhood tugged at the corners of her mind. *Tyger! Tyger! burning bright in the forests of the night, what immortal hand or eye dare frame thy fearful symmetry?* Honoria was a tiger. Patiently she had stalked Coppelia down through the years, waiting till the time was right to pounce and rip her heart out. How could she have known that Coppelia had begun to stalk her too and had similarly been biding *her* time?

Bitter-sweet memories came back to haunt her,

as she thought back to the very beginning, her affair with Henry, Honoria's husband. She had seduced him, of course, if one could call it that. Seduction implied some effort, after all, but he had just fallen into her lap.

They had first met at a big race meet in the Curragh when Henry came in to celebrate a rather large loss with the traditional champagne and strawberries. Right from the start, that was one of the things she loved about him, his mischievous sense of humour. In no time at all she had secured both an introduction and an invitation to stay and 'celebrate' with him. At only twenty-three, compared to his not-far-off sixty years, Coppelia was certainly young. With her golden limbs, fiery mane and green eyes, combined with a rare intelligence, she was well equipped to go to war on Henry's heart.

What she hadn't factored in was falling in love with him. Henry was easily old enough to be the father she had never known and Coppelia was clever enough to recognise that his paternal qualities were part of his attraction. But Henry was also funny, kind, gentle and guileless, and so completely the antithesis of herself it was wonderfully refreshing. Almost before she knew what had happened, Coppelia had lost her heart for the very first time in her life. She was in love. Real love! Not to be compared with the usual lusty grapplings and sexual gymnastics that had so far passed for romance in her life. When Henry announced that he was prepared to divorce Honoria for her, it was the happiest day of her life. And then, fulfilment within her reach, the old witch had bested her at the final fence and robbed her of any chance of a normal life. Henry had 'drowned' in the lake at Carrickross and the love in her heart had died too, whilst hatred moved in and stayed for good.

Henry had been Honoria's victim, not just in the way he met his end, but right from the start. Honoria had never loved him and to his shame he'd known that. She had nothing but contempt for his weaknesses – his love of gambling and high living – which had resulted in the dissipation of his own fortune. But Henry still had the one thing Honoria wanted: the Granville name to go with the estate she had inherited, Carrickross. And so he'd sold his soul to the devil, dutifully fathered three children, and coped with the lack of affection by having one empty affair after another. Till Coppelia came along. But the price of their love had been Henry's death.

But what Honoria hadn't known, what Henry hadn't known, what even Coppelia herself hadn't known until the day of the funeral, was that Henry had left a little complication behind.

Ashling.

Coppelia arose and left her hotel window to seek her bed. Memories still surged in her head as she shed her wrap and lay down, and she knew they would not leave her.

Henry had what the locals called a 'great send-off', with people travelling from far and wide to attend his funeral. The family graveyard at Carrickross remained open the entire day to enable those who missed the church service to come and pay their respects at the graveside.

Coppelia waited till twilight to make her own visit, carefully picking her way between the low mounds of grass-covered earth and lichen-embossed gravestones to where a lantern had been left lit to show the way. Bats swooped low over-head, silhouetted against a sky rose-tinged by the last rays of the dying sun. Yew trees hunched on either side of the graveyard like little groups of black-clad mourners.

Slightly unnerved, she reached the grave and sank to her knees. An overpowering scent of lilies wafting from one of the wreaths decorating the grave almost made her retch.

Tentative, she reached out, touched the cold earth below. It was wrong, so wrong, and so unfair that someone as warm, as vibrant as Henry should be laid to rest in so dismal and dank a place. Henry, who was the very definition of life, with a soul that embraced laughter, champagne and good company. Reduced now to inert marble flesh, with only the rotting bones of his ancestors for company. Overcome with her loss, Coppelia covered her face in her hands, rocking backwards and forwards, almost keening her grief. A stone dug into the soft flesh of her knee. She welcomed the pain.

Why was it that happiness seemed always to elude her? For a short time, all too short, she had dared to be happy but in doing so she had tempted Fate and Fate was not, nor had ever been, a friend of hers. Such defiance had a price and the cost was Henry, her beloved, kind, gentle, funny darling.

Above, the sun sank and died. A night mist fell softly. Her feelings of loss mingled with feelings of guilt. Why should she be warm, with the hot blood pulsing in her veins, and her love be lying there cold and stiff? Oh, it wasn't fair! It wasn't fair! Soon the mist turned to rain and still Coppelia knelt by the graveside. She looked up only when a pebble, disturbed by a footfall, rattled against another and rolled away.

Honoria Granville stood on the far side of the grave.

It was the first time Coppelia had encountered her face to face and she greedily devoured her with her eyes, willing that the image be imprinted on her brain for ever. Then, stiffly, she rose to her feet and faced her across the flower-strewn pyramid of earth. Even in the diffused light of the lantern, the older woman was a formidable sight, her heavy, almost Victorian mourning garb and bone-white, angular face lending her a draconian look, her eyes peculiarly piercing, giving the impression that she could see right through Coppelia's flesh and into her soul.

'He is gone,' Honoria said. 'And all your tears

will never bring him back. I knew you would come and I wanted to see the Jezebel who sought to lure my husband from me and my sons and steal their inheritance. The painted whore who tried to steal away everything I had struggled to build.' She nodded, as if confirming something to herself. 'And now I have seen you and I will make sure I never forget you. And I will make sure that you never forget me either. And one day, some day when you are least expecting it, believe me, I will extract my pound of flesh.' Her eyes went to the grave. *'To every thing there is a season, and a time to every purpose under heaven.'*

She walked away and Coppelia watched her approach the great mass of Carrickross, erect, dignified, sure of her place in the world.

Pressing the tips of her fingers to her lips, Coppelia bent and touched them once more to the cold earth of the grave. 'Rest in peace, my love,' she whispered. But she knew he never would, no more than she would, until they were both avenged.

The discovery that she was pregnant with Henry's child knocked Coppelia for six. At first she was shocked, mainly because, never having been troubled by maternal instincts, she had been almost paranoid about taking precautions. But the shock had rapidly been overtaken by delight because now she had the tangible evidence of Henry's love and suddenly those previously suppressed maternal instincts came clamouring to the fore. The child would be half-Granville. In theory, he or she might even have a legal claim on the Carrickross estate and fortune. And wouldn't that rattle Honoria's cage! But as Coppelia knew to her cost, Honoria Granville was ruthless. Any perceived threat and she would not hesitate to do whatever was necessary to eliminate it. Even if that threat was an innocent child. That was why she had left Kerry and the secret little love-nest she had shared with Henry, on the morning after the funeral. If the child was to be kept safe, nobody must ever put two and two together and come up with Henry. Especially not Honoria.

Without hesitation, she threw a few things into a suitcase and took the first train to Dublin. There, she went into self-imposed purdah, venturing out only when necessity dictated. Armed with the money she had inherited from James, her former lover, she procured the best medical attention from the most discreet obstetrician in the whole of Ireland and settled down to wait.

The pregnancy itself was uneventful and after the initial three months, when Coppelia found that morning sickness actually meant morning, noon and night sickness, she began to feel physically much better. But gradually it dawned on her that she couldn't risk keeping the baby.

After many nights, tossing and turning in bed, with the scene at the graveyard playing over and over in her head – Honoria vowing to make her pay – she conceded defeat. Broken-hearted, she realised that the safest course for the child was to give it up for adoption. But it would be an adoption approved and overseen by Coppelia. If she could not be mother to her own child and Henry could not be father, then the woman and man who would have that privilege would need to be very special indeed.

In strictest confidence, she eventually broached the subject with the midwife sent to monitor her in the later stages of the pregnancy. Within days, the woman returned with the names of a likely couple. Seeing their names and reading about them gave her something of a jolt, made the adoption seem that much more of a reality and brought yet another loss that much closer. On paper, though, she had to admit they sounded perfect, exactly the kind of people she would have wished for. Edward and Margery Morrison. Good, solid, unpretentious names – he, a local politician, well heeled, not high-profile enough to attract much in the way of media attention, but with sufficient clout to ensure that the adoption could proceed on a private basis – she, a former fashion model, with a long history of miscarriages and stillbirths and an overwhelming desire for a child. Coppelia gave the go-ahead and the midwife arranged for them to come to the house.

On the appointed day, she watched covertly as they drove up to the front door in their stylish black Mercedes. Classy, but not flash. That was good. Flash always attracted attention. The woman got out first. Coppelia watched her glance nervously at the windows of the house then quickly over at her husband for reassurance. Mid-thirties, she guessed – blonde, slender, strawberry-and-cream pretty as opposed to stunningly beautiful. Her dress was elegant, designer, her heels classic court, mid-height. The overall look screamed respectable. That was good. Every child deserved respectable parents to give them a decent start in life.

The man, Edward, was older than his wife, probably by a decade or so, and his black hair was turning silver at the sides. Formally dressed for the occasion, he wore a suit, tie and spotless white shirt, which Coppelia guessed acted like his armour. As he too turned and looked up at the house, she saw his eyes were an incredible gentian blue, thickly framed with black lashes. She liked the way he took his wife's arm, protective, guiding her up the steps.

The first impression was good, which was almost disappointing, because Coppelia was looking for a reason, any reason, not to give up her precious child. But the good impression continued all through the meeting and, by the time they left, Margery was looking considerably more animated and less Bambi-shy than when she'd first arrived and Edward seemed to have grown a good six inches or so taller than his already six-foot-two. They were good people, kind people. A child would be the pinnacle of their world.

With tears running down her face, Coppelia watched as her unborn baby's new parents drove away. She prayed she had made the right decision.

For almost two years, Coppelia followed her daughter's progress from afar. Edward and Margery sent photographs, crowing with delight over Ashling's small achievements, every wave of her fat baby fist or smile on her chubby face was carefully recorded and regurgitated for Coppelia's benefit. They were appeasing her, she knew, living in fear that she would change her mind and come storming into their settled, happy family home, demanding her baby back. And they were right to be nervous. Sometimes Coppelia wanted to do precisely that. It was only the ever-present vision of Honoria Granville that restrained her.

And then the dream fell apart. Margery, her body already weakened from the strain of repeated miscarriages and stillbirths, contracted ovarian cancer and died when Ashling was just shy of her second birthday. At first Coppelia was devastated at the unravelling of her carefully laid scheme. Ashling needed both a mother and a father. That had always been the plan. She had wanted something different for her daughter. The security she, herself, had craved but never had. But how to achieve that now, given this latest obstacle? Then one night, unable to sleep for worrying, she picked up a copy of Jane Austen's *Pride And Prejudice* and

started to read. *It is a truth universally acknowledged that a single man in possession of a good fortune
must be in want of a wife.*

Coppelia rocketed up in the bed. Of course! The
solution was right under her nose. Wasn't it equally
true that a widower in possession of a small child
must be in want of a wife? And who better to fulfil
the role? The more Coppelia pondered the matter,
the more she realised this could be a win-win situation all round. Edward would get a brand-new
wife – he already admired her, she had seen it in
his eyes when they met – and Ashling would get
a brand-new mother. The beauty was that, apart
from Edward who would not be anxious to publi-
cise the somewhat dodgy adoption of his daughter,
nobody else would know that she was Ashling's
real mother. If Honoria should ever stumble across
her, she, like everyone else, would believe that
Coppelia was the girl's stepmother and Ashling
would be safe. Her lips curved in a satisfied smile.
She would let a decent amount of time elapse and
then, with apologies to the late Margery Morrison,
she would move in for the kill. Coppelia Morrison!
It had a rather nice ring to it.

CHAPTER 24

A more than usually frail-looking Honoria sat on a recliner on the lawn at Carrickross, watching the younger members of the family playing a game of croquet with an old set they had unearthed from somewhere or other. The sun was already sinking and leaving long shadows on the grass.

On the face of it they were just like any other family – just that bit better looking, that bit richer and, Honoria couldn't help but reflect bitterly, that bit more complicated.

Speculatively, her eyes went to Rossa who was playfully threatening Ashling with his wooden mallet. He was flying back to Thailand in the morning to cover for colleagues who had fallen ill. Or so he said. Ashling might fall for that but Honoria wasn't fooled. Not that it mattered any more. Soon she would have to make the announcement that the wedding was off, without revealing the fact that Rossa and Ashling were blood relatives or that she had known of this all along. She had used that knowledge as a stick to beat Coppelia with, never for one moment dreaming that Ashling's mother had in her possession a far deadlier weapon. Of course, the ideal solution would be for Ashling to somehow discover Rossa's true colours and call it off herself. A swifter end would be for Honoria to renege on her deal with Rossa, thus removing his motive for marrying Ashling. He shouldn't be too surprised – after all, she had changed her mind before and Carrick had become the loser.

Her gaze shifted to her eldest grandson, who, judging by body language alone, seemed to be engaged in some kind of altercation with Maggie O'Keefe. His dark head bobbed up and down furiously, his hand slicing through the air to emphasise some point. Silly, silly boy! In love at last and unable to recognise it. But why couldn't the vivacious Maggie have come on the scene a little sooner? Everything would have worked out so naturally and so differently. And what lovely children they would have! Honoria could visualise them now, some raven-haired like Carrick, some inheriting the distinctive wine-red curls of their mother. Laughing brown eyes or thoughtful blue ones. Bright, articulate, a combination of both their parents. She wished fervently she could be around to meet them.

There was a sudden cheer and Honoria shaded her eyes to see what all the commotion was about, then quickly looked away again as she saw Jaspar envelop his Maasai lover in a joyful embrace. Ah, well, nothing to be done there, of course. Some things one simply had to endure.

Just as one had to put up with the twins, Sapphire and Indigo, sitting under a nearby tree, thick as thieves and no doubt plotting further mischief. Their stay in custody didn't appear to have done them any long-term harm and both were confident that they would be cleared of the murder of Kate O'Leary, despite the police being no nearer to finding any other suspect. As she watched, Indigo rose to his feet and pulled Sapphire to hers, the sun forming a halo round both their golden heads. *Fallen angels*, she thought, her eyes following them till they disappeared from sight into the shadow of the rhododendrons.

'Grandmère? Are you all right?'

A shadow fell across her, blocking out her light. Once, in a distant land, in a happier time, another shadow had fallen across her at the foot of an old banyan tree. And her world had fallen off its axis and rolled away into madness.

'Are you warm enough? Would you like a drink?' Fin was standing there looking concerned.

She smiled and pointed to an empty sun lounger next to her. Until a short while ago it had been occupied by Rajesh, but he had left to consult with Noreen about something or other.

'No, thank you, Fintan. But perhaps you can keep me company for a while.' She smiled at this youngest and least complicated of her grandsons. He and he alone had never given her a moment's cause for concern. Despite his nonchalant attitude to his schooling, she was confident he would excel in his Leaving Certificate examination.

Fin plopped down on the lounger. He felt mellow and relaxed. For a short while he had been worried that Carrick had replaced him in Coppelia's affections, but she had assured him that her dealings with his brother had been strictly business. Her dealings with him, on the other hand, were strictly pleasure. And the fact that Carrick, despite trying to hide it, was more interested in Maggie O'Keefe certainly seemed to give that credence. Fin looked forward to having further reassurance tonight: long, delightful, physical reassurance. Stretching out his arms up above his head, he soaked up the last rays of the sun. All was well with Fin's world and he could afford to give the old girl some attention.

'So, Grandmère,' he said, 'fancy a game of croquet before dinner?'

Honoria reached across and patted his hand gently. 'I think my days of game-playing are over.' She smiled sadly. 'These days, I always seem to lose.'

From her seat at the top of the table, Honoria eyed Jaspar with distaste. He had arrived for dinner just as the main course was being cleared away.

'Sit down, Jaspar,' she commanded in a voice of steel. 'We delayed dinner on account of your tardiness and then had to eat without you. No, Noreen,'

337

she added crisply as the cook hesitated before removing the remains of the roast, 'Jaspar will *not* be eating. You may serve dessert.'

'But, Mother,' Jaspar lowered himself into a chair next to Fintan at the other end of the table, clearly more than a little sozzled, 'the twins aren't here yet and I—'

'The twins are feeling poorly and have been excused,' Honoria cut across him, 'but you have no excuse. Punctuality is clearly not a word in your dictionary. Or sobriety.'

'Unlike homosexuality,' murmured Fin with a smirk. 'Speaking of which, where is Ehu?'

'Banished!' said Jaspar loudly. 'Mother will insist that I leave him downstairs, well below the salt, so to speak.' His mouth pruned. 'He's not one of the *fembly*, dontcha know? Not accepted like the lovely Ashling here – no offence, my dear!'

'None taken, Jaspar,' Ashling said with a smile.

Jaspar suddenly spotted Maggie at the table. 'Ah, Maggie! How delightful! Always like to see your cheerful face! Maggie doesn't give a damn for hypocrisy and pretension – do you, Maggie?'

Maggie grinned in response, relaxed now that she had managed to reach the dessert course without mishap, such as confusing her butter knife with her steak knife or her red-wine glass with her white.

'Shame I don't fancy you, Maggie,' Jaspar rambled on, 'but, alas, my radar is permanently set to gaydar. What can one do?'

'Spare us your gibberish, Jaspar!' Honoria thundered. 'You are a *disgrace*!'

Noreen had reappeared and begun to serve dessert while Rajesh circled the table pouring a golden dessert wine.

'But who invited Maggie?' Jaspar wanted to know, an exaggerated expression of bewilderment written on his face. 'Was it me? I can't remember!'

'No, Jaspar, Mrs Granville invited me,' said Maggie.

Noreen reached over Jaspar's shoulder to place a double-sized helping before him with a covert wink.

'Ah, thank you, Noreen! What a sterling woman you are!' He made a bib of his napkin and tucked in.

'Mother thought Miss O'Keefe should dine in the bosom of the family to properly appreciate the Granville Experience,' Carrick offered, irony ladled on lavishly.

'Bosom? A bed of nettles, more like!'

'Or murderers,' said Fin through a mouthful of ice cream.

A thought struck Maggie. 'Was there ever a murder at Carrickross before?'

'Oh, yes, or at least manslaughter,' said Rossa. 'A dismissed servant tried to burn the house down. The cook was killed, a kitchen maid and a monkey, I kid you not, brought back from Africa by a globetrotting ancestor.'

'Oh no! Poor creature!' said Maggie. Somehow

the murder of the hapless monkey dragged from his native habitat to Kerry affected her more than that of the poor cook or kitchen maid.

There was a sudden rapping as Jaspar banged his spoon on the rim of his crystal glass, startling them all. He struggled to his feet, swaying slightly.

'Ladies, gentlemen – and Mother! I have an an*nounce*ment to make.'

'Jaspar,' Honoria surveyed him with a cold eye, 'sit down immediately!'

Rajesh, who had withdrawn from the table to stand behind Honoria, visibly tensed.

'No!' Jaspar shook his head like a recalcitrant child. 'Not until I have my say. Now, do I have everyone's attention? Good! You're going to like this, Mother.' He tapped his chest. 'Me, that's to say, I, Jaspar Granville, am – going – back – to – Kenya.' He spaced out the words to give them emphasis. 'But – before – I – do, I am going to get married.' He waited for their reaction but was met with a stunned silence. 'And you're all invited! Especially Maggie, because it was her idea in the first place!'

Flushing to the roots of her hair, Maggie felt a strong impulse to slide under the table as incredulous faces swung in her direction. Her idea? What did he mean? Then suddenly she remembered their conversation when Jasper was guilt-ridden over his dalliance with Seán and she had encouraged him to make it up to Ehu in some special way. But marriage? Not in a million years!

'Nonsense!' Honoria exploded. 'Just who is the happy bride-to-be, may I ask?' Her voice dripped scorn.

'*Moi.*' Jaspar smiled beatifically. 'I shall look a treat in tulle.'

Unable to control himself any further, Fin burst into laughter. 'Which makes Ehu the groom, I expect! Well, Ehu laughs last, laughs longest, I suppose!'

'Enough! Fintan, this is no joking matter.' Enraged, Honoria scrunched her linen napkin into a ball. 'Dear God, Jaspar, what new idiocy is this? How much further will you go to drag this family into the mud?'

Slightly more sober, Jaspar set his lips. 'Mother, I am going to marry Ehu and there's an end to it. We'll stop off in Amsterdam and have a civil partnership ceremony. Carrick, you can be my best man—'

'No more!' Enraged, Honoria got to her feet. 'You will stay at Carrickross, Jaspar, and learn to live a decent life, or I swear I will cut you off with not a penny piece to your name. I will not, repeat *not*, have any more scandal attaching to the Granville name.'

Belligerent, Jaspar stuck his chin out. 'Screw you and your money, Mother. I am going to marry Ehu and there's nothing you or anybody else can do about it!'

'Hey, come on, Uncle Jaspar!' Carrick sought to bring a modicum of calm to the table. 'Can't we at least discuss this? To say it's come as a surprise is rather understating the case. Grandmother, calm down before you do yourself a mischief. Jaspar's not married yet.'

'And won't be if you cut off his money, Grandmère,' said Fin mischievously. 'After all, why else would Ehu want to marry the old soak?'

'Ehu is not a gold-digger!' yelled Jaspar. 'He is my soul mate!'

'Oh, chill, Uncle Jaspar, I'm only kidding. I'm sure he was swept off his feet with the romance of it all.'

Jaspar tried to focus on one of the two Fins that he could see. 'In truth, dear boy, I haven't proposed yet. I only got the idea this morning. A one-knee jobbie, do you think?'

Fin smirked. 'Oh, most definitely!'

'Fintan!' Honoria banged her fist down on the table, two red patches of colour burning on her cheekbones. 'Do not encourage him! That uncouth African has spent his last hour at Carrickross. Go and tell that creature to pack his bags at once and put Tom on notice that he is to drive him to the airport. I shall pay for the ticket. Get Tom to check that he hasn't stowed any valuables in his suitcase.'

For a moment or two, rage silenced Jaspar, then he gasped, 'How dare you! How dare you insult Ehu. Why, he's got more honour in his little finger than you have in the whole of your vicious old body.'

'That's enough, Jaspar!' Carrick cut in. 'Before you say something you might regret.'

But the reins were off and there was no stopping the pent-up resentment Jaspar had harboured for so long. 'Look at you, *Mother*, the epitome of righteousness glaring down the length of your nose at the rest of the world – but who's been living a double life all these years, eh?'

'Jaspar!' Honoria gasped, visibly blanching.

'Oh, yes, you vile old hypocrite! I *know* your secret!' Like a divining rod, Jaspar's finger swung to Rajesh. 'Ah, dear old Daddio, my surrogate father! Lord Protector of Clan Granville. Let me ask: what mare is in your stable? With what filly do you have your wicked way?' He widened his eyes. 'Lemme see, could it be – no – impossible – or is it – my beloved Mummy?'

A chorus of gasps rose from around the table.

Rajesh said not a word, just stood like stone, hatred leaping from his eyes.

Still trembling with fury, Jaspar concluded his speech with a final dramatic flourish. 'I hereby vow to shake the dust of Carrickross from my soles, never to return! Carrick – Rossa – you're welcome to this rotten dump. May the best man win!' His mouth scrunched up in a vicious mimicry of Honoria. '*That Ehu creature! Check his luggage for stolen valuables!*' He reverted to his own voice, low and menacing. 'I've had it with you, you *bitch*!'

Knocking his chair over, he strode to the door,

flung it open, then turned dramatically to deliver a parting shot.

'Take one long, last look at me, Mother. I, Jaspar Granville, do hereby solemnly declare that, having met the love of my life, *I am getting married immediately* and nobody, not you, not the Pope, not God himself is going to rip me and my beloved asunder!'

With that he turned on his heel, his eye falling on Ehu who had been waiting there for him but who, thanks to the heavy mahogany doors, had heard not one word of the contretemps in the dining room and was now scrabbling to make sense of the speech delivered by Jaspar at the door.

Jaspar pointed a trembling finger at the bewildered Maasai as he strode past and made for the main door. 'Ehu! Pack! Pack for Africa!' he roared. '*Now*! Say your goodbyes to Carrickross!'

Jaspar tore past a gaping Tom McCarthy on the drive outside and, fuelled by his temper, headed off across the lawns, not stopping in his headlong rush until he had reached the lake where he curved left towards the boathouse. Reaching it, he strode up and down in a fury on the paved stone walkway that overlooked the lake. Eventually his anger wore itself out and, as it wound down, his steps slowed and his breathing became less ragged.

There is no going back, he thought. This bride is not for turning. Amsterdam, here I come. Bugger you, Mother! Bugger you, Carrickross!

He halted at last and gazed out at the lake, drawing in deep refreshing breaths, reluctant to go back to the house just yet. With a bit of luck, Ehu would be getting on with the packing.

Jaspar stepped into the boathouse, his eyes slowly adjusting to the gloom. He was surprised to notice it wasn't its usual shipshape self. There were a few champagne glasses and empty beer bottles on a shelf among the ropes and tackle and one of the boats was bedecked with green and yellow streamers. He remembered that there had been a jazz band playing here the night of the ball. It looked like the servants hadn't quite finished the clean-up operation. Then, lying on a shelf as if it was waiting for him, he spied a single cigar, a guillotine cutter and matches beside it. Just the thing to soothe his nerves.

Although he had stopped smoking many years before, this was surely a gift from the gods and he didn't hesitate, just got to work with the guillotine and in a matter of moments he was drawing the spicy, peppery smoke into his lungs.

He threw back his head, eyes closed, the better to savour it and so, unwittingly, made it extremely easy for the attacker to flip the ligature over his head and tighten it before Jaspar was even aware he was no longer alone.

As cigar smoke burst from his lungs in a violent blast and he clawed at the garrotte, Jaspar was forced to his knees by the assailant. His eyes blurred as he struggled for breath. Less than thirteen seconds passed before he lapsed into unconsciousness.

Tom was standing on the gravel drive outside the house, debating whether he should follow Master Jaspar to be sure he was all right, when he heard the purr of a car engine. He swung around and couldn't believe his eyes: there was Mrs Granville's Beauford convertible creeping out from around the side of the house, Sapphire kneeling up on the passenger seat and Indigo at the wheel. Grinning, Sapphire waved to him.

'Master Indigo!' Tom's voice skittered into the high octaves. 'Master Indigo! Bring back that car at once! At once, do you hear me? Jaysus Christ, you're not insured to drive it! Your grandmother will have your guts for garters – and mine!'

Despairingly, he tore off his hat, pitched it onto the ground and stamped on it as, with a great roar, the car skidded like a bat out of hell out along the driveway.

'Bye, Tom!' Sapphire thumbed her nose at him.

Tom kicked his flattened hat away. Bloody head-cases the pair of them! Friggin' looney-tunes! The local jail had been the right place for them! Pity they ever got out!

Sapphire turned round and righted herself in her seat. 'Isn't this cool?' she giggled. 'The Terrible Two ride again, eh?'

'Just like before, Sapph, just like forever.' He

smiled and ran a hand up her bare thigh, up, up under her miniskirt.

She slapped it away. 'Mind the road!'

A warm evening breeze caressed their faces, playfully catching tendrils of Sapphire's long hair and setting them to stand snake-like atop her head like Medusa. She spat and wiped her mouth, as they drove through a cloud of midges, a big dis-advantage of an open-top car at that time of the year.

'So where would yer ladyship like teh go?' Indigo imitated Tom's thick accent.

Sapphire shrugged. 'Dunno. The Drop Inn, maybe? There's always something going on there.' It was a bit of a dive, but they'd been there with Sean on and off. It had a late licence, a bad repu-tation, and was where all the young locals hung out.

'The Drop Inn it is, then.' Indigo made a kind of lassoing motion round his head, floored the accelerator and a few minutes later amid much whooping and yelling, the twins rode into town and screeched to a halt in front of the pub.

Meanwhile Tom was dithering on the driveway, hoping against hope he would hear the roar of the Beauford coming back. Surely it would? He could hardly believe they had the gall to take it. He turned his dusty hat round and round in his hands. Little beads of sweat rolled down his brow. Those little bastards might have cost him his job, maybe even Noreen's and Sean's too. He looked to the sky for inspiration.

No sign of them. He'd have to go looking for them and hope to God he got them and the Beauford back before the mistress found out.

Minutes later, he was sitting in the jeep at the main gates faced with the dilemma of which way to go, right or left. Left to The Kerry Eden and the village beyond? Or right to the Drop Inn and the road over the mountains? Faced with Hobson's choice, Tom tossed a mental coin and turned left.

Inside the Drop Inn, with its saloon-style doors, the twins stood for a moment getting their bearings in the dim light as every head in the place swivelled to observe the infamous Granville twins, both of whom, judging from their hugely enlarged black pupils, were already as high as a pair of kites.

'What a shit-hole!' Indigo delivered the observation in a loud drawl, deliberately designed to stir up trouble with the locals. 'Smells like something crawled in and died here. Oh, sorry, is that your aftershave?' He honed in on one youth in particular.

'Fuck off!' Bristling, the boy jumped off his bar stool and took a menacing stance, making it clear he was quite prepared to punch Indigo's lights out.

'Sorry.' Sapphire quickly interposed herself between the two and shot the lad a killer smile. 'Don't pay any attention to my brother – he only got out of the zoo today.' She ran her hand down the front of his shirt. 'Besides, I need you to conserve your energy.' She licked her lips suggestively. 'After all, I might have something far better for you to expend it on later. Come on, Ind.' She dragged her brother away. Tamed, the youth subsided back onto his stool, basking in his mates' envy and admiration. The lucky bastard! Everyone knew Sapphire's reputation and the fact that she had recently been up on a charge of murder only added to her air of dangerous mystique and desirability. There wasn't a man present that night, married or single, that wouldn't have sold his soul to give her one.

'Hey, what did you do that for?' Aggrieved, Indigo allowed her to haul him away to the bar where, with a snap of her fingers, she ordered a double G&T with instructions to the barmaid to 'just set up a drip and keep 'em coming'.

'Because the night is young yet, stupid!' She whirled about and kissed him full on the mouth. Tonight the shadow of Kate O'Leary seemed very far away and Sapphire, coked to the hilt, felt invincible, irresistible, as if every sinew, every muscle in her body, was alive and tingling.

On a makeshift stage at the far end of the room, a small group of musicians were shifting about, the discordant twanging of an out-of-tune guitar signalling that they were tuning up for the Take That tribute night advertised on the amateurish flyers tacked to the wall outside.

Indigo eyed up the lead singer, who was patting the mike like he knew what he was doing. Gary Barlow? Not in a million years. But he was kind of cute and had a very nice ass.

'Hey, Sapph, what do you think?'

Sapphire followed his gaze. Their favourite game, not played since . . . since the night of the ball.

'Mm, good choice.' She nodded approvingly. 'He's definitely got prospects. Your move or mine?'

'Yours. Buy him a drink at the interval, maybe. Pull your top down a bit more. Give him an eyeful. Work it, Sapph – you know how.'

Sapphire pulled the low-cut neckline of her tight black Karen Millen mesh top just that little bit lower – she wore no bra – swivelled about on her seat and faced the group, catching the lead singer's eye without too much trouble. Slowly, deliberately, she hoiked her leather miniskirt further up her slender bare things.

'Slut!' Indigo chuckled approvingly. 'So, what's it to be? Threesome or foursome?'

Suddenly alert, Sapphire sat up straighter. 'Ah, so who's number four?'

'Hayseed at nine o'clock.' Indigo drew her attention to where a young farmer type was propping up the bar, his pumped-up muscles straining beneath a T-shirt emblazoned with the words, *Real Men Do it in Tractors*.

'Hm.' Sapphire's carefully plucked eyebrows

arced. 'In the mood for a bit of rough, are you? Seán not good enough any more?'

Assessing, Indigo narrowed his eyes, took a long swallow of his G&T. 'Getting a bit clingy these days, which is tiresome. Besides, Young MacDonald over there looks like he's playing with a full deck of pecs.' A sudden flurry of notes announced that 'Take That' were ready for action and a moment later they launched into their first song of the night, 'Could It Be Magic'. That was followed by 'Re-Light My Fire' and, on cue, Sapphire put a match to the lead singer's fire by inching her mini, Sharon Stone style, all the way up to her crotch. She knew she had him when he almost dropped the microphone.

At the interval, she went outside to the Beauford and waited, counting down from ten as she always did. On six, the door opened on a burst of noise and laughter and there he stood outlined in a shaft of light, his head twisting about.

'Over here,' she called, already moist with anticipation. This was the kind of scenario she loved. That hint of danger. The thrill of the unknown. 'Ready, willing and waiting.'

As he strode across, clearly hampered by tight jeans, made tighter by a rather magnificent erection, she wondered briefly how Indigo was getting on with his farmer boy. Moments later, as her bare bottom came in contact with the soft leather of the car seats and Gary Barlow

351

dove into her, the thought was replaced by wondering what Honoria would say if she could only see just what her granddaughter was getting up to in the stately Beauford. The idea added an extra frisson to the proceedings and she bucked and squirmed with enthusiasm beneath the singer who was proving to be a pretty good all-round entertainer.

Five minutes later, just as she was embarking on her second orgasm of the evening, the pub door crashed open and Indigo came racing out at full pelt. A few seconds later the door crashed open again to reveal Young MacDonald and a great gang of his mates in hot pursuit.

Unceremoniously, Indigo yanked the singer out of the car, leaving him sprawling on the ground with his trousers round his ankles and a rapidly dwindling erection.

'Quick! Quick! Move over, Sapph! They're going to kill me!'

Galvanised, Sapphire struggled into a sitting position, not easy when one foot in its spike-heeled boot was caught up in the spokes of the steering-wheel.

Regardless, Indigo was already in the driving seat and fumbling with the ignition. He swore as the engine refused to turn over, tried again and swore again, this time with relief, as the engine sputtered into life. The Beauford shot off but not before several hurley sticks and pool cues succeeded in raining savage blows on it.

'I take it he didn't fancy you?' said Sapphire as she straightened herself out and shunted along the seat.

'Didn't fancy having his ass pinched.' *Dear God,* he prayed, *don't let the old crock conk out, not after sixty years of reliable motoring.* If ever there was a need for speed it was now as the pursuing posse jumped into an assortment of vehicles to continue the chase.

Not half a mile on, the speeding Indigo braked vigorously as he rounded a corner – luckily, as it turned out, since he drove head-on into an oncoming jeep with an ear-shattering bang.

'Jesus Christ, Master Indigo!' the other driver yelled, jumping out – it was Tom and he was apoplectic. 'I warned you not to take that vehicle! Holy Mother of God, your grandmother's going to flay me alive!'

Other than a bloody lip, sustained by Indigo, and some bruises, all three had got off lightly. But the front grille of the Beauford was completely caved in. Ignoring the smashed headlights and mangled bumper of the jeep, Tom surveyed Honoria's car in horror.

'Sacred Heart of Jesus, she'll fuckin' kill you, Indigo!'

'Well, she'll have to get in the queue like everyone else!' Sapphire giggled, still on a coke high, as the lights of several other vehicles suddenly lit up the scene.

'Oh, Christ, do something, Tom, or I'm a dead

man!' Frantic, Indigo ran round the jeep and tried to hide.

Seeing immediately which way the wind was blowing, Tom yanked open the back of the jeep. 'Lucky for you, I was out shooting rabbits today. I'll have this lot on their way in no time.' He reached in and grabbed a shotgun.

'Right!' he yelled, as the lead vehicle drew to a halt and the occupants tumbled out. 'Who wants a taste of lead?' Shotgun in hand, he stepped menacingly forward.

CHAPTER 25

'You must come,' said Rajesh calmly, as he leaned over Honoria's bed, laying a gentle hand on her plaited hair. 'There has been an accident. But do not distress yourself. No great harm has been done.'

She had only just drifted off to sleep, her copy of *Daughters of the Empire* still on her lap, her reading-glasses fallen to the counterpane. She was alert now immediately. He reached a lean brown hand towards her and she accepted its familiar support gratefully. Stiffly, she climbed out of bed and with his help slipped on a warm charcoal-grey dressing gown and slippers. Then he lifted her boar's-head walking stick from its gleaming brass stand and handed it to her.

She made no attempt to question him, weary of the shocks and stresses visited upon her daily and loath to suffer another one. She would find out soon enough. Too soon for her liking. With a deep sigh she took his arm and once more they moved as one to face a crisis together.

On reaching the main staircase, they paused as Honoria looked down into the hall where a little group was assembled: Carrick, Ashling, Noreen, Seán and Ehu, all bending solicitously over someone who lay prone on a settee.

'Who is it?' she muttered, almost to herself.

The figures below straightened and turned as one towards the stairs, raising apprehensive faces, white in the light of the chandeliers, and she saw that it was Jaspar who was lying there.

'Jaspar!'

His head turned slightly and his eyes opened blearily to focus on her as she and Rajesh began to descend.

So, she thought, he was alive and conscious. Was he drunk? Most likely. Rajesh had called it an accident. Had he had a serious fall, perhaps?

Carrick came forward to meet them as they reached the last step.

'What is it, Carrick? What has happened? Is he drunk?'

'No, Grandmother. He has been assaulted.'

'Hmph! So who had the gumption to attack him? I applaud the effort. Considering the gibberish and insults he flung about at dinner, I only wish I had the strength myself!' A threatening shake of her walking stick signified she might yet have a go at him.

'We don't know who,' said Carrick, 'and he doesn't either.'

'Why not?' She moved forwards, the better to view the prone Jaspar.

'He was attacked from behind – he never saw his assailant.'

'Attacked from behind indeed! By one of the village louts whose company he has always craved!'

'Mother, you bitch!' croaked Jaspar weakly, clutching his throat.

'Grandmother, for God's sake!' said Carrick fiercely. 'A little sympathy wouldn't go amiss!'

'Sympathy! I think not! Jaspar, enough malingering! Get him to his feet, Carrick! Seán, lend him a hand.'

'No, Grandmother, let him be,' said Carrick. 'We've called for the doctor – and the gardaí.'

'The gardaí! Whatever for?'

'Memsahib,' came gently but firmly from Rajesh, 'your son has been garrotted. Do you not see the marks?'

Honoria recoiled as Rajesh placed a steadying arm around her. Then she steeled herself to bend over Jaspar, and only then saw the livid marks around his neck.

'We found him down at the boathouse, Grandmother,' said Carrick, 'barely conscious. He had been missing since dinner time.'

'A poacher?' Honoria demanded loudly, but her voice was shaken.

'It might have been, ma'am, it might have been,' said Seán, nodding vigorously. 'Cut your throat as soon as look at you, that lot!'

Honoria shook her head. 'More scandal!' she grieved. 'More damage to the family reputation!'

'Your son has nearly been killed,' said Carrick in disgust, 'and you think only of the scandal!'

'It is my *duty* to protect the family name!' she shot back.

'*Damn* your duty! And *damn* the family!' -countered Carrick.

'I second that!' croaked Jaspar.

A silence fell.

Honoria made no response. She stood, immobile, leaning on her walking stick, eyes hooded, gazing at the floor.

Disconcerted, they waited for the thunder to roll and the lightning to flash. To their astonishment, calm prevailed.

At last she stirred. 'Carrick.'

'Yes, Grandmother?'

'Establish what time this assault occurred as best you can. Then check where every family member and servant was at that time. Report to me.'

'Very well.'

She looked about as if only now belatedly registering the absence of some family members. Rossa, of course, had left for Thailand. 'When exactly did Rossa leave?' she asked.

'Immediately after dinner,' Carrick replied. 'You know what he's like. He always has to get to the airport hours before it's necessary. Still, that's dedication for you, I suppose.'

'And Fintan?'

'In his room, I believe.'

'Make sure that he is. But, Carrick . . . go to the

twins' rooms immediately – *immediately* – and check that they are safe and sound.'

'Em, Mrs Granville . . .' mumbled Seán.

'Yes?'

'Em . . .'

'Speak up!' Honoria snapped.

'Eh . . . my father just rang me on his mobile. The twins went out . . . and they've have had an accident in – in – um, a car accident – nothing serious like – no injuries. Only . . . well, anyway, Da is dealing with it . . .' He had dealt with it good and proper all right, shotgun blasting away.

'They went out? *When?*' Honoria asked urgently. 'When did they leave?'

'I don't rightly know, ma'am . . . I wasn't here . . . Da tried to stop them and then he followed them . . . and he, eh, met them . . .' On cue, Seán's mobile rang as he floundered, startling the company. 'Sorry . . .' He turned aside to answer it. 'Yeah?' Then he ended the call without another word. 'They're outside now, ma'am. That was my da.'

When Seán threw open the heavy oak doors a sad sight was revealed. A now abject pair of twins came moving into the circle of light outside, heads hung low, Sapphire limping along, a broken boot in her hand, Indigo clutching a bleeding nose, a craven Tom in their wake, hat twisting between his hands in classic guilty pose. Behind them, at the edge of the circle of light, the two mangled vehicles.

'I'm sorry, ma'am, I'm sorry,' said Tom, sidling forward.

'Where have they been?' demanded Carrick.

'They were up at the pub – the Drop Inn – I followed them up the drive but I went the wrong way – I went looking for them in the village first and—'

'Don't ramble on, man!' Honoria cut in brusquely. 'Did you see them leave?'

'Yes, ma'am, and I told them not to take it—'

'What time did they *leave?*' Honoria snarled.

'When ye'd just finished dinner, ma'am – I remember because Master Jaspar came out of the house and tore off across the lawn like the hounds of hell were after him. I was just wondering whether I should follow him, to see if he was all right like, when I heard the purr of the Beauford and there they were trying to sneak out behind my back, the little fuckers. Oh, excuse me, ma'am.'

Fortunately, Honoria took no notice of the slur. A silence fell as they all stared apprehensively at her.

She, in turn, was staring at her beautiful Beauford, repository of so many precious memories, now battered and broken. Next she shifted her anguished gaze to the twins. Then for the second time that night, she astonished her listeners.

'Thank God,' she said, 'thank God.'

Carrick knew exactly what she meant. This time the twins had an alibi.

CHAPTER 26

The clock on the spire of Southwark Cathedral showed the time to be just gone seven o'clock. From the window of his hotel on London Bridge, Rossa gazed out at the panorama of London, a veritable smorgasbord of architecture that would have had his older brother creaming his boxer shorts. Across the Thames the impressively carved stone-topped dome of St Paul's glistened in the rays of the early-morning sun and a bit further beyond he could see St Bride's Church, the tiered spire of which was said to be the inspiration for the modern-day wedding cake – appropriate, since a wedding was taking up a great deal of his thinking time lately. As if in stark contrast to all this history, or even in protest, the incredible Gherkin building, correctly known as 30, St Mary Axe, raised its amazing glass head proudly into the skyline, looking for all the world like a rocket about to launch.

To his left, the river, a dusty emerald green, snaked its way towards Westminster, the Houses of Parliament, Big Ben and the impressive giant

Ferris wheel, the London Eye. To his right it wended its way towards the great Thames flood barrier, passing underneath Tower Bridge and the permanently docked HMS *Belfast*, which was flanked on one side by the grim Tower of London. With its bloody history and tales of murdered princes, the Tower swung his thoughts reluctantly back to Carrickross.

It had been so nice to get away from it all, so nice to spend a couple of precious days with Priti. He turned and looked at her as she lay sprawled naked across the bed in a most un-ladylike fashion, mouth open, snoring slightly. Despite his somewhat sombre mood, Rossa grinned. She would be horrified if she could see herself. Despite her penchant for Anglo-Saxon expletives and her fiery temper, she was usually very careful to act the lady. That was part of her appeal, he supposed, turning back to the window. What you saw with Priti wasn't necessarily what you got.

As if she sensed something of his thoughts, he heard her shift slightly and a moment later, she had padded across and wrapped her arms around his waist. He felt her lean her face against his back, her breath warm on his bare skin.

'Honey.' Her voice was slightly muffled, but there was no disguising the wheedling note that meant she was after something. 'Come back to bed. Is early still.'

Rossa reached down and stroked her slim strong

hands, encountering the hardness of the diamond ring he had given her as compensation for his engagement to Ashling.

'It's no good, Priti. I can't sleep.'

'Sleep? Who said anything 'bout sleepin'?' She punctuated each word with a tiny kiss on his back.

As usual the magic worked and he felt a twitch of interest from down below, aided a moment later by her slipping one hand down to cradle his balls and the shaft of his already growing cock. Almost angry at his powerlessness to resist her, he spun round and pushed her roughly onto the bed.

'You bitch,' he groaned, falling on top of her and burying his face in the perfumed depths of her hair. 'Why do you torture me so? And why must you always disobey me? Have you any idea how difficult it was for me to get away from Carrickross?'

'I worth it,' Priti pouted, rubbing her breasts against his chest.

'Of course you are,' Rossa said. 'But God, you don't half make life difficult for me.'

Priti's eyes filled with tears. They didn't mean anything. They were simply a trick she had perfected to ensure that she always got her own way. It generally worked, on men, anyway. 'You are angry with me?'

'Bloody furious,' Rossa confirmed.

'Why?' Priti's bottom lip trembled alluringly.

'Oh, don't play the innocent. Your insane jealousy. The way you don't trust me. You're a naughty girl, Priti, and you know what happens to naughty girls?'

She made her voice tiny. 'Yes, master, they get little bit punished.'

'Exactly!' With a deft movement, Rossa flipped her onto her stomach and in another moment she was on all fours before him. His cock reared proudly, nudging against the cheeks of her bottom.

From outside somewhere came the tolling of a church bell. Southwark Cathedral? St Paul's? St Bride's? At that moment London Bridge could have fallen down all over again for all he cared.

Maggie was sitting by Jaspar's bedside, feeding him ice cream, red grapes and sips of champagne, pleased that at last he had recovered his appetite to some extent – and his sense of humour.

Ehu had peculiarly chosen to sit on a mat outside the door. The mat was no surprise – he had often said he preferred a mat to a chair. But why outside the door? Maybe he imagined himself as a faithful guard dog. Or maybe he just couldn't bear to look at Jaspar in so much pain.

She kept a pleasant expression on her face as she fed the patient but inside she was downcast. So much for her theory that Ashling was the target. It was utterly futile and groundless – unless the murderer was truly mad and practising on the

Rose and then Jaspar before attempting the big hit on Ashling.

'So the downside,' croaked Jaspar through a mouth of ice cream, 'is that my nasty little niece and nephew are off the hook. What a pity!'

'Looks like it. The twins were committing another felony while you were being throttled. But cheer up, no one else has an alibi. So it could still be a family member that tried to do you in.'

'I like it! I like it!' chuckled Jaspar, then winced and clutched his throat in pain.

'Even Tom could have done it before he rushed off to follow the twins. If he was nifty. Or Sean.' She noticed the shadow that crossed his face at the mention of the younger Mr McCarthy. With a glance at the open doorway, she mouthed, 'You think it was Sean, don't you?'

He grimaced and nodded, then whispered, 'But I couldn't tell the gardai about the threats he's been making against me – miming throttling and all that – I'm still terrified he'll tell Ehu about *you know what*. Besides, it could have been Dear Old Daddio – Rajesh – in revenge for my exposing Honoria before the whole family. All in a day's work for him.'

A sudden gloom darkened Maggie's mind as she wondered whether she was morally obliged to let the gardai know about all of this. If Sean was the killer it looked like he was set to continue with his murderous rampage. A thought struck her. Was it possible Sean was *with* the twins the night of the ball when they had sex with Kate O'Leary?

'Maggie . . .' Jaspar protested weakly.

She was dripping ice cream over his pyjama top. 'Oops, sorry!' Diligently, she spooned the remainder into his mouth.

'Maggie, to think it could have been curtains for me! Cut off in my prime!' croaked Jaspar. 'Which reminds me – there's something I must do without further delay.' He swallowed and grimaced with pain. 'And I want you as witness.'

Maggie rolled her eyes. 'You don't mean your will? Oh, for God's sake, Jaspar, you're not dying!'

'No, no, not my will – that's already sorted.' He chuckled throatily. 'I've left Mother my vast collection of gay porn.' Weakly, he raised himself on one elbow. 'Ehu! Ehu!' he called rustily. 'Ehu, where are you?'

The door opened and Ehu appeared. Almost fearfully he approached the bed.

Again, Maggie's eyes sought the heavens. What a pair of drama queens!

Grasping one of Ehu's hands, Jaspar smiled up at him through bloodshot eyes while Ehu, apparently expecting Jaspar to pronounce his last words, gazed at him, lips trembling, eyes flooding with tears. 'Ehu, my darling boy . . . will you make me the happiest man in the world by doing me the honour of marrying me?'

Ehu gaped in astonishment, while Maggie laughed. He had actually done it. He had proposed to Ehu.

'And, Ehu,' Jaspar added faintly, 'will you do

it before somebody finishes me off once and for all?'

Falling to his knees, Ehu placed his head on Jaspar's chest and cried like a baby.

Maggie made a discreet exit.

CHAPTER 27

Honoria was unable to sleep. As the anniversary of her sons' deaths approached it was always the same – she grew restless and fitful. Please God, she would be strong enough to make the annual pilgrimage up the mountain in the pony-trap with Rajesh. In her heart, she feared it would be for the last time. Next year the responsibility of scattering white roses and lilies on the surface of the deep black lake that had devoured them might well fall to someone else.

Her own death didn't frighten her. In some ways she would be happy to lay down the mantle of what had in many ways been a difficult life, made even more so recently by the murder of Kate O'Leary and the vicious attack on Jaspar. What was it about Carrickross and its inhabitants that attracted, perhaps even inspired, such violence? She, herself, was both its mistress and its slave. Whenever it had come under threat, she hadn't hesitated to strike, whatever the cost.

But now, at the end of her life, all she wanted to do was to hand the reins over into safekeeping. And had Fate not interfered, it would all have been so simple. William and David would still be alive and, upon her death, William would have stepped into her shoes and the estate would have been secure for the foreseeable future. But Honoria knew she was tilting at windmills, searching for a utopia that existed only in fairy tales and the minds of fools.

Carrick could have given her the happy ending she so desired, had his idealism not stood in the way. Stubborn fool, she both adored and despised him for it. Pray God he still might give Carrickross an heir, now that Maggie O'Keefe had so fortuitously come on the scene. Sadly, idealism was something of a foreign word to both Jaspar and Rossa. Although Fin had the makings of a fine man, he was very much a boy still, victim to his raging hormones and not to be relied upon. As for the twins! Honoria ran a weary hand across her eyes as she considered the pair, those aesthetically beautiful but fatally defective works of art.

They had been effectively cleared of the murder, thank God. The case would never stand up in court now that another near-lethal assault had been committed, one for which they had an alibi. But, if they were not guilty, then who was?

From somewhere within the house a clock chimed. Two o'clock. A light breeze stirred the summer muslin curtains, setting them to billow slightly, spectral white in the gloom. The thought was fanciful, morbid. She shivered. Although it had been a warm day, with the temperature in the high twenties, the night air felt chill, cold as a step-mother's kiss. The old saying brought Coppelia to mind. Coppelia and the Sword of Damocles she held poised over Honoria's head. She shivered again. She was old, under pressure, conscious of her hourglass running down, mere grains left. The curtains billowed again. The ghosts moved a little closer, swayed like restless souls, reached for her. She set her lips, something of the old fire coming back into her eyes. Yes, she would join them soon enough. But not yet!

Slowly, she sat up, wincing as the arthritis in her hip dug its teeth in, eased her legs over the side of the bed, then walked stiffly over to the window to close it. Outside, the grounds of Carrickross were clothed in night, palely, almost eerily lit, by a waning moon. Black on black, the trees, indistinguishable from each other, seemed to crouch like vigilantes on the perimeter of the estate, poised, watchful, ready to invade on command.

Impatient, Honoria shook the notion away. It was true what they said about the night. Thoughts became magnified, disproportionate, gloomy. Her eyes travelled across to the middle lake, over which a slightly phosphorescent mist was hovering, lending an insubstantial, illusory feel to the panorama. A small rowing boat was bobbing at the lake's edge, black in silhouette, though she knew it to be blue. *The Free Bird.* Carrick's first boat. Her eyes hardened. Left by the twins who couldn't be bothered to return it to the boathouse, no doubt.

Henry! Unbidden his face rose up before her, as he had appeared on that last night, his mouth moving silently, forming words she couldn't hear, or at least that was how it had seemed at the time. In truth, it was simply that she couldn't take them in, had no wish to take them in. The import was just too great. And then at last they had penetrated.

I'm sorry, but I'm leaving you, Honoria. I've fallen in love with another woman. Her name is Coppelia.

The words seemed to quiver in the air before her, erratic as dancing fireflies, imbuing themselves with a life force that made her gasp and clutch at the window ledge. She had begged him not to go, to stay and dine with her one last time. To drink to old memories, old times, to William and David, to their grand-children and to Carrickross. Solicitous, she had filled and refilled his glass. The condemned man had eaten a hearty supper. Then, for Auld Lang Syne, one last tour of the lake, with Rajesh in close attendance.

And Henry had drowned, swallowed up by the vast dark lake.

The summerhouse! Something drew her eye to it now. A flicker at a window. A candle? A torch? Immediately on the alert, Honoria strained to see more clearly. Yes, there was a faint wavering glow. Someone was in the summerhouse. The murderer? A sudden burst of adrenaline making her forget her pain, she shrugged on her dressing gown and went to rap sharply on the door connecting their two bedrooms. 'Rajesh?'

It opened almost immediately, showing that he, too, had had problems sleeping. Odd how her heart still skipped a beat when she looked at him, even now when her mind was occupied with other things. He was old now too, of course, though far more agile than she, his black hair sprinkled through with the essence of silver, deep lines of worry traversing his brow, not a few of which had been pinned in place by her. His eyes, though, were as bright, as alive, as ever, verdigris almost in the muted light of the bedroom.

'What is it, Rani? Are you ill?'

'No. No.' Honoria pointed a trembling finger at the window. 'Somebody is in the summerhouse. There's a light! I'm frightened.' Only now that the words were out did she realise it was true. And only to Rajesh, her friend, her lover, her confidante, would she ever admit to such a weakness.

'Sssh!' He placed a reassuring finger on her lips. 'Do not be anxious. It is only Sapphire.' He held up a pair of field glasses. 'I saw her in the doorway against the light.' He frowned disapprovingly. 'She was dancing.'

'Dancing?' Honoria's eyes narrowed. 'All alone? And perhaps with a madman on the loose. Rajesh, we must go to her at once.'

'No, Rani, I will go. I am already dressed.'

'I'm coming too,' Honoria said firmly. 'I demand to know what the child is up to.'

Rajesh knew better than to argue. While Honoria

372

got dressed, he tucked a wickedly curved, bone-handled dagger into the broad sash encircling his waist. Just in case . . .

Night rushed to meet them as they stepped outside the house, breathing mist, cold and wet, on their faces. Rajesh laid a reassuring hand on Honoria's arm, sensing her unease. His touch was enough. Confidence returned. Carefully they made their way down through the grounds, keeping to the dew-soaked grass so as to make no noise, wending through the herb-garden redolent still of the oils of rosemary and lavender diffused by the earlier heat of the day, and skirting past the koi-carp pond. When they came to the little wooden footbridge that led to the summerhouse, they slowed almost to a halt.

Suddenly Rajesh whirled round and laid a finger across Honoria's lips, a gesture that was unnecessary, given that she was already trans-fixed by the scene unfolding through the open door of the summerhouse. Candles had been placed all around the interior, throwing the naked body of one of the young maid-servants into yellowish relief. Bound and gagged, she had been tied to a chair. Plainly terrified, her eyes rolled back to where Sapphire was standing behind her – casually snipping off long brown strands of the girl's hair with a pruning shears.

'He loves me.' Snip! 'He loves me not.' Snip! 'He loves me.' Snip! 'He loves me not.' Her voice carried clearly on the night air, the lilting singsong of a child reciting a nursery rhyme.

Indigo, stark naked, except for a ridiculous Red-Indian headdress and daubs of red lipstick on his cheeks meant to resemble war paint, was dancing crazily round them both. In his hand he carried a long horse-whip, which he cracked menacingly every now and then. There were red stripes on the young girl's breasts and stomach – blood? Empty bottles of alcohol littered the floor, some of them broken, and an acrid smell hung heavy on the air. Music was playing softly in the background. Church music: 'Nearer My God To Thee'.

Honoria suddenly felt the ground give way beneath her feet. Her knees buckled and she would have collapsed, were it not for Rajesh catching her in his arms.

'It was them!' The words ripped from her throat like the agonised screams of a dying animal. At the sound, the twins froze in surprise, their faces turning in perfect unison to where Honoria and Rajesh were watching them. Tears rained down Honoria's face. 'Oh, Rajesh, it *was* them! They murdered that poor girl.' She hammered at her own breast. 'God help me, I've known it all along!'

She fell silent as Sapphire, her face lit up and beaming like a child, came skipping towards her.

'Granoria!' She presented her with a lock of the maid's brown hair. 'Look, he loves me!'

In the background, Indigo, wildly out of control,

threw back his head, pranced about and howled like a wolf. Deranged! The word clanged a death knell in her brain. Her beautiful gilt-haired, jewel-eyed grandchildren were clearly deranged. Quite, quite, unsalvageably mad! It was no shock really. She had known it for years. The difference was that only now was she prepared to concede defeat, to hold her hand up and admit the awful possibility that, throw money at it as she might, and importune the best doctors in the world as she might, the twins' insanity was here to stay.

'Take Sapphire back to the house.' Urgent, Rajesh catapulted her back to the immediacy of the situation. There would be time enough later for lamenting. 'I will deal with Indigo and the girl.'

Perfectly docile, Sapphire threw down the shears. Then, placing her hand in her grand-mother's, she skipped merrily along by her side, the tress of shorn hair still dangling from her other hand. Thank God for Rajesh, thought Honoria. There would be no trouble from the maid, she knew, no scandal ensuing, no tales of the Granvilles' madness would filter through the doors of Carrickross. The poor frightened girl would, by turns, be further frightened, bullied, coerced, coaxed and bribed into silence and no one except those present would ever know the evil work wrought by the twins this night.

But they could no longer remain at Carrickross. As soon as was humanly possible, she would send them to Sweden, to the private secure clinic where

Agneta, their equally mad mother, had once been treated.

'Come, child!' Honoria urged, as Sapphire stopped to rip the head off a buttercup. 'Come, let's go home.'

Back at the house, Honoria put her still docile granddaughter to bed as if she were a little girl, having persuaded her to take a couple of sleeping pills with a warm glass of milk. She then sat by the bedside, stroking Sapphire's forehead until the girl sank into a deep peaceful sleep.

Finally, chilled, exhausted and overwrought, she made her way to her own suite, thankfully laid her aching bones down in the comfort of her bed and closed her eyes.

But sleep, when it came, was anything but peaceful. Instead it was troubled, full of fearful images. Tossing and turning in bed, Honoria grew feverish.

Once, when she awoke briefly, it was to find Rajesh sitting by her bed, his face riven with concern.

'Rajesh.' Even to her own ears her voice sounded distant, tired, as though it had travelled a long way. 'Don't leave me.' She felt his hand cool on her forehead.

'Never, Rani; never will I leave you. We two are bound to each other, as surely as the moon is fastened to the sky.'

'Dear Rajesh,' she murmured. 'I was dreaming of the past.'

'I know,' he whispered. 'And secrets, yours and mine, were spilling from your lips.'

He raised her head gently and helped her to take some paracetamol.

Her eyes closed again and then she was falling, falling once more and the past was rising to meet her.

Rajesh sat on by her side, cooled her brow and listened to the telltale mumblings escaping her parched lips. He, too, was haunted by images of that tragic, pivotal event that still tortured her.

The monsoon had come late that year, the year Honoria had given birth. The period known as 'The Longing', directly preceding the rains, stretched out interminably. Unremitting, the sun beat down, scorching the earth to a barren dryness. It rose earlier and set later. Shade shrank to nothingness. No life-giving breeze ruffled the trees. Rivers dried first to muddy streams, then to dusty trails. Plants shrivelled and died. Birds fell from their nests, dead before they hit the ground.

In the late stages of her pregnancy, Honoria sometimes felt she too would die if the rains didn't come soon. Hot, sticky and uncomfortable in the little hideaway bungalow Rajesh had procured for them, she longed for an ending to it all. At last, like a blessing, the sky turned dark, wind filled the black sails of storm clouds and sent them billowing across the sun. Fat drops of rain splattered against the windows of the verandah. Then the rain began in earnest, torrential, great sheets shaken from the sky. The grasses, flat, brown and desiccated, turned emerald almost overnight. The monsoon had come, and with it 'The Release'.

Release came for Honoria, too, but not before pain seized her in its jaws and shook her about like a rag-doll. Helpless in the face of her distress, Rajesh did his best to soothe her. He brought cold compresses for her forehead and gently chafed her hands and feet. He massaged the cramp from her calves and moistened her lips with ice-cold water. He sang lullabies in Hindi, uttered words of nonsensical comfort, prayed to Shashti, the goddess of childbirth. Thunder banged and crashed and shook the house. The bare lightbulb in the middle of the ceiling swung back and forth, casting eerie shadows round the room. Lightning bleached the sky to silver.

Her hair and face soaked with sweat, Honoria screamed and thrashed about. Shards of darkness gathered before her eyes, slotting together, then drifting apart again, blessed unconsciousness cruelly eluding her. At last, as the world of ghosts drew nearer and the world of men receded, the child emerged, her tiny hands punching at the air, angry at the indignity of her birth, an exquisite Anglo-Indian princess.

The baby smelt sweet, like honey and jasmine. She was warm and soft to the touch. The weight of her against Honoria's breast felt right. For a newborn baby, she had a surprising amount of hair, russet and soft as thistledown. Her skin had the patina of old gold.

Honoria loved her, but that wasn't enough to save her little girl. Rajesh took her away – it was what they had agreed.

Now, so many years later, in her bedroom in Carrickross, Honoria wailed and reached her arms out to nothingness. Then she struggled to the surface, batting away the darkness that had her in its grip. Her face was wet with tears.

Light spilled into the room and Rajesh, still beside her, was grey with exhaustion but smiling.

'It is morning, Rani. Your fever has broken and the bad dreams have fled with the darkness.'

But Rajesh was wrong. The dreams would never leave her. They had been with her since the day she had watched him walk away with their daughter wrapped in a blanket in the crook of his arm. In her mind, that period of her life had become synonymous with 'The Retreat', the third and final phase of the monsoon. She had retreated too, back to her husband, Timothy Villiers, longing always for the time when she would be free to go and reclaim her Indian daughter.

CHAPTER 28

It was just after half past seven on the day appointed for the visit to Carrick's island retreat when Maggie swung off the road into the main entrance of Carrickross and skidded to a halt.

The gates were closed. In fact, as far as she could see, they were chained and padlocked. She jumped out and went to pull at the chain. No go. She was too bloody early. She tried the side gate: locked. Why hadn't Carrick warned her? Should she wait? But she had no idea when anyone might arrive to open them up and she couldn't risk Carrick taking off without her – which she believed him quite capable of doing if only to prove a point. She took out her mobile and scrolled to C – only then realising she didn't have a number for him. Should she ring the house? Not at this hour.

Nothing else for it. She parked the car near the gates and, grabbing her rucksack, slung it across her back. Then, with great difficulty, she awkwardly climbed over the side gate, nearly impaling herself on the spikes on top and tearing a small rent in her skirt as she jumped down.

Then she set off for the house, the rucksack banging rhythmically off her lower back as she strode along. The drive seemed very long and secluded. Not the ideal spot to come face to face with the serial strangler and his garrotte. She gazed nervously into the dark woods on either side of the drive.

Her thoughts shifted back to Carrick Granville and the coming trip. It had taken her an hour that morning to decide what to wear. What in God's name was the right outfit for a female journalist invited on a helicopter ride to the private island of a gorgeous multi-millionaire architect still on her list of suspects? Feminine? Sporty? Sexy? Sensible? She'd finally settled on a compromise: skimpy brown strappy T-shirt and a mid-length taupe skirt with a centre pleat, which she felt was reminiscent of the kind of safari skirt worn in decades past.

At last the house came into view. No smoke from the chimneys. Nothing stirred. She walked on and then stopped in her tracks and stared as a young guy on a bike came suddenly around the corner of the house and rode towards her. He passed her at speed and flew off up the drive. She thought she remembered him from the night of the ball – one of the foreign waiters. And now, no doubt, he was off to open the bloody gates! Blast! If only she had waited a few minutes!

She walked on and, as she came nearer the house, she spotted Ehu down by the lakeside, waving frantically at her. He began to trot in her direction.

'Hi, Ehu, what's up?' she asked when he came to a halt before her, dripping, a Maasai version of Mr Darcy having just emerged from the lake, his long white robe clinging to his skin.

His hand rose to clasp the charms hanging from his neck. 'My poison, it is gone,' he said urgently.

'Gone?'

'It is lost.'

'Lost! How?' Maggie asked in alarm.

Ehu shrugged. 'I have it before I go swim in lake. Then, when I come out, clothes still there, necklace still there, poison all gone.'

'And you're sure you had it? Maybe you dropped it earlier in the grass or somewhere?'

Stubborn, Ehu shook his head. 'No, I have it – then I don't have it. Something come take it.'

'Well, I'm sure you would have noticed if a person was mooching around. Maybe it was a dog, a bird even. Magpies like shiny things.'

'No!' Ehu insisted fiercely. 'No dog, no bird!' His eyes darted past her. 'Today, Ehu feel some evil spirit watching. Yesterday I feel him in the woods.' He shuddered, raising a forearm and pointing at the goosebumps that suddenly stood out on it. 'Look! My skin did like that!'

'You think somebody planned this, that they were actually waiting for an opportunity to steal your poison?'

'Not some*body* – a spirit – an evil spirit – or maybe a witch!'

Or maybe the murderer, thought Maggie in alarm. She laid a hand on his arm. 'Be careful, Ehu, please. You must get Tom or Seán to search with you, just in case it did get dropped somewhere. But, the poison, is it truly as dangerous as you said?'

'Very bad!' Ehu nodded. 'Nobody live.'

'Shit! Well, in that case we need to warn everyone to be on the look-out.' She gazed earnestly in his eyes. 'Look, you go and tell Jaspar and ask him to warn the family. Okay?'

Ehu nodded and loped away, drops of water still glistening on his ebony skin.

Feeling anxious, Maggie set off along the terrace, heading for the rockeries and the helicopter pad beyond in search of Carrick. She wended her way through a maze of little pathways and found him at the top of a small rise, seated on a stone bench . . . waiting, presumably, for her.

He stood up and to her surprise kissed her politely on the cheek.

She might have been embarrassed at the un-expected contact if it weren't for the fact she was so worried about Ehu's lost poison. She told him about it and, taking the matter seriously, he pulled out his mobile phone and spoke first to Tom who was apparently awake and alert and then to Jaspar who had already been informed by Ehu and was now a hysterical wreck.

Carrick flicked off his mobile. 'Right. Tom's going to organise a search of the grounds and woods and will keep me posted, so there's no need to cancel our plans. Let's go.' Lightly placing a hand on the small of her back, he led her off through the rockeries to the helicopter pad.

CHAPTER 29

Ashling had woken that morning with an intense urge to get away from Carrickross and all its inhabitants, even Rossa, for a while. *Especially* from Rossa. Since he'd returned from his latest trip, her feelings were all over the place, her thoughts see-sawing wildly from one extreme to the other. He loved her. He did. He told her so. And that made her happy. But then . . . then sometimes he looked as though he was in a world of his own, a world in which she had no place. And that worried her. Lately, she had found herself assailed by uncertainty, wondering at the veracity of that old adage 'marry in haste, repent at leisure'. The doubts she had managed to put to rest rose up and prodded her once more. Why had he not told her from the start that he would inherit Carrickross upon their marriage? It was hardly something trivial, something you would overlook, and it had placed her in a very awkward position with Carrick. It was almost as if Carrickross was her dowry. 'And would he want you without it?' her inner mischief-maker asked. Of course he'd want me. He'd love me if I had nothing but the clothes I stood up in, she wanted to snap back. And yet, she hesitated. The words wouldn't come.

On top of all that anxiety, she desperately needed to get back to Dublin and her work. Moira, her assistant, had been holding the fort well in her absence but her queries and requests for advice were increasing in volume by the day. Ashling's office diary was apparently already bristling with rescheduled and new appointments and, if she didn't get back soon, the business and her career would begin to suffer. Yet how could she leave with all this uncertainty, with Rossa behaving so erratically, and Coppelia still present, circling Carrickross like a vulture?

She was beginning to feel trapped, beginning to feel too much taken over both by the whole Granville family and the craziness that was infecting the estate. Like she was being subsumed by them. In order to touch base with herself again, to redefine who she was, she needed to be free of this house and its people for a while.

Quietly, so as not to disturb Rossa, she rose, dressed and made her way to the kitchen, where she cobbled together a thick bacon sandwich and helped herself to one of the bottles of Noreen's homemade lemonade from the fridge. She was in the stables before the house stirred, nervously saddling up Morrígan. Nervously, because no one could forget that a young girl had been murdered, Jaspar had been half-strangled and the attacker was still on the loose – and yet she simply had to get away.

It was still chilly as she emerged from the stables with the mare, eager to get going, prancing along beside her.

'Sssh,' she soothed, adjusting the bridle buckle and checking that the bit was correctly in place. 'Hang on for just one moment, girl, and then you can let loose and gallop to your heart's content.'

About to mount, she remembered she had left her sandwich and drink on a bench by the stable door. She retrieved them quickly and slid them into the saddlebag, soothing Morrígan as she did so. She was edgy too, nervy. The skin crawled on the back of her neck. She had a strong sense that she was being watched. Glancing back at the house, she scanned the many windows but there was no face to be seen and no movement anywhere.

Shaking off her fanciful feelings, she mounted and set off, waiting for the forest path before giving Morrígan her head, in case the thudding of her hooves woke anyone.

As they climbed higher and the house receded into the distance she lost her nervousness and felt the stress slip from her shoulders like a shroud. The first cobwebs blown away, Morrígan slowed to a walking pace and Ashling allowed her to wander at will. Almost before she knew it they had reached the small clearing, scene of her ill-fated picnic with Rossa. She tethered the horse loosely to a tree, walked across and looked out over the view. Only the timeframe had changed. There was Carrickross, shrunk to miniature in the distance, a plume of white smoke rising up from one of its chimneys. Above she could see Carrick's helicopter on its way to his island. She had heard he was taking Maggie O'Keefe there. Maggie O'Keefe of the vivid imagination and mad conspiracy theories. The only other signs of life were the black Kerry cattle grazing in the rich parkland. Rays of light shone out across the lake, mirror-smooth.

Miles from the house now, she decided to stop for a moment and dismount. Once more her thoughts turned to Rossa. His face rose up before her, more than handsome, with those leonine looks, that tawny-teak complexion from so many hours spent under hot Eastern skies, those amazing turquoise eyes that looked back at her with such . . . such what? With humour, yes. Thoughtfulness, yes. Interest, yes. And love? Her stomach sank. Usually, he looked at her with a kind of patient fondness. Her fiancé, her great love, the man she had promised to spend the rest of her life with, looked at her fondly. How had she not noticed it sooner? Ah, but you did notice it before, Ashling berated herself. You just didn't want to *see* it. The signs were all there. But she had been caught up in the drama of it all, encouraged by awe-struck friends. Rossa Granville, what a catch! Lucky, lucky girl to have fortune single her out. And yet, pre-Rossa, her own life had been pootling along quite nicely. She was comfortably off, had her own loft-apartment, a swish sports car and the kind of looks other women would die for. She had more offers from interested gentlemen than she could shake a stick at. *And* she was pretty much at the pinnacle of her game career-wise. Ironically, just before Rossa had popped the question, she had been given the chance to go to the States for a year to work alongside Annie Leibovitz, taking photographic portraits of the Hollywood elite. All the big stars – Nicole Kidman, Harrison Ford, Jack Nicholson. She had turned it down with scarcely a pang.

A sudden rustle in the bushes behind her and the sharp crack of what sounded like a twig snapping brought her head spinning round. Nothing, probably just a squirrel. Still, it had caused her pulse to race and reminded her again that a murderer was on the loose. She went back over to Morrígan and stood by her side, drawing comfort from the closeness and warmth of the great beast. She experienced a strong impulse to fling herself on Morrígan's back and gallop away. But she also felt a stubborn urge to stand her ground, eat her little picnic as planned and go only when she was good and ready. Retrieving the food from her saddlebag, she sat down. She ate the sandwiches to the last crumb and washed them down with some of the lemonade, though it was tart on her tongue. Upending the bottle she poured the remains of the lemonade into the grass.

By the time she had finished, the sun was riding high in the sky. She tossed a mental coin. Should she continue with her ride, higher into the pines, where the view would be spectacular from the next spur of the mountain, or should she return to Carrickross and Rossa? And suddenly she wanted nothing more than to look deep into those green-blue oceanic eyes of his and reassure herself that her doubts were unfounded and it was all down to pre-wedding nerves kicking in. Idly, she plucked a daisy, picked off the petals in clumps. He loves me. He loves me not. He loves me. With a smile, she tossed away the stalk, gathered up the empty bottle and tin-foil wrapper and went to untether the horse.

'You see, Morrígan,' she said, hoisting herself up onto the saddle, 'he does love me. Rossa does love me. Let's go home, girl.'

She was halfway down the mountain when she began to feel queasy. She wondered if perhaps the bacon or the butter in the sandwiches had been a bit off. At first, it was just a slight nausea, but then her head started to pound and sweat broke out all across her forehead, dripping into her eyes and making it difficult to see. A searing pain ripped across her stomach, doubling her over. Inadvertently her heels dug into the horse's side. Morrígan took offence, bucked and threw her rider. Winded and disorientated, the earth spinning round her, Ashling lay where she fell for a moment, then struggled to her knees and was violently sick, retching again and again. Just before losing consciousness, she thought she heard someone laugh.

'Ash – ling! Ash – ling!' called Rossa urgently, his voice echoing back to him from the mountain rocks.

When an overwrought Jaspar had awakened him with the news that Ehu's poison had disappeared, Rossa had been assailed by panic and had gone charging off to look for Ashling. Since Morrígan was not in her stable, it was an easy deduction to make that she had gone for a ride and most likely to their favourite picnic spot.

Beneath him, The Sheikh skittered and pranced, practically jumping out of his skin at everything sound, every shadow. At one point a rabbit or some other small animal rustled in the trees nearby and he shied wildly, almost dislodging Rossa from his back.

'Easy, boy . . . easy . . .' Rossa patted him on the neck, his eyes searching through the trees for signs of Ashling.

He found her a little less than halfway up the mountain path, spread-eagled on the ground, deeply unconscious, telltale patches of froth at the corners of her mouth and Morrígan quietly champing the grass nearby. Rossa didn't need to be a doctor to know that Ashling had been poisoned.

★   ★   ★

'It's all my fault!' Rossa dropped his head in his hands as, siren blaring, Ashling was driven away in the ambulance. 'It would never have happened if it wasn't for me and my selfishness.'

'Fuck's sake!' Fin said in alarm, starting up the car to follow it. 'It's probably just food poisoning or a bug or something. She might even have been thrown from Morrígan and hurt her head. Accidents do happen, you know.'

'No, you're wrong.' Rossa slammed his fist against the wall, relishing the pain. 'It's all down to me. I got her into this mess. I should never—'

'Jesus!' Fin rolled his eyes. 'Quit the emotional disembowelment, will you? It's not helping.'

'You're right.' Rossa fell silent, but inside an awful suspicion was gathering.

CHAPTER 30

The helicopter ride had been quite brief, Carrick's special lake and island being near. Though the first nosedive, which Carrick performed quite nonchalantly to point out a stag on a rise below, was enough to scare her to death, Maggie was soon breathless with delight as she viewed the lake and woodland through the pristine glass floor of the chopper.

They swooped over a mountain ridge and her stomach lurched for a moment.

'My lake!' Carrick pointed downwards.

Then the island came into sight, quite small, thickly wooded, almost perfectly round apart from the minor indentations of tiny coves. Shortly afterwards they landed on a helicopter pad, which from above had looked no bigger than a coin.

The silence when the noise of the machine subsided was delicious to Maggie's ears. She was surprised to find herself quite rubber-legged when Carrick helped her to alight and she sat on a flat rock taking in her surroundings while Carrick busied himself with checks around the copter. The landing-pad was on a low-lying grassy open area by the edge of the water but no more than twenty feet away a track led into thick woodland.

Maggie twisted around and looked out over the lake, hemmed in by mountains on the far side. She heard Carrick approaching and turned round – to find herself confronted by a slavering panting monster of a beast. Two beasts.

'Wolfhounds!' she said, in stupefaction.

'Meet Barakiel,' said Carrick, smiling, 'one of the seven archangels, who has dominion over lightning. Barakiel! Bow down!'

The giant grey dog bowed, head on forepaws.

'And this is Zerakiel. The name means "God's command". Zerakiel's job is to lead souls to judgement. Zerakiel! Bow down!'

The second dog bowed and Maggie laughed. 'I know I'm crazy, but you are quite quite mad!'

'They won't rise until you give them permission. Touch their heads.'

'Arise, Sir Barakiel!' said Maggie, laying a hand on his shaggy head. He sprang to his feet. 'Arise, Sir Zerakiel!' At a touch Zerakiel sprang up.

'Zera is actually a girl,' grinned Carrick.

'Lady Zera then.'

'Zera and Bara for short. The Irish wolfhound motto: *Gentle when stroked, fierce when provoked.*' He gave her a meaningful look, eyes glimmering with what looked suspiciously like laughter.

Maggie reddened at the implication. First blush of the day. She tried to distract his attention away from her burning cheeks. 'So, who looks after them?'

'Me, during the summer if I'm home, but if I'm coming and going all the time there's an older clone of Tom who rows out and stays here as caretaker – and in winter we batten down the hatches and they come back to Carrickross with me. Does that meet with your approval?'

Good, her cheeks had cooled. 'I won't be calling the ISPCA just yet.'

He pulled her to her feet. 'Right, let's go.'

And with the long-legged Bara and Zera lolloping before them, they walked into the trees.

A few minutes later she gasped as the house came into view. Nothing had prepared her for the flair and originality of the building before her, with its glowing honey-coloured wooden walls, its great glass windows fronting the lake and the high steep white roof with its overhanging eaves, which seemed to float above the building rather than be attached to it.

'It's like a ship somehow!' she exclaimed. 'It's poised there, looking as if it's just about to move – like a ship on the point of being launched into the lake!'

'Got it in one!' said Carrick, looking genuinely pleased. 'Come inside and you'll see just how right you are.'

As they climbed the stone steps and entered the house she saw that her impression was correct. The roof *was* floating, suspended above the structure by wooden rafters.

Carrick allowed her to take it all in, soaking up

her pleasure. She gazed in delight at the lofty airy interior. Light poured in through large velux windows, making the whole interior glow. The timber frame of the house crested overhead – there were three great arches, shaped like church windows – again making her feel as if she were on the polished deck of a sailing ship with the masts and sails rising above her.

'Well?' he asked, looking at her intently.

'Wow!' Maggie used her favourite expression of awe. 'Wowee!'

'The cruck frame,' he pointed at the great wooden arches, 'is made from curved pieces of oak – this was how many medieval buildings were constructed. Of course, in those days they really knew how to work wood.'

Light glimmered everywhere on the polished wooden surfaces, and Maggie couldn't resist stroking them, instinctively knowing without asking that everything had been lovingly hand-carved.

'Who was the craftsman?' she asked, as she admired a glossy banister.

'Me.'

'Really? I am impressed.'

'No need to sound quite so surprised.' Carrick gave a dry laugh. 'What do you think I spend my time doing out here? Seducing women, as Indigo would have it? Believe me, the women I normally seduce would have no appreciation of such a building.'

Despite the implied compliment to Maggie's taste, the thought of Coppelia Morrison and her ilk darkened her day. She patted Zera, then moved off to explore further. It was open plan but full of twists and turns and surprises: a cosy nook with a stone fireplace, a little spiral staircase leading to the loft-like bedrooms with stunning views, and, best of all, what Carrick called his crow's nest – one could exit from one of the bedrooms and cross a little wooden bridge onto a wide railed platform built around the trunk of an oak tree. A polished bench encircled the tree and Maggie could easily imagine Carrick here with his book and a drink, the dogs at his feet. By nature or design the branches of the great oak parted in such a way that every time he glanced up from his book he'd be able to gaze out across the lake.

'*Swiss Family Robinson*!' she exclaimed.

'Maybe,' Carrick confessed. 'A childhood fantasy. But don't publish that!'

Maggie sighed. 'Imagine if your fantasy had been of King Arthur and the Knights of the Round Table. You might have ended up with a whole castle.' She gave an impish grin. 'And by the way, there will be no censoring of my article. Freedom of the press and all that!' Not that she'd written a word of it yet. Somehow, she just couldn't seem to concentrate.

CHAPTER 31

Coppelia was livid. Someone had tried to kill her daughter. Sweet innocent Ashling, whose only crime was to fall head-first into the trap set by Honoria Granville. But Honoria was not to blame for this attempt on her daughter's life. Of that Coppelia was certain. Not so long ago, she wouldn't have hesitated to point the finger, but not now. After all, she had Honoria over a barrel, terrified that the world would learn about her extra-marital love affair and the child that was the result. She wouldn't dare lay a hand on Ashling now.

The shadows of evening lengthened, creeping across the floor and the bed upon which Ashling lay, marble-pale beneath her healthy outdoor tan. Purple bruises decorated her slender arms where blood had been taken and where the IV drip had been attached. All was silent except for the sound of her shallow breathing and the low comforting bleep from the various pieces of medical equipment responsible for monitoring her vital signs.

Picking up her daughter's limp hand, Coppelia pressed her lips gently to the back. Amazing how childlike they still were, those hands, smooth, unlined, soft, but for a callus on her right index finger, caused by endlessly clicking the camera. Her oval-tipped nails were unvarnished, buffed to a shine, and kept to a practical length. There was the faint mark of her engagement ring on her finger. The nurses had taken it off and given it to Coppelia for safekeeping. A Granville heirloom, two carats of flawless, marquise-cut solitaire, in a heavy solid gold setting, worth a king's ransom. Well, Honoria could have it back now, and good bloody riddance.

A tear glimmered in the corner of her eye, trembled for a moment, then tipped over, leaving a feathery charcoal trail of mascara down her powdered cheek.

Was there really some madman on the loose, a serial killer, an opportunist who had struck lucky, if that was the right phrase, on the mountain? Or was it someone with a personal grudge against Ashling? And if so, why?

The door to the room opened and a nurse came in, checked both Ashling and the medical equipment, threw Coppelia a brief, compassionate smile and left again.

Carrickross! Coppelia concluded. What other reason could there possibly be? Of course that didn't explain the murder of Kate O'Leary or the attack on Jaspar, but what if they had just been red herrings and the real target was Ashling? What if someone didn't want the marriage to take place because the estate would then go lock, stock and barrel to Rossa, who, unlike Carrick, would see it as his own personal piggy bank and run it into the ground in no time at all? Great! That put all of the Granvilles, barring Rossa and Honoria, squarely in the frame.

Round and round went her thoughts, but nothing was clear except the fact that Ashling had been poisoned. An unidentified toxic substance had been found in her bloodstream and traces of the same substance had also been found in the lemonade bottle she had taken with her that morning on her ride. A sample had been rushed to Dublin for identification, but everything seemed to point to Ehu's little gourd, which had gone missing. He had given the police the secret Maasai name for it, breaking a taboo, or so he said, though the Irish police held no truck with that kind of nonsense. They hadn't arrested him and even Coppelia had to admit it was highly unlikely that he would have used his own poison. And if his motive had been to protect Jaspar's interests, well then Jaspar had been attacked too. So that made no sense. Unless it was some kind of incredibly clever double bluff.

Still, whatever the truth about Jaspar and Kate O'Leary, Coppelia was sure that Carrickross was at the root of the attack on Ashling. And what made it even more likely was that no one apart from Honoria, her acolyte Rajesh and Coppelia herself knew that the marriage wasn't actually going to happen.

She kissed her daughter's hand again and her heart gave a little kick of fear. What if Ashling had died without ever knowing the truth and without ever knowing how much she really loved her? Oh, God, it didn't bear thinking about.

Fortunately, she had been found in time, thanks to Rossa, and the doctors were optimistic she would make a complete recovery. All going well, the hospital had agreed that in a few days' time she could be transferred to Carrickross, under the care of Honoria's private physician and with a private nurse guarding her at all times. Coppelia would have preferred to have whisked her straight back to Dublin, but had to agree that undertaking such a long journey at this stage might be unwise. Coppelia intended to stay on at the Kerry Eden hotel, so she could be on hand at any moment if Ashling needed her. Weary beyond belief, she sighed and clutched at her brow in despair. At the sound Ashling moved a little. Her eyelids fluttered briefly open, then closed again.

'There, there,' Coppelia crooned, as if Ashling were still a child. 'Mummy's here. You're safe now. And, believe me, this time I'm not going anywhere.'

CHAPTER 32

Maggie was living a dream. With a leaping log fire, a squashy armchair and a glass of luscious Shiraz in hand, Irish wolfhound at her feet and Carrick Granville sitting large as life and twice as gorgeous opposite her.

It wasn't perhaps the best time to engage upon a formal interview, given her mood of wine-induced indolence, but she couldn't afford to lose sight of the fact that she had an article to write. She placed a digital voice recorder on the table between them and leaned forward with what she hoped was an expression of professional intent. But, damn, if he wasn't laughing at her, his eyes all twinkly and glimmery as if he was humouring her, as if she was just *playing* at being a journalist. She sent him a glare in response. Maggie O'Keefe took her career seriously. She was nobody's fool, least of all his.

'Right,' she said, having checked that the recorder was set to 'on'. 'Carrick Granville, you are being touted as one of the foremost "green" architects of the day. What steps do you feel we as a nation should be taking to reduce our carbon footprint? And what steps are you taking personally?'

Maggie sat back, as Carrick, plainly on a hobby horse, launched into a long explanation about how we could learn from China and its long-term green housing policies. The firelight played across the beautiful chiselled lines of his face and intent on his subject his eyes were bright and fervent. His hands, graceful, strong and artistic, illustrated his points in the air. Here again was the charismatic man she had met at the fountain the night of the Midsummer Ball.

'So you see,' he smiled as he came to the end of a passionate monologue, 'they would be green buildings both inside and out.'

'Um, yes, that brings us to a question I have been meaning to ask you since I saw an article on you in the *Indo* a while back. There was a picture of a building you designed in Tokyo. An oblong box of concrete and steel stuck between two office-blocks at the side of the street, and not a plant or tree in sight. So where does this brick box fit into that green vision of yours?'

'Ah! But there was a garden *inside*, Maggie. It was for an exclusive jewellery company so the offices and craft rooms were arranged around the garden in two storeys. So instead of looking out to a hostile city, it looked inwards to its own centre. I imagined it as holding the city at bay, protecting its own calm space.'

'What a lovely concept,' Maggie breathed.

'You sound surprised.'

'Well, I had misinterpreted the design,' she said slightly guiltily.

'And I think you have also misinterpreted *me*, Maggie.' Carrick's gaze held hers.

God, it was true. She had. She really had.

'Well, it's hardly any wonder, is it?' she defended herself. 'Look how *you* misinterpreted *me*. Seeing me only as a ruthless journalist, ready to use and abuse anyone who comes within reach.' She gave him a straight look. 'Can I take it you've changed your mind about me?'

'I suppose I have,' he said wryly. He was silent for a moment, gazing in the fire, swirling the wine around in his glass. 'Well, my Uncle Jaspar likes you enormously. I know we treat him like a court jester a lot of the time but Jaspar has a good heart and can be very perceptive under all the bluster and campness.'

Maggie was surprised and touched by his answer.

Then he added playfully, 'Will you be using all of this in your article?'

'Of course not!'

He pointed at the recorder, eyebrow raised.

Maggie leaned forward to stop the recorder, then let it run instead. 'Never mind. I can wipe it later.'

Embarrassed, she felt obliged to return to formal interview mode and go on the offensive. She was in danger of losing her street cred.

'Right. Back to your image as an environmentalist. How do you square it with that gas-guzzling chopper sitting out there on the landing-pad? Is it a case of do as I say, rather than do as I do?'

The softer mood was immediately broken and Carrick looked annoyed. 'Unfortunately, until the scientists come up with an alternative fuel, I'm afraid I'm rather stuck with it. I need it. Quite often I have to be ready to dash to projects at a moment's notice and it's absolutely necessary for overseeing the estate.'

'Ah! The estate.' The word seemed to trigger something in her and she heard her voice sharpen as she went on. 'That reminds me. How does an environmentalist live in a house decorated with the heads of dead animals?'

'Don't be ridiculous!' he spluttered, taken by surprise. 'They've been there for centuries. *I* didn't shoot them. Besides, animals prey on each other in nature.'

Maggie flushed, felt her heart begin to quicken. 'That's no excuse for you and your kind to participate in the slaughter!'

'Me and my kind? What "kind" is that?' Carrick's face had darkened.

'You so-called gentry! Considering yourselves superior while living on the backs of the poor for centuries past!'

Carrick was outraged. 'Now you're holding me responsible for the sins of my ancestors?'

They were both sitting on the edges of their chairs, heads jutting forward belligerently. The wolfhounds had fled – out of the line of fire.

'My God! You really do have contempt for me, don't you?' said Carrick scathingly. 'So you consider yourself morally superior? You know, you're the one who's a snob – you've treated me and my family with contempt from the start just because of our ancestral history!'

Mortally stung, Maggie leaped to her feet. 'That's it! I've had enough!' She snapped her recorder off. 'Look, I can't be doing with this. This just isn't my world. Why should I even *want* to relate to the likes of you?'

Carrick stood and confronted her, his face thunderous. 'Is this how you usually conduct your interviews, Miss O'Keefe?'

The use of her title and surname felt like a slap in the face. Maggie felt suddenly close to tears. She turned and strode out of the house.

As she walked towards the lake the tears began to stream down her face. Her feet drummed on the planks of the little wooden pier and then, on an impulse, she climbed into a small rowboat moored alongside it. The boat swayed alarmingly and she sat down abruptly.

She wiped the tears from her eyes and stared out at the placid lake. Her heart ached. She was also conscious of having made an utter fool of herself. She had crossed an invisible line and there was no going back.

After a long while, some instinct made her look back over her shoulder at the house. He was walking slowly towards the pier.

Then he was standing there, his boots at her eye level.

'Maggie?' His voice was low.

'What?' She didn't look at him.

'I've been thinking . . .' he said softly. 'That was supposed to be an interview. But it didn't seem like one to me.'

She sat silent, staring at the glossy surface of the lake.

'You know what it felt like?' he went on almost conversationally and squatted down to her level. 'It felt . . . it felt like a lovers' quarrel. Now why do you think that might be?'

It was the moment of truth.

Maggie shrugged. 'Maybe . . . maybe it's because I do care for you,' she said and her heart plunged at the risk she was taking.

'And I care for you.' He reached out to her. 'Maggie, take my hand.'

She did. It was warm and strong and sent delicious shivers racing up her arm and through her body.

He pulled her up onto the pier and into the blissful comfort of his arms.

They held each other close for a long long while, then Carrick gently led her back to the house.

Inside, she put her hands on his shoulders, looking up into his eyes earnestly.

There were tear tracks still on her face. Gently he reached out with his finger and traced them all the way down along her cheeks to the side of her mouth.

'I really am sorry,' she said, her voice slightly choked, little more than a whisper. 'I . . . I'm . . .'

His finger touched her lips, silencing her, and suddenly she was in his arms again and their mouths were seeking each other's with a passion neither had known before.

CHAPTER 33

Maggie woke once more to feel Carrick's body slide over and into hers. Murky light was filtering through the blinds and she could hear the wind whipping at the trees close to the house. She wrapped her legs around him as, amazingly, she began already to orgasm. His thrusts deepened as he felt her respond to him, she arched backwards and thrust too and they came together in a perfect, shuddering, achingly sweet climax.

Eyes closed, she savoured the delicious after-shocks, and slipped back into sleep.

She woke again to warmth and wonder and skin against skin and Carrick's voice as he murmured soft loving words and nuzzled her neck.

He had been wonderful – the sex had been mind-blowing. She had expected that – after all, he'd had lots of practice – but she hadn't been prepared for the depths of tenderness, the feeling of being treasured and precious . . . of being *loved*.

Carrick sat up abruptly, every line of his body tense.

'What is it?'

'Christ, how could I have forgotten!'

Oh no, Maggie thought cynically, her heart suddenly aching in her chest, this is where he remembers an urgent appointment in Moscow . . .

'God, I'm sorry, Maggie, but I've just remembered. It's the anniversary of my parents' death.'

Maggie sat up too. 'Oh! Poor darling. How awful!'

He took her hands between his own, his eyes dark and troubled. 'Maggie, our parents' deaths damaged us all beyond repair. If I sometimes seem as if I live a bit on the dark side, it's because of that. I'll tell you all about it another time. But we need to get back now. Grandmother always goes up to the mountain on this day – she and Rajesh – and when she returns we hold a memorial service.'

Maggie kissed him. 'No problem, I'll be ready in two shakes.'

Carrick picked up his mobile, switched it on and waited as it searched for a signal. He grinned, a little shamefaced. 'I had it turned off all the time we were here – I didn't want us to be disturbed. What's the betting there's already half a dozen messages?'

Maggie had turned hers off too for exactly the same reason, not that she was going to tell him that. She admired him all over again as he listened intently to a message.

'Oh my God!'

Maggie jumped. 'What?'

Carrick looked at her disbelievingly. 'It's Ashling! She's in hospital! She's been poisoned!'

Ashling! All the alarm bells began to jangle again for Maggie. 'Christ! Is she okay?'

'I don't know.' Frantic, Carrick scrolled through a number of messages, his face clearing slightly. 'Yes, yes, she's okay. Thankfully she doesn't appear to have ingested all the poison.' His expression darkened again. 'They think it might have been Ehu's poison . . . the one he lost . . .'

Honoria gazed with dread at the lofty rise of rock that cradled the corrie lake and the phantom mist that was scudding in the rising wind over the summit of towering cliffs. A sickly perfume rose from the huge bunch of flowers she carried in the crook of her arm, white roses and lilies, funeral flowers.

They were following the track Honoria had commanded be hewn out of the mountain when she was no longer able to ride up to the lake for this yearly remembrance. The pony-trap breasted the outer lip of the corrie's deep cradle and then they were looking down at it – the treacherous lake. Dug out of the lap of the mountain by the cruel glacier, it seemed to brood – bottomless, icy, dead. What chance had her innocent sons stood of surviving its rocky depths, roped to the women as they were?

Sheltered in the mountain's deep hollow, the lake was barely ruffled by the wind. Rajesh drew

411

the pony to a halt, set the brake on the trap, then helped Honoria dismount. He kissed the back of her hand, looked deep into her eyes, reassuring her without the need for words that he was there for her today, just as he had been on every anniversary of William and David's deaths. She acknowledged the gesture with a half-smile. He took her arm and together they walked towards the edge of the corrie and stared down into its hypnotic depths.

A gust of wind caught Honoria and she swayed a little, Rajesh's grip fastening on her arm.

Time, everyone had advised; give it time. But they hadn't understood. Nobody but Rajesh had understood the magnitude of the loss her heart had sustained. Three children lost for ever. She raised her hand and scattered the flowers into the lake below, the wind tossing them as they fell to the smooth dead surface.

'Sweets to the sweet. Farewell!'

The next lines of the quotation came unbidden to her: *I thought thy bride-bed to have deck'd, sweet maid, And not have strew'd thy grave.* And with the words, the wan face of Ashling, *Henry's daughter* Ashling, slid into her mind like a reproach.

She shivered as the cold – it was always cold here – bit through the folds of her thick black coat. She might never come here again. The hour-glass was fast running out. But not quite! There was still one thing left to do before she would go easy to her grave, one final deed to ensure that her secret, that dreaded secret that had haunted her for half a century, was buried with her. She would have to silence Coppelia, by whatever means possible.

'Let us continue to the summit, Rajesh.'

Rajesh gazed at the much rougher, steeper and treacherous track that led to the edge of the cliff towering over the corrie. It had always been part of their ritual on this day to climb to the top where they would stand at the edge, hand in hand, and stare down into the dizzying drop to the lake below. Now he noted how the rough grass and heather was flattening against the wind and how the storm clouds were still gathering to the west.

'Rani,' he said uncertainly, 'I fear a storm is on its way. Perhaps, this time, this year, we should go back.'

She faced him as he had known she would, chin raised, defiant.

'No, Rajesh. I *will* not let my sons down. I will climb to the spot where they fell, just as I have always done and always will do for so long as I have breath in my body.'

'Well, at least let us rest awhile and gather our strength,' he suggested soothingly, diplomatically, leading her to a seat on a nearby rock in the hope that she might change her mind. 'My legs are not as young as they used to be.' He would try to dissuade her gently before opposing her outright, which might have the contrary effect of steeling her resolve.

'Five minutes, then,' she agreed, trying but not quite managing to suppress a little groan.

Worried, he reached for her hand.

In the early-morning light Ashling opened her eyes and smiled to see her mother there sleeping on a bedside chair, leaning on the bed, still somehow managing to look elegant.

As if sensing the change, Coppelia opened her eyes.

'Ashling! You're awake!'

'Hello, Mother,' Ashling said weakly, gazing in wonder at the various tubes attached to her and the saline drip over her head. 'What am I doing? Oh, I remember . . . I was sick, wasn't I . . . on the mountain?'

'Hush, darling!' Coppelia tenderly stroked her face. 'The doctors seem to think that lemonade you drank was spiked. But don't worry about that – we have plenty of time for both questions and answers – the important thing now is for you to save your strength and concentrate on getting better.'

'I thought it tasted odd. Bitter,' Ashling whispered. 'I poured half away.'

Thank God for that! Coppelia suppressed her gasp as she realised that her daughter's life had been saved by that one simple fact.

'Was I really ill?'

Tears sprang to Coppelia's eyes. 'Yes, I won't lie to you. At one point it was pretty much touch and go.' She gave a strained smile. 'But you're a fighter, Ashling. Just like me. And you're going to be fine. I promise you, everything's going to be all right.'

Ashling looked at her then in wonder, lying quietly, savouring the rare pleasure of her mother's hand on her skin and hair and the equally rare soft expression on her face. Then her eyes closed and she drifted into a peaceful sleep.

When she awoke later, sunlight was slanting across the bed, its rays making Coppelia's hair glow like fire against the white bed-cover where she had again laid her head. Ashling stretched out a hand and gently stroked one glowing tendril, then let it curl around her finger. And suddenly she felt that this was a good place to be, here with her mother. A better place than she had been for a long time. And the thought came unbidden: *Somebody tried to kill me!* And then, *Maggie was right.*

After a long time Coppelia stirred and raised her head, smiling to see Ashling's eyes fixed on her.

Ashling spoke, her voice faint. 'Mother?'

'Yes?'

'I think I'd like to go home.'

Coppelia reached out and stroked her hair. 'And we will, very soon, just as soon as the doctor gives us the go-ahead. Rossa would like you to return to Carrickross where you can be treated by their family doctor and I—'

'No, definitely not,' Ashling interrupted. 'I want to go *home*, Mother, back to Dublin. For good.'

Coppelia's heart gave a little jump. Maybe matters were going to resolve themselves after all. 'But . . . what about Rossa?' she asked tentatively.

A wetness appeared at the corners of Ashling's eyes. 'I love him still only . . . only I'm not *in* love with him any more. Do you know what I mean?' Her fingers plucked anxiously at the edge of her sheet. 'And I'm not even sure when that change took place.' She gave a little wry smile. 'It wasn't ever right for me . . . but it was the whole fairy-tale thing, I guess. I got carried away by the glamour, the excitement of it all. But you know, fairy tales are probably best kept between the covers of a book.'

Coppelia smoothed Ashling's tears away with her fingers. 'I'm sorry, darling. Truly sorry. I know I've made mistakes in the past, but I've only ever wanted you to be happy. And Rossa Granville is not, nor ever was, the man to make you so.'

Ashling dipped her head. 'I know that now, but I had to learn it for myself. Still, it was a nice dream while it lasted.' She gave a rueful little grin that quickly faded. 'But now the scales have fallen from my eyes at last. You were right – something *is* rotten in the state of Carrickross. Whether it rests with the place or the people themselves, I'm not entirely sure. I know it sounds dramatic, but I think it would devour me if I stayed. It has already *begun* to devour me.'

And like a dagger through the heart, the realisation hit Coppelia: she herself had had a role to play in that dark fate, the evil that had now spread its tentacles to ensnare her daughter. She had played a part in keeping the hatred alive and that had almost cost her lovely daughter her life.

Appalled at the revelation, she staggered to her feet.

'Mother!' Alarmed, Ashling's eyes flew to her face. 'What's the matter? You look like you've seen a ghost!'

Coppelia brushed away her concern. 'No! No! I'm fine. Don't worry. Just – just a bursting bladder and pins and needles – a nasty combination.' She tried to laugh but it emerged as a gasp. 'Must just go to the loo.'

Grabbing her handbag en route, Coppelia hurried out of the room.

Locking herself into a cubicle in the ladies', she sat on the toilet and let the harsh sobs rack her, stifling the noise with her hands.

Ten minutes later, wan but composed, her make-up once more immaculate, she returned to Ashling's room to find the consultant, surrounded by a bevy of trainee doctors, at her daughter's bed.

Typically, the old Coppelia would have waded in, scattering his minions like flies, confronting him with demands and questions. Now, possibly for the first time ever in her life, she hung back.

The consultant stopped as he left the room and smiled at her sympathetically. 'Well, you'll be pleased to know, Mrs Morrison, that most of the poison has left Ashling's system and her kidneys and liver are functioning as normal. All she needs now is to rest and regain her strength.' He gazed keenly at her. 'And if you don't mind me saying so, it will do you no harm to follow the exact same prescription.' With that he turned abruptly on his heel and led his gaggle of students down the corridor.

'Mrs Morrison?' It was the staff nurse, a kindly woman, her face full of sympathy. 'You heard what the man said. Off you go now – your daughter is in safe hands and on the road to recovery.'

'But—' Coppelia started to protest, unwilling to leave Ashling's side.

'But nothing, Mrs Morrison. If you collapse with exhaustion you'll be no earthly use to your daughter at all. Now off with you at once. We'll take good care of her for you.'

'Yes, go on, Mother,' said Ashling weakly from the bed. 'Don't worry about me. I'll be fine here. Go back to your hotel and rest, then come back later when I'm fit for a chat.'

Coppelia hesitated, then dropped a quick kiss on Ashling's forehead. 'All right, bossy boots. I'll take your advice, but I'll be back before you have time to miss me.' Turning to the nurse, she added, 'You have my mobile number. You will call me, won't you, if anything . . . changes?'

'Like greased lightning,' the nurse promised. 'But she's out of the woods now. And a lucky young woman she is too!'

CHAPTER 34

Coppelia pulled up outside the Kerry Eden and waved away the flunky who came scuttling up to the car, his jacket flapping in the rising wind.

For a while she just sat and brooded, her eyes drawn to the nearby spruce trees whose heavy branches were rhythmically lashing to and fro. It was true that she should grab a few hours' desperately needed sleep and then get back to Ashling's bedside. But now she felt another need, another compulsion, stronger even than her desire for sleep.

It was the need to cast off this burden she had carried for so many years. Revenge is a dish best served cold? But now it seemed Coppelia no longer had the stomach for it. Until now, she had always pictured the hatred that consumed her as a fiery and exultant force, bright and beautiful in its raging power, and she, the Joan of Arc, transfigured at its centre.

Then those devastating words from Ashling . . . 'something *is* rotten in the state of Carrickross. I think it would devour me if I stayed . . . it has already *begun* to devour me . . .'

There it was, plain and simple. She and Honoria Granville had joined hands in mutual hate, nurturing that darkness, that evil. But the truth stood revealed now in all its naked ugliness. Primitive. Raw. Hatred was not the bright and avenging sword of her imaginings, the raging fire that purified all in its path. No, it was a cold, putrid, cancerous thing corrupting all those who sought to use it for their own gain and endangering the lives of the innocents unwittingly caught up in its path. 'Oh God!' Coppelia struck the steering-wheel with her fist, welcoming as a punishment the shaft of pain that shot up her wrist. To think she had been so deluded. So stupid! So utterly, utterly wrapped up in her own sense of injustice that it had almost cost her innocent daughter her life. But no more! Someone had to make the first move and if not Honoria, then it had better be she. And so she would confront her old enemy one last time. Let the volcano erupt and spew out its long-held secrets. The truth would set them all, including Ashling, free. And if there was a price to be paid, she would pay it, whatever the cost.

She flung the car into gear, the wheels skidding on the gravel as she tore through the hotel gates and onto the main road.

'Today it ends, Honoria!' she vowed. '*This* is Judgement Day for both you and me!'

The urgency she felt now to get to Carrickross pushed her to ignore the speed limit on the outskirts of the village, her hand hovering in frustration over the horn of the Lotus as she barely restrained herself from blasting a crawling tractor out of her way.

When she was past it, she floored the accelerator, careering onto the side road that snaked through woodland beside the stone walls of the Carrickross estate. In no time at all she found herself swinging through the main gates and sliding rapidly down the winding drive that was sheltered by ancient trees and tangled greenery. Only when she emerged from the woods and was on the approach to the house did she realise that the sunshine of earlier had fled and the blue of the sky had taken on a sombre scowl. A fitting stage set for the scene about to unfold, she thought and smiled grimly.

She braked to a halt outside the main door, surprised to see the housekeeper, her large apron billowing about her, together with her surly looking son, standing on the steps like a welcoming committee of two. But whoever or whatever they were waiting for, it was not her, for the pair barely glanced in her direction. Instead they were straining their eyes to the west where storm clouds were amassing like great black soufflés in the sky.

Coppelia swept up the steps.

'I wish to see Mrs Granville,' she said without preamble. 'Please tell her I'm here.'

Noreen pressed her hand to her chest. 'Oh,

Mrs Morrison, you've not come about . . . ? Is Ashling okay?' She forgot herself so far as to grasp Coppelia's elegant hands, squeezing them in sympathy.

'She's fine.' Awkwardly, Coppelia pulled away, her habitual poise shaken by this unaccustomed warmth. 'On the mend, I'm pleased to say. Now, I really must see Honoria Granville. At once.'

'Oh, you can't, I'm afraid. The mistress is not here.' She nodded towards her son. 'Sure, isn't that why Seän and me are worried sick? She's up on the mountain. Her and Rajesh.' Seeing the look of blank incomprehension on Coppelia's face, she gestured to the mountain that towered a few miles to the west of the house. 'Ceanngairiff. That big one over there. Today is the anniversary of the deaths of two of her sons and their wives. It's a pilgrimage that she makes every year. All a bit morbid, if you ask me—'

'I didn't ask you,' Coppelia said, reverting to her usual imperious self. 'Pilgrimage or not, I need to see her and I need to see her now. I must get back to my daughter. I assume you have her phone number?'

'A mobile phone number, do you mean?' Noreen shook her head. 'Indeed I do not. The mistress doesn't hold with mobile phones or the like. Newfangled nonsense, she calls them. You'll just have to wait till she comes back down, Mrs Morrison.'

'And even if she did have one, you'd get no signal up there anyway,' added Seán.

A wave of fury and frustration sent Coppelia rocking back on her heels. This could *not* be happening! She strove to control the angry shake in her voice.

'When is she likely to be back? You must have some idea!'

'Well, that's the point, you see.' Noreen frowned, picked up the corner of her apron and began to wring it nervously. 'They're usually back long before now.' She glanced at her watch. 'They're cutting it a bit fine if they're to get back for the family gathering at three o'clock – there's always a bit of a special ceremony to mark the occasion.' She cleared her throat. 'I'd be a liar if I said I'm not worried. I am. Very. Especially with the way the weather's taken a turn for the worse. I don't like the look of those clouds at all.' She shivered. 'And that wind is rising by the second. And if it's bad down here, it'll be magnified tenfold up on that mountain.'

'Well, if you're that worried, how come you've not sent someone to search for them?' Coppelia gritted her teeth. 'Surely that would be the logical thing to do.'

Noreen went on the defensive. 'Wasn't I just going to send Seán? Tom's taken one of the dogs to the vet's and none of the Granville lads are here. Besides, I didn't want to be phoning and causing panic without good reason. Haven't we all had enough of that lately, thinking there might be a serial killer on the loose?' The wringing of her apron became even more fast and furious. 'Jesus Christ! Mrs Morrison, do you suppose the serial killer could have got the mistress and Rajesh? There'd be a hundred and one ways to kill them on the mountain. Sure, what are they only a couple of OAPs? They'd go down without too much of a fight, I'd say.'

I pity the serial killer who'd cross Rajesh's path, thought Coppelia. Impatient, she rolled her eyes. 'Oh, don't talk rubbish, woman! You should have sent someone to look for them. There's no excuse.'

Noreen bristled. 'It's not as simple as that. The mistress doesn't like being spied on, as she calls it. She went ballistic once before when they were late down and my Tom went up looking for them, worried that the pony might have cast a shoe or—'

Coppelia was incredulous. 'The pony? Do you mean to say Mrs Granville has *ridden* up there?'

'Ridden, no,' said Seán. 'Sure, Honoria's ancient! They've taken the pony and trap.'

'Mrs *Granville*, you mean,' Coppelia said pointedly, reminding him of his lowly position. 'I can see somebody is going to have to take charge here.' She swung on her heel and marched back down the steps, gesturing for Seán to follow her as Noreen stood open-mouthed in their wake. 'You! Get in the car. You can take me up the mountain to this lake.'

'Not in *that* car!' Seán faced her across the roof of the Lotus. 'We wouldn't make it five yards up that track. The suspension would be ruined. Sure, it's little more than a dirt track pitted with rocks and ruts.'

Furious, Coppelia hammered the car roof with a fist. 'Well, you must have something more suitable then. A Land Rover? I tell you, I have no time to waste!'

Sean shrugged as Noreen came panting down, apron flapping, the wind flattening her mop of hair across her head.

'Mrs Morrison, Seán could saddle up and go look for the mistress. That's the best thing all round. Go on, now, Seán! Go on – saddle up one of the horses, while I go and make Mrs Morrison a nice cup of tea!'

Seán shrugged and slouched off unwillingly. Noreen lowered her voice conspiratorially and rattled on in an undertone. 'Lord, he's in fierce form since the twins went away to that madhouse in Sweden! I don't know what to do with him at all! He's neither eating nor sleeping nor—'

But to her alarm, Coppelia left her standing there mid-sentence and took off like the hounds of hell after Seán.

'Oh, Christ, she's going to go with him!' Noreen muttered, crossing herself. And God only knew what devilment she was up to. Honoria Granville would be fit to be tied if the Morrison woman was to show up today of all days, when she was in mourning for her two sons. Battling against the wind sweeping round the corner of the house, she followed the pair of them, almost falling to her knees in gratitude as the whirr of approaching rotary blades sounded above the wind! Thanks be to Christ, Carrick was home! He'd know what to do. Turning on her heel, she headed back to meet him.

But her relief was short-lived as another sound reached her ears, competing with the chatter of the helicopter blades: the pounding of a running horse accompanied by a familiar rattle.

Pony and trap had returned home, safe if a bit shaken. But of the mistress and Rajesh, there was no sign.

While Seán led the pony and trap around to the stables, Coppelia ran to meet Carrick as he emerged from the helicopter, Maggie O'Keefe by his side. Then the heavens opened and the rain came down in torrents.

'Carrick! Carrick!' Coppelia yelled.

He grabbed her by the arm and leaned an ear down to listen as she screamed the news above the wind. Then throwing an arm about her and another around Maggie he hurried them to the front porch of the house.

'Maggie, tell Noreen to give Seán some blankets and Thermos flasks of hot drinks if she can manage that quickly and get him to meet me at the front of the house.'

'He's gone around to the stables with the trap,' Coppelia told her.

'Okay.' Maggie hurried into the house.

'You wait here, Coppelia,' Carrick said. 'I'll get the Land Rover and we'll search the mountain.'

Coppelia nodded, frozen to the bone, but grateful and relieved that someone was capable of taking charge.

A short while later the Land Rover hurtled around the side of the house and braked to a halt in a shower of gravel. Coppelia hurried down the steps only to find herself outstripped by Seán who had burst out of the house behind her, his arms full of blankets and Thermos flasks. He jumped into the passenger seat and slammed the door. But it wasn't until the Land Rover revved and began to move that Coppelia realised Carrick had no intention of taking her with him after all.

With a scream of outrage she threw herself at the car and grabbed the door handle. Carrick was forced to brake with a suddenness that flung himself and Seán forward and jerked Coppelia like a rag-doll. But she hung on and tried to open the door. It was locked. Inside, a pale-faced Seán signalled urgently to her to let go.

Shaking in fury, strands of her red hair clumping together in thick Medusa-like tendrils, Coppelia clung determinedly to the handle.

'Carrick, open the door! Don't you understand? I need to see Honoria and I need to see her *now*!' Oh why had she left it so late? What if Honoria had met with an accident? In that moment she felt that her own future would be rendered meaningless if Fate robbed her of her ultimate confrontation with Honoria Granville.

'Back off, Coppelia!' Carrick revved the engine warningly. 'This is family business and *you* are not family.'

'Neither is he!' Coppelia screeched, pointing to Seán.

Carrick glared angrily out the window. 'Jesus, woman, will you let go of the door! My grandmother could be seriously injured up on that mountain and I really can't be doing with your hysteria.' He gunned the engine again. 'Look, if I have to drag you along, I will. So, do us all a favour and get out of the way!'

'Fuck you, Carrick!' Eyes wild, Coppelia aimed a flurry of kicks at the door of the Land Rover. 'I swear to God, if you don't take me with you, I'll follow you on your best horse. That's right,' she threatened, as she saw his face pale. 'I'll take The Sheikh and if either he or I break our necks, the blame will lie firmly at your door.'

Carrick's face suffused with angry colour. A blue vein popped up, zig-zagging along his right temple. 'Just you do, Coppelia, and I'm warning you – I'll – I'll—'

Coppelia kicked the door again. 'You'll what? I'm not joking, Carrick. I'll do whatever it takes to see Honoria. And I can assure you, if she has had an accident she *will* want to hear what I have to say.' Her eyes filled with tears in a mixture of rage and frustration. How she loathed having to beg. Her hand tightened on the door handle as he slowly began to move off, then braked again as he saw that she was quite capable of allowing him to drag her under the wheels of the Land Rover.

'Get in out of the rain, Coppelia!' he roared, losing his temper. 'Fetching though you are in the wet-shirt look, the running makeup ruins the effect! And, by the way, if I have to choose between you and Seán – no contest. His muscle-power will be a great deal more useful than your bullshit!' With a quick forward, then backward jerk of the Land Rover, he contrived to loosen her grip and sped off.

'Bastard!' Helpless, Coppelia danced up and down in fury. She *had* to see Honoria. She ran towards the stables.

A mile up the road, as Seán got out to remove a branch brought down by the storm, a horrified Carrick caught sight in the rearview mirror of Coppelia pursuing them on The Sheikh! She had carried out her threat. White with rage, he leaped out, waited till the horse drew level and grabbed the bridle. Hanging on with all his strength, he brought the stallion to a halt.

'You stupid bitch!' Roughly, he reached up and dragged her from the saddle. 'Risk your own foolish neck, if you must, but this is a valuable horse.' His lips drew back in a snarl. 'If I wasn't so pressed for time, I swear I'd put you across my knee right now and give you a damn good hiding!'

'And no doubt enjoy it,' Coppelia sneered, wrenching herself free. Her chin came up, rebellious, the light of battle still hot in her eyes. 'I warned you, Carrick. I warned you but you just wouldn't listen.'

Despite his anger, he felt a reluctant admiration for her spirit, her determination to get her own way at whatever cost. He patted The Sheikh's neck, quieting him. Coppelia had ridden him hard and he was drenched with sweat. He threw the reins to Seán. 'Take him home and make sure he's well rubbed down. And give him some mashed bran. *Lead* – don't ride,' he instructed.

To her credit, a flash of something close to remorse crossed Coppelia's face as Seán led the horse away. 'You left me no choice. I was desperate.'

Carrick turned back to the jeep. 'And for the life of me I have no idea why. And I can't admit to caring overly much either.'

Coppelia grasped his sleeve. 'Oh, but if you'll just let me come with you, Carrick, I'll explain everything.' Rain streamed down her face and the elements battered her but she willed herself to focus her energy to a clear point of concentration. 'This is truly important, I swear it.'

Afterwards, Carrick was never sure if it was the urgency of the situation, the inclemency of the weather or the sudden unmistakable sincerity that rang in her voice that caused him suddenly to capitulate.

'Get in,' he ordered, climbing into the jeep. 'But, if you give me any trouble, Coppelia, I won't hesitate to chuck you out, storm or no storm.' He turned the key and the engine roared into life. 'Now, what was it you were going to explain?'

Coppelia brushed a hand across her wet face, took a deep breath and began to fill Carrick in on her long and turbulent history with the Granvilles.

CHAPTER 35

Lashed by the driving rain and buffeted by the howling wind, the Land Rover finally made it to the lip of the corrie. Coppelia leaped out almost before the car had rolled to a halt and frantically began to search the area for any sign of Honoria or Rajesh. But there was no trace of them at the lake and nothing to indicate that they had ever been there. She cupped her hands around her mouth and shouted their names, but the wind stole the words and tossed them unheard into the yawning depths of the dark evil-looking lake.

Carrick pulled her into the shelter of the looming cliffs, turning her to face him so that she could read his lips. 'Coppelia! They're not here!' He jerked his head towards the Land Rover, indicating they should go back, and when they had once more gained its sanctuary, both of them shivering, he turned on the ignition and flicked the windscreen wipers into life.

'Turn the heat up, will you?' Coppelia begged through chattering teeth.

'It's up to the limit, I'm afraid.' He nodded

towards the rear seat. 'Grab one of the blankets Seán threw into the back. Not exactly Calvin Klein but still . . .'

Coppelia stretched round and took one, a red tartan rug. She wrapped it about her like a shawl, grateful for its warmth.

'Carrick? Shouldn't we be getting a move on?'

She turned a puzzled face towards him as he stared almost hypnotically at the rain streaming onto the window and being rhythmically brushed away again in a sweeping arc.

'What? Oh, sorry.' He gave a start. 'I'm still trying to get my head around those revelations of yours – and failing miserably. Carrickross, the House of Secrets, eh? Or the house of cards. I feel as if somebody has come along and pulled the foundations out from under me.' He gave a short bark of mirthless laughter. 'The family tree seems to have turned into Spaghetti Junction with roots and branches shooting out all over the place. Nothing is as it seems.' He slid a sideways look at her. It would be a while before he could knit all the loose ends together, and make some sort of sense of them. Outside the wind gathered momentum and the Land Rover rocked slightly, reminding him of what he was doing out here in this storm in the first place.

'It's a shock, I know.' Coppelia laid a hand briefly on his arm in comfort, feeling a mild surprise that Fate had led her to this point where she, Coppelia Morrison, was offering comfort to Carrick

Granville . . . to any Granville . . . and yet, she had loved a Granville deeply. Henry.

He slammed the Land Rover into gear. 'I only hope they didn't follow the track to the summit before the pony bolted,' he said. 'If that's what happened I fear the worst. There's no shelter up there.' He pointed and she discerned a rough steep track leading upward among the rocks. 'Do you see the track – over there?'

Coppelia strained to see through the sheets of rain and sweeping mist. 'Surely Rajesh wouldn't take her up there in these conditions? That would be suicidal!'

'No,' Carrick agreed. 'I may not be his number-one fan, but I credit him with more sense. Perhaps they went up before the rain came.' A pulse twitched in his cheek. 'My . . . my parents fell from the edge of the cliff up there and it's become something of a pilgrimage for Grandmother. Every year without fail, no matter what the weather, she comes and stands in that very place, surrounded by the sad, long-dead ghosts of her memories.'

Despite herself, a shaft of pity found a hole in Coppelia's armour. She too knew the workings of a mother's heart.

'Carrick,' she asked tentatively, 'what if the pony bolted *while* they were on their way up there?'

He threw her a swift look. 'Best not to think about that.'

'It's very steep. Can the Land Rover make that climb?'

Carrick nodded. 'Yes, but with any luck it won't have to. I have a notion of where we might find them. I hope to God we do, anyway!' The jeep protested noisily as he swung the wheel to the right, then bounced and jolted around the rim of the lake, plunging downwards so sharply that Coppelia gasped and her hands shot out instinctively to brace themselves against the dashboard.

'Relax,' said Carrick, his gritted teeth giving the lie to the word. 'I know this terrain.'

But Coppelia hung on for dear life. 'Oh, God, how much further?'

'Not far, I promise. Look ahead and to the left.'

She peered through the windscreen, just about managing to make out a dark rectangular shape ahead of them. A building of some kind? 'What is it?'

'It's a stone hut. A hill-walkers' shelter, designed for occasions just such as this when the weather springs a trap for the unwary.'

'And you reckon that's where they'll be?'

Carrick nodded. 'I certainly hope so.'

The hut was set on a small incline sheltered from the worst of the elements in the lee of a rugged outcrop of rock. Carrick parked as close as he could, then they got out and continued the rest of the way on foot, keeping their heads well down and struggling to keep their footing. Carrick reached out and caught Coppelia's wrist, pulling her with him till they reached the hut. They hesitated for a moment, then Carrick raised his hand

and pushed. The wooden door creaked open and they stepped inside, Coppelia hardly daring to breathe. Then, with immense relief, she felt the blast of heat and saw the welcoming lick of firelight.

Rajesh was on his knees feeding turf into a small stove on top of which a kettle was boiling and, in the dim light of the hut beyond him and the amber glow cast by the open door of the stove, Honoria lay on the lower level of a set of makeshift bunk beds, blankets draped across her. Her eyes were closed.

Coppelia was unable to suppress the tiny flicker of triumph at the sight of her bitterest enemy laid low.

Carrick sprang forward, torn between relief and urgency. 'Rajesh, thank God we found you.' His eyes darted to Honoria. 'Jesus, is Grandmother all right? She looks like she's . . .'

Rajesh raised a finger to his lips in caution but, at the sound of Carrick's voice, Honoria's eyes fluttered open. She turned her head, seeking him out.

'Carrick!' she called weakly. 'Is that you?'

'Yes, it's me, Grandmother,' he said, swiftly moving to kneel by her bed. 'How are you? We were so worried!'

Unobserved by Honoria, as Carrick was blocking her line of vision, Coppelia had quietly sunk down on a low wooden stool just inside the door, the tartan blanket still clutched about her.

Rajesh, his eyes narrowed in a mixture of hatred and suspicion, glared at her. Unblinking, she glared boldly back. Rajesh looked away first, his feelings once more concealed behind his hooded eyes.

But, in truth, this was never how Coppelia had envisioned it. Now that the moment had come, she was completely at a loss as to how to proceed. Far from being a proud and equal opponent, Honoria had been reduced to a frail, possibly injured old woman, her kingdom a filthy, cold walkers' hut on the side of a bitter mountain. And in becoming a victim, Coppelia conceded, she had robbed her of what should have been her finest hour, her greatest triumph.

'Carrick, I prayed I would not go to my Maker until I had had the chance to speak to you, the chance to right some wrongs.' Honoria freed her grandson from a weak embrace, then clasped his strong brown hands between her own age-dusted ones. Her voice was thin, a mere thread of its former self.

Alarmed, Carrick looked questioningly at Rajesh.

'There was an accident.' Rajesh met his look calmly. 'She fell from the trap. Nothing is broken, I think, but she also—'

'Fell from the trap?' Carrick echoed angrily. 'How could you have let such a thing happen? You were supposed to look out for her!'

'Enough, Carrick!' Honoria ordered, with a

touch of her old asperity. 'Rajesh had nothing to do with it. It was I who insisted on taking the trap to the summit though the weather was worsening. I had to have my own way. I *always* have to have my own way.'

'Rani,' Rajesh interrupted, 'please, it is of no matter. Do not distress yourself. Rest. You must rest.'

'I will rest,' she promised gently. 'But you must not be tarred by my sins. I was angry, Carrick. I wanted to go on and so, in defiance, I pushed Rajesh from the trap, grabbed the reins and whipped the pony up the track myself. The wheel hit a boulder. I fell. So it was my own stubbornness that was to blame. Rajesh did nothing wrong.'

Carrick shook his head. 'Madness, Grandmother!'

She cackled faintly. 'Perhaps. But desperation and foolish pride make madmen of us all. And as we all know, pride comes before a fall – literally in my case!'

Carrick smiled and squeezed her hands, not for the first time getting a glimpse of the spirited young woman his grandmother had been. 'And then the pony bolted?'

'Yes,' said Rajesh who was now lighting some candles and placing them around the hut, 'but we knew she would return home and so we waited for help.'

Honoria chuckled grimly. 'Rajesh wanted to go for help himself, but I refused to let him leave my side. What a pigheaded old tyrant I am! Am I not, Rajesh?'

'It is true, Memsahib,' said Rajesh, smilingly.

'And tell Carrick how we then discovered that his heartless grandmother has a heart after all . . . but a broken one . . .' Tiring, she closed her eyes.

Grim, Rajesh nodded. 'Your grandmother has had a minor heart attack. The shock of the fall . . .'

'No no, not the fall,' whispered Honoria, eyes closed, 'not the shock alone . . . but the terrible events at Carrickross . . . that is what has weakened me . . .'

Tentative, Coppelia stepped forward. Honoria's eyes flickered open again, widening in astonishment.

'Hello, Honoria,' Coppelia said softly, coming to stand over her, but this Coppelia, her cheeks flushed with cold, eyes glittering even in the dim light, hair wild, darkened to scarlet by the rain, was not a woman Honoria recognised. Gone was the power-dressed, immaculate socialite, her place taken by this wild-looking creature, a rough red tartan shawl around her shoulders. Honoria flinched and Rajesh shot forward, his hand going instinctively to the dagger at his side.

Carrick stayed his hand. 'No, Rajesh! Coppelia, the timing is all wrong. You have waited so long, a while more won't kill you, but the shock might kill . . .' The sentence resonated, incomplete, on the air. 'Besides, there's no time to be lost. I must get my grandmother back to Carrickross without delay.' Though how this was to be accomplished without causing further harm was not immediately clear.

'No!' Coppelia hissed, pushing past Rajesh. 'I cannot risk . . . she might . . . she *must* be told now!'

Honoria licked cracked dry lips. 'What? What must I be told?'

Carrick hesitated then sighed. 'Grandmother, there's something you need to know. Believe me, it's important and Coppelia hasn't come in anger, so please try to remain calm.'

'Not in anger? Then she's not the Coppelia Morrison I know!' Honoria struggled weakly to raise herself on an elbow, but Carrick gently eased her back on the bed and adjusted the blankets over her. Her brow creased in annoyance. 'Let me sit up, Carrick! I'm not dead yet and if I am to confront this virago, I will not do so lying down!'

As Carrick obediently propped her, half-sitting up, against his arm, Coppelia felt relief. It was reassuring to see the old witch still had some spark left in her and wasn't about to pop her clogs just yet.

'Well, what is it that is so urgent that you need to speak to me on my very death bed?' Though it was plain she was still very weak, she found enough energy to glare at Coppelia.

'Your death bed?' Coppelia scoffed. 'Hardly. But Carrick is right, I did not come here in anger.' But even as the words left her mouth she was denying them in her head. She *did* feel angry. How could she not? How could she feel anything but sheer violent rage towards this woman? Then she thought of Ashling, lying wan and ill in her hospital bed, and the anger evaporated once more. 'I just ask that you listen. Will you, Honoria? Will you listen to what I have to say?'

Specks of spittle flew from Honoria's mouth, as she dredged up whatever reserves of strength remained and struggled to sit up straighter.

'Me listen? Goddamn you! *You* listen and listen well.' She shushed Carrick, as he tried to calm her. 'You already tried to ruin me once by seducing and seeking to lure away my husband. But that wasn't enough for you and so you dug, grubbed about in the mud and sewers, to see what other ammunition you could find to use against me.' Her voice was icy in tone. 'Oh, how you must have gloated when you finally hit pay dirt and uncovered my poor secret!' She pointed a bony shaking finger at the other woman. 'And now you want to revel in your victory, to expose and revile me to my family and all the world, to uncover my shame and besmirch all I hold dear – the Granvilles and Carrickross. You plan to make my remaining days on earth a living hell!' The finger transferred itself to her collar, pulling it away from her throat as though she were choking.

'Rani!' Distraught, Rajesh fell to his knees beside her. 'Please, this is not good for you. Let the vixen say her piece and be gone!'

But Honoria hardly heard him. For her, only one other person existed in the room – Coppelia. Her mouth twisted. 'But what do you know of what I went through, Coppelia Morrison? Who are you to set yourself up in judgement on my soul? I *paid* for my transgressions over and over and over again, till sometimes I thought I would go insane from the pain of it all. If it weren't for Rajesh, I would have *gone* insane. But I couldn't allow myself that luxury and part of me, a part that got smaller and smaller and more and more hopeless over the years, never stopped believing that one day . . . one day it would all come right.' Breathless, exhausted, a hand pressed to her chest, she closed her eyes for a moment. 'Praying that one day I would find . . . but it wasn't to be . . .'

'Grandmother,' Carrick eyed her anxiously, 'are you in pain?'

'Pain?' She nodded. 'I am always in pain. I have been in pain for years, running from it, Carrick. But, clearly, I didn't run fast or far enough.' Her mood changed swiftly, became almost admiring as Coppelia continued to face her out. 'We had planned to kill you, you know,' she said, almost conversationally. 'After all those veiled threats of exposure. The sleepless nights you gave us! Those who are dead can no longer hurt the living.'

Carrick's eyes widened in shock, as he thought of his grandfather, Henry, and the rumours that surrounded his death.

For a moment, there was silence, punctuated

only by the sound of the rain beating on the roof of the hut and the wind wailing like a banshee through a gap in the cliff. Then Honoria spoke again in a measured tone.

'But your triumph is empty, Coppelia, just as, I dare say, it will be short-lived. Nothing you can do to me matters now. My heart is winding down. If God is good enough to spare me a while longer, I shall make the trip back to India. I was happy there. If only for a short while. Carrick?'

She gave him her hand. It felt light and fragile, desiccated and twig-like in the warmth of his own.

'I give Carrickross into your care. It was always destined for you. Forgive a stupid old woman for trying to manipulate Fate for her own ends.' She lay back exhausted, but strangely serene. 'Now, go do your worst, Coppelia Morrison. Expose my shame to whomsoever you wish.' She paused, waited, ready to face her worst nightmare head on. 'Come now, Coppelia,' she taunted as Coppelia made no move, just continued to stand silent, her gaze fixed on the floor. 'You have waited so long. Don't disappoint me now.'

Outside, the wind howled louder than ever. Inside, the fire hissed and crackled; it seemed as though the whole world was holding its breath.

At last Coppelia heaved a huge juddering sigh. 'You lost a daughter, Honoria. In some ways, I lost *my* daughter. Because of my fear of you and of what you might do to her if you discovered her existence, I embarked upon a charade, I became her "stepmother", forbidden from openly claiming her as my own flesh and blood, the tangible evidence of my love for Henry and his for me. To play the part convincingly, I had to suppress all those maternal feelings. I had to hide my love for her, even from myself. Yesterday, I almost lost her again – this time for ever.' To her shame she felt her eyes well up. She blinked furiously to bring Honoria back into focus. 'I hadn't realised it until then but now I know that pain would have been too much to bear. You say you've suffered, suffered for years, because of your loss, but you didn't lose your child, Honoria – you *gave* her away, just as I gave Ashling away.' Anger flashed for a moment, then she controlled it again, drawing her tartan shawl more tightly about her, as if by imprisoning her arms and body she could control that anger. 'But there is one very important difference: I gave Ashling away to *protect* her. You gave your daughter away to protect *yourself!* More accurately, you *dumped* your innocent but unwanted daughter in the slums of India like – like garbage! Oh, I'm not suggesting that you didn't agonise over it, if only a little. Even you, Honoria, can't be devoid of all human feeling and I dare say you even managed to rationalise it. Perhaps you thought it was for the baby's own good.' She waved a hand as Honoria tried to speak. 'Oh look, Honoria, we've been over this road before. Remember? There's no point in denying it. I *know* about the baby and I *know* the baby wasn't your husband's. He was a

444

sick man. Too sick to father a child. So, to avoid divorce and disgrace and to save your reputation, you gave your poor little bastard daughter away. Banished her from home and hearth.' Her voice hardened. 'But Timothy, your husband, died when your daughter was still just a baby. So why, in all that's decent, did you not retrieve her then, whilst you could still go some way towards undoing the grievous wrong you did her? Pride, was it? That unpardonable Granville pride that puts a family name and an old pile of stones in the arsehole of Ireland above human life itself?'

'Coppelia, please!' Carrick protested, as the last remnants of colour drained from Honoria's face leaving her waxen as a corpse. 'Her heart! Don't draw this out – it's cruel and unnecessary. Get to the point and be done.'

'Cruel and unnecessary – do you think so?' Coppelia looked at him with disgust. 'Get your facts straight, Carrick. Abandoning an innocent child is cruel and unnecessary.' Her eyes went back to Honoria's, boring through her skull as if they could expose the thoughts lurking beneath, her voice ragged '*Why? Why* did you do it?'

'What is it to you?' Honoria screamed suddenly, tears beginning to pour down her face. 'Why do you persist in torturing me so, raking over old ashes? Why do you *care* why I did it?'

'Because . . .' Coppelia's knees seemed to buckle suddenly. She took a deep breath, steadied herself. 'Because . . .I am that daughter. *Your* daughter.'

There. It was said. At last it was said.

The words dropped like a stone into a pond, sending out ripples that would continue to spread, long after she had fallen silent.

Frozen in shock, Honoria stared white-faced, then her mouth opened in a terrible howl of rage and denial. 'No! No! No!' Her hands bunched themselves into claws.

'Rani!' Rajesh's cry was anguished. 'Rani!'

'Enough! Do you want to kill her, Coppelia? Wait outside, please!' Carrick caught hold of her elbow and tried to hustle her from the hut, but Coppelia pushed him violently away.

'No, Carrick, I don't want to kill her, not now, although up till recently nothing would have given me greater pleasure.'

Honoria was sobbing now in Rajesh's arms, great harsh sobs shaking her frame, as the burden of guilt she had carried all these years finally burst the dam. 'Why would you say such a thing?' she wailed. 'My daughter is dead!'

'Have you proof of that? Did you see her dead body? Did you mourn at her graveside as you do for your sons?' Coppelia shook her head. 'No, of course you didn't!' She gave a rueful grimace. 'Now, if this was a fairy tale, I would roll back my sleeve to reveal the cute crescent-shaped birthmark that would mark me out as one of the Granvilles, or I would produce a gold locket left to me at birth by my mother, and we would fall on each other's breasts, reunited at long last. But this is no fairy tale; this is a horror story of abandonment, cruelty, even . . .' she paused, her voice catching suddenly, '. . . even sexual abuse.'

The words fell like an executioner's axe.

Honoria raised her tear-drenched face, a mask of horror.

Rajesh leaped to his feet, hands clenched by his sides. 'Do not say such things!' he hissed. 'You will kill her with your lies!'

Carrick held up a hand. 'Stop, Rajesh! Grandmother, I know this is very hard for you, but Coppelia spoke to me earlier and although I was shocked, I don't disbelieve her. There is a ring of truth about it. Please, listen.'

'No! It's a trick!' Honoria snapped through dry lips. 'Coppelia Morrison is a hard, cruel woman. She's using my secret, my awful burden and guilt to torment me!'

'Rubbish!' Coppelia glared. 'Why on earth would I want to claim kinship with you if it wasn't true? Of what benefit is it to me?'

'Enough!' Honoria cried, childishly covering her ears. 'Stop her, Rajesh! Stop her lies, for truly I cannot bear any more!' She reached out her arms in appeal to him.

And froze. Staring in shock at the two pairs of green, so-familiar eyes turned on her, one pair with contempt, the other with love and grief and pity, but each with the truth plainly written within their emerald depths. Dear God in Heaven, how could she have missed the resemblance all this time? Overcome, she swayed back against Carrick's arm.

'Ah!' Coppelia watched the penny drop, though she'd no idea what had caused the sudden shift. 'You believe me now. I can tell.'

Then, Honoria's eyes fastened greedily on her face, searching her every feature for family likenesses. Spittle flew from her mouth. 'Where is your proof?' she asked urgently, eagerly.

'Yes, where is your proof?' asked Rajesh, his breast heaving with emotion. 'It is not enough to make spurious claims. You are clever – but we are not stupid.'

'Proof!' Coppelia snorted. 'You shall have your proof. I shall tell you everything and you shall decide if it is proof enough. But not while you stand confronting me in that fashion.'

'As you wish.' Rajesh waved a hand inviting her to proceed, then knelt by Honoria's bed, his eyes fixed on Coppelia's face, almost greedily, all the while.

'Everyone sitting comfortably?' Coppelia mocked. 'Good, then I shall begin. Once upon a time in India, in a little village called Puttaparthi, an Englishman – we shall call him James – rescued a little girl from the hell to which she had been condemned by her mother.' Her finger shot out, accusing. 'That little girl became his *fille aux yeux d'émail*, after the ballet *Coppelia*. His girl with enamel eyes! He loved me in that twisted way some adults have for children, but it was the first time anyone had shown me kindness and, for all that it was wrong in society's eyes, he truly did love me.' Her chin came up. 'And I will have no one condemn him for it. Were it not for him, who knows what would have become of me?' Her voice broke slightly. 'He bought me, you know, like I was an object, goods to be traded, *not* a flesh-and-blood person. Oh, don't shed those crocodile tears, Honoria! And spare me the mock stricken looks, Rajesh! It was the best thing that could have happened to me at that time – short of my real mother showing up, of course, and that wasn't going to happen.' Coppelia continued, relentless. 'And because he loved me and because of my unusual looks – red hair and green eyes – he knew there was a story there. A story that I would want to hear some day. That story began and ended with you, Honoria.'

'When did he tell you?' Honoria whispered through cracked lips.

'Oh, not straight away. How could a child cope with such a heavy load? He was a wise man, James. And a sensitive one. He recorded my whole story in a diary, which he left to me when he died. At twenty, I was no longer a child, but a strong woman. He knew I could deal with whatever brick-bats came my way. And eventually, I came searching . . . and found Carrickross.'

'But you kept your identity secret. Why?' Honoria wailed. 'Did you not realise I would have thrown my arms around you! What joy, to have my long-lost daughter restored to me!'

449

Coppelia shrugged coldly. 'Why should I think that? You had *abandoned* me, for God's sake! And then I find you in Carrickross – beautiful, magnificent, historic Carrickross, seat of the Granvilles for generations past – playing at happy families. A happy family that didn't include me! I hated you then, Honoria, with every fibre of my being. I vowed to make you sorry.'

Honoria gasped as the first piece of the jigsaw slotted into place. 'Henry!'

Coppelia nodded. 'You better believe it. Yes, Henry. I deliberately set out to take him from you, but that particular piece of scheming turned around and bit me on the bum. I fell in love with him, Honoria, deeply so, as I have never been before or since. I hadn't planned on that. But I don't regret it for one moment. *You* never deserved him! Neither did I plan on getting pregnant with Ashling.' She drew herself up, proud as a queen in the tatty old red blanket. 'But, unlike you, I never regretted having my daughter. Never once did it occur to me to get rid of her.'

Honoria's eyes turned from Coppelia to fasten themselves eagerly on Rajesh. But his face was now masklike once more, his eyes hooded. 'Rajesh, Rajesh, don't you see?' Her voice turned into a wail. 'It is my baby – it is she – come to find me! Can you doubt it?'

At this, Rajesh uncoiled himself from beside the bed and again confronted Coppelia. He held himself tensely, his face taut, as he strained to rein in an overpowering emotion. His hooded eyes flickered over her. 'I've listened to your story and indeed, on the face of it, it fits the circumstances. But this is not proof. It is, after all, a story, a story such as anyone might learn. Anyone *clever!*' He paused, flashed her a glittering, challenging emerald look. 'Show me. Show me you are a daughter of India. *Ap kis des ke hain?*' The last words were spat out, a verbal gauntlet chucked down in a challenge.

Coppelia threw back her head and laughed. 'Oh, please! What country am I from, indeed! Oh well, if it makes you happy. *Mein Bharata se hoon.* I am from India.'

Rajesh visibly reacted to the Indian words, then challenged her again. '*When* did this man, this James, buy you in Puttaparthi? What was the year? How old were you?'

'Rajesh, please!' Honoria objected, but he raised a hand and she fell silent.

'What is this – twenty questions?' Coppelia jibed. 'You really have missed your vocation, Rajesh. Chief Inquisitor would have been right up your street. But, tell you what, since you've started, why don't I finish? The man James bought me from was a filthy child trafficker – his true business disguised, of course, by a plausible cover. To those not in the know he was a "carer" of orphans, and the gullible even donated money to his "charity"! The year was 1969 and I was about twelve years old, on the verge of womanhood.' As Honoria gasped on hearing the date and age, Coppelia continued venomously, 'Forgive me for not being more exact, but you see my *mother* took care not to leave documentation of any kind.'

She turned back to Rajesh, to find his face transfigured.

'I believe you are she.' The admission was clearly painful. He had been so long without hope. It was difficult to believe his dearest wish had finally come true and was standing body and soul before him.

Tentatively, he held out his arms as if he would embrace her, then let them fall uselessly back to his sides.

He turned to Honoria, his voice laden with grief and guilt. 'Yes, the date is right, Rani, and the age. And there was such a man as this child trafficker in Puttaparthi. Whispers came to my ears and I found him – twice I searched for her among those poor children he bought and sold, but she was not there. But I should have gone back! For now it seems he acquired her in later years – after I had already been there. Oh, how cruel Fate has been to us! I never mentioned him to you, Rani – I didn't wish to hurt you more.'

'I see,' Honoria said, her eyes full of tears. 'Dear Rajesh, you have sought always to protect me, but perhaps you should not have. Actions have consequences and I deserved to wallow in my guilt.'

A thought struck Coppelia like a thunderbolt. Appalled, she wrenched at Rajesh's still-damp sleeve. There was a tearing sound as the material ripped. 'You, you venomous reptile! You were in Honoria's employ even then! And who else could she entrust to do her dirty work? Who else was so slavishly devoted?' Her brows drew together in a fierce scowl. 'But perhaps not so devoted that you didn't think of feathering your own nest, you bastard!' She drew back her hand to slap him, but Carrick caught her wrist. 'You sold me, didn't you? You sold me to that evil man. *Usne tumhen kitna paisa diya?*' she spat at him. 'How much did he pay you? What was the going rate for an innocent little baby?' She lost what was left of her composure then, dissolved into a near hysterical mess in front of them. She flung her hand out at Honoria. 'Then, after Timothy Villiers died, you panicked and told Honoria I was lost! Perhaps that I was dead! It was your greed that kept me from my mother!' She shook Carrick off. 'Get your hands off me, Carrick. Don't worry – I'm not going to hit him. I wouldn't soil my hands!'

'It is not true!' Rajesh groaned, his body curling in on itself like one struck in the heart by a dart.

'Oh, no, Coppelia!' cried Honoria weakly. 'Rajesh would never—' Suddenly she pressed a fist to her chest and gasped. 'Look at him, Coppelia! Look closely at his eyes. You have seen them before – every time you look in a mirror!'

Rajesh raised his eyes, flooded with tears, to Coppelia's. Time stood still as green eyes looked into green and a stunned Coppelia at last learned the truth.

'Forgive us, my daughter,' he said huskily. 'Forgive if you can.'

But Coppelia, her whole world shifting, stared dumbstruck and could not answer.

As Rajesh threw himself down beside Honoria again, clasping her age-spotted hands and raining kisses on them, crooning soft words in Hindi, Coppelia gazed aghast at the elderly couple who had once long ago conceived her in love, then left her to her fate in a foreign land. Rajesh! Honoria's lover? My God, in retrospect it all made perfect sense, but proud, well-heeled Honoria and a lowly native? Never! And yet the proof was within herself, her golden skin and emerald eyes, legacies of her father. And her fiery temper and unforgiving nature, a legacy of them both.

As Coppelia's head reeled, Carrick was watching his grandmother and her faithful Indian servant. *My God, he really loves her*, he thought in wonder. Sorrow shot through him. *Oh, Grandmother, Grandmother, what have you done with your life? How many lives have you ruined because of your pride and foolish stubbornness?*

He glanced at Coppelia and his heart ached for her. He put a supportive arm around her waist and felt her trembling.

'Be strong,' he whispered. 'At least you now know the truth.'

Honoria had caught the words. 'Not all of it,'

she said. She stretched out an arm towards her daughter. 'Come closer, Coppelia!' Her voice crackled like dry autumn leaves. 'Come sit by me and . . . and your father. There is so much you do not yet know.'

Propelled gently by Carrick, Coppelia moved forward like an automaton.

Honoria's eyes blazed like those of a young woman. 'Firstly, you must believe we did not abandon you.' She took Coppelia's hand in hers. Coppelia did not pull away. 'Indeed, we took great care to place you in the hands of a good family, confident that they would give you a good life. Sadly our trust was betrayed. For reasons we shall never know, they passed you on to another family, whom we could never trace – and so you were lost to us.'

'After we left India,' Rajesh joined in, 'I returned year after year to search. But always in vain. There was never a trace, never so much as a whisper or a rumour. It was as if you had never existed.'

'But you existed for me – for us both,' said Honoria, 'every second, every hour of every day, year after year, right up to this moment. It has always seemed as though part of my heart was still in India. My darling daughter. I am so, so sorry.'

And there they were, the words Coppelia had longed to hear all her life. With a small cry, she sank to her knees beside the bed and for the first time since she was a baby felt the caress of her mother's hand on her head. Like a blessing.

Carrick quietly left the hut. But as he closed the door behind him, he stood gazing in for a moment, savouring the scene. The light of the little stove and candles lit up a glowing image as Honoria and Rajesh welcomed their daughter back into the fold.

Climbing into the back of the Land Rover, he began to arrange the blankets to prepare a warm nest where Honoria could lie in Rajesh's arms for the journey back to Carrickross, then went round and sat in the driving seat, where he idly watched raindrops chase each other down the window. He would give the three of them five minutes, no more. Whatever questions they still had could wait until later. Inside the hut, bridges that had been burned were being rebuilt. Shame it couldn't last, though. Musing, he chewed at a ragged cuticle. In the heat of the moment they were all forgetting one thing: Henry and his unfortunate demise.

CHAPTER 36

The flames leaped and lamplight glowed, catching the amber tones of the brandy in the bulbous glass in Honoria's hand and the copper tones of Rajesh's skin where he sprawled on the hearthrug at her feet, leaning on a bunch of tasselled silk cushions. A storm raged outside, reminding Honoria of their horrible ordeal in that dreadful mountain hut only two weeks before. She gave an involuntary shudder.

'Are you cold, Rani?' Rajesh was immediately solicitous.

'No, no. A goose walked over my grave.'

Now he shuddered. 'Do not speak of graves, Rani.'

'Too close to home?' She chuckled grimly.

But not close tonight. She sighed in contentment as she savoured the warmth and comfort of her luxurious room and the sight of Rajesh who, in the muted glow of the fire, looked once more almost like a young man. It also helped, of course, that her sight was failing. She gave a half-smile, rueful.

She was beginning to feel good again, happy in

her own skin, in a way she hadn't been for years. If nothing else the mountain, which had taken so much from her, had also brought a resolution of sorts. At last it was time to leave the past behind and look to the future – the little that was left to her.

There had been no recurrence of the heart attack – though she still suffered from a few twinges of angina if she over-exerted herself. But she did not fool herself. Death was almost upon her. But for now these last few drops of life were extraordinarily sweet. There was no more effective medicine than having all one's desires fulfilled.

'I've been thinking,' she murmured. 'Things have panned out quite nicely, all in all. Everyone's a winner.'

Rajesh looked up at her, musing. 'We have found our long-lost daughter.'

'And she has found her long-lost parents.'

'She has also "found" the long-lost love between her and *her* daughter.'

Honoria nodded, then chuckled. 'Ashling has escaped from Rossa's and my clutches. How wrong I was to use her like that! How misguided!'

'Jaspar has gone happily back to the plains of Africa,' Rajesh smiled, 'with Ehu.'

'Carrick has achieved his destiny – Carrickross.'

'And a wife perhaps?' Rajesh's eyes gleamed mischievously in the firelight.

'Perhaps,' Honoria concurred. 'But I wonder if I shall live to hear the patter of tiny Granville feet?'

He reached up a reassuring hand. 'You will, Rani, but while you are waiting, we are free now to go once more to India.'

She smiled, her face softening. 'India, yes. Yes, we shall go soon, my love.' She paused. 'And Rossa will return to his nefarious pursuits . . . whatever they may be.'

'And Fintan?'

Honoria frowned. 'Fin is still but a young foal, unsteady on his feet as yet, but one day I believe he may jump higher than all the rest.'

'And the twins? Hardly winners – locked up in that clinic in Sweden.'

'It is not for ever, only until such time as their broken minds are healed.' She smiled faintly. 'But you know, they are winners too. After all, they have escaped a murder rap.'

'But you do not still believe that they killed that young woman, do you, Rani? After all, they had alibis for the attempts on Jaspar and Ashling.'

'No, I don't believe they did it, but ask me if I believe they are capable of murder and I will say yes. Yes, they are. It seems we will never know for certain. The police themselves admit to being no further along with their inquiries.'

'That poor young beauty queen,' Rajesh reminded her. 'She lost everything.'

'She was not a Granville,' said Honoria.

'And therefore doesn't matter,' murmured Rajesh.

Honoria threw him a sharp look but said nothing.

They were silent for a little, watching the flames dance.

'And Henry was certainly a loser,' said Honoria then.

'Ah, yes, Henry!'

'He was an old fool! We would do the same again.'

A pause.

Then Rajesh spoke ruefully. 'Coppelia will never forgive us for Henry's death.'

'No. She won't. But she should. That was her fault after all,' Honoria stated unreasonably.

Rajesh shook his head. 'No, Rani, the sin started with us. Her hatred started with her abandonment. That brought her to Carrickross – and to Henry. We can only hope her heart is big enough to find forgiveness.' He sat up, gently took her veined hand and kissed it. Then he lay back on his cushions and gazed again into the heart of the fire.

'So,' said Honoria after a pause, 'it seems my grand scheme worked out beautifully after all.'

Rajesh raised an ironic eyebrow. 'More by good luck than good management – isn't that the expression?'

'Nonsense!' She waved a dismissive hand and continued with great satisfaction. 'Carrickross is safe for the future. And Coppelia Morrison is . . . disarmed. My two aims achieved.'

They were silent again, both thinking of the spectacular daughter who, until recently, had been their greatest enemy.

'I think she takes after me,' said Honoria eventually.

Rajesh smiled, but kept his own counsel.

'Rajesh?'

'Yes?'

'Bring me the diary. I can hide no longer.'

'Now, Rani?'

'Yes. Now.'

Rajesh got to his feet and went to fetch James Mayhew's diary from the bureau. Then he topped up Honoria's brandy and stretched out again in front of the fire.

Then, with Honoria listening intently, he began to read.

Puttaparthi village, India – 4 July 1969
I pulled my car up beside a jacaranda tree, got out and stood beneath the shade, as I had done every day for the past four days. Blue trumpet-shaped blossoms littered the dusty, hard-baked earth. From somewhere close by a roller bird gave the harsh chack-chack cry that went so ill with his colourful blue and lilac plumage. I checked my watch, angling the face away from the sunlight. It was hot today, hotter than Hades. An insect spun past on multi-coloured gossamer wings, returning to dive-bomb my face. I swatted it away and leaned my back against the trunk of the tree, feeling the bark rough and warm

461

through the thin material of my cotton shirt. Any moment now. My eyes followed the line of the dusty street, bordered on each side by box-like shanty houses, welded together by a peculiar mixture of mud, broken planks, torn sheets of plastic and odd rusty bits of corrugated iron. The dogs were already gathering. I eyed them with distaste – filthy, mangy-looking animals, ribs visible as bicycle spokes beneath their skinny, half-starved bodies. Probably rabid.

A shout went up. A door opened, disgorging a handful of dirty brown ragged children into the street. The show was about to begin. I stiffened, my heart starting to pound, blood rushing dizzyingly in my head. I was surprised no one else could hear it, but they were intent on their game and oblivious to me. The dogs stiffened too, the sinews in their necks tightening to snapping point, their muzzles up and already salivating. Who would win today? I craned my neck and then I saw her, being pushed and shoved roughly ahead of a much bigger boy. Other children danced along beside them, taunting, grabbing, pulling at her hair. She was skinny, lighter-skinned than the others, and she was proud. I could tell that even from a distance. Her small chin was up, defiant, even as they goaded and bullied her into the middle of the road. There were sores on her emaciated arms and legs, the rags that covered her body barely adequate. Her hair was incredible, waist-length, Titian, its richness undimmed by the filth and dirt, though probably lice-ridden. Her eyes were green. Large. Flat. Hopeless. I called her Coppelia, *la fille aux yeux d'émail* – the girl with enamel eyes, after the ballet of the same name. For a moment she looked straight at me and my heart leaped. Had she noticed me watching her for the past four days? Had she been watching out especially for me? The boy thrust her roughly into the centre of the street and her glance fell away. The others moved back to form a circle around her. Knowing what was expected of them, the dogs moved in, slowly, picking their paws up carefully from the ground, alert, knowing from past experience that danger, a kick in the ribs, could come out of anywhere at any time.

It was as if the world suddenly stood still. Time froze, telescoped into just one moment. Then one of the children threw a chicken carcass into the circle and the spell was broken as with a yell that was almost primeval, both girl and animals fell upon it. Whoever won would eat that day. The children yelled and cheered. The girl lashed out, screamed and snarled, feral as a wild cat. The dogs barked, growled, fought her and each other. Someone pushed a stick into her hand. She swung it like a mace, brought it down on one dog's head. He yelped. Blood appeared at his ear and muzzle. He fell over, twitched, stayed still. The other dogs scattered. Triumphant, her dress ripped so badly it hung open, she stood silent for a moment, searching me out again, a mini-Boadicea. Then, her eyes locked on mine, she picked up her trophy, turned on her heel disdainfully and walked gracefully away.

I bought her.

There was no haggling. The 'caretaker' of the children seemed glad to be rid of her. 'Tatti' he called her and even with my limited knowledge of Hindi, I knew that it meant 'shit'. The word clawed at my heart. My beautiful Coppelia, my Titian-haired goddess-child to be so denigrated! I would have bought her whatever the cost. As it happened, a handful of rupees and my gold watch was enough to make her mine, in body, if not in soul and spirit. I recognised that from the outset. Those would always be her own.

She was feral, this young girl, a wildcat. Ill-treatment had made her cautious, vicious, ready always for flight or fight, and yet when I took her to my house she made no attempt to run away, although I left the door unlocked. But what were the alternatives? Where would she go? Back to the people who had abused her so badly, the people who had sold her to me with no thought for what kind of a man I might be. India! Scorching, dusty, poverty-stricken, dangerous. It was no place for a young girl, barely past childhood, to fend for herself alone. Her natural intelligence must have told her as much.

And so she stayed, and little by little we grew used to one another's presence.

Rajesh looked up when he reached this natural pause and found Honoria silently weeping. He made a move towards her, thinking to comfort her, but she waved a trembling hand, signalling him to go on. He hesitated, then obeyed.

He read on, read through the whole disturbing and astonishing story, while Honoria listened motionless, silent. Read how it took time for James Mayhew to gain Coppelia's trust, read how she flinched away whenever he came too near. How only once did he make the mistake of going too fast, when drawn as a moth towards a flame he reached out to stroke her tumbling locks and she sank her teeth into his arm so hard she drew blood. She had scuttled away then, crouching down in a corner, warily watching him for hours above her folded arms, her eyes sharp, back-lit like a fox, wired to his every movement. Patience won the day. Patience, good food, slow movements and a soft voice.

But despite the difficulty of those early days, James never had any doubt that she was a prize well worth the waiting and so he bided his time, taming her step by step. The process took years. But he waited.

Eventually, Coppelia came to his bed, slipping in quietly beside him, not speaking but making it plain from her actions that she knew what she was doing and the kind of effect her adolescent body was having on him. It was what he wanted. She gave herself willingly. And he took.

James went back to the child-trader only once, to learn her story. He figured he owed her that much. With a little financial encouragement, the man was only too happy to spill his guts. The girl, he believed, was the love child of a European lady. He knew this because once an Indian servant of that lady had come from Bangalore, searching for a red-haired green-eyed child, but that was two years before he, himself, had acquired her. Even now he cursed his luck! If only she had come into his hands sooner! The European mother would no doubt have paid a small fortune to have her back! When the girl had later been sold to him, he had remembered the Indian's visit and had considered making attempts to find the parents and reunite the family. But it was too dangerous. He could be accused of stealing the girl or jailed for child-trafficking. He had abandoned the idea.

He gave James Mayhew the name of the family who had sold the girl to him.

With this information James had continued to trace back Coppelia's history. It was extremely difficult but he had at last arrived at the name he sought: Honoria Granville. But by then it was already too late. He *could* not, *would* not give her up to anyone. And so he kept what he had learned locked between the pages of a secret diary.

Those hours not engaged in his work as a diplomat, James spent teaching her English and French, about the 'green and pleasant land' that was England itself, about the literature of Shakespeare and Dickens, the poetry of Keats and Wordsworth, the art of Constable and Hogarth. He enjoyed imparting his knowledge as much as she enjoyed learning. When she was fifteen, three years after he bought her, he took her to England, passing her off as his daughter, Coppelia Mayhew.

But then James was struck down in his prime by the cancer that plagued his family. He won the battle temporarily but decided to take early retirement in his remote country house in Hertfordshire, where he was careful always to keep a low profile and discourage callers. Both saviour and lover to Coppelia, James was in no doubt that others would be anxious to cast him in the altogether different roles of pervert and paedophile. He held his hands up – he was what he was – but that didn't mean he was anxious to go to prison, for what would happen to his *fille aux yeux d'émail* then? His girl with the enamel eyes.

In the last year of his life, when Coppelia was twenty, he relaxed the rules – what could it matter then? – and began to prepare her for life in the outside world upon his death. Along with teaching her how to cope with the everyday minutiae of life, he took her to meet his lawyer and to go through the contents of his will, which would make her a very wealthy young woman. He bought her a car and taught her to drive. In the only way he could, James was trying to atone, trying to give her back her life.

She had nursed him in his last weeks, was on her knees by his bed in his last days urging him to stay with her, begging him not to leave her alone in the world. She was his angel, his tower of strength, his reason for existence. To the end she outstripped him, giving him more than he could possibly give back – even if he had not run out of time.

The diary ended abruptly, after a series of disconnected and hardly legible entries obviously recorded with difficulty in his last days. But thrust into the book was a letter, clear and carefully written.

It read:

Coppelia, my green-eyed darling,
I thought long and hard about leaving you this Pandora's box.

468

So much hurt, so much pain and betrayal you have already suffered in your short life. And I, the wolf in sheep's clothing, as guilty as all the rest. But, Coppelia, it is your story and your right to know the truth.

God grant it will set you free.

Forever, your James

Honoria sat long and silent, eyes hooded, after Rajesh's voice was stilled and he laid the diary on her lap. Each was lost in bitter regrets and thoughts of what might have been.

So much hatred, so much hunger for revenge. In the last analysis, thought Honoria, the gods had been good to them, choosing at the eleventh hour not to inflict the ultimate punishment – so nearly had Coppelia been the sacrificial victim on the altar of their mutual hate. In fact, more by luck than management, the only victim had been Henry. And Henry was an old fool.

Yes, there was much to be grateful for. The outcome was better than they deserved.

'For all that, she is remarkable,' said Rajesh then.

'Yes. She is everything we could have hoped for.'

They smiled at each other and fell silent again.

'Rajesh, I am weary for my bed,' said Honoria at last. 'The fire has gone out.'

CHAPTER 37

MIDSUMMER, 21 JUNE 2009

Laurel Canyon – Hollywood Hills

Ashling shook the droplets of water from her hair as she emerged from her swimming pool. Although still early morning the temperature was already nudging the mid-70s and today promised to be another LA scorcher.

It was midsummer, the anniversary of the infamous ball at Carrickross. As she patted herself dry with a towel, it was difficult not to reflect on what a huge difference a year made. She had taken up the offer of working alongside Annie Leibovitz and look at her now! These days she felt like an altogether different person, a phoenix who had risen from the ashes, honed, toned and made of tempered steel. The woman who had become engaged to Rossa Granville was nothing to do with her. That was a different lifetime, one she had no wish to revisit. She had been foolish, easily led, seduced by a dream that had all too rapidly turned into a nightmare. But something good had come from the mix. She had learned who her mother really was – oh, not just the fact that she was *really* her mother, but who she was as a person, what made her tick, the fact that she was a survivor – a trait which she, herself, had clearly inherited. Her chin came up, unconsciously. Yes, she was a survivor too and wow, when she looked around her luxurious hacienda-style villa in the Hollywood Hills she had to admit that the girl done good.

Yes, the Midsummer Ball had changed her life – had changed all their lives. Coppelia, having sold the town house in Dublin and settled into a loft-style apartment in Manhattan, was moving on with her life. And very successfully, if the latest tabloid story about her and a new young American actor was to be believed!

Honoria had gone off to India with Rajesh to revisit their past. Another strong woman, Honoria, her grandmother. Now, a year later, she had just about managed to forgive her for using her as bait in a trap – an incestuous trap, although she had to believe that Honoria had genuinely never meant for her to sleep with Rossa and that the separate rooms at Carrickross had not simply been for form's sake. One day, some time in the future, maybe she could even learn to love her. How they had suffered, her mother and grandmother. But that was all in the past now and that's where it must remain.

Of course, they never had discovered who killed the Kingdom Rose and attempted to murder Jaspar and herself. Rumour was still rife at

Carrickross. One lobby had it that the mad bad twins were the murderers after all and that Seán McCarthy had strangled Jaspar. Others voted Rajesh. While 'that wild African' was odds-on favourite with the bookies.

Would anyone ever know? Poor Kate O'Leary, the Kingdom Rose, was she fated to go down in the annals of unsolved Irish murders?

Ashling walked gracefully over to the wall of her property and gazed down at the City of the Angels, Los Angeles, nestling like a precious jewel in the valley below. Behind her was the great dry desert-baked ridge of the Santa Monica Mountains; in front of her: a brand-new future.

Nyambeni Lodge, Kenya

'Oh, bliss!' Jaspar relaxed back in the outdoor jacuzzi, the Kenyan sun deepening his already tanned naked skin, an ice-cold glass of G&T within easy reach. From nearby came the staccato chatter of a monkey climbing an acacia tree and from the plains below, the distant reveille of an elephant. 'I am never leaving this place again, dear boy, never ever.' He said this at least once a day but today he was pontificating at great length on the theme, it being the anniversary of last year's Midsummer Ball. 'Not for anything! I have found my heaven, my Nirvana, and this is where I will stay.' He smiled lovingly across at Ehu, reached for his hand and kissed the dull gold of the

472

wedding ring he had placed there during the most wonderfully romantic civil marriage ceremony in Holland. 'You and this place are all I need. Remind me of that, won't you, especially if you ever hear the word Carrickross pass my lips again.' He mock-spat to one side. 'Though I must admit the matriarch left all of us more than amply provided for before she departed for the subcontinent. *Quelle surprise!* I never expected such largesse from that quarter.'

Ehu smiled and allowed Jaspar to prattle on as usual, as he too cast his mind back to that dark period in his life. Luckily, Jaspar would never find out that he was the one who had tried to murder him at Carrickross. And all because of a stupid misunderstanding.

He remembered as if it was yesterday how the blood had sung in his head as he moved stealthily through the rhododendron bushes, keeping Jaspar in sight, after he had announced at the dining-room doors that he was getting married, then shouted at him to pack and say goodbye to Carrickross.

It seemed he was to be kicked out like a dog because Jaspar wanted to marry a white woman, Maggie, who had pretended to be Ehu's friend while trying to steal Jaspar from him. But he had known – he had seen them embracing in Jaspar's room.

Used to stalking wildlife in his own land, it had been a simple matter to follow the inebriated Jaspar, to creep up on him in the boathouse and garrotte him with the leather thong of one of his many necklaces. He was a member of the Maasai. He was a warrior. He would not be humiliated. Jaspar had to die.

Only when Jaspar's eyes had begun to bulge and turn blue had Ehu come to his senses. What was he doing? The terrifying prospect of being locked up for life in an Irish jail made him tremble. Leaving his unconscious lover on the ground, he had run swift as a gazelle back to the house. Jaspar had not seen him. Nobody had seen him. Everyone would think it was the work of the person who had murdered that beauty queen. Later he had raised the alarm and joined the search for a missing Jaspar.

But he had very soon realised what a terrible mistake he had made. It was he, Ehu, that Jaspar wanted to marry. Not Maggie. But, of course, he had never heard of men getting married before.

'Ehu?' Jaspar's voice snuffled into his shoulder. 'You do love me, don't you?'

Ehu nodded. Since that terrible time at Carrickross he had come to realise that he did. He proceeded to demonstrate his affection in exactly the way Jaspar liked best.

Le Meridien Hotel – Piccadilly, London

'Ready, Sapph?' Indigo poked his head into the hotel room, where Daniel Galvin was putting the final touches to his twin sister's hair-do. Sapphire

474

smiled her thanks at the celebrity coiffeur as he patted the last strand into place and then hurried away to attend to another star.

'So whaddya think, Ind? Eat your heart out, Sienna Miller, or what?' Gleeful, Sapphire tipped her head to one side and grinned.

'She'll be gutted,' Indigo laughed, stepping into the room. 'The press will be all over you like flies.'

'Yes, but this time it will be for a good reason. No more "Twin Freaks in Swedish Freak-house!" headlines for us, eh?'

'No!' Indigo chuckled. Standing behind her chair, he massaged her shoulders gently. 'No more Twin Freaks, indeed!' He made a little moue. 'It's an ill wind, Sapph, and we turned that notoriety to our advantage. Just look at us tonight – you and me – the famously infamous Sapphire and Indigo Granville, ready to take the world by the balls. Ready to shimmy up the red carpet with the best of 'em.' He went to the line of coke that Sapphire had already laid out in readiness on the table and helped himself.

Sapphire tapped her hand against her throat, round which nestled a collar of amethysts and diamonds. 'Notice the rocks?'

'Fabulous. Antique, I should think. Wait a minute – aren't they—'

'Granoria's? Yes, the ones she gave me before she left for India – as some kind of pay-off for incarcerating us! I wasn't sure whether to wear them tonight . . .'

'No, they're perfect,' Indigo assured her, recalling that the last time he had seen them around Honoria's neck had been a year ago at the ill-fated Midsummer Ball. 'And it's kind of fitting that we should have something of the old girl along with us tonight.'

Sapphire got to her feet and did a little twirl. 'And, what do you think of the gown, eh, Ind? Will I do? Only a cool three thousand quid's worth of pure Gianni Versace. Small change!'

Indigo wiped the residue of the coke from his nose, pursed his lips and let out a slow appreciative whistle, as his eyes ran leisurely over the svelte, midnight-blue-velvet-gowned form of his twin sister, cut to hug in all the right places, the heart-shaped neckline showing off her high round breasts to perfection. 'Sis, you look incredible! Good enough to shag! You, dear heart, are a work of human architecture most wondrous to behold.' Indigo put his arms around her slender waist and drew her to him.

'Do you think there's time?' His voice was husky, hypnotic.

'You'll muss me up.'

'Can't be helped and it's in a good cause.' Scooping her up, Indigo carried her to the bed and within moments his beautifully cut Armani tux had gone to join her Gianni Versace on the floor.

Outside the Odeon Leicester Square, fans pushed and shoved on either side of the roped-off

476

red carpet, desperate to catch a glimpse of the stars of *Plucking the Rose*, the blockbuster film loosely based on the horrific killing of an Irish beauty queen that was set to break all box office records.

A hush fell upon the crowd, expectant faces turned towards the white stretch limousine pulling in by the kerb. Then a roar broke out as Indigo Granville, the star of the film, stepped out of the car, escorted by his stunning twin sister, Sapphire, and his handsomely rugged bodyguard, Seán McCarthy.

As they sashayed through the doorway, illuminated by the light of a thousand flashlights and borne aloft on the waves of admiration from the Indigo Granville fan club, the famous statue of Eros in nearby Piccadilly Circus looked a little forlorn. When it came to Sapphire and Indigo Granville, his arrow had been blown way off course.

Hua Hin, Thailand

'So, now we get married?' Priti asked. 'No more excuse.'

Rossa laughed, stroking Priti's long brown thigh as it lay draped across him. The air was thick with the smell of sex. 'Yes, Priti, now we'll get married. Do I have a choice?'

Priti pulled herself up and straddled him, pushing her shoulders back so that her small round breasts stood proudly at attention. 'No! No, Mr Rossa, you don't have no choice.' Play-fighting, she grabbed his arms and pinioned them high above his head. 'Cos you know what Priti capable of . . . think little bit 'bout what happen this day last year?'

'Don't remind me!' Rossa's voice was suddenly taut with tension.

'The first one, she is a mistake,' Priti continued, almost conversationally. 'It is dark. Same dress. Same hair. Same stupid face! Hey, I'm sorry I do that, but it is for you, Rossa. I jealous.' She batted a fly away. 'And I not succeed with the other one anyway. That black man poison is shit. Not even kill a cat!' She punched him lightly in his chest. 'But that Jaspar – that is not me, Rossa. You believe me?'

'I believe you,' Rossa said, and he did. Priti had no motive for trying to murder Jaspar. He sighed deeply and relaxed back onto the bed.

It had been a terrible experience, so terrible that the discovery that Ashling was actually a close blood relative paled by comparison with all the other horrors. But, now, one year on, life was pretty good, especially since Honoria had opened the coffers and paid him a substantial amount of 'guilt' money.

'Come here, you!' Reaching up, he pulled Priti down into his arms.

'No, wait.' Priti struggled back into a sitting position. 'You want me to dress as waiter again, like I'm doin' at Carrickross? It turn you on, no?'

'No!' Rossa roared, sweat breaking out on his forehead as he recalled the merry dance she'd led him, following him to Ireland and getting herself employed as a waiter. Christ! He'd nearly shit himself when he'd rumbled her at the Midsummer Ball – his engagement party. He'd packed her off to Thailand immediately after the Rose had been found, but she'd sneaked back again. And when he met her in London, the crafty mare had only flown out from Ireland, then promptly returned once more.

'Oh, Priti,' he sighed, 'you've put me through hell, but I love you. I'd die for you, you know that?'

Priti smiled. 'Yes, Rossa, my darlin'. And I would *kill* for you.'

With the lightning-quick change of mood inherent in her nature, she flung off his arms and stood naked by the side of the bed. 'But what we gonna do about this, eh?' Angrily, she indicated her groin, swishing at it in disgust. 'You make me big promise. Priti, when I have money, I gonna make you operation.' A note of pure longing entered her voice. 'Okay, so I got boobies now. But, oh, honey, Priti no want be lady-boy no more. I want be lady, proper lady.'

Rossa reached out and caressed her small male member, the part that made her so miserable, the part that stood (literally) between her and her

dreams of being a *real* woman. The part that, ironically, made her special to him. His voice was soft.

'Oh, Priti, as far as I'm concerned, you're once,
twice, three times a lady . . . and I love you.'

Carrickross

'And who's a cute little boy? Look at those
gorgeous eyes! Carrick, hand me a nappy there.'

'I'll do it while you fix his bottle.' Carrick laid
the bundle of press photos he had been perusing
on the table, grabbed a nappy and bent to his
task.

Maggie came scuttling back. She and Eddy had
bonded to such an extent that she hardly had time
to pee these days. But that was the name of the
game, wasn't it? She took the freshly changed
Eddy from Carrick and placed him on her hip.
'Carrick, could you mash a little banana?'

'Coming up!'

Life was good at Carrickross. A new wind had
blown through the estate, sweeping all the old
spider's webs away. Of course, Honoria would
return but she intended to live out her days in the
dower house on the estate, she and the faithful
Rajesh, and leave the running of Carrickross to
Carrick and Maggie.

When Carrick had first proposed Maggie had
had qualms about accepting, lost in love though
she was. She truly felt she could not live a life of
privilege, felt that the Carrickross land and wealth

belonged to the Irish people from whom it was stolen in colonial times and bestowed on the likes of the Granvilles. She couldn't be part of all that. It would only make her unhappy.

And then Noreen had her big idea. After that, compromises had been reached.

'Carrick.' It was Tom, looking furious. 'Mrs Granville.'

Maggie had long since tired of trying to get him to call her Maggie.

'Yes, Tom?' said Carrick.

'Those blasted apes have escaped again. Two of 'em. They jumped from the top of the fence to the oak tree and they're up there now. Luckily I saw it happen or they'd have been in Tralee before we even noticed.'

'Good man, Tom! I'll bring the Land Rover around in case they run but let's hope we can lure them down with fruit like the last time.' He came and tickled Eddy and kissed his silky hair. 'Daddy will be back soon, little man!'

'Good luck, love!' said Maggie. 'Oh, where did you put the photos Fin brought? I want to have a look.'

'On the piano.'

Fin had brought a pile of press photos from last year's dread Midsummer Ball. He thought they might finally have the stomach to look at them.

'There's a hilarious incriminating one of Rossa on top!' Carrick called as he left. 'Bending a lustful eye on one of the waiters! Uncle Jaspar always did

481

claim Rossa swung both ways. That Thai mistress of his had better be versatile!' And with that he was gone.

Tom paused on the threshold to deliver his own exit line: 'And to think it was my own Noreen who brought all this trouble on us with her notion of bringing in monkeys!' He shook his head.

'You're like a broken record, Tom, with your complaints about Noreen's brilliant scheme,' Maggie scolded. 'You know they're a great attraction for the public on Sundays.'

'I don't know which is worse, the bloody apes or the bloody public!'

'Ah, Tom, it's a privilege to be able to house these poor orphaned animals – like sweet little Eddy.'

'*He'll* just grow up to be a blasted ape too!'

After she had fed the little chimpanzee his bottle and mashed banana, Maggie went to look at the photos. She had to steel herself and gave a shudder as she picked the first one up, the one Carrick had referred to. It was a large black-and-white photo, a close-up of two faces. On the far right, in perfect focus, was an oriental waiter – the one Rossa had been tearing strips off outside near the fountain. Yes, it was definitely him, his long hair drawn back tightly in the same way. Head turning to his right, he was making eye contact with Rossa who was staring right at him, full-force, from the left-hand side of the frame.

But what a strange look! 'Bending a lustful eye'?

There was nothing lustful about that gaze. It was urgent, hugely significant. Whatever Rossa was communicating it sure wasn't a request for more canapés or a spot of slap and tickle. He actually looked as if he was gazing on his worst nightmare. As for the waiter . . .

Maggie sucked in her breath.

The waiter was beautiful. Delicate.

And she had seen him before, apart from the night of the ball. On a bicycle. At Carrickross. The morning Ashling was poisoned.

What was it that Carrick had just said? *That Thai mistress of his had better be versatile.*

Versatile? She most certainly was.

'Oh my God,' breathed Maggie. 'I know who killed the Kingdom Rose!'

Family Graveyard, Carrickross

Coppelia knelt by the grave, sweeping some rogue leaves and twigs away with the palm of her hand and replacing them with fresh flowers purloined from the gardens at Carrickross. Nearby stood the two black marble headstones where the brothers she had never known, William and David, lay with their wives, Ella and the deranged Agneta.

The headstone on this grave was made of the same plain black marble, the gold-lettered inscription as untarnished as if it had only been etched the day before. Just as her memories were untarnished. Dear Henry! What a lot of water had flowed under the bridge since that fateful night Honoria and Rajesh had lured him to his death. Rajesh – her father! She had difficulty still in absorbing that particular piece of information, although every time her green eyes stared back at her from the mirror, so did he. She felt regretful now that she hadn't had a chance to get to know him properly, since he and Honoria had departed for India soon after the great revelation. Perhaps they felt they needed time to take stock, there where it all began.

But she would see them again – on their return to Carrickross. She wondered how it would be to meet her father again. After all, he had killed Henry and had planned to kill her. But, looked at in a certain light, who could blame him? He had long made up his mind that his baby daughter was lost for ever, and made it his role in life, thereafter, to protect her mother from further threat. And both Henry and later Coppelia Morrison had been threats to Honoria's honour and peace of mind.

A shadow slanted across the grave as a gentle breeze whispered across her face, soft as a lover's promise.

'Goodbye, Henry!' Coppelia patted the grave in farewell. 'Until we meet again.'

Back at the Kerry Eden, she quickly finished packing her suitcase, settled her bill at the reception desk and without bothering to wait for the porter carried her own suitcases out to the car.

'Here, let me give you a hand with those, *Aunty* Pelia!'

'Fin!'

He pushed himself away from the wall he had been lounging against, hands in pockets, and came towards her grinning. Taking the suitcases, he heaved them into the trunk of the Lotus.

She smiled ironically. *Aunty* Pelia indeed! Her mouth twisted at the emphasis he had placed on the word.

'Thank you, Fin. It's good to see you.' He looked good, more mature. Fortunately, not too much so.

'Why didn't you tell me you were coming?' he asked reprovingly. 'Lucky I spotted you. I was in the bar when you came in.'

'I didn't know you would be at Carrickross – I was told you were away at college.'

'It's the summer holidays, Aunty Pelia, as you well know. But I don't spend much time here now. I just came back to see Carrick and Maggie . . . it being the anniversary of you know what.'

She placed a hand on the sleeve of his jacket for a moment. 'I came to visit Henry, Fin. I'm afraid I wasn't thinking of anything else. I'm sorry.' She got in and settled herself in the driver's seat, winding down the window.

He squatted, placed his hand on the edge. 'So, this is farewell again. Back to the Big Apple, eh?

Scene of some of our greatest exploits.' He chuckled ruefully. 'Oh, but what a wonderful double bluff you played. What a shock when I found out you really *were* my aunt!' A glint of speculation in his eye. 'The end of a beautiful affair, eh?'

'Hmm.'

'A real shame. We were *soooo* good together.'

Coppelia stuck her head through the window and kissed him lingeringly on the lips. '*Plus ca change*, baby, *plus c'est la meme chose*.' With a twiddle of her fingers and a naughty wink, she put the sports car into gear and screeched away.

'*Plus ca change . . . ?*' Fin plundered his brains, dredging up his limited stock of schoolboy French. Yes, he had heard that saying before: '*The more things change, the more it is the same thing*.' A great grin spread across his face as he realised what she had meant. He and his Aunty Pelia would live to lust another day.

'Yes!' He gave a great shout and a joyful punch into the air, startling a newly arrived pair of hotel guests.

'Game on, Aunt Pelia!' he shouted as her car disappeared round a bend. 'Game on!'